Taking a Chance on Love

By Erin Green

Erin Green was born and raised in Warwickshire, where she resides with her husband. An avid reader since childhood, her imagination was instinctively drawn to creative writing as she grew older. Erin has two Hons degrees: BA English literature and another BSc Psychology – her previous careers have ranged from part-time waitress, the retail industry, fitness industry and education.

She has an obsession about time, owns several tortoises and an infectious laugh! Erin writes contemporary novels focusing on love, life and laughter. Erin is an active member of the Romantic Novelists' Association and was delighted to be awarded The Katie Fforde Bursary in 2017. An ideal day for Erin involves writing, people watching and drinking copious amounts of tea.

For more information about Erin, visit her website: www.ErinGreenAuthor.co.uk, find her on Facebook www.facebook.com/ErinGreenAuthor or follow her on Twitter @ErinGreenAuthor.

Taking a Chance on Love

Erin Green

H

REVIEW

First published in Great Britain in 2020
by HEADLINE REVIEW
An imprint of HEADLINE PUBLISHING GROUP

1

Cataloguing in Publication Data is available from the British Library

ISBN 978 1 4722 6357 5

Typeset in Sabon by CC Book Production

Printed and bound in Great Britain by
Clays Ltd, Elcograf S.p.A.

Headline's policy is to use papers that are natural, renewable and recyclable
products and made from wood grown in well-managed forests and other
controlled sources. The logging and manufacturing processes are expected
to conform to the environmental regulations of the country of origin.

HEADLINE PUBLISHING GROUP
An Hachette UK Company
Carmelite House
50 Victoria Embankment
London EC4Y 0DZ

www.headline.co.uk
www.hachette.co.uk

To every 29 February – what a difference a day makes!

Chapter One

Friday 14 February – Valentine's Day

Carmen

I tap in the security code to void the boutique's alarm system, automatically flicking on the light switches as I stride through the room towards the red velvet curtain which hides our small kitchenette.

I fill the kettle, plug it in and wait.

It doesn't take long, just enough time to remove my coat, grab three mugs from the draining board and spoon in the necessary coffee and sugars before the front door opens admitting the first arrival of the day.

'Hellllllllo, how are we?' calls Trish, her cheery tone confirming my fears. Her slender frame nips around the curtain divide and it's obvious – her husband, Terry, has come up with the goods *again*!

'Bloody miserable,' I moan, hating myself for allowing it to affect my mood. 'And you, need I ask?'

'Breakfast in bed, a bit of a cuddle *and . . .*' Trish sucks in her pale cheeks and rolls the words around her mouth before continuing. She's carefully selecting the next piece of information, knowing it could push my mood further along the 'woe is me' scale.

'Go on,' I urge, eager to get this conversation over and done with.

'Thirty-six long-stemmed roses – one for each month we've been married.'

I perform my usual head tilt and sigh. I love her husband. Why can't I have a man as attentive and as thoughtful as Terry?

'Sorry, Carmen,' says Trish, rubbing my forearm as I suddenly turn to busy myself with pouring boiling water and stirring mugs. 'Dare I ask?'

'Go ahead, ask away,' I mutter, grabbing the milk from the mini fridge.

'Hiya!' calls Anna, sweeping aside the velvet curtain to join our conversation. 'How are we this beautiful morning?'

Trish and I exchange a fleeting glance. Neither of us answers the teenager, whose cheeks are aglow, eyes sparkling like diamonds and bursting with delight.

'Well?' asks Anna, her asymmetric black fringe swinging as her head turns to each of us.

'I received thirty-six beautiful red roses,' repeats Trish, a coy smile brightening her delicate features. 'You?'

'A card from my ex . . . which is nice. My mum says I need to distance myself and not encourage him, but it's still nice to receive a Valentine's card.' Anna turns to me, her expectant face eager to hear of my Valentine bounty.

'Me? Oh, I got a card, the tiniest card ever produced and probably picked up from the local petrol station on his drive home last night and written whilst in the bathroom this morning, I imagine,' I say, my voice monotone. Hearing it, I want to kick my own arse for being so miserable.

'Ah never mind, maybe tonight . . .'

I interrupt her by raising my palm. 'No! Please don't make excuses for Elliot's sorry effort by suggesting that a candle-lit meal for two, or a table booked at a swanky restaurant, or rose petals strewn across our bed awaits my arrival home . . . eh-eh! *That's* not Elliot's style.'

'Yeah, but . . .'

Trish interrupts her this time. 'Nah! He's definitely lacking in the romance department . . . Carmen's had this every year for . . . seven years?'

'Eight,' I correct her.

'Eight years . . . She knows him well enough to know what to expect when she gets home.' Trish gives her habitual knowing nod.

'But this year might be the year when . . .' mutters Anna.

'No,' we say in unison.

'You'll only make the day harder for me by suggesting that there are treats waiting for me at home. I know there aren't, so let's not pretend.' I ignore my scalding coffee and swill the teaspoon under the tap, knowing that both my employees are watching my every move for fear of a delayed reaction.

'Can I ask what you got him?' asks Anna.

'A card . . . from the petrol station . . . bought two nights ago,' I mutter, drying my hands.

'There you go then!' exclaims Anna, about to put my relationship to rights.

'I'll leave Trish to explain why.' I leave the kitchenette, safe in the knowledge that Trish will recall my disastrous Valentine of six years ago when I vowed to 'see how he liked it' and got him nothing but a cheap card. Elliot didn't even notice and so, sadly, I've continued. And he's never changed or learnt what I truly want. So how can I go back on my word?

The velvet curtain swishes into place separating me from

their conversation and I begin my morning routine. I inhale the smell of the fresh rose petals that decorate our reception counter. I make a lap of the boutique, my eagle eyes searching for anything out of place. I briskly straighten the rails of cellophane-covered gowns, ensuring they look presentable for our first appointment at ten o'clock. I inspect the large gilt mirrors, strategically positioned to enable a wedding gown to be viewed from every angle, for smears or fingerprints. I titivate the tiara display, straightening each to ensure the overhead spotlights highlight each delicate bead or crystal droplet. I pick a thread of cotton from the burgundy chaise longue, on which a row of family and friends will perch, eager for a first glimpse of the chosen bridal gown. A box of tissues sits close at hand on the nearest table, ready to frantically dab at their tears of joy.

I check my own reflection in the nearest mirror: smart green suit, natural-looking russet-toned make-up and a mane of vibrant red hair, which I quickly tease into place.

Once I'm satisfied, I flick the 'closed' sign to 'open'.

Another day begins at The Wedding Boutique.

I love my tiny empire, situated near the upper end of the High Street, nestled between the travel agents and what was once the local department store – now empty. A pretty high street of honey-coloured stone buildings, each dominated by aged bay windows, and a cobbled walkway.

I love my job, which makes days like today so much harder to handle. I don't resent Trish's moment of loved-up joy – honestly, I don't. I'm not asking for grand gestures, just slightly more than a garage forecourt card.

Staring out of the front window, between two mannequins adorned in ivory tulle and beaded satin, I watch the passers-by striding to work. I can't help but pick out individuals and wonder.

I bet she received flowers.

I bet he sent a fancy Hallmark card.

I bet he received chocolates.

I bet even those schoolkids received a proper sturdy card and not a cheap, flimsy effort.

Valentine's Day is a cruel, twisted reminder that I, Carmen Smith, am the owner of a successful bridal gown boutique and am unmarried despite being in a committed relationship for eight years. Every day I hear about beautiful plans for amazing weddings days. I don't begrudge my brides their moment of joy, their detailed wedding plans, their dream day or even their handsome husbands. I simply want my very own slice of wedding happiness and a gold band, which I believe is overdue by approximately five years. I may seem self-centred, maybe a tad impatient, but in my world, when you commit, you commit properly.

We, Elliot and I, have acquired a joint mortgage. We have joint ownership of a border collie, Maisy, despite him never walking her. We have joint bank accounts, a king-size bed, matching toothbrushes, and the automatic alternate-year Christmas dinner at each other's parents. We even have a couple of joint promises regarding godchildren, who we've vowed to raise in a morally correct manner should anything happen to our dear friends, which we share too.

We have everything apart from a shared surname and a wedding certificate.

The name situation is neither here nor there; I could rectify that quite easily, with one legal document, a swift signature and – bingo! – I could officially sign his name. It's the certificate I want. The commitment shown to me. I need to build the future I've dreamt of – a family home, children, the future I thought would automatically come my way, in the circle of life. I want finger paintings covering the fridge door, the dead goldfish drama and the frantic extra-curricular activity time-table. I wouldn't mind him getting a man shed, the end of date nights because of no babysitter or even the growing old and pottering around together stage. But nothing can officially start without a commitment.

How do you get the man you love to propose to you? Without forcing the issue, creating a marriage minefield or patiently waiting while he gets his act together?

If, indeed, he ever does!

The boutique is empty and we're busy steaming a delicate lace bridal train ready for collection when the door opens. We each hold our breath and pose like mannequins as the local florist struggles to get through the door carrying a cello-phane-wrapped bouquet.

Trish looks at me, her eyes wide with excitement. I curtail any reaction, acting calm and serene whilst my heart pounds a little faster.

Really?

'Flowers!' cries Anna, glancing between us two older ladies. I say older because when you're the tender age of eighteen, my thirty-nine years and Trish's forty-one seem ancient. Anna will arrive at our age in a blink of an eye; she simply doesn't know that yet.

'Delivery for Anna Chaplin,' announces the florist, her eager gaze switching from face to face to identify the lucky lady.

'Mine?' beams Anna, dropping her end of the lace train and dancing on the spot, her excitement overflowing, before dashing forwards to collect the bouquet. 'A dozen long-stemmed roses!'

The florist leaves us open-mouthed and staring as Anna rips open the accompanying card.

'Who from?' I ask, knowing full well I'm being nosy. Eighteen, single and yet she receives roses – go figure!

'That would be telling,' she teases, tapping the side of her nose.

'Oh no, missy . . . if you're going to flaunt your Valentine spoils in the kitchenette's sink all day and deflate me even more, you need to be prepared to share on the info front,' I say, putting the steaming nozzle down. Trish releases the layers of delicate lace as we await the announcement.

'Cody? That's the guy from the bathroom store, isn't it?' she explains, her fingers pinching the simple card.

'He's cute . . . he walks past here most lunchtimes,' says Trish, nodding in admiration.

'I know. I've seen him round town in local pubs, we've chatted once or twice but this . . . wow!'

'Who's a lucky lady?' I say, curbing my jealousy on seeing her delighted face.

'I don't know what to do . . . How do I thank him?'

'Mmmm, believe me, if he's forked out for roses on Valentine's Day, he'll be seeking you out tonight, so don't worry,' laughs Trish, lifting the next layer of lace so I can resume steaming the delicate train.

Dana

I read the website's payment page. I'm hesitant to enter my debit card number and press the send button. It might be nerves but I suspect it's the remnants of my dignity disappearing into the World Wide Web never to be seen again if I conform to society's expectations and sign up for a dating site. I, Dana, vowed never to join a dating website, under any circumstances, regardless of my situation or lifestyle. I was never going to follow the lead of the other single chummy-mummies at the school gate and seek love via a dating app. I'm proud that I've confidently upheld that vow for five long years. Five busy years. Five devoted and yet lonely years, during which I frequently reminded all who'd listen – mainly at birthdays, New Year, Easter, midsummer's parties, summer holiday fortnights, midwinter nativities and, finally, Christmas – that I would find a man the old-fashioned way. In the flesh. In real life. Someone tall, dark and handsome and in need of a decent, law-abiding yet slightly sassy – especially after wine consumption – loving woman. A loving woman with an adorable young son.

Sadly, I haven't succeeded.

My computer screen flickers, flashes and somewhere inside my head I hear a million tiny padlocks open as the gated entrances to millions of warm, loving relationships are potentially flung wide if I enter my card number and press 'send'.

Or, I could sign up and find it's all an almighty scam, taking twenty-five pounds a month by direct payment and eons of my time should I ever attempt to cancel my membership. Much like a gym membership can do . . . once did, many moons ago in my previous life. And what for? So I can join the chummy-mummies complaining about meeting endless morons – who I'd never give the time of day to in real life but who I feel the need to converse with politely, should I be lucky enough to receive the offer of a date, just because I've paid for the privilege each month. Then, in time, I'll also be a skint chummy-mummy, venting about the conniving, cheating bastards who lose my number once I've organised a costly babysitter, bribed the child to be good and curled my hair. Only to have to return home after being stood up.

I pause and check the computer clock: 9 p.m.

I listen to the silence, and see myself as others would, should they enter my house at this precise moment.

Suddenly, the prospect of being stood up by an internet nobody feels slightly more desirable than my current situation: a lonely single mum, wearing joggers and a messy bun, cradling her second glass of cheap wine, who, after a long day creating and delivering beautiful bouquets to excited customers, now relaxes by signing up to a dating service on Valentine's night.

'Bloody cheers!'

Such a fine achievement for a thirty-nine year old.

I instantly correct myself – my finest achievement is fast asleep upstairs in the front bedroom, dressed in his favourite Spider-Man pyjamas, minus his tiny glasses and clutching the raggedy ear of a toy elephant.

But I still really don't want to sign up and pay hard-earned money for a dating app.

And that's when I spot it, in the right-hand side panel, edged in a glimmering gold border.

Do you want experts to help you find true love?
Are you prepared to be honest, open and frank
about your future desires?
Would you participate in a social experiment
to identify 'the one'?
If so, click here for further details . . .

I click. I wait and read the next screen, which introduces Channel 7's new TV programme *Taking a Chance on Love*, and calls for the enrolment of singles who'd like to participate. I read with interest: the blurb offers qualified psychologists, psychometric testing, personality matching, feedback and support to the carefully selected few destined to find out whether true love can be scientifically engineered.

I've watched many reality shows – the big ones with voting lines and a huge public following – but this online advert suggests a small independent TV production, nothing too risky. I'm not sure I'm up for the public scrutiny of a major fly-on-the-wall documentary, but I doubt that a small independent programme will get a decent audience or a prime-time slot and I could do with the panel of experts and their various tests. Anything that will curtail the time-wasters, the two-timers, the players . . . need I carry on?

It takes me five minutes to answer a set of basic questions about me and my situation. Even less time to read the terms and conditions, and one click to submit my enrolment form.

I sit back. Now that feels better than the dating website. Enrolment in a social experiment conducted by professional people fills me with confidence. Plus it's a free application, debit card not needed, so I can't be scammed.

Some confidence.

A smidgen of confidence.

A wave of guilt flash-floods over me.

Am I being fair to Luke?

Fair to myself?

I really must stop doing this self-flagellation routine, having to justify myself every time I choose to chase a desire. Something for me. Something I want . . . need . . . would like . . . I beat myself up purely because I feel guilty for wanting something outside my relationship with my child.

My eyes well, the screen blurs. Who am I trying to kid? Thousands of people will see the very same advert, fill out the questionnaire and be selected ahead of me. Interesting people, with fabulous stories, overflowing with confidence . . . because, let's face it – I never win anything.

An incredible urge to hug my son envelops me. I put my wine glass down.

As if in a re-enactment of the chummy-mummy one-hundred-metre final frantic dash for a front-row space at the school railings, I take the staircase two at a time. Luke won't wake, he never does.

I stand on the landing and stare at the sliver of shadow around his door, left slightly ajar because he's scared of the dark. This allows the cute snuffles of my sleeping son to be heard on the quiet landing. I touch the door gently, knowing it'll swing open freely without noise to reveal my sleeping child. He's a pyjamaed lump of sprawling chubby limbs; his face is turned to the wall, a crumpled duvet kicked to the bottom of his bed. His elephant, snared by its right ear, stares back at me. His tiny blue glasses sit by his bed, awaiting a new day of fingerprints and smears.

I don't need to see Luke's face. I've examined his features every day, they're committed to my memory for life: his stumpy button nose, slanting inquisitive eyes, and his indelible smile, freely available to everyone he greets.

My boy.

My baby.

My son.

Snuggled and dreaming in his own precious world, where elephants and Spider-Man fight for justice and peace for all by giving a little extra to this world. Just like Luke, who gives a little extra to everyone he meets.

Ensuring that I must do the same.

I lean against the door jamb, admiring the image as he noisily slaps his lips and snuffles into his pillow, unaware that this world, with its cruel reality and harsh society, does little to justify his good nature. One day, when he's a little older, I'll attempt to explain the chance meeting of human cells, the forging of a new being in a moment of love, even the strength and disposal of such love once issues arise. I know I'll fail miserably, science will evade me. No doubt I'll cry. No doubt he will too. How wrong that a child so loving, boisterous and bright – every quality I'd have chosen for my son – is destined to walk a slightly different path in life from his classmates, destined to have to give a little extra focus and effort to everything he achieves or desires in life. Ironically, his little extra is contained within chromosome twenty-one.

Polly

'Is that it?' sneers our son, pointing at our mantelpiece, as he watches the early evening news. 'I know you're a pair of old fogies, but even so, that's pretty pathetic. Where's the romance?'

'Oy, cut it out, Cody! Since when have we ever done the whole Valentine's Day guff? You shouldn't need to be told when to tell someone you love them, worse still, do it en masse as a nation, all on the same day,' I say, ironing his white shirt, which I should have done last night but forgot to – or rather couldn't be bothered to when I did remember, given that it was quarter past ten. 'Where's the romance in that?'

'You would say that though, wouldn't you?' grunts Cody from the sofa, feigning interest in our simple cards standing side by side. Fraser has signed his usual 'Fraser X'. I've been slightly more extravagant with a simple message of 'Love always, Polly xx'. Neither of us feels the need to declare undying love inside a Hallmark card, just because the calendar dictates we should. We've survived the sunshine and shadows of twenty-one years together, paid off a mortgage month by month, both worked around the clock to hold down full-time employment and raised the aforementioned son – though the fact that he can't iron his own bloody shirt at nineteen years of age probably speaks volumes regarding the layer of cotton wool we've wrapped him in.

'It's a commercial ploy simply to line the pockets of florists and card manufacturers, you know that, don't you? Over the years, I've saved your father a small fortune by refusing to allow him to buy me roses on Valentine's Day. And believe me, he's grateful. I've always said . . .'

'I'm happy as long as I receive a nice card and a kiss,' interrupts Cody, mimicking my voice, though I know I don't sound half as whiney as he makes out. I sound genuine, I sound like a woman who is sure of her man and his affections, a woman who wants real day-to-day love, not some bullshit idea created by the admen.

'I'm glad you've heard me say it. I know your father loves me, and he knows I love him. We don't feel the need to be mushy or gaze adoringly at each other, unlike your aunty Helen and uncle Marc! How would you fancy having those two as your parents, bloody smooching and snogging all over the place?' My older sister and her husband have never been any different. They've never matured from the arse-groping stage of a relationship, despite three years of courtship, twenty-five years of marriage plus two daughters.

Helen and I have always been close, although given our seven-year age gap, we were always at different stages. As teenagers, she and Marc used to scare the life out of me when I watched them through the crack of the kitchen door, terrified that they'd die of asphyxiation as they French kissed for a whole ten minutes, while our parents sat in frosty silence watching *Tomorrow's World* in the front room. I'd squirm whilst peeking, like watching a David Attenborough nature programme but without the long lens, decorative ferns and billowing long grass – though the Moulinex mixer and a Sodastream were their camouflage backdrop. It probably explains why I've never been one for public displays of passionate affection. With my first boyfriend, I was content with hand-holding, pecks on the cheek and a cheeky arse-feel when a private moment arose, 'There's a time and place for everything' being my favoured line. How I ever kept that first boyfriend and made him my live-in lover just three years later I'll never know, but he didn't complain. And now here we are, two decades later, and our beloved Cody, into whom we have ploughed all our hopes and energy, mocks our attempt at being romantic. As if he's the bloody Casanova of Lansdowne Crescent!

'Urgh, the very thought of it.'

'Exactly, so be thankful for small mercies.'

'Old people snogging – yuk!'

'More importantly, wait until you see the price of twenty long-stemmed roses plus the delivery charge – then you'll be hoping your future partner has my attitude. So don't knock it, OK?'

'They're not that expensive. A dozen red roses delivered locally only costs . . .' Cody's words fade on seeing my stunned expression. I automatically lift the iron to ensure no burning.

'How on earth would you know?'

'Mmmm, wouldn't you like to know?'

'Cody, have you . . . ?' I daren't finish my sentence. I want to, I am desperate to, but I can't bring myself to ask for fear of the answer.

Iron held aloft, face still stunned, I take in the sprawling frame of my son. He might be six foot one, with size eleven feet and a collar size which matches his father's but an invisible umbilical cord sits comfortably between us. Stretched as it might be at this current moment, still it is present and correct.

They tried to convince me nearly twenty years ago that it had been physically cut, but I refuse to believe it. In my book, it gives me an innate right to ask my son questions, though Fraser tends to disagree with me about this on a fairly regular basis, usually in hushed tones behind a closed kitchen door. But, hey, what do the Y chromosomes in this house know? Not as much as the X chromosome does, *that's* what I've learnt over the years.

'Don't worry, I wasn't ripped off.'

I give a weak smile and resume ironing, my mind spinning faster than a weather vane in a tornado.

Bless him, he thinks I'm bothered about the cost. As I said, what does he know? Bugger the cost! I'm more bothered about who the recipient was and whether she's actually worthy of the affections of my strapping lad! Or – and I really don't want to venture down this line of thinking, but here we go, needs must – dare I ask if it was his ex-girlfriend, Lola?

Shall I?

Should I?

Surely not!

No, it really isn't my business. It shouldn't be my problem, but it feels like it could be. I shouldn't ask. He's entitled to a private life, away from his parents' scrutinising gaze. At nineteen, I'd have hated my mother interfering in my love life, asking questions and prying, although maybe her quizzical stare over the rim of her glasses, her persistent tutting and her subtle 'little chats' did guide and influence my choice.

Oh dear, I've turned into my damned mother!

I continue with my ironing, *his* ironing.

Out of the corner of my eye, I observe him watching the news.

Maybe I should ask purely to show interest? It isn't being nosy. How many times do parents get slated in the media for not taking an interest and, boom, their kids end up taking drugs on the way to college, being arrested for illicit internet activity or fathering three babies in the space of two postcodes!

But what if he confirms the return of Lola? Who, whilst absent from our lives, has no doubt dated another ten men since she wrangled with our son, has perfected her repertoire of bad behaviour and now plans to make a grand comeback into our lives.

The last time I saw her she'd fallen over on the dance floor at my father's sixty-fifth birthday bash, her legs akimbo, flashing her lime-green gusset whilst congratulating herself for holding aloft her oversized glass of cheap plonk, of which she hadn't split a drop. Hoorah!

'Cody, anyone I know?'

He looks at me surprised: there's been a lengthy pause while my brain wrote a pros and cons list. I half expect him to ask what we are discussing.

'Nah!' He returns his attention to the TV as I finish ironing his shirt.

'Praise be for small mercies,' I chunter. My relief is instant, I can't hide it. Such a glorious confirmation erases my fears – much like my reaction when he received his A-level results. Though given his current employment at a local bathroom showroom, he's hardly made good use of the qualifications that took such graft to earn. One day I might wave him off to uni, here's hoping it's soon.

Not Lola anyway. Excellent. No fear of repeating the string of embarrassments endured purely by association then. The half-nakedness, her slovenly drunkenness, her nocturnal phone calls disturbing our sleep and the constant worry that our son is being drawn into a social vortex of her erratic lifestyle and make-believe.

So, someone new.

Someone lovely.

Someone I don't know.

Bloody great! So the allowance which his dad and I provide him with in order to top up his low-paid job has been blown on a dozen roses and a delivery charge! I congratulate myself on completing seven hours of overtime last week at the travel agents purely to provide an unknown girl with a doorstep delivery and a rush of teenage pheromones. I hope she enjoys my gift and fully appreciates the care and consideration I showed towards her. Whereas I happily settle for a solitary card with a simple sentiment and single kiss.

'Here . . . here's your sodding shirt.' I fling it in his direction, narked that the realities of motherhood frequently bite me on the arse, and his carefully ironed shirt crumples into his lap.

'Cheers.'

Chapter Two

Friday 21 February

Polly

'Mum . . . I've been thinking,' says Cody, entering the kitchen as I dash about; juggling burnt toast and boiling kettles is the norm at breakfast time in our home.

'Sound ominous,' offers Fraser, nabbing the least blackened piece of toast from the bread board and settling at the breakfast table to consume it alongside his morning coffee.

I stop in mid-action, butter knife held aloft, with two burnt pieces awaiting camouflage. I sense what Cody's about to say before he even says it and I will want to bloody scream if it's what I think.

'Go on,' I say calmly, knowing full well that my ordinary working day at the travel agents is up the swanny if I'm right.

Cody stands beside me at the countertop, nodding at the burnt toast as an indication that he's waiting. I slowly resume my task, aware that his casual manner is hiding something.

'You're right . . . for once,' he says, watching my hand busily buttering. 'Having a party for my twentieth would be pretty neat – given that I didn't get an eighteenth party.'

He can't look me in the eye.

'I bloody knew it! Why didn't you say before now? I asked you back in October ... that's four months ago. But oh no, Mum's making a bloody big fuss about nothing and now ... now with –' I glance at the kitchen calendar for confirmation – 'eight days to go, you decide I had a good idea.'

Cody snatches a piece of toast from beneath my knife and drifts towards his father, crunching.

'Just saying, that's all ... nothing posh, but somewhere decent with music, drinks and a few laughs – but not the old scout hut like my mate Josh had ... that wasn't a great night.'

'Well, that narrows it down, Cody,' I say. 'How about a back room in a local pub?'

'A classy pub?'

'Such as?'

'The Red Lion is pretty decent but not the Welfare Club.'

I stare open-mouthed at Fraser, who comically lifts his eyebrows as if questioning why I am surprised by my offspring.

'Can you believe it?' I mutter, as if Cody weren't present at the table, munching his toast.

'He's never been any different, Polly,' says Fraser. 'He's always been last-minute.'

'Isn't that the truth!' I say, buttering my own piece of cold toast, as Fraser finishes his coffee, plants a kiss on my temple and heads out for work.

'You love me,' mutters Cody, as laid-back as ever.

'Fraser ... Fraser, how much do you think we are talking?' I call, from the kitchen. There's no answer, just the sound of the front door slamming.

Carmen

My hand reaches for the heavy curtain and I give the bride-to-be a knowing smile as she takes a deep breath. My aim is to pull back the curtain in one fluid movement, enabling her mother and three sisters to view her wedding gown, fitted to perfection, for the first time.

'Ready?' I whisper, seeing a mixture of nerves and excitement surface as she fiddles with her flowing veil.

She gives a nod. My hand dramatically sweeps the curtain aside, revealing all. A princess-styled ballgown with a sweetheart neckline in ivory with a sequined panelled bodice.

The gathered females, sitting and standing around the chaise longue, give a simultaneous gasp, then ooh and ah as my bride-to-be lifts her hemline and gracefully steps into the open space of the boutique. Trish and Anna linger in the background to admire. I move in front to help her step up on to the circular platform set before our largest gilt mirror, in which her gown can be viewed from every angle using the reflections in other mirrors.

I quickly bend to titivate the hemline to ensure it hangs correctly, as she views herself for the first time.

This is a wondrous moment for any woman, whatever her age. Over the years I've witnessed instant tears, open-mouthed gasps and shrieks of delight.

In any working day, this is one of my favourite moments. One which twangs at my heart strings every day. To witness the parental pride, the sisterly excitement and the thrill of a bride-to-be – knowing that this image will always be treasured – is so very special. I've been known to shed a tear or two myself when a family have shared a touching story or a specific history with us during their visits.

Thankfully, today's bride is no different.

She stands and stares, a look of bewildered delight etched upon her face, as her mother and three sisters frantically dab at tears of joy and repeat endless adjectives, none of which seem to accurately describe the radiant vision before them.

This is when I know I've done my job right. If a bride-to-be ever attends her final fitting and stands staring into this mirror without such a reaction, I will assume the worst. And hastily attempt to put it right with another gown.

Every bride should have her moment of joy – where her dreams begin to come true.

'Doesn't she look fabulous?' I ask the family as I quietly back away to enable photographs and memories to be made.

'It's exactly what I'd dreamt it would look like,' says the bride-to-be.

'You look like an angel. I can't wait for your dad to see you,' sniffs her mother through a handful of crumpled tissue. 'Suddenly this wedding has become very real.'

'Who'd have thought that in just one week you'll be walking down the aisle to be married in that gown,' sobs a sister.

'I know!' The bride smiles. 'And yet you all doubted me when I asked him.'

My ears prick up. This conversation has taken a slightly different path to the usual script for a final gown fitting.

'So true,' replies her mother.

I look from bride-to-be to mother and back again, interested to hear the story.

The bride-to-be begins to giggle.

'Go on, you might as well say,' urges her mother.

'We'd been dating for six years and I wanted to get married. Every birthday and Christmas I thought, this will be the time he'll propose ... but he didn't. So, I kept waiting, dropping hints, as you do, but eventually I took matters into my own hands and proposed to him last leap year,' explains the bride-to-be. 'Which is why we've waited four years to get married on the twenty-ninth of February.'

'*You* asked *him*?' I stutter, unsure if I heard her correctly.

'Yeah! I was the biggest bag of nerves ever but I'm glad I did it.'

'She'd still be waiting otherwise, wouldn't you?'

'I certainly would, Mum.'

'You *proposed* to him?' I can hear the shock in my own voice, so I know my expression must be a dead giveaway. It might seem old-fashioned in today's age of equality but it's still not the usual proposal story we hear in the boutique.

'Absolutely. I went with the tradition of a leap year.'

'And he said yes straight away?' I'm now all ears, my shock subsiding.

'Oh yeah, he was surprised to be asked but he gave me an answer there and then.'

'Wow, you're braver than me. I could never do that,' I say.

'I didn't think I could, but I'm glad I did.'

'But what if he'd said no?' I ask.

'I'd have had my answer, wouldn't I? As I said to Mum, "If you don't ask, you'll never know,"' says the bride-to-be, her face beaming. 'And now look what's happening, all because I asked him.'

'Exactly! I'm glad, even though it isn't the norm,' adds her mother.

I fall silent as Trish tops up their champagne glasses and Anna offers around the tray of delicate petticoat tail short-bread.

Extending my hand as a support, I walk our bride-to-be back to the curtained changing area and help her remove the gown.

I'm following my usual final fitting routine: conversational pleasantries about how delighted the family were, how exciting that the date is so near and instructions on how to hang the gown ready for the big day, but my mind is elsewhere. My mind is spinning with one sentence: 'If you don't ask, you'll never know ...'

Females proposing isn't the norm; surely it's the male's job to propose in a heterosexual relationship? Isn't it up to him to show true commitment towards a woman by proposing?

It might be tradition but ...

I baulk at the very idea.

It's not the right thing for me to do.

Cinderella didn't propose to her prince. And how different would the fairy tale be if she had?

Would Elliot say yes, like this woman's fiancé?

Knowing Elliot, he'd be too shocked to answer me. Or he'd be offended that I'd questioned his masculinity with such a request. I might ruin a future plan that he's been concocting for my birthday, our dating anniversary or Christmas.

I pull myself up sharp, as I unzip the gown and the bride-to-be carefully steps out of its sumptuous folds.

If there was even a remote possibility that Elliot might be planning a proposal, I'd be happy to wait but ... surely me proposing isn't the answer.

It shouldn't be.

It couldn't be.

Could it?

Dana

'Hello, can I speak to Dana Jones please?' asks the woman politely.

'Speaking.' I'm cautious – I didn't recognise the mobile number which flashed up on the tiny screen. I never get phone calls from unknown numbers, not even PPI calls.

'Hi there! I'm Tamzin Edwards from Happy Productions TV and I was wondering if you could spare me a few minutes to discuss your application for our new dating documentary *Taking a Chance on Love.*'

'Oh right, yeah, of course,' I stutter.

'I have your details in front of me . . . Let's see . . . mother of one . . . boy or girl?'

'Boy.'

'How old?'

'Five . . . nearly six.'

'Good, good, and it says here that you haven't ventured on to the dating scene in quite a while. Is there a reason for that?'

I hesitate. How honest do I want to be?

'Kind of . . . I had my little boy – I'm a single mum, so I wanted to focus on him during the early years. I wanted to establish a strong bond between us, ensure he had my full attention and that we both developed as a tight little unit before I began sharing my time with others . . . That probably sounds very selfish of me but, you know, first-time mum and all that.'

'Absolutely. I get your drift, nature and nurture are both crucial in those precious formative years,' says Tamzin. 'You never get them back, you know – never.'

I imagine she's hastily writing down every word I say, like a crazed journalist at a news conference, though given my status of self-employed florist I doubt she'll have to quote me on *Newsnight*.

'And finally, Dana, is there any chance you're available this Saturday for an interview with a couple of our production team and the professionals? An hour or so is all we'll need to ask a few vital questions and get to know you a little better.'

I swiftly glance at our kitchen wall calendar, which is always up to date and the deciding factor for any arrangements in this house. I can see Saturday is entirely blank, which equals free: no birthday parties, no christenings and no play dates. Though I do have to prepare for the wedding fayre taking place the next day. I know my parents will have Luke for an extra hour or two in addition to our arrangement for Sunday; I won't leave him with anyone else. I spy Luke's visual timetable pinned beside my calendar, which shows his morning and bedtime routines in picture form – I will need to rearrange the images for the weekend so he has prior warning of what is happening otherwise he'll be thrown by a change to our usual routine. I will have to put his 'going to Grandpops's' image on there, which will please him.

'What time were you thinking and where?'

'Midday. We've booked a meeting room at the Red Lion Hotel, do you know it?'

'Oh yes, along the High Street.'

'That's the one ... So, you're OK to attend?'

'Yes. OK. Midday on Saturday at the Red Lion. And who do I ask for?'

'Ask at reception for Happy Productions TV ... and I'll look forward to meeting you, Dana.'

'Yes, me too.'

'Oh, Dana ... could I ask that you bring along your birth certificate, your passport and any qualification certificates you may have?'

'Oh OK.' I'm taken aback as she reels them off as if in a practised speech.

'Purely a formality, you understand . . . So we'll see you on Saturday. Ciao!'

The line goes dead at her end. Wow, she didn't wait for me to say bye. Maybe she's got numerous phone calls to make, and it's such short notice.

I tap the mobile screen and return to the sink unit where I'd been working when my mobile rang. I have three buckets sitting on the draining board filled with cut oasis, which needs soaking in cold water before I can use it. I've just spent the last twenty minutes cutting the green foam, all the while cringing at the awful sound it makes against the metal carving knife blade. Since day one as a trainee florist, that dreadful squeaky noise has always given me the heebie-jeebies.

I glance at the wall clock: 9.45 a.m.

I'll fill the buckets with cold water and leave the oasis soaking while I prepare my orders for tomorrow. If I can get the Taylor birthday arrangement and the Willets' wedding posies made, then, once I've collected Luke from school, done teatime, bath and bedtime, I can make a start on the flower arrangements and bouquets ready for my stall at the wedding fayre on Sunday. If I store them in a cool dark garage they'll look as fresh as if I'd created them on Saturday evening. That will ease my workload so that I can attend tomorrow's meeting.

That sounds like a plan.

Gingerly, I hold each plastic bucket beneath the kitchen sink tap and fill them with cold water, before heaving them on to the tiled floor. I really should get an outdoor tap fitted in the garden as it would cut down on me dragging heavy buckets of cold water back and forth each day to the kitchen sink. Firstly, it'd save wear and tear on our hall carpet – which get splashed on a daily basis from me slopping buckets through the house. Secondly, it would save my back, which takes a hammering from the heavy lifting. But, like many jobs, I keep meaning to get around to it.

My stomach flutters with nerves.

What have I agreed to? It might be fun – or a complete nightmare. Either way I'll get a sense at tomorrow's meeting and, if needs be, I'll pull my application out of the mix. Anyway, what's the likelihood of them picking me from the scores of women who also applied? Pretty low, I imagine. I know what tomorrow's meeting will be: it'll be the opportunity for them to give me the once over, check out whether I look like my application photograph, ask a few questions and then decide. Decide that I'm a definite no-goer, given my lack experience and confidence about finding love. No doubt they'll class me as permanent singleton material and be eager to wave me goodbye.

My innards continue to jitter. I won't think about the outcome; I'll simply turn up, accept a cup of coffee, show my documents and come home after a nice chat. Simple. Even I can do that.

Polly

I switch the 'closed' sign to 'open' and pray that no one accepts the invite to walk in until at least one o'clock, when my co-worker Stacey will arrive to join the shift. I need the next four hours on the phone moonlighting from my job to organise a family affair, rather than an all-inclusive package holiday for a family of four.

My coffee mug awaits my swift return to my desk as I straighten the travel brochures on each display shelf, repin a falling poster advertising the Maldives to the back wall and then ditch my work responsibilities, knowing at least that the shop floor is respectable should anyone drop by, be it a potential customer, a mystery shopper checking the quality of our service or the regional boss. If the regional boss did surprise us with a visit, he'd be amazed by the complicated staffing rota, all part-time workers who pass like ships in the night at various hours ensuring a smooth service.

I settle at my desk, sip my steaming coffee and grab a pad of paper to make my to-do list for the party.

But first I need to ask the all-important question of Fraser.

It's naughty of me but, given my endless years of service, unplanned overtime and lack of co-workers on a Friday morning – which always ends up being a busy day – I'll use their telephone and not my mobile to make the necessary calls. I have until Stacey arrives bang on time at one o'clock for her four-hour shift. Till then, I'm on my own.

Fraser answers his mobile immediately.

'Fraser, you didn't hear when I asked you earlier ... what are you thinking should be our maximum spend for this party?'

I wait as he mentally calculates. I imagine him sitting at his planning and design desk, pulling his serious thinking face, the one where he looks up and stares as if the answer is written upon the stippled ceiling. His mouth will twitch, as if he's talking to himself, and then he'll eventually answer. I've learnt to wait, not to interrupt the process. He's so methodical, logical and usually precise on his upper limit, so it won't be worth trying to force another hundred once he's said. Fraser has never worked that way. He does the accuracy and figure work in our relationship; I do the caring stuff, the running around and the family commitments. The balance can often be skewed but it works for us, despite what others may think.

'Fifteen hundred quid,' he says, surprising me by how quickly he's answered. I was expecting to hold for a few more minutes. 'Given the cost of his present ... Is that about what you're thinking?'

'Perfect. Bye.' I can't afford to waste time; Fraser will know I'm on a mission.

October seems like a distant memory, when planning a size-able party could have been enjoyable, but no, Cody wasn't interested back then.

A twentieth birthday party probably isn't the norm in most families, but in ours it was – he'd forgone the possibility of a proper eighteenth celebration due to my inability to push him through a birth canal on 28 February. After a sixteen-hour labour, I failed miserably, missing the deadline to avoid having a leap-year baby by eleven minutes, unlike the other three women in the labour ward, who didn't go on to deny their children an annual birthday.

My midwifery team, family and close friends were thrilled with his unusual birth date, Fraser simply relieved he had a son with ten fingers, ten toes plus a healthy set of lungs. Me, I was never quite taken with the date. It was always a conversation starter, when his birth date or certificate was asked for, lots of oohing and aahing over something a little different. We'd opted for the 28th as his annual celebration, given he was a February baby. Everyone played ball and duly accepted it, apart from my in-laws, who frequently pointed out that Cody wasn't actually here on earth on the said date so 'surely the first of March is more logical'. March didn't belong on his birth certificate, so it wasn't logical to me. Each year it riled me, and never more so than when Cody did the circuit of celebrating eighteenths with each his mates. We offered to organise a bash for the 28th, but he'd refused and went boozing with his mates around town instead.

So when Cody gets a true birthday on a leap year, we need to make the most of it, which is why I mentioned it last October. Yet here I am, with just eight days to organise an event that can't appear as if it has been thrown together in such a short time.

I scribble my to-do list:

> Venue
> Food/buffet – hot?
> Bar
> Music
> Invites – family, friends, mates?
> Decorations

How the hell am I going to get a party booked and organised in a week? As well as complete my usual weekly routines as a dutiful homemaker, mother, daughter and daughter-in-law alongside my part-time hours at the travel agents?

I punch Cody's number into the phone and wait while it rings for an age.

'Mum, what? I can't really talk at work, you know that!'

'Cheers, son, but I need to get started if next Saturday is going to materialise. Does the venue need a dance floor?' I ask.

After Cody's affirmative, away I go on to the internet in search of phone numbers for so-called 'decent' local pubs.

In one hour I've drunk three coffees and researched and called four local pubs, of which only one answered, given the early time of day. And, luckily, received no customers but the crowds passing the window are growing – it's the school half-term holiday, so I know my time is running out.

As I wait on hold to speak to a local company about the cost of hiring a photo booth complete with amusing props and dressing-up regalia my mobile begins ringing from inside my handbag. I juggle the landline and finally retrieve my mobile from the bottom of my bag: my mother.

I stare at the illuminated screen.

I'll call her back once I'm through with this supplier.

As it's Friday morning, I know exactly what she's calling for. If I had a choice, I would refrain from returning her call, but that wouldn't be the action of a dutiful daughter, would it?

'Hello, we wouldn't be able to confirm the final cost without knowing the venue, in order to take travel costs into consideration.'

'Can I pay the deposit and get back to you?' This might blow the party budget but still, they're fun, it gets people up and involved.

'You could ... but if you felt the final quote was too high, you might prefer to go elsewhere.'

'And my deposit?'

'That's non-refundable.'

Great! Do I chance it or not? Book entertainment without a venue secured?

'Would you still like me to take the card details over the phone?'

I take the gamble. The idea of ticking one thing off my to-do list feels like an achievement.

I linger over the call, once my card details are given, knowing what awaits me.

In fact, I make another coffee, check the weather report and then, when there's really no other option, return my mother's call.

'Hello, darling, I was wondering what you're doing next Wednesday at midday?' she asks immediately, continuing without giving me a chance to speak or confirm if I am free. Knowing my part-time work pattern of Mondays, Tuesday and Fridays, she assumes I am. 'I've booked myself a treat with Derek – you remember Derek, don't you?'

'Oh yes, I remember Derek,' I reply. Or Derek the Deviant, as our household nicknamed him after he and my mother attended a series of dodgy evening classes where a state of undress always seemed a prerequisite, alongside the usual course fee.

I hold my breath, awaiting her next line.

'Anyway, it's called tantric intimacy . . . have you heard about it? Derek says it's all the rage at the moment amongst our generation.'

I cringe, not fully understanding the term but my skin has learnt to crawl at any of Derek's suggestions. Why and how my mother has involved herself is beyond me.

'Polly . . . are you there?'

'I'm waiting to hear what that involves, Mum, that's all . . . It'll no doubt shock or surprise me. I thought that tantric related to sexual activity, but I thought you'd previously said that you and Derek weren't . . .' I can't find the words or at least can't bring myself to say them aloud to a sixty-four-year-old woman who's vigorously fighting to retain her youth.

'Polly, stop being so timid, my darling! Life doesn't have to be so defined, sweetheart. You need to allow yourself to be free from the trappings of social norms. Derek and I can be whatever we choose, from one week to the next.'

My stomach reacts and a bit of vomit burns the back of my throat. This is not what I need to hear from my own mother at this – or any – hour of the day.

'Thank you, Mum, but Fraser and I are more than happy as we are. We're not looking to go against the norms of society . . . unlike yourself and dear Derek.'

'Anyway, I need you to drop me off for midday and then collect me afterwards,' she continues.

'Where from?'

'The Bed Shop.'

'The Bed Shop on the High Street? Are you serious, Mum?' My mind fills with the quaint image of our local, eponymously named bed shop, manned by the softly spoken Mrs Jenkins, established thirty years ago and maintained by her nearest and dearest.

'Sorry, correction, I read the leaflet incorrectly . . . the studio *above* The Bed Shop.'

'Oh, I'm glad to hear it. I was concerned for a second . . . I'd have never bought from there again if it was the *actual* bed shop staging such an event.'

'Oh Polly, humour me for once. My days are drawing nigh and I do as I please.'

'Why can't you be happy with flower arranging or painting watercolours?'

'Listen, darling, when you're older, I hope you never have to justify your decisions to Cody.'

'Mum, if I ever reach old age, I'll make sure I never give Cody anything to question me about, OK? I'll happily potter around my garden deadheading the dahlias.'

'Mmmm, *anyway* . . .'

'Pencil me in for Wednesday, though I bet you didn't consider asking Helen if she's available, did you?'

'Helen's got her hands full with the two girls. Bye, darling, speak to you later. Mwah, mwah.'

I end the call and shiver at the thought of any intimacy lesson in a room full of strangers, tantric or not.

I glance at the clock; I have barely thirty minutes before Stacey arrives, but a quick chat with my sister won't hurt.

She answers within two rings.

'Hi, Helen, how's things?'

'Good, good . . . you?'

'A quick call for two things: are you still OK for Sunday lunch and save the date for the twenty-ninth as Cody's now decided he does want a twentieth party.'

'Yes to Sunday but . . .'

'No buts, Helen.'

'Oh Polly, I asked you about that weeks ago and you said . . .'

'I know what I said, but he's only just changed his mind this morning over breakfast. What can I do, Helen?'

'Oh Polly . . . we were . . . we wanted to . . . we need . . .'

'Don't you dare let me down, Helen! You're the only normal relatives the lad has so there's no way you and Marc are squirming out of attending!'

'But, Polly, I did ask . . . you remember me asking, right?'

'I do, but tough. You're his aunty and Cody wants you there.'

'He or you?'

'Both, you silly arse. What other plans have you got anyway?'

'I wanted to book a weekend break away for just me and Marc.'

'And I wonder who you'd have asked to babysit the girls over the weekend? Me, by any chance?'

'Well, yes, I wouldn't trust anyone else, but it looks as if that idea's gone for a burton.'

'Sure has. Instead you'll be dancing at your nephew's twentieth, alongside your husband – why don't you book yourself a couple of rooms at the Travelodge overnight and make the most of it?'

'Are the girls invited?'

'Of course.'

'Oh . . . just with his mates there and the amount of drink I assume will be flowing . . .'

'Helen ... listen to yourself, will you? It's a family celebration. There'll be the usual family, close friends and, yeah, some of Cody's mates – his good mates, who he's grown up with.'

'OK, I'll see what ...'

'No, not I'll see what Marc says!'

'*Polly.*'

'*Helen.* Tell me, how many nephews do you have?'

'One,' says Helen, her dulcet tone rattling my cage.

'How many sisters do you have?'

'One.'

'There you go then, decision made ... Saturday the twenty-ninth of February, arrive sometime around seven-thirty – I'll let you know the venue when I've booked it. Love you. See you on Sunday.'

I end the call before she devises another excuse.

I start tidying away my to-do list and grab a pile of customer filing, making it appear as if I have *actually* done some work this morning. I can do fifteen minutes before Stacey arrives at one.

Cheeky bugger. One nephew, one sister and she thinks she can shirk her duties. Did I say 'I'll think about it' when she asked me to be Evie and Erica's godmother? No. And did Fraser complain about being dragged into the godparent mix purely by association? No.

I silently chastise my older sister for her slack notions about family obligations. I rely on her to counterbalance the lack of normality in the handful of other relatives that Cody has: a grandmother who has reverted to her youth and a grandfather obsessed with his ex-wife covers my side of the family, apart from my great-aunty Doris, who I can never remember or explain the family connection to. As for Fraser's side, his parents always smother Cody – he's the only grandchild on their side, which is sad given their hopes for their other two sons.

His uncle Rory and uncle Ross are both good-looking chaps yet neither has ever settled down. So all the more reason why my older sister had better step up to the plate!

The door chime sounds, interrupting my thoughts.

Smile in place, I look up to greet the customer.

It's Lola, Cody's ex-girlfriend.

My smile fades.

'Hi, Polly, I was wondering . . .' Her heavily made-up lips pout as she speaks.

'What do you want, Lola?' My voice is flat, but the volume is high.

I sit back as she lets the shop door close and steadily makes her way to settle in one of the customer chairs in front of my desk. Her heavy-looking boots unbalance her skinny proportions; she's poured into tight jeans and a skinny-ribbed top beneath a plume of synthetic cream fur. She drops her oversized handbag to the floor. At eighteen, did I ever look that sultry? Or was I always sunshine and smiles?

I'll wait. I'll allow her chance to say what she wants and then I'll say my bit.

'I was thinking, with it being Cody's birthday in a week or so, is there anything he was particularly wanting, like, as a present?'

'A present? You wish to buy Cody a present?' I'm stunned. This is the last thing I thought she was about to say.

'Yeah, something nice.'

'*Something nice*,' I repeat, my brain playing for time. 'Something nice like a social media posting circulated amongst all his mates and co-workers suggesting that he cheated on you? Or an actual gift?'

'Polly . . . that wasn't me. I've told you, my account was hacked and before I knew it . . .'

'*Really?* In which case, it was *so* good of you to deactivate your account after only forty-eight hours, once numerous people had added their remarks and shared the details several times causing my son much embarrassment at work.'

'Polly, his workmates were fine with him afterwards.'

'That's hardly the point, Lola.'

'Anyway . . .'

'*Anyway . . .*' I mimic, knowing I sound pathetic given my age, but my angst goes unnoticed. 'What else can I help you with?'

'Oh, nothing. I was just passing and wondered what Cody might like, that's all.'

'I'm sure he's quite all right as he is, thanks, Lola. Now, if you wouldn't mind . . .' I say, glancing around the store. I really wish there was a queue of impatient customers right now, as then my comment would seem apt. Given there's no one here, it makes me feel daft.

Lola follows my gaze around the empty shop and looks back at me, puzzled.

She gets the message though and stands, grabbing her handbag.

'If there's anything you can think of, just let me know, OK?'

I smile and nod politely as Lola talks and walks backwards towards the shop door. I have no intention of passing on any message or encouraging this young woman in any way.

'Polly, please,' she says opening the door. 'It's been so long since I spoke to him and . . .'

'Did you not get any flowers last Friday?' I ask, having hit my irritability limit.

Her kohl-edged eyes widen as I knew they would.

'No!'

'Oh!' I give a tiny shrug.

'Cody sent flowers to someone on Valentine's Day?' Her jaw drops, her petite frame frozen.

'Oops, sorry.' I busy myself with my computer. I know that was a cheap shot, but necessary to erase her intentions regarding my son.

As Lola's head drops and the door closes behind her, a wave of guilt washes over me, chased away immediately by a wave of sheer relief.

Dana

I button my coat as I near the crowd of parents standing by the metal railings at the top of the school driveway. There was a time we were allowed down the driveway to congregate nearer the school exits but not since Tyler's mum showed her annoyance at him coming second in the 'design a Christmas card' competition to Miranda-with-the-most-gold-stars when her mum rudely sneered. Mrs Huggins, the school's cuddly head teacher, was having none of it and put a stop to parents standing anywhere where the children might see adults having a fist fight through a classroom window. As a result, we now gather at the metal railings, which means our little ones have a trek and a half, accompanied by one or two knackered teachers, to reach us at the end of the school day.

I stand on the outer edge of the parental crowd, mindful not to ignore others but definitely not willing to join the ranks of the chummy-mummies, who haven't a nice word to say about anyone, even each other!

I smile at Bethany's mum standing a few feet away, rocking her brand-new baby stroller; obviously her first outing since baby girl number three arrived. I mouth 'congratulations' and she smiles. I'd go over and have a coo but I daren't risk that newborn baby smell wafting up my nose and setting me off being broody. Hankering after a non-existent newborn is the last thing I need right now, so I stand well clear and smile politely. I'll leave it a week or two, then ask for a cuddle when the new arrival smells a little more milky, of baby sick or of Johnson & Johnson talc. Then I can compliment her on how well she looks in her slim-cut jeans, which she'll feel obliged to squeeze into before long given the twice-daily scrutiny of the chummy-mummies.

I give a polite nod towards the Two Dads of Dudley, who always attend the school gate delivery and collection despite one being the dad and the other the mum's current partner, a devoted stepdad. I'm always intrigued how their love triangle works, because the Two Dads of Dudley appear and leave at the same time. Dudley goes home and arrives with a different dad and his car each day. I suspect there is one ultra-organised mum as the kingpin, with both dads doing their duty regardless of the other's presence. But, hey, if it works, it works. Dudley has three doting parents to cater to his every need, which can't be bad. I wonder how and where you find such obliging dads and stepdads, as Kingpin Mum has obviously cracked it. If I ever spot her, I'll be sure to ask. Luke's father, Andrew, jumped ship just three days after the positive test – not the pregnancy result but the amniocentesis at seventeen weeks.

Ring, ring, ring!

The faint sound of the school bell can be heard at the gate. At this point most, though not all, parents cease chatting and prepare for the dash. Not the dash of little ones racing up the driveway but the dash to grab your little ones' hand and quick march faster than their little legs can move to your precariously parked vehicle, on double yellows, if needs be. Before anyone else has chance to bundle their children in, fiddle with car seats, indicate and pull out – which will block you in for at least ten minutes because some people have insufficient status amongst the parents to break into the traffic once it is jammed solid along the school road. If you're not part of the in-crowd, no amount of PTA attendance, birthday party promises or inching your bumper out will get you the green light to cut in or a friendly headlamp flash.

Me, I walk. I walk every day with Luke as it gives us chance for a lovely end-of-school-day chat and gives him a little extra exercise. Plus I get to carry his heavy rucksack, providing me with an extra little weight-training session on top of the heavy water buckets I move each day. I love it. This walking routine of delivery and collection to this sweet little primary school is one of the highlights of each day, which is why I refuse to let others ruin it for me. I'm a mum. Luke's mum. And I love it.

A tsunami of tiny bodies, white shirt tails flapping, snotty noses running, plaits unplaiting, flow up the driveway towards us waiting parents. You see their little blank faces react and respond to the familiar face only when they recognise it amongst the crowd. It's like a light-bulb moment, from off to shining, from blank expression to 'Daddy!'. It never ceases to amaze me, the instant transformation on their tiny faces. Around me a sea of 'Hello, cupcake', 'Jake, I'm over here' and 'Oh dear, how did you do that then?' fills the air.

And here's my Luke. Why are his little glasses always skew-whiff? He never straightens them so the tilt of the blue plastic gives him a permanently cute but slightly daft expression.

His coat is wide open, flapping as he runs, his little legs are pounding; in one hand he's clutching a large piece of paper – no doubt it's another painting for our fridge exhibition. In the

other is a black bin liner. I know that inside will be a wet pair
of pants and maybe one pair of school trousers. Despite Luke's
best efforts, despite everything he has managed to overcome to
attend the mainstream school allocated by our local authority,
he still leaves it a little late regards peeing. Potty training was
one of our biggest struggles; thankfully he managed the main
business, just not the peeing. Sadly, most days he leaves school
clutching a bin liner. I'm grateful that the school accommodate his needs but I really do wish they wouldn't send him
out clutching the evidence, notifying every other parent of
his continued accidents. I'd much prefer to walk down to the
school office or the classroom and collect the bin liner myself.
Peeing and speech are his areas of weakness, and I don't know
how many times I've discussed both with the primary school.
I'm used to his lack of articulated words but until he receives
his allotted speech therapy sessions, I can't see this weakness
improving.

'Mummy!' he cries in his own fashion, thrusting the large
piece of paper at me while I crouch down and attempt to steal
a wet kiss, grabbing the bin liner from his clutches. 'Look ...
I painted a panda!' His lack of self-consciousness melts my
heart; my boy doesn't care about bin liners or skewed glasses,
just his painting.

I take his offering and stare at the blobs of red and blue paint
which has seven sticky-out fingers on each hand and a long tail.
Not recognisable as any panda I've ever seen, but what do I
know? I'll leave it to my little expert.

I'm about to praise him, coo over his efforts, when Tyler's
mum chips in unexpectedly, as she's still waiting for her little
cherub to appear.

'That's quite good,' she remarks, peering at his painting.
'Considering.'

Instantly, the hairs on the back of my neck bristle. My head lifts in slow motion, as her final word hangs in the air between us.

'*Considering?*' I repeat, my right eyebrow arched and primed for trouble. I'll give her a chance to quickly correct herself, a moment to gather her insensitive thoughts or swiftly deliver her apology, as necessary.

I slowly stand tall, my chin lifted.

She shuffles on the spot. Blinks rapidly. Her mouth works non-stop and yet fails to produce a complete sentence. She swiftly looks around for parental back-up, but the others have all quickly taken one giant step away from her for fear of association.

'Well, yes, you know . . . considering.' She murmurs the final word softly.

My eyebrow lifts higher. I glance down at Luke, who is happily admiring his handiwork.

'Considering he's five? Considering he hasn't used black paint or considering he has Down's?' I ask, my voice steely, my manner too.

'Mummy!' Tyler arrives and interrupts the drama, his hands instantly reaching for his mother's neck and today she is very willing to bend down to his level and receive a snotty kiss – unlike other schooldays when her precious make-up can't *possibly* be ruined.

I remain statuesque, unmoving, waiting. The crowd collectively release their held breath. I can sense the ripple of relief that Tyler has had perfect timing today; more often than not he's kept back by his teacher for a naughtiness talk, despite his intelligence.

His mother slowly stands, straightens his shirt collar and exhales.

'I'm sorry, Dana – I just . . . I didn't . . . think. Sorry,' she says stroking the right forearm of my coat as if that makes the world a better place.

I simply stare. Words fail me every time this happens. One day, when they stop looking at Luke as the little one who is different from the rest of the class, they will finally get to see what I see: a vibrant, beautiful, smart young boy who has the world at his feet and can do anything – and I mean absolutely bloody anything – he chooses to put his mind and effort to. And just as well as any other child who attends this school. One day. 'One day' has sadly become my mantra for my Luke. One day others will see the shape of his heart before they notice anything else: his features, his speech, his condition. One day they'll see his continual kindness, happy smiles and laughter, and then they will realise that Down's syndrome is just an element of his make-up, much like his eye colour, his hair colour and potential shoe size, nothing more.

Simply a child, like any other.

One day.

One day can't come soon enough for me. Or Luke.

'Come on, Luke, let's go home,' I say, turning away and smiling down at my son's upturned face. 'Guess what we've got for tea?'

I take his chubby hand in mine and we walk, just as we've walked every day: together amongst the crowd.

'Sausage, egg and chips?' he asks eagerly.

'Is that what you want?' I've bought a sliver of fresh fish and vegetables for our tea. I have to monitor his daily nutrition and digestion in order to counteract the biological impacts of his condition. Thankfully, we have a few supplements to rely on when a boy wants chips. 'OK, you win!'

Luke nods, his dark fringe bouncing above his tiny smiling eyes, his glasses tilting even more.

Carmen

Elliot's already home by the time I pull into the driveway. I can see his outline through the kitchen's open blind as he moves about making dinner.

Instantly, my mind quietens and my heart softens.

I undo my seat belt and watch him.

He'll be listening to his blaring boy music with a thumping bass whilst rhythmically moving – he won't ever admit to dancing – and conjuring up another of his fabulous meals without effort or fuss. I know he'll flick the switch on the kettle as soon as I come in the door, plant a kiss on my forehead and make me a hot coffee as I settle at the table and reel off the details of my day at work. He'll nod, he'll comment, and if I sound drained, fed-up or overly tired, he'll ditch the coffee and pour me a glass of white wine from the fridge.

I know all these things, and yet I don't know if he wishes to marry me. Commit to me. Make a life with me and try for a family.

How do I not know that after eight years? Because we've never talked about it. I've never dared to question his intentions, and I get the impression he doesn't wish to ignite the wedding touchpaper prematurely.

How does he not know that I am desperate for *this* scenario to change and for us to become Mr and Mrs Cole? Mr and Mrs Elliot Cole – that has a certain ring to it.

Our next-door neighbour Nile pulls into his drive, leaps from his car, sees me sitting here and gives a warm yet awkward wave. I raise my hand to acknowledge it. Even next door got married two summers ago and are expecting a baby in two months ... we moved into this street years before they did. I watch as Nile unlocks his front door and enters. What made him ask in the end? Did Nessa give him an ultimatum – I doubt it, given her mild-mannered nature – or did he suddenly mature overnight and decide he wanted to commit?

Immature, that's my mum's excuse for Elliot each time we discuss it: 'He hasn't matured yet, it's as simple as that,' she'll say, sharing her expertise on the male of the species having married one and mothered four. 'Your father was the same.' After which she'll outline how my own father went from Casual Keith to Commitment Keith literally overnight, thanks to maturity. It frequently irks me that my parents dated for only two years before Commitment Keith showed up proposing marriage; I've waited four times that long already and still nothing, despite laying the foundations which now stand before me.

I watch Elliot cease moving, glance at his watch and then separate the kitchen blinds to stare out of the window, puzzled by my stationary car.

Wow, he even senses when I'm slightly late home and yet . . .

I give up. I know what I want. I can't see me waiting much longer for what I'd like, but I can hardly bring myself to say it, to think it, let alone do it. Could following the leap-year tradition deliver the goods?

I climb from my car, collect a box of paperwork from the back seat and make my way into the house.

Every day, I uphold tradition: the silver sixpence, orange blossom and something old, something new, but would this tradition be one step too far? Wouldn't I be missing out on a special moment? Haven't I been dreaming, wondering about, expecting that proposal for my entire life?

I sound so old-fashioned but the Leap Year Bride-to-be will never have that unexpected moment of delight knowing her man wanted to commit to her. She'll never have the assurance that he matured, made a choice, a decision and planned a proposal just for her . . .

My mind pauses mid-flow.

I enter our kitchen, wince at the thrash of music blaring from Elliot's phone, smell the delicious aroma wafting from the stove and receive a hasty peck on the cheek as Elliot grabs a colander and a boiling saucepan from the hob and begins straining cooked pasta over the sink.

. . . She'll never have that dream fulfilled of simply being a girl being asked by a boy to share his life.

I remove my coat and watch Elliot dodge the billow of steam from the pasta.

Apart from two gold rings, how different would this scene be if we were married?

It wouldn't be . . . so why the devil won't he just ask me?

Dana

'Please, Mummy . . .' whines Luke sleepily, as I close his favourite story book after the final page. 'One morrrrre.'

'Not one more, not tonight. You need sweet dreams because you're visiting Grandpops tomorrow to play in the garden and feed his billy-birds.'

'Billy-birds,' mumbles Luke, drifting beneath half-closed eyes.

'Yes, darling, billy-birds,' I whisper, as I tuck his duvet around his tiny body and make sure his toy elephant is close at hand. Luke rarely falls asleep without clasping the toy's tatty ear. I check his nightlight is correctly switched on, then plant a kiss on Luke's forehead. 'Night, night little man. Mummy loves you.'

I creep from the room; tiptoeing isn't really necessary because once Luke's down, Luke's down for the night. There are very few times when he wakes. Even as a tiny baby, he only woke for his night feeds and then went straight back off to sleep, which was a blessing given our circumstances, then and now. I'd be run ragged if he was one of those up-every-fifteen-minutes children who think bedtime is a game. I've seen them on the TV being trained by the Supernanny brigade. How parents keep their wits about them on the nine-hundredth time of calmly coaxing their child back into bed, I will never know. I'd crack on the fourth occasion, ranting, raving and pulling my hair out in sheer frustration that my nine, ten and eleven o'clock wind-down time had been absorbed by coaxing my child back into bed.

I reach the bottom of the staircase and switch off the landing light as a well-meaning phrase from six years ago whispers in my mind: 'We're only ever given what we are strong enough to love' – bloody right. I love what I have and thankfully that love isn't tested on the nine-hundredth time of kissing him good night.

Within ten minutes, I've rearranged the furniture in the lounge, carried in half the contents of my workbench from the garage and am settling down for a couple of hours of floristry work in front of Friday night TV.

It's not ideal, but I can work like this on occasion when needs must. And tonight – if I'm going to deliver on time tomorrow morning, attend a meeting at midday and present myself in a professional manner with samples of my work at Sunday's wedding fayre – needs must. I was happy with the two orders I created earlier in the day, I know both customers will be delighted when I deliver early tomorrow.

I carefully lift a piece of soaked oasis from the water bucket, and hold it aloft, allowing the excess water to drain without making a mess on my carpet. This is my downfall – I try to do too much too quickly and then create more work for myself.

I'm grateful that my Dutch supplier considers me as important as the high-street florist. My flower orders are tiny in comparison but still, if I order online by four o'clock, my wholesaler guarantees delivery by nine the following morning, travelling through the night from Holland. Their warehouse operates twenty-four hours a day – all high-tech and efficient with robots packaging each delivery on to the lorry, or so the driver tells me. More often than not, he unloads my delivery straight into my workshop, as per the delivery notice, while I walk Luke to school. If I can secure a few orders for this year's wedding season I'll be in a better position to plan for next year.

My hands work busily as my eyes flick back and forth towards the TV screen. I'm not really following the weekly serial, as I can never be sure I'll have time each week to watch the next episode, so I'm simply watching a male chat to a female, the female starts to cry, the male comforts the female, then kisses the female – all very random and pointless given that I don't understand any backstory or the build-up to their scene together. But it looks intense, it appears pretty positive for them both and, oh yep, there they go, heading towards the bedroom . . . eventful too.

I laugh to myself. I'm sitting here, surrounded by wedding work, taking the mickey out of a storyline where two actors are doing what I would like a piece of in my daily life. Not a huge piece, nothing too intense, but definitely some company, some kissing and, who knows, maybe some sex if he's the right fella.

I blush.

What am I like?

I'm blushing and there's no one around to be embarrassed in front of. Oh Dana, get a bloody grip, woman! But the reality is this: it has been so long since . . . well, since there was a man in my life that I'm virtually back to acting like a schoolgirl when a half-decent guy is a metre away. Or not ... my cheeks are still burning.

My stomach begins to flutter.

What am I going to be like attending this meeting if I feel nervous sitting here alone? Earlier, I'd promised myself not to think about it but now ... I stare at my hands working on autopilot – they are visibly shaking, causing the white lily bloom to quiver as I wire it.

Don't think about it, simply do it, Dana.

Polly

'Tell me you didn't!' whines Cody, glaring from under his brows as I peel potatoes at the kitchen sink.

'I'm sorry, I couldn't help myself. She did that sultry walk, trying to be all vulnerable and pally-pally towards me. I was having none of it. You said it was over and now, well, there's no need for her to be hanging about, visiting me at work seeking suggestions for a present, is there?' I wince as I wait for his answer.

Cody peels himself from the countertop he was leaning against and makes to leave before stopping to answer me.

'I just wish you hadn't, that's all.'

I know he's annoyed, I've stepped on his toes.

'Help me out here – the girl made you as miserable as sin. She was barely pleasant towards you for the whole time you dated and now, when it's clearly over, she's willing to shower you with gifts! Seriously, Cody ... it's calculated.'

'I know, but still. You'd come down hard on any parent who sniped at me that way.' He raises one eyebrow, reinforcing his tone.

Am I actually getting told off by my son?

Has our relationship crossed a boundary where mutual respect equates to his disapproval of my actions? Bloody hell! When did that happen?

'Sorry.'

Cody nods an acknowledgement, much like Fraser's manner of receiving a sentiment when delivered, good or bad. And since when did Cody become a replica of his father? He's always been my double!

'You forget she has a nice side too.'

'Mmmm, pity I didn't see any of it during the – how long was it? – eight months that she messed you about for.'

Cody shrugs, as if the hurt had been water off a duck's back. I know it wasn't.

'I'll be upstairs . . . shout when dinner's done,' he says, ending our conversation.

I continue to peel the potatoes, my fingers nimbly rotating each one.

A shout upstairs, a quick conversation over dinner and a slam of the front door will be the routine as he leaves for another Friday night out, going God knows where, to see God knows who for a few beers. Only to return when I'm tucked up in bed, though Fraser will still be up, watching late-night TV. I'll lie beneath a warm duvet listening to the murmured chatter of two males downstairs, much like I listened to the sounds of the TV drifting up through the floorboards when I was little. And then the arguments, which increased as I neared school-leaving age – not about Helen pushing her unspoken-curfew time, which she often did when she was out with Marc, but my parents' marriage unravelling. Is that the circle of life, lying in the darkness, listening to your family, from childhood to adulthood, in various situations?

I rinse the peeled potatoes and grab a saucepan.

I assume this is how mothering feels once your children truly find their independence. This is the reality of letting go and allowing my son to build his own life. I can't choose his friends any more, needless to say I shouldn't try to choose his girlfriends . . . but still, I couldn't sleep at night if I thought he hadn't learnt his lessons regarding that young lady.

I load the stove with various pans, putting a light under each gas burner.

He'll be twenty in just over a week, and being one of 'those mothers' was never my intention. I'll need to be careful in future. Having to apologise to my son isn't something that I wish to repeat too often. I couldn't name a single incident before where I've felt it was necessary to apologise. Was that his maturity, or the weight of my mistake in saying what I had to Lola?

'Your dad's on the phone, Polly,' says Fraser, bringing my ringing mobile to me from the lounge. 'Are you OK?'

'Yep, fine.' I tap the screen and accept the call. Fraser peers at me before returning to the lounge. 'Hi, Dad, are we still OK for tomorrow?'

I mentally change hats, from concerned mother to dutiful daughter, and buzz about the kitchen, bringing together our evening meal whilst chatting to my dad about his pet dog, Fido.

Carmen

'How does this sound, Elliot?'

Elliot mutes his TV drama and waits while I adopt my announcement voice and read the scribbled notes which I'm preparing for a business proposal. This is our usual routine most nights, him lying on the sofa, me across the way in the armchair.

'Thank you so much for attending. As you all know, I'm Carmen Smith, owner of The Wedding Boutique. I'm creating a new venture, bringing several wedding services together. My hope is that we'll be able to cater for all areas of wedding preparation in one place rather than expecting our couples to go in search of suppliers and goods offered in various locations.' I pause and look up to check he's listening. Elliot is looking up at me. 'OK so far?'

'OK apart from the owner part. I think "proprietor" sounds more sophisticated.'

Fair dos, I'll change that later.

I continue to read aloud.

'I'm currently in discussion to take over the property adjoining this and the new shop would become a one-stop wedding centre enabling an entire wedding to be booked in one visit, dependent upon availability, of course . . .' I wait for Elliot's feedback.

He nods.

'No other changes?'

'No.'

I'm not convinced.

'Just the one change, then?'

'I'd say so but, hey, you know these people better than me. Are they having difficulties in securing wedding bookings or not? They might be making a decent living doing what they're already doing.'

'But if we bring the services together under one roof, it will make the planning process so much easier for everyone!'

Silence descends while I wait for his opinion.

'You done?' he asks, indicating the TV with the remote control.

'Yes. Done.'

Elliot hits the button and the TV blares back into life.

Thanks a bunch.

I lower my head, pretending to be busy working, but instead I watch his profile. His brown eyes are fixed on the plasma TV screen, his wavy brown fringe is pushed further to one side than usual and his mouth twitches amidst the beginnings of tomorrow's shave. He seems content, sprawled on the sofa having completed a day at the bank, but who knows what's truly going on inside someone's head? I've never heard him complain about his lot in life. I've never heard his mates rib him about being the last bachelor standing.

Some of his mates haven't got the deposit for their own home, as we have, and yet they have young children. I glance around our lounge: we have decorated it, have every soft furnishing, every gadget necessary for our daily lives – the entire house is homely. Anyone walking into this property right now would see us as a contented couple with a comfortable lifestyle ... and yet we're not committed.

The only thing missing is the framed wedding photograph on the bookshelf.

Go figure. I can't.

I'm stuck for an answer.

I'm no further forward in figuring out the complexities of men than I was in my last relationship. We didn't last as long as Elliot and I have but it was no less intense. I'd pinned my hopes on him being 'the one' ... only for the relationship to flounder, fail and me to be left broken-hearted. He became my lost love, a forgotten ache in the memory book of life.

I love Elliot to bits. We're good together. We make a fine couple in everyone's eyes so why aren't I the one choosing a wedding venue, ordering bridesmaids' shoes and checking off

RSVP replies? Instead, despite the late hour and having completed a full working day at the boutique, I'm trying my hardest to put together a new business venture so my little empire can grow into something more lucrative. It's not guaranteed to work – it's a risky business stepping out of the proverbial comfort zone – but needs must if I'm to expand and invest in my own future. I don't pretend to be a wedding entrepreneur, but I've got my head screwed on regarding ambition. From a tender age, I realised that hard work never did me any harm, which is why I work hard in all areas of my life: home, business and personal development.

Still, what I *really* wish I was doing right now is investing in our future family by planning a wedding.

'What?' asks Elliot, glancing up and seeing me staring.

'Nothing. Sorry, I was in a world of my own,' I confess, shuffling papers and returning to my task.

Elliot goes back to his TV drama.

If you don't ask, you'll never know ... says a tiny voice in my head.

Mmmm, and that's the problem: I don't *want* to ask. I don't think it's my job to ask.

Chapter Three

Saturday 22 February

Carmen

I skim my index finger down the list of today's appointments as Anna hovers beside me, looking over my shoulder.

'Are you OK?' I ask her, having taken in the busy nature of our day ahead. Saturday is always booked solid with appointments and fittings accommodating those who work full-time during the week. We have an appointment every hour on the hour from ten o'clock until five. By closing, we'll have kicked off our shoes and be tidying up or vacuuming in stockinged feet.

'I was wondering if I could go a little earlier tonight? Not much earlier, just fifteen minutes?'

I raise an eyebrow inquisitively.

'I know we're busy but if I can leave early, I'll happily make it up at lunchtime or work over on another day,' she adds, twisting her fingers into knots.

'Who is it?'

'Remember last week, the guy from the bathroom shop who sent me the flowers? Well, he wants to catch up for a quick drink straight after work and ... I was thinking that ... well, if ... you know ... Carmen, please?'

I give a gentle nod.

'Oh, to be young again,' I call to Trish, who is busy tidying the rails of bridal gowns ready for our first appointment.

'No, thanks. I'm past all that fuss. When I think of the number of hours I wasted on men who really were not worth my time, let alone spending eons washing my hair and getting dressed up for ... oh no, I'm happy as I am, thanks. You enjoy yourself, Anna, while you can – but don't get too bogged down with men at your age. Have your fun.'

Anna gives her a hard stare from under her asymmetrical fringe.

'Cody's OK, he's worth bothering for.'

'I used to think that at first but then they'd stand me up, or let me down at the last minute and I used to feel so depressed about it. In reality, they were proving to me that I should be doing other things rather than dating and waiting for them. My priorities should have been having fun with my girlfriends and achieving my own dreams. You need to read the signals based on how he treats you, then decide if he's worth it. Don't you agree, Carmen?'

'Not really. I wasn't asked out that often and when I was, I made the most of it, until Elliot came along.'

'You went steady for ages with that one chap ... what was his name?'

'Connor? Oh yeah, but I outgrew him so it didn't go any-where, did it? My first serious love. We were too young really, but at the time I thought he was "the one for me". He made everyone smile with his funny one-liners or his favourite saying, 'I'm in no rush' – and he wasn't, was he?'

'He was nice though, good-looking too ... but, yes, very

immature compared to you,' says Trish, adding, 'You've always been beyond your years though, Carmen.'

Trish is right. I should take it as a compliment, but I never have. When other girls giggled through biology class I was transfixed and learning, when others failed their driving tests seven times over I studied every page of *The Highway Code* and passed first time and, yes, when it came to boys, I was always the level-headed, sober girl holding everyone else's hair back while they puked in a nightclub loo. That's me: sensible, mature and now, looking back, maybe a tad boring in my teenage years.

'Anyway, Anna, what did you say to him about the Valentine roses?' asks Trish, swapping sides of the boutique to neaten the other rail of gowns.

'I just thanked him when we ran into each other in the Cross Keys, and he asked if I wanted a drink, so we chatted for a bit before his mates moved on to another pub.'

'And you didn't follow them?' asks Trish, her hands swiping and pushing yards of white, ivory and champagne fabrics neatly into place.

'Nope, my crowd had pitched for the night at a table and we stayed there . . . I don't go chasing guys into other pubs just to get attention. What kind of girl do you think I am, Trish?'

'Phew! We used to, didn't we?' giggles Trish. 'Many a night I've trekked from pub to pub, checking if a certain guy was in there before rushing out and into the next.'

'That sounds desperate,' mutters Anna, wincing at the idea.

'Yep, I'll give you that. We thought we were upping our chances of getting chatted up by the guy we fancied, nothing more. We must have looked like a right bunch dashing from pub to pub before settling in one and buying a drink.'

Anna glances at me. She's wondering if Trish's 'we' refers to me too, but it doesn't. I was rarely asked out on dates, so limiting my chances by setting my sights on a specific guy never appealed.

The church clock of St Peter's strikes the hour and I check the wall clock, ensuring it is time before I flick the door sign to 'open'.

Our first appointment will be here within minutes, from which point we'll only have time for quick toilet breaks and staggered solo lunches.

As I stride away from switching the sign, the door's buzzer sounds. Anna rushes to the reception desk to release the automatic catch as Trish and I, professional smiles in place, turn to greet our bride-to-be. We know that first impressions count; we've been in the wedding business long enough to know that every little interaction goes towards ensuring that a bride-to-be and her associated family have the very best experience in our boutique. We give each bridal appointment our undivided attention; I would never allow two brides to share the limelight – it isn't what I'd want for myself – so I insist one appointment, one bride. I've taught Trish everything I know and I don't doubt that if I were absent for a matter of time she would continue to run my business in the exact manner in which she sees me do it on a daily basis.

As we both smile at the incoming party we instantly recognise our lady. This is not her first time visiting us. This is not our typical bride. I recall the surname written into our appointment book and step forward to welcome her, for what I believe could be the ninth time in my boutique, but manners must prevail on every occasion, to every prospective bride, real or not, sale or not.

'Hello, Miss Ingram, how are you today?' I ask, still smiling, though I know that the next hour will be a total waste of our time and effort. I might send Anna into the kitchenette to make

Trish and me another cup of coffee – we'll need it once this appointment is through.

'Hi, this is my mum, my nan and my cousin who is brides-maid,' says Miss Ingram, pointing to each in turn as the ladies gather inside the boutique, ignoring my question.

'Welcome,' I say, recognising each of the females from last time. 'Please come and take a seat and we'll get some details.' The family know the routine: four females scurry towards the chaise longue as Trish brings across our appointment clipboard and the form into which I usually add many details regarding our bride-to-be. But not this one. I have long ceased taking notes about this young woman and her associated family. On her first visit I was eager to please, on her second visit I was helpful and polite. On the third, fourth and fifth occasions I was dubious. On the sixth, seventh and eighth visits I was non-committal, not convinced that this bunch had a conscience, indulging in this absurd behaviour. For Miss Ingram – a different name from the one she used last time – is a serial appointment bride. A wannabe bride who does the rounds of bridal boutiques making appointments on busy Saturdays simply to try on numerous gowns and pretend that she is one of the lucky ones who has a wedding to plan for. In fact, she never pays a deposit, never chooses a specific gown and never appears to be getting married, despite having a wedding date, venue details and a wealth of information about a fiancé – though I suspect he is also fictitious.

But still, once she's here, we have to honour her appointment.

Just twenty-five minutes later, Anna watches the boutique door close, open-mouthed.

'How come . . .'

'Don't ask. We've seen that one at least eight times before. She's been coming in here and trying on bridal gowns since she was your age and the conversation then revolved around how young she was to be getting married,' I explain.

'She hasn't got a wedding booked, she simply wishes she had,' adds Trish, biting into a custard cream and handing out our coffees.

'She had an engagement ring on . . . it was a sapphire and diamond cluster,' says Anna.

'Yes, she always has an engagement ring on. I think that's part of the act,' I reply.

'It's a bit sad that she hasn't anything better to do on a Saturday morning. I blame the family for encouraging her – they should be taking her in hand rather than complying with the obsession,' says Trish, leaning on the reception counter.

'Exactly. In the future, if she *does* receive a genuine proposal of marriage and comes looking to purchase her bridal gown, her special moment has been marred. She's ruined it for herself by playing games.'

'She's desperate for attention,' says Trish, before sipping her coffee.

'I feel sorry for her . . . she's obviously desperate to get married,' says Anna, slurping hers.

'Mmmm, she's not the only one but we don't all go around faking bridal appointments, do we?' I say with a chuckle, glancing towards Trish.

'Some simply wait years and years until it happens,' says Trish, grasping my meaning.

'Or like the bride-to-be yesterday, she proposed to him,' interrupts Anna. 'It's a sign of modern life.'

'Not so modern. Queen Victoria proposed to her cousin, and I think that's the greatest love story of all time,' swoons Trish.

'Only because she was Queen!' I add quickly, not wanting to mislead Anna. 'It's hardly a fair comparison.'

'Even so, she *still* asked him.'

'Did he say yes?' asks Anna, showing her lack of knowledge.

'Obviously,' pouts Trish.

'If you don't ask, you'll never know . . .' I mutter softly, more to myself than the other two.

'Exactly, Carmen . . . but are you willing to ask?' says Trish, a smile dawning.

Dana

'Everything OK, love?' asks my dad, as I drop Luke off at half eleven on my way to my meeting. Dad's instantly curious given that I'm wearing a blouse and trouser combo, which was the only thing in my wardrobe that looked remotely interview-ish. It's been a long time since I've needed to smarten up my appearance: my days revolve around a five year old, cold water and flower pollen. Fingerless gloves, a baggy fleece and a messy bun are more my style.

'Fine, Dad, just meeting friends for a quick lunch. Nothing fancy but I wanted to . . .'

I don't finish my sentence, Dad simply nods and takes Luke's rucksack containing his spare set of clothes, his toy elephant in case a nap is necessary and, I have no doubt, a packet of half-eaten sweets shoved in for good measure by Luke when I wasn't looking.

'Your mum's nipped out to the shop, but you'll see her when you get back,' he says, kissing me on the cheek and taking Luke by the hand and hauling him over their doorstep.

'Luke, give Mummy a kiss,' I say, kissing his soft, plump, upturned cheek. 'Now, be good for Grandpops, OK? Mummy will be back by the time you've had some cake, fed the billy-birds in the garden and watched your favourite elephants programme, OK?'

Luke nods, eager to disappear with Grandpops into the garden on the hunt for wild birds and the big bag of bird seed which he knows lives inside the shed.

'Thanks, Dad,' I mutter, as I turn to go.

The pair remain on the doorstep as I walk the length of the path towards my car. Luke waves enthusiastically, as if I'm leaving him for a fortnight – which I never have: six hours is probably the longest separation we've endured in nearly six years.

'Bye, Mummy!' shouts Luke, holding my dad's hand. My heart melts.

I reach the car door, give one final wave, and breathe. I can focus ahead now that I know Luke is settled. He's never usually a problem, but on occasion he'll become clingy, like all children do, and then throw a paddy-fit, which always makes it so much harder to leave him.

'Afternoon, I have a meeting with Happy Productions TV,' I say to the attractive receptionist sitting behind the wooden desk. She has the brightest smile. The large vase of decorative lilies have a few days more life in them, though I would have placed more eucalyptus leaves amongst the flower stems as a colour contrast.

'Straight along this corridor, fourth door on your right,' she says, pointing as she speaks.

'Thank you.' I turn, about to follow her directions, then instantly turn back. 'Can I ask where the toilets are?'

'Along the same corridor, second door on your right . . . you can't miss them.'

I quickly dash to the loo, check my appearance and am back in the corridor within a few minutes.

I locate the fourth door and knock.

I'm early, but I'll wait if necessary.

'Hello ... Dana, isn't it?' says the man who opens the door. 'I'm Jez. Come on in and take a seat.'

'Hi,' I reply. He beckons me into the room and I am greeted by a sea of smiling faces sitting in a row behind a table covered with a linen cloth and a scattering of teacups and papers. I know I am blushing profusely but still I repeat, 'Hi.'

There's a Mexican wave of greetings as I ease myself into the single chair on this side of the panel. There are so many faces I can't count; more than eight but less than twenty.

'Guys, this is Dana Jones ... welcome, Dana. Can we go along and each give a brief introduction before we start?' says Jez. 'I'll go first. Hi, Dana, I'm Jez, as I mentioned, and I head the production team for Happy Productions TV. The documentary is my idea.' His blond crew cut bobs as he talks as if reinforcing his own answers.

I nod and smile at each person in turn, but I'm lost already. My mind is awash as they continue to throw a register of names and job titles at me: clinical psychologist, a lifestyle coach, a sociologist ... the panel of people seems endless. I don't remember any apart from Jennifer.

'I'm Jennifer, a relationship and dating counsellor.' She has a soft Australian accent and gives a little wave as she speaks, causing her tie-dye top to slip seductively from her right shoulder.

All the 'ologies' remind me of an old TV advert for British Telecom recalled and re-enacted by my dad's generation: 'Oooh, he got an ology!'

'So, before we begin, Dana, do you have any questions?' asks Jez.

'Where's Tamzin, the lady I spoke to yesterday on the phone?'

'Tamzin is running late unfortunately but, hey ho, that's Tammy for you. She'll arrive when she arrives. She's great at her job, just can't set an alarm properly.'

The panel chuckle. Some smile, some openly peer at me, taking in the head-to-waist view above the table. I fiddle with my hands in my lap.

Jez gives me another smile, faker than the first one.

'Are there any other interviewees today?' I ask, unsure whether Jez's smile was to encourage me to ask more questions. I had imagined they'd be asking me plenty, not the other way round.

The panel glance at one another, swapping little smiles before turning back to me.

'Can I answer that one?' asks Jennifer, her Australian accent coming across broadly.

'Sure,' says Jez, gesturing between us.

'Well, you completed an online application form for a new documentary following the journey of individuals finding true love. We had –' she pauses, grabs a pile of papers from the table, shuffles through them before continuing – 'two thousand females apply and we've spent the week whittling those down and ... well, we're delighted to say we've chosen you.' She smiles on her final word.

'Oh!' is all I can manage as the butterflies in my stomach spin about.

'Don't worry, we've collated a whole host of males, but we need to get to know you a little better, Dana. Then later today or tomorrow, we'll be reducing the male applicants to just three. The experts here are sure you'll be a good match for all of them and then, as the dates progress, you'll be able to stipulate which you would like to get to know better. By the finale night, we're hoping that there'll be a very special someone in your life and, well ... things might develop naturally from there onwards. All we ask is that you don't exchange contact details with any male until the week is complete.'

Three males?

'Of course, we'll all be on hand twenty-four-seven for you to discuss any issues or concerns you may have with us,' adds the woman who I believe is the lifestyle coach.

Concerns?

'You seem a little surprised,' says the psychologist.

No shit, Sherlock, however did you pick up on that!

I give a weak smile.

'You can be honest, Dana – this whole process is being offered to support your search for your Mr Right-in-Life,' she continues, tapping her pencil on the table.

They all wait for me to speak.

The meeting room is near silent, except for the tapping pencil.

'Sorry, sorry, sorry, I can't say it enough times – you know what I'm like. I make the bloody arrangements and then sodding oversleep ... and ... oh, hello ... I'm Tamzin. You're Dana ... I spoke to you yesterday.'

I jump at the interruption that bursts into the meeting room. A mass of orange and yellow dyed hair in tight zingy spirals, wide eyes and an enormous smile enters my personal space.

'Dana, yes, I am,' I say.

'You bet! And given it's a leap year – are you up for popping the big question come finale night?' says Tamzin, plonking herself on the edge of the table and beaming at the panel.

Polly

'And she's interested in that, Polly?' asks my dad, his mild-mannered features grimacing like I've never seen before.

'Yep, it seems so.' I slowly push the trolley along the aisle as he saunters beside me.

'And . . . you're taking her?'

'Yep, looks like it.' I stop to grab a couple of tins of his favourite soup before continuing to guide the wonky-wheeled trolley.

This is our weekly routine. A slow walk around the supermarket while I do Dad's shopping and he catches up with the wonders of my mother's world. I can't say it is the healthiest conversation I have, but it's all part of the juggling act which is my life.

'Do you need any sauces?' I ask, pointing to the ketchups. A quick shake of his head enables us to continue but I know he's lost in a world of how they used to be. Married. This isn't how I expected my aged father to live out his later years. I always thought that their arguments were a side-effect of her early menopause or maybe his mid-life crisis. I assumed that the sniping and bickering would one day cease and they'd resume being the loving couple they once were, when I was a child and we took day trips traipsing through the Forest of Dean or unravelling mysteries at Berkeley Castle. Sadly not. Not long after my sixteenth birthday, they officially divorced, though thankfully the dust settled just in time for Helen and Marc's wedding. But twenty-three years on, still he asks about her.

'I've run out of shaving foam,' he mutters.

'OK.'

'I don't understand the attraction ... he's older than I am,' says Dad as we turn the corner of the aisle.

'He makes my skin crawl and I've only met him twice,' I say, picking a couple of items from the shelf as we pass. I don't stop; there's no need to browse as we buy virtually the same items every time. Shaving cream is the anomaly purchase for this week.

'And is he joining her at Sunday lunch?'

'He bloody isn't, Dad. Sod that for a game of soldiers! I'm not encouraging Mum and Derek in any way. Fraser would have a fit at the very thought of them being in our house. It takes him all his effort to ignore what my mother's up to, let alone her ... friend.'

'Friend?'

'I think so ... she hasn't said anything else so friend sums them up.'

'Mmmm.'

We continue in silence, only broken by the clunk each time I place an item into our trolley.

'Can you take Fido to the groomers next week?'

'I can if you make it around Thursday,' I say, knowing he dislikes such tasks. Though it's a grooming parlour for dogs, he sees it as a beauty parlour, full stop, and not a place for his generation to frequent.

'I'll phone on Monday and let you know.'

Family life with married parents seems such a breeze. Growing up, I never imagined this scenario. I attempt to spend time with each of my parents, soothing their disgruntled feelings about the other and encouraging them each to lead an active and healthy lifestyle. My mum has her friend, Derek – who I'd wish she'd exchange for a nice gentleman with shared interests. I'd say 'normal' interests but Fraser would say my mother's partly to blame for the ludicrous ideas. My dad deserves a kindly female companion, someone who could share his days and weekends, if nothing else. I know he'd love to spend quality time out of the house, visiting garden centres, going to the pictures once in a while and enjoying some company. He's a proper gent is my dad, his manners are innate. He deserves to spend time with a wider social circle. I keep hoping he'll meet someone at his bowls club, but it hasn't happened.

'What's it to be afterwards? Pie and chips or a cream cake?' I ask, wanting to steer the conversation away from my mother.

His face breaks into a genuine smile. I watch his wrinkled cheeks lift and partly cover his eyes. This isn't the life he'd planned either, but he makes the most of it.

'Cake it is, then.'

'You're sure?'

'I'm sure.'

'Do you want me to write it on the calendar?'

'Do you think I'm an imbecile? I can remember my only grandson's birthday. Though could you order me a taxi? I'd like to be there early.'

'Fraser can collect you as we drive by, Dad. There's no need for a taxi.'

'But I don't want to stay out late. I don't like the loud music these kids play – it gives me a ringing in my ears even when I'm back home.'

'We'll find you somewhere away from the DJ to sit and enjoy yourself.'

'A DJ, not a band?'

'No, not a band – if we had a band, there'd be only one type of music all night, and with a mixture of friends, family and Cody's mates we need a bit of variety.'

'Boom, boom, boom then?' mutters Dad, as I unpack his shopping and he makes the cuppa.

'I'll request Louis Armstrong partway through the night if that makes you happier,' I say, emptying the plastic bags for life for another week.

'And how's your mother going to get there?'

He never ceases to think about her, does he?

'Don't worry about Mum, Dad. I've asked Fraser's parents to drop by as they pass – it's all worked out to ensure everyone is where they should be on the night.'

'Is her friend Derek too busy?'

'Her friend Derek isn't invited, Dad. I'm trying to discourage that acquaintance, not strengthen it.'

'And Helen?'

'Yes, Helen, though she's none too keen on the idea. She fancied a weekend break without the girls, though as I said, they can always go the weekend after – we're free to have the girls at ours. Which reminds me, she hasn't asked me to keep that free now she knows our plans. I'll phone her later.'

'And Marc?'

'Yes, Marc too.'

I settle at his small Formica table, with Fido fussing about my feet, and Dad passes over my drink.

'I can't invite my sister without her husband, surely!' I tease, knowing Dad's always been a bit nonplussed by Marc, unlike Fraser, who Dad treats as the son he never had.

'He'll make an excuse not to attend, you watch. He always has something better to do. Long hours at work, an emergency call from his own parents or . . . what was it that he said that one time?'

I feign boredom by fussing over the aged cream poodle but it's no good, Dad's going to continue.

'Your sister's fortieth, wasn't it? His mate was stranded on the M103 motorway ... M103, I ask you! It doesn't bloody exist! Who the hell does he think he's kidding?'

'Dad, you don't know that – he might have said it wrong. He might have meant to say ...'

'Ask your Fraser. Both he and I clocked it straightaway, as soon as Marc said it. We all know what he was trying not to say, don't we? Marc thinks we're all as bloody blindly loved-up as our Helen. Well, we're not. How do you miss your own wife's fortieth party when it's being held at your own bloody house?'

I've listened to this tirade countless times and Dad's patter never changes. He is correct though: it had been the first thing Fraser had said once we'd waved our goodbyes and climbed into the car that night.

'Bloody M103 doesn't exist ... he's playing away.'

'Fraser! Little piggies have big ears,' I'd shushed him, because Cody was present on the rear seat.

'Like he knows what playing away means,' had been Fraser's final remark.

I sip my tea and stare at Dad over the rim of my mug as he settles.

'Is there anything you want me to pick up for Cody as a small gift?' I ask, knowing the week will fly past and already my days are being filled what with the party, Fraser's plans and my mother's social life.

'No, I'm sorted.'

'You are?' I'm surprised because for countless years I've picked up the Action Man boxed figure, the football, the latest games controller, and wrapped them in beautiful paper before attaching a name tag for my father to sign and give to his only grandson. Even once Cody hit puberty and all he ever asked for was vouchers, I was the one who'd queue and deliver them to

Dad, complete with the mini card and envelope. It was safer and easier than him walking his legs off around town, wasting his money on the wrong gift, only to provide me with another job: returning them to customer services for a credit voucher. 'How?'

My dad gulps, his head giving the slightest nod – with which he covers a multitude of emotions.

'Dad?'

'He's old enough for my watch ... He'll take good care of it, I know.'

'Oh Dad ... are you sure?'

I watch as he continues to gulp, his eyes moist as he focuses on his mug of tea.

I reach for his hand and squeeze.

'Thank you. I know how much that means to you.'

'It was my dad's before mine,' he says, before breaking the moment by gulping his tea noisily.

We sit in silence and an image of the gold watch fills my mind. I know Cody will look after it; it was never destined to be anyone else's but his from birth. But still, I know how long Dad has waited to gift his watch to my son.

Carmen

'Would *you* propose, Trish?' I ask, as I perch on reception, quickly swallowing my lunch before our next bridal party arrives at two o'clock.

'Nah. I mentioned Victoria earlier but still I think it's romantic when a man finally makes up his mind and takes action.' She eyes me closely as Anna hands her several Mori Lee gowns, heavily decorated with crystal droplets. 'Are you seriously thinking of ... you know?'

I purse my lips and avoid looking at her.

'No, well, not exactly ... possibly ... maybe.'

'Bloody hell, you need to be more certain than that!' she laughs.

'It shouldn't be such a big deal ... but it is! In my opinion, Elliot should have asked me three years ago. And now I'm thinking of doing the one thing that had never popped into my head until yesterday's bride-to-be told her story.'

'I thought she sounded a bit desperate.'

'Well, isn't that exactly what I am? Desperate to get married, start a family, create our future together. But I don't want it to *look* like a desperate act.'

Trish raises her eyebrows at my torrent of words.

'I even sound desperate, don't I?'

'You did just then.'

'Why can't life be easy and follow the natural course of events?'

'Because that would be too simple, Carmen. And what's the natural course of events any more? Times have changed.'

There's a lengthy silence as they finish arranging the gowns.

'So, you have just one week to organise a proposal,' says Trish.

'Mmmm, one week,' I say, my mind spinning faster than a wannabe bride planning a fake wedding.

'Are you not sure?'

'I'm sure. I can't wait forever. I just have to let go of the dream in my head where Elliot proposes to me. There needs to be a whole change of scene, the same characters but a role reversal and it has to be me that comes up with a proposal speech.'

'You'll be fine, Carmen.'

'Says she who is already married and received the perfect proposal,' I tease.

'Ah, it was wonderful . . . he'd thought it through properly, knew the exact location, time of day and had a ring.'

My mouth falls open.

'Do I need a ring to offer Elliot?'

'I'd imagine so.'

'What bloke wears an engagement ring?'

'Carmen, you can't make a proposal without one, surely?'

'Plenty of men do.'

'Yeah, but I always assume those are the spontaneous pro-posals, that the suggestion spilled from his lips on impulse. If you're planning a proposal, you'll need a ring.'

'Couldn't I buy him a nice pair of gold cufflinks or a diamond tie pin?' I ask, trying to avoid obstacles.

'Would *you* have liked a nice pair of engagement earrings instead of an engagement ring?' teases Trish. 'Or an engagement brooch?'

I grimace at the very thought.

'Exactly.'

'And *how* do you propose I do that without knowing his ring size?' I moan, as Trish smugly gloats.

'Easy . . . simply measure his finger with one of your rings.'

'Are you joking? Elliot would never fall for something as obvious and, may I say, as tacky as that trick . . . "Hi, Elliot, please come here a minute, I'd like you to try one of my rings on but if it doesn't fit I'll try another and another and maybe . . ." Honestly, Trish, can you see that happening?'

'Even *I* can't see that happening and I've never met him,' pipes up Anna.

'OK, so stick with the principle. How else could you measure his finger?'

'Trish, if I knew that I wouldn't be asking for ideas!' I

chunter. 'I'll simply have to forget the idea of presenting him with a ring at the proposal.'

Trish purses her lips tightly and shakes her head.

'I know, but without an accurate fit what's the point?' I say, adding, 'Or I could buy any ring as a token gesture and get it fitted, stretched or made smaller when we arrive back home?'

'Not ideal, if you're going to do it properly,' says Anna.

'Quack, quack, oops! You pair are officially as useless as me,' I joke. 'Back to the drawing board.'

'If I think of anything, I'll text you,' offers Anna.

'Cheers, babe, but maybe it's a sign.'

'No, it isn't. It's simply another obstacle which you've got to get overcome to achieve what you want,' says Trish, straightening the chaise longue. 'You'll find a way.'

'So, a ring, a location and a speech?'

Trish nods tentatively.

The boutique's door chime interrupts our conversation as a party of four females bustles in.

I quickly hide my empty lunch box under the countertop.

'I've got plenty to plan then, haven't I?' I mutter, before my professional smile is in place and I greet my new clients. 'Welcome, can I take your coats?' And I usher them towards the seating area.

Dana

It's five o'clock and I'm dashing along my parents' pathway to collect Luke. I'm practising my apology as I stagger under the mental exhaustion of question after question, quickly fired at me by what seems like every professional in the United Kingdom. At one point, roughly two hours in, one of the experts actually phoned some else who asked me yet more questions via her hands-free mobile. In the last four and a half hours I have completed numerous questionnaires, undertaken isometric tests, intelligence and personality tests, and I have been asked every question that can possibly exist. What's my dream holiday destination? What's my family background? What qualities does my ideal man possess? What's my view on religion? Culture? Politics? Would I like more children? Do I neatly fold or scrunch toilet paper before using it? Even what's my favoured sexual position? I was damned if I was answering that one to a panel of complete strangers on a Saturday afternoon! Though, upon my refusal to answer, I did notice several of them instantly scribble a lengthy note on their writing pads.

I ring the doorbell, hoping to hell that my parents have had a good afternoon with Luke and aren't frustrated with me.

'Hello, lovey,' says Mum, her tone easing my fraught nerves immediately. 'We're hoping you've had a good time with your friends.'

I want to come clean. I want to be honest. But, given all the talking I've done in the last few hours, I don't really want to go into the whole thing.

'Thanks, Mum, we did. I'm so sorry, I don't know where the time went and ... hello, my little man, have you had a good afternoon?'

'I fed the billy-birds,' announces Luke, as he scuttles along the hallway to greet me. I open my arms and crouch down to meet his hug.

'Chased them more like,' corrects my dad from his armchair beside their coal fire, as I enter the lounge. 'Though he sat still when I played his elephant DVD.'

'Did you?' I say, tweaking his button nose.

'Tea?' asks Mum.

'Please, I'd love one.' I remove my coat and so begins the routine at my parents. Mum makes tea, Dad stares at the TV and Luke runs back and forth as if he owns the place, touching everything in sight that I was never allowed to touch as a child, because now, in this house, grandchildren have special rights.

'Mummy, look,' says Luke, climbing on to my lap and thrusting a plastic car under my nostrils.

'Lovely, where did you find that?' I ask, unsure whether I've seen it before or it's a new purchase from the newsagents when Dad collected his Saturday lottery ticket.

'Rucksack,' says Luke, pointing towards the bottom end of the lounge where his bag has been placed. Luke darts from my lap, I assume to retrieve it.

Dad and I exchange a glance and a shake of our heads, both constantly surprised at what he finds in the bottom of that bag.

'I really must clean it out.'

'I wouldn't bother, it contains everything he needs,' mutters Dad.

'Look,' repeats Luke, waving a piece of crumpled cardboard at me, as he climbs on to my lap for a second time.

I turn it over and smooth it out on the arm of the sofa. A huge red heart beams up at me; out of the corner of my eye I can see Luke's smiling face watching me.

'Yours,' he says prodding me in the shoulder.

I take in the crayoned image: a big red heart, lots of kisses and a scribbled word beginning with a 'V'.

'What's that?' asks Dad, leaning forward in his armchair.

I can't speak. A knot of emotion lifts to my throat and tears spring to my eyes.

Dad half stands and takes a couple of steps nearer to peer at the crumpled card.

'It looks like a Valentine's card to me,' he mutters before sitting back down.

I want to cry with joy. My baby drew me a Valentine's card and it's been stuffed in the bottom of his rucksack for a week and a day.

'Good boy, Luke, well remembered.' I lower my chin, resting it on the top of his head, as he bobs about with excitement, and inhale the smell of my son.

My one true love.

Carmen

The Cross Keys is jampacked on a Saturday night. We sit as a cramped party in an upholstered seating booth constructed for eight adults and not the actual ten we are. Our thighs and bottoms are somewhat squashed together in the horseshoe-shaped built-in bench around a wooden table sporting an array of drinks and half-filled bottles. Behind my head, which I keep inadvertently banging, is a stained-glass panel decorating the dark wooden partition; designed in a previous era to offer privacy, it nowadays provides a viewing rail over which those without a seat enviously peer to check if our group is moving anytime soon. Hasty looks of 'sorry' answer impatient stares each time we catch their eye, making me feel irrationally guilty that we arrived early enough to hog the only desirable space for any large group, forcing them to stand and keep vigil. I fear our departure will cause a pub riot as all those standing with tired legs try to seize the chance of being seated.

This isn't how I'd planned to spend our Saturday night. After a long day on my feet, I'd hoped for a quiet night in, a calorie-rich takeaway and a film on TV; instead we are with

Elliot's crowd of mates and their wives, drawn together at the last minute for one final pub night before Monty and Michelle's wedding in two weeks' time. They're a happy crew; despite one or two of Elliot's mates being blessed with uncouth manners or a snooty wife, the majority are a good laugh. This is the group that, when we first began dating, I wanted to impress and fit in with the most. Those early days when you're not yet an official couple but you know you're being tested, watched, compared to previous girlfriends as to whether you'll 'fit in' with his crowd or you're giving off warnings that you'll be putting a stop to the Sunday lunch quick half. Obviously I passed the initial test, but over the eight years we've been together I've seen his mates introduce numerous candidates who haven't.

'What's the occasion?' I'd asked earlier, as Elliot vacated the bathroom, a towel wrapped about his waist, so I could take a quick shower, having just arrived home.

'Monty's called everyone together as it's been a while and, with the wedding in two weeks, he thought it would be nice to see us all together for one final time.'

'I thought you guys met up just a few weeks ago for grooms- men's suit fittings – which Monty turned into an all-day affair.'

'We did but that didn't include partners, did it?'

'Aren't you all going to the stag do?' I say undressing and tying my hair up for speed, knowing full well that the three-day event in Cardiff is this coming Wednesday to Friday, taking up three days of Elliot's annual leave.

'Yeah, but again that doesn't include partners either.'

'So, without any prior notice, he's chosen tonight?'

'Carmen, when was the last time we all got together, eh?'

'Bank Holiday Monday,' I mumble, remembering the head- ache I had the next morning.

'Exactly, and not the August Bank Holiday; it was way back in May,' he says, disappearing into our bedroom.

I run the shower and gather my towel.

'Magoo wasn't there that night nor at the fitting the other week . . .'

'He wasn't at his own brother's suit fitting?'

'No, something cropped up. So I haven't caught up with him since . . .'

'Before they had the baby,' I shout over the noise of the shower, peeling off my spent clothes and throwing them into the laundry basket. Monty and Magoo are the brothers of the social group yet you wouldn't know it, given their lack of interaction.

'We have.'

'No, we were meant to go round but Magoo cancelled at the last minute as Judy wasn't up to visitors after seeing a lot of people earlier in the day. Our baby present is still sitting in the front bedroom despite me asking you to take it round next time you're passing.'

'Take it tonight.'

'Elliot, a romper suit for a six month old isn't going to fit a one year old now, is it?'

There's a pause from the bedroom.

'They had a girl, yeah?'

'No, a boy . . . Hugo.'

There's no hiding it, I'm his social PA. There was a time when a weekly night out with the crowd meant me reminding Elliot of the names of his mates' partners, or current girlfriends as we were back then. It was a dodgy game of remembering names and faces in an attempt not to call Magoo's new girl-friend – now his wife – Judy, rather than Marnie, who'd been his *previous* long-term girlfriend. A task of high importance to ensure a carefree and enjoyable night for us and not a week of the silent treatment for Magoo – because woe betide any error igniting Judy's high level of jealousy. I was pretty skilled at it, having been around the longest, so I held a fairly central place amongst the females. Though I'll admit Haughty Hannah is now self-appointed leader of the female pack, given that they married first and got pregnant first – but still, she couldn't keep up with the name-changing as well as I had. Nowadays, I catalogue and confirm the names of their babies as they arrive in the same meticulous manner.

So we're here in the Cross Keys, spending a night with the couples: Monty and Michelle (soon to be newlyweds), Magoo and Jealous Judy, plus baby Hugo, Andrew and Haughty Hannah and, finally, Steve and Nicole. Nicole is my safety net within the social group, the one with whom I have the most in common. It's strange to think that we females only socialise because of the males we are partnered with; yet more concerning is the fact that we're only a social group because of the deep connection the males shared when aged six over a love of skateboards and Transformers.

'Hi, Elliot, hi, Carmen,' giggles Judy, hitching the afore-mentioned Hugo up on her hip bone, freeing herself from the cramped party in the alcove to soothe the baby.

'Hi, hasn't he grown?' I swoon, knowing full well that we've never seen the little chappy before but estimating that the gurgling bundle looks much heavier than the seven pounds mentioned in Magoo's excited baby-arrival phone call.

'He's such a gutsy boy, aren't you? Yes, you are . . . you are a gutsy boy!' coos Judy at a dribbling Hugo.

Elliot wears a rabbit-caught-in-the-headlights expression as we sit and listen to Judy continue to talk in a silly voice to her son. I want to interrupt her, I want to ask her to stop, because I know that her display of motherhood is frightening Elliot senseless as he imagines me doing the exact same thing with our baby in years to come. I know, deep down, that mummy-talking Judy is scaring Elliot's sperm and, therefore, further ruining my chances of starting a family. By the time Judy ceases her ninth rendition of 'yes, you are a gutsy, wutsy, chubby, wubby, Mummy's little munchkin', I know she's probably set my course to motherhood back by about a decade. Cheers, Judy, I owe you one.

'Why has she brought the baby to the pub?' asks Elliot the second Judy moves away to be seated by Magoo, who had flashed us both a knowing smile which we accept as an apology.

'Couldn't find a babysitter, perhaps?' I answer, seeing I need to tread carefully given his current state of mind.

'It's Saturday night! I thought that important role was assigned to grandparents,' mutters Elliot.

'It is usually but not always.' I want to continue my sentence but know I can't admit that some women simply can't leave baby with anyone, even their own parents for a child-free night with their husband.

'Great, well, the gang's never done that before,' says Elliot, snatching up his pint and taking a sip. 'I remember when Monty walked in and put his first packet of legal fags on the table next to his pint. Now, that was a milestone in growing up. But this . . . this is . . . are babies even allowed in pubs at this time of night?'

'Elliot, please forget it,' I whisper.

'Magoo, how the devil are you, my man? We haven't seen you in ages!' he says calling to his mate.

I give a sigh of relief as Elliot's dear friend moves others to settle beside us and begins a hearty chat about his accountancy work, the regretful sale of his beloved motorbike and the re-organising of his loft complete with additional insulation.

'How are you, Carmen? Busy at work?' asks Nicole, who leans

across the table, saving me from the boredom of loft insulation.

'It's just picking up after the winter slump, to be honest, Nicole. After Christmas engagements, many brides-to-be like to get started on picking their gowns, even if they are unsure of the exact wedding date.'

'I can imagine, especially given the price of some,' she responds.

'Exactly, it gives them more leeway for saving and budgeting, even if the wedding is a couple of years away.'

'Oh, I'd love to plan ours all over again! It was such a special time, though Steve's sister acted like an utter brat, refusing to wear certain colours and styles; eventually, she gave me no other choice but to cull her from the wedding party.'

'I don't remember that!'

'Oh yes, his mother went berserk at me but what do people expect when somebody causes so much drama? She's forgiven me now, but only since we've given her two adorable nieces to obsess about. For a while, though, she was a nightmare about letting her brother fly the nest.'

I listen and nod. I've witnessed many a stressful situation during a gown appointment, bitchy sniping between females or bitter resentment rallied back and forth along our chaise longue. Once, Trish and I thought we'd be seeing fisticuffs between two agitated matriarchs, but at least we've never had to physically separate any adversaries or call the police. I suppose most families try to keep the in-house bickering to a minimum – it's not really a spectator sport.

Polly

Fraser unwinds the second he arrives in his mother's immaculate lounge.

'Fraser,' I hiss, as he sinks into the armchair nearest the fire, slips off both his shoes and scrunches his stockinged feet into the thick hearth rug.

We aren't stopping; we'll be heading back out of the door in a few minutes once Olive, his mother, has finished dressing and is ready to depart. Malcolm, his father, is busy locking the back doors and checking all windows are securely closed. It's a ten-minute routine.

'What?' Fraser's brow creases as I hover by the lounge door, not bothering to even sit.

I can almost see the five-year-old child he once was in his expression. I bet that this was what he looked like if he was disturbed whilst watching cartoons, asked if he'd completed his homework and informed it was time for bed – all of which occurred in this house.

I've always felt like the guest in the Evans' home, from the first moment of being introduced to his parents to the night we sat huddled on the sofa to confess that a baby was on the way, and ever after. His mother has never lost that look she wore on hearing our news. A silence had lingered for ages before any discussion occurred. No congratulations, no hugs and no kisses – just a stern telling-off by his mum. His father had sat in that very armchair staring into the fire, much like Fraser is now.

Was that the last time we'd sat side by side in this lounge? Probably. Since that night, Fraser has chosen the spare armchair, and Cody, from baby to teenager, and I have occupied the sofa. Olive's resistance softened slightly once there was a baby for her to hold and coo over but there have never been any hugs or kisses in my direction. I'm simply the silly girl who got pregnant and snared her son.

I'm her Lola. The thought pulls me up sharp. I am Olive's Lola!

'Hello, darling,' says Olive, bustling through the door, her outfit perfectly over the top for a charity quiz night at the Unicorn, heading straight to Fraser to pop a kiss on his forehead. 'How are you?'

'Fine, Mum, and you?'

'Hello, Polly. Oh, you know how it is, Fraser . . . your father's fussing about an MOT needed for next week and I couldn't book my usual girl at the chiropodist.'

'Not good . . . can't you go another time?'

'Oh no, my feet need doing . . . badly.'

I listen. I wait. I know the routine. She won't ask, she never asks me. Fraser never asks either – he knows how busy I am – but I know he appreciates every time I offer; and I always do offer, given they haven't any daughters of their own. Though, of course, their sons could easily drive to the chiropodist's too, but they never have. They never will. I've always done the job, much like I do for my own parents, and it's a result of my love and commitment to Fraser, not Olive.

We have a similar unwritten rule regarding Mother's Day cards. I always select a card befitting both mothers and buy two. I assume Fraser's feelings for his mother match the same quiet sentiment that I feel for mine and so I duplicate the cards. I address both but we each write our own; I'd take a stance if he decided not to – it's the least a mother can expect. I'll be hurt if Cody's future partner ever writes my card.

'Which day is it booked for?' I ask, catching a thank you glance from Fraser.

'Thursday afternoon, the usual time,' answers Olive, checking her appearance in the mantelpiece mirror.

'I can do that . . . if you need dropping off,' I say; it's my usual line.

'Could you? Perfect.'

Fraser gives a small smile. He gets her just as much as I do.

She's grateful, but she never lets it register on her face or in her level of warmth towards me.

'Are we all ready?' asks Malcolm as if we hadn't arrived ready some ten minutes ago.

No one answers, we simply drift towards the front door. Fraser puts his shoes back on and grabs his car keys from the bottom of the stairs.

Tradition dictates that I will sit in the back next to Olive, Malcolm will take my place beside Fraser, as he dutifully drives us – them, more specifically – to the monthly quiz night at the Unicorn pub. An evening which both his parents enjoy immensely despite the stupid answers offered by me and routinely ignored without ridicule by them.

'How's work?' asks Malcolm, his standard question to anyone, family or not.

Olive and I listen as Fraser outlines his previous week, his focus being the difficulty on designing for a client unsure of what his own requirements are, a situation which Fraser never copes well with.

The drive to the Unicorn only takes five minutes but it feels much longer, given the stunted conversation in the back. I don't worry any more. I don't panic because I know that once a large dry sherry hits her tastebuds Olive will begin to soften, especially if there's a quiz round on baking, cooking or geography. I much prefer the questions on celebrity chefs or gardening. Other than that, for me, the evening is a chance to chill out and enjoy being with Fraser, alongside his parents. I know how much they like spending time with him but not in a casual Sunday-lunch-around-the-table, let's-all-eat-together kind of way, which is what my family prefer. The thought of cooking a Sunday roast for Olive fills me with dread. I know I wouldn't be able to prepare and serve mint sauce correctly, let alone impress her, even with my best roast tatties, fluffiest Yorkie puds and seasoned onion gravy.

Carmen

I spend time moving around the group, conversing with everyone, even Haughty Hannah who, after delivering two children in four years, acts like a mother hen to the rest of us. I wouldn't be surprised if at any moment she whips out a tissue, licks the corner and wipes something from one of our faces whilst muttering, 'It's clean, honest.' Hannah's never been overly keen on me, but it's not my fault that I was around when Andrew had a previous partner. I witnessed their happiness and dramatic break-up, which none of the other WAGs did, and I'm not prepared to badmouth Andrew's ex, much to Hannah's disgust, because I think Dana was a decent woman. She did the right thing in my opinion.

I'm happy, content and slightly woozy – this is now my third white wine on a virtually empty stomach. The minute I settle next to Haughty Hannah, I sense she's going to ask the one question I've been dreading all evening. The question that the other women have probably considered asking me but thought better of it, knowing how they'd felt in my position. For, despite the fact that these five guys happily reached thirty-five years of age before Andrew introduced a wedding band into the merry mix, it goes without saying that from 7 March Elliot will be the only bachelor remaining.

'Any sound of wedding bells yet?' Hannah gives me an instant head tilt and simpering smile. I'm not overly sensitive, but if Nicole or Michelle had asked, I'd have known they were taking a caring interest in my relationship with Elliot. Haughty

Hannah only ever thinks about herself and Andrew, so I know this is her killer putdown. Great, I now wish I'd spent longer chatting to Michelle about her wedding plans, even though her final fitting is at my boutique next week.

The woozy effect of my wine suddenly disappears.

'Actually, no, not yet, Hannah.' I go with my usual line and place the blame firmly at Elliot's door, as if suggesting she goes and asks him and not me. 'You know what Elliot's like, there's no rushing him, is there?'

'Pity. Because you know you need to get a move on, right? None of us are getting any younger, are we? If you know what I mean . . .' She whispers the final few words.

We always know what you mean, Hannah, and if we don't, you'll repeat it, often with added depth of explanation to ensure everyone in the frigging pub gets the gist of your insinuations.

Blast it! Try as I might to ignore it, her comment hits the bull's eye like an emotional stomach punch.

'Mmmm, I get your drift . . .' I pause and ponder. I fight the urge to retaliate. I so badly want to ask her how many couples get divorced nowadays? Or even how many stitches she had during her last Mother Earth all-natural birth? Or, worse, remind her oh-so-subtly of Andrew's drunken and uncouth remark whilst wetting the baby's head when he announced to his best mates that her 'nether regions' looked like 'a ripped-out fireplace'! I know boys will be boys but surely to God the man can be respectful towards the mother of his child, rather than insult her for a cheap laugh.

But I don't say any of this, because I'm not as unkind as Haughty Hannah. I can think it but refrain from saying it. Damn my mother for raising me with good manners! I wouldn't lower myself to her level and I certainly wouldn't take a cheap shot of emotional enjoyment by aiming the dreaded question to the soon-to-be only unmarried female in our group.

She pats my hand and gives it a squeeze as if I were her tearful three year old; she's silent but her implied 'There, there, never mind' comes across loud and clear.

That is the moment. My moment of decision-making. It might be very wrong of me that my undying devotion towards Elliot isn't my prime motivation, nor the sheer beauty of the life we have created together, but, instead, Haughty Hannah and her incredibly patronising hand pat and squeeze seals the deal. The deal that, by this time next week, I will have proposed marriage to Elliot Cole.

I'm going to push aside all my hang-ups regarding females proposing. I'll be open-minded regarding my ability to exercise equality in such a traditionally male task and fully embrace the leap-year tradition. I, Carmen Smith, will ask my boyfriend, partner, lover, best friend and backbone to my life if he will marry me.

Of course, should anyone ever ask me in the future when I made my mind up to propose, I will lie. If my potentially wide-eyed daughters want to know 'how come Mummy proposed to Daddy?', I'll concoct a beautiful story about the depth of our love and an overwhelming connection one romantic evening, when the moon was high and nightingales sang. I will eliminate Haughty Hannah altogether.

My mind is suddenly awash with necessary plans; I have so much to organise if I am to pull off such a huge life event at such short notice. I don't want to talk to Haughty Hannah any more, especially now she's stung me with her barbed comment. I'd much prefer to be at home, making lists and planning so that I do the very best job of proposing I can, given my initial lack of enthusiasm or interest.

I might even be able to plan the proposal of my dreams: a romantic location, a pitch-perfect speech – the only difference will be a slight twist on who answers 'yes' in the final scene. What's so controversial about a woman organising her own proposal in this day and age? Hardly a huge sacrifice really, or not as much as I originally imagined, but a sure way to guarantee that it'll be the proposal of my dreams.

I glance over at Elliot, absorbed in his conversation with Magoo.

This time next week, we will be engaged. We will be en route towards becoming Mr and Mrs Cole. I no longer care that it isn't the traditional version of all the fairytales … I am an independent, modern woman who established her own wedding business from a mere two hundred pounds of savings kept in a Post Office account. If I can do that, I can do anything!

I can feel my inner goddess rising from deep within. If I wanted or wished to, I could propose to Elliot right here, right now! But I choose not to; the Cross Keys pub is the last place that I imagined him proposing to me. I also hadn't planned on his best mates having front-row seats. Plus I wouldn't give Haughty Hannah the satisfaction of seeing my knee-jerk reaction to her insensitive comment.

'Lovely chatting with you, Hannah. We'll have to make a date soon for a visit to ours,' I quickly say, patting her on the hand before collecting my drink and leaving her side. Once standing, I quickly seek refuge elsewhere. My options are limited: I can sit with Judy, who is currently baring one breast and feeding her son in the middle of the crowded pub. Or I could return to Nicole, who appears very involved in a conversation with bride-to-be Michelle, with whom I have very little in common, but wedding chat is always a safe bet.

'Hi, you two look deep in conversation,' I say, sidling up to them, only to realise my social faux pas as they abruptly cease talking and jump apart. In my desperation to escape Haughty Hannah, I've landed myself in the middle of a situation. Both pairs of eyes widen and the women stare at me in silence as I read their body language. Clearly whatever the topic of their conversation, it isn't about to include me.

'Catch you later,' I whisper and back away.

I have three choices: return to Haughty Hannah for round two, join Judy and study breastfeeding for the next ten minutes or join the men.

I join the men.

I slide in beside Elliot and receive a fleeting glance of confusion as he spies the other women seated and standing on the far side of the table and tries to read my expression. Our table now looks like a teenage disco, boys one side, girls the other . . . and I am the rebel girl who has dared to cross the invisible line.

'You all right?' he whispers, unnerved by my return.

'Yeah, fine.'

I can see by his continued observation of Hannah, Judy, Nicole and Michelle, he isn't convinced.

'Is she feeding?' he suddenly asks, nodding towards Judy.

I give a quick nod, not wishing to have Elliot linger on Judy or the topic of breastfeeding given his earlier reaction to her mummy talk.

'Elliot, it's natural.'

'So is having a crap but I don't do that in public. You won't be doing that, will you?'

I suck in a hurried breath. This is the first time that Elliot has acknowledged that at some time, in the future, we – he and I – might actually have a baby.

I need to play it smart and keep my cards close to my chest. I need to assert my desire for potential motherhood in this conversation.

'I may, I may not ... we'll decide when the time comes, won't we?' I bluff.

I give his thigh a gentle pat.

Elliot gives a nod of acceptance.

Wow, maybe the universe is suddenly playing ball with my desires and aligning itself in my favour! Maybe my proactive decision in light of Haughty Hannah's question has unlocked a psychic gateway enabling me to take charge of our situation.

I snuggle beneath Elliot's left arm, picking a piece of cotton from his jumper sleeve. I wind the single thread back and forth through my fingers, like a bored child feigning interest in adult talk. Elliot switches conversations and is totally engrossed by Monty's detailed explanation about his engineering work but I was lost a long time ago by such a mind-blowing topic. Now might be a good time to begin playing with Elliot's fingers, sizing them against mine, reckoning his digits against my index finger, middle finger, ring finger.

I gently ease the length of cotton around his ring finger, noting the circumference by carefully withdrawing the thread and tying a simple knot to mark the length. Purely as a pre-caution, almost reinforcing the game, I move on and measure his middle finger, before repeating the exercise with his index finger. Elliot doesn't seem to notice. He remains enthralled by Monty's description of a newly acquired operating system installed at his work.

Polly

The charity quiz ends just after eleven o'clock; we didn't win but we didn't collect the booby prize either. I'm grateful that I only suggested two utterly stupid answers to our team of four, though realistically it's a team of three with an ignorant plus one. Fraser attended the local grammar school; sadly, my secondary education left a lot to be desired. But hey, it wouldn't do for us all to be the same, would it? Kindness is my strength and the world needs that too. The event helped to raise a fair sum for the Gloucester and District Samaritans, which is the main aim of the evening, so I take comfort in that fact.

Fraser ushers us towards the exit.

'Careful that you don't trip, Mum,' he warns, his arm outstretched, pretending not to steer her away from the dodgy step now she's consumed three large sherries and is slightly unsteady.

I smile. It's behaviour such as this which reminds me that Olive really is human and not the uptight matriarch she pretends to be every other hour I'm in her presence.

I also love Fraser a little bit more for showing he cares; he never complains, he's always attentive and dutiful ... unlike me who performs some tasks begrudgingly as it pinches time out of my free day.

'I take it you're picking her up on Thursday?' whispers Malcolm, linking his arm in mine and giving it a squeeze. I give him a smile. 'Thank you, you are a good girl.'

Malcolm regularly praises me with 'good girl' despite my age; my sister says it's an endearment you'd use for a dog but I willingly accept it as his way of expressing affection. He's used to three boys and Olive's harsh manner, and this is his special phrase for me. It gives me a warm fuzzy feel inside to know he appreciates what I do.

Chapter Four

Sunday 23 February

Carmen

'Have you got any holiday days still to take?' I ask, as Elliot and I lounge sleepily in bed following a late night of drinking and an early morning of tender loving.

'A few days, but I was planning on using those for the fishing trip my brother wants to take at Easter. Why?'

This is the moment when I need to hold my own without Elliot suspecting or questioning me about anything.

'I was thinking we could do with a mini break, that's all.'

Silence.

I wait patiently, snuggling into the crook of his arm. I'm determined not to start an argument; I can do without any upheaval occurring while I plan for next Saturday. So I wait.

And wait.

The silence lingers, then lengthens uncomfortably.

Elliot repositions his arms, putting his hands behind his head, which causes me to have to move from my comfy position. I can see from the corner of my eye that he is staring at the ceiling.

Is he thinking?

Ignoring me?

'When?' asks Elliot suddenly, just when I am convinced he is asleep.

'Next weekend.'

Silence.

'Where to?'

'I was thinking of a weekend in Paris ... neither of us have been there before.'

I'm waiting for a simple 'yes' – but nothing.

'Are we busy next weekend?' I ask finally, for fear that I am about to fail at the first step in arranging our marriage proposal.

'Nope, but I wasn't planning on a weekend trip away either. We've only had two free weekends since the Christmas break and next weekend's the only free weekend until Monty's wedding.'

'I get you're tired, Elliot – you're right, we have been pretty busy, non-stop since New Year. Maybe we can have a stay-at-home duvet weekend on the weekend after the wedding?'

'A stay-at-home duvet weekend?'

'Yeah, a whole weekend filled with films, with music, take-aways, chilling out at home.'

'Promise?' He eyes me cautiously, as if I'm tricking him.

'I promise.'

'Not the typical Carmen promise where you say it but then our plans keep changing ever so slightly and end up nothing like the original promise?'

'Elliot!'

'What? Are you denying that you change our plans all the time?'

'Things happen, plans change. I believe you swiftly changed our plans last night the minute Monty called you. Did I moan? No, because that's life.' I can hear that my tone has an edge but

I am doing all I can to remain snuggled beneath a warm duvet and not throw a hissy fit that Elliot isn't jumping on board at the suggestion of our mini break. If it had been the other way around and he'd suggested a weekend break to Paris, I'd have been thrilled to bits. But no, Elliot is cautiously staring at me as if I've just asked if he'd like round two of some loving.

'So, Paris it is, then?' I ask, hoping to ignite a spark of interest.

'But the weekend of the fourteenth we stay at home, just us two, and chill out, yeah?'

'Yeah. I've already promised.'

'OK. I'd asked for overtime on Saturday morning, given that I'll be away from work on the stag do Wednesday to Friday, but I'll take my name off the rota on Monday morning.'

'So you were planning to be at work anyway on Saturday morning and not chilling at home?'

'Yeah, you work every Saturday at the boutique so why not?'

'I'm not at work next Saturday, which is why I want us to make the most of going away on a mini break.'

'OK, let's do it then.'

I fall silent. The conversation hasn't flowed as I'd hoped, or maybe I'm being too harsh? Surely I can class it as a success, given that he has agreed, even if it feels like an arm-twisted-up-his-back kind of agreement. I silently replay the exchange, wavering between rejoicing and full-blown annoyance that he didn't jump at the chance to spend a romantic weekend in Paris. I know men who would be chuffed to bits to be invited for some fun-filled days away. As I lie here, I can't actually name any at the moment – it's been a while since I met up with my male friends who are just *my* friends and not ours jointly, but still, I know they exist, somewhere. Elliot could actually do with a reminder that my men friends aren't extinct. I could give one a call for a catch-up and a coffee anytime I like. Which I haven't done for a fair while, given that I'm juggling Elliot, home, business and life in general . . . but I could, if I wanted to.

I decide to keep the peace and not air my grievance. Experience has taught me that we rarely see situations the same way. I can predict if I backtrack, mentioning my surprise at his reluctance, we will disagree on how our conversation actually played out. Within a matter of minutes, one of us, usually me, will say the wrong thing and we'll have the makings of a full-blown argument. An argument which I know will ruin Sunday, result in him withdrawing into his shell, like he always does, while I begin to cry, frustrated that he's not listening to me. All of which will taint our memories of the next seven days: seven days of planning, seven days paving the way to our engagement.

Dana

I am drowning in guilt as I unpack the boot of my car and make the umpteenth trip into the Castle Hotel's function room carrying my flower boxes. I rarely drop Luke at Mum and Dad's two days on the trot, and today he threw the clingy tantrum I had expected yesterday.

'Mummy . . . no!' cried Luke, lying on their hallway floor whilst hanging on to my leg for dear life.

'The billy-birds are waiting for their breakfast,' called my dad from the back door, attempting to distract him.

'Mummmmmm-y!'

I bent down to comfort him; it breaks my heart every time this happens. I know it's what every child does at some point but when my Luke does this, I simply want to cancel everything, hug him tight and tell him I understand. Part of me always blames his condition for such outbursts; I figure his affectionate nature can't bear the separation. Or am I simply using it as an emotional excuse?

'Mummy needs to go, sweetie. Look, Grandpops is waiting for you.' I point towards the back door.

Luke had lifted his head, his tears suspended, and stared through the open kitchen door towards my dad beckoning him into the garden.

'That big robin is back,' Dad called.

'Robin!' cried Luke, releasing my leg and clambering from the carpet to dash towards the garden.

'Go, go, go!' ushered my mum, hastily kissing my cheek. 'He'll be fine, you know he always is. We'll watch his elephant DVD, that always settles him.'

'Thanks.' The front door was quickly fastened before I'd stepped from their doorstep.

I drove off feeling dreadful; a wedding fayre was the last thing I wanted to attend – this wasn't how I'd imagined today would start.

But now here I am, amongst the throng of other wedding industry suppliers, and I need to up my game if I'm to secure some floristry bookings. I've already spied another florist, who I believe owns the largest shop in the town, amidst the stationers, the photographers, limousine hire and talented milliners. Thankfully, my prices reflect my low overheads and self-employed status, so I'm fair competition for any commercial florist. I've no doubt we're both talented in our chosen profession, but for some couples the price is the bottom line.

I carry the large flower box to my assigned stall space, drop it and immediately return to my car. I believe we have just one hour for the vendors' vehicles to park near the hotel steps before they want the entrance cleared and the red carpet rolled out ready for the arrival of potential wedding couples and their excited families. I start unloading the interior, which is as crammed full as the boot was.

'Hi, Dana!' calls a male voice. I quickly turn to see Kevin Knightley, the wedding car specialist, passing by dressed smartly in his chauffeur's outfit.

'Hi, Kevin you're looking very smart today,' I call back, straightening from my crouched position.

'You never know what bookings you'll take at these affairs, do you?' he replies, striding towards his highly polished Bentley. 'Let's hope it's busy if nothing else.'

He's got a point. You prepare as much as you can, bring as many sample materials as you can and a gallery of photographs showing what you can't physically bring, and yet a potential wedding booking will still outwit you by saying, 'You're not quite what we're looking for.' I've attended so many wedding fayres; some are worth it but others are a total waste of time, where no one is booking, everyone wants a freebie and the time you've spent standing and smiling at the passing parade could have been spent with your child at home.

Thankfully, I've been stationed in the hotel's main function room, without a competing florist in sight. Every couple and their family have to walk past me in order to get to the cake decorators and the wedding photographer. Therefore, I've been rushed off my feet answering questions, suggesting flower combinations symbolising specific meanings and have secured three bookings for May, June and a massive wedding in August. All deposits paid in full!

'Can we have navy blue flowers?' asks a young woman, staring at the large fresh bridal bouquet of white lilies which I created on Friday evening.

'You can have whatever colour you wish. I can dye the flowers to match a piece of fabric from your wedding colours,' I explain, instantly flipping my gallery of photographs looking for a Cadbury's purple bouquet I once dyed flowers especially for.

'And it doesn't rub off on to your dress?' she asks, eagerly glancing between her bored fiancé and me.

'No. The technique works really well, giving a rich colour, which is sustained if the bouquet is later dried and displayed as a picture.'

'Any colour?'

'Yep.' I point to my Cadbury's purple bouquet and the bride-to-be squeals in delight.

'That's exactly what I wanted. Look, Danny, look!'

The fiancé looks but fails to show any interest.

'I want . . . a large teardrop bouquet, with a mass of trailing foliage that touches the floor as I walk . . . like the royal family have,' she says, her hands wildly gesturing shape and size.

'Mmmm, can I suggest that your wedding bouquet doesn't quite touch the floor? My great-grandmother always blamed the failure of her marriage on that small detail. Could I suggest' – I flip through my gallery of images to a beautiful bridal bouquet with delicate tendrils and variegated ivy which almost touches the floor, stopping an inch or so above the bridal gown's hemline – 'something like this?'

'Yes, that! Oh, I love that idea!'

Sold. Another floristry booking secured: one large bridal bouquet plus six bridesmaids' posies for August, and a deposit paid.

I'm on a roll today!

Polly

I run around the dining room, folding fabric napkins and rearranging hard-backed chairs, nudging them sideways to squeeze in two garden chairs for my nieces, avoiding the legs of our dining-room table, which will ruin their enjoyment of the Sunday lunch.

'Fraser, I don't know why I offer to cook for everyone – we haven't the room, the cutlery or the patience for such big family occasions, and yet . . .' I say, bounding back into the kitchen to grab the condiments.

'You do it every other month in the name of sisterly love. I've said it before: she never invites us to their house in return,' says Fraser, uncorking two bottles of red wine in preparation. 'Everything goes in her favour; she gives very little to you, Polly. Helen cares about Helen and her own.'

'Fraser, please don't.'

'Mark my words . . . I can predict the entire conversation from the moment they arrive until the moment we wave them goodbye from the doorstep.'

'Oh, Fraser, she's my sister. If you were tighter with your brothers, we'd be inviting them over.'

'But still . . . she should appreciate you a little more than she does. Anyway, if either of my brothers could maintain a relationship for longer than a week or so, we could invite them and their plus ones – but they don't so, we can't.'

'Much to your poor mother's disgust,' I mutter, as I buzz about preparing the table, dashing back and forth from kitchen to dining room. 'Though she continues to pray for a wedding for either of them.'

Fraser's right; I can admit it without feeling disloyal to Helen.

I know he's always got my back where she's concerned. He's pointed out so many things over the years, but it boils down to the simple fact that she is my sister, and I only have one. Unlike Fraser, whose two younger siblings we see very little; it seems like his relentless act of big brother, with the comfortable home life and child, isn't always what younger siblings wish to see. They'll be settled one day, and maybe we'll see more of them then.

I replay Friday's phone call to my sister in my head. I know Helen would prefer to go on a mini break with Marc than be at Cody's party; worse still, she'd probably prefer me to be at home babysitting her two girls than be at Cody's party – but we all have our flaws.

I pull myself up sharp – look how rude I was to Lola. By the time she'd reached the end of the High Street, no doubt striding past the bathroom showroom and craning her neck to see our Cody in his suit, I felt mean. Mean for mentioning the flowers. Mean for flexing my maternal instincts on a slip of a girl who simply had eyes for a specific male. Hadn't I been that girl once? How would I feel if a grown woman had treated me that way?

I stop in my stride. Yep, Olive was . . . is cold, but she's never verbally mean towards me.

And Malcolm's always been approachable, but men don't do that sort of thing, do they?

'What?' asks Fraser, dragging me from my thoughts. 'You look like you're mithering away inside your head.'

'Nothing. Could you find suitable background music whilst we eat dinner? And no Pink Floyd,' I say, to pre-empt his questioning.

It's one thing to admit to myself what I'd done to Lola, but quite another to confess it to Fraser. Fraser would never have let anything as trivial get under his skin like that. He'd have maintained a dignified persona, but no, not me.

'I think Marc would appreciate a bit of the Floyd,' mumbles Fraser, disappearing through to the lounge to flick through his collection.

'That may well be . . . but the rest of us will have indigestion before dessert arrives. Oh shit!' I exclaim, scrambling to the freezer, remembering that I hadn't taken out the pavlova to defrost last night as I'd planned.

'You haven't defrosted the dessert, have you?' calls Fraser, his voice muffled with his head buried in his music collection.

'Nope, but you knew that!' I drag the strawberry pavlova from the freezer drawer and check that the mint Viennetta remains intact as a feasible substitute.

Why I do this to myself every other month I do not know. Fraser has a point: Helen never invites us to hers. In fact, Helen never invites anyone to hers, including our parents, though they do need inviting on different days in order to keep the peace. I invite each one alternately to join bi-monthly; today's my mother turn to join the happy throng, though if she brings up the subject of Wednesday's tantric session in front of her grandchildren, I will be stepping in to silence her.

I glance at the clock: half twelve.

'Fraser, will you give Cody a call, please? He needs to be up, washed and dressed before they arrive at one o'clock.'

I hear Fraser's muffled cry up the staircase and hope Cody's forgiven me for mentioning the Valentine flowers to Lola.

Dana

'Have you got a pen to jot down some details?' Tamzin's voice sounds even zanier and more frantic on my mobile hands-free.

'Sure,' I say, grabbing a pen from my pocket, struggling to hear amidst the wedding fayre chaos.

'So, we're looking at the following: Monday, Wednesday and Friday afternoon for a date with each male A, B and C which allows us early evening for editing. Tuesday and Thursday lunchtime until about four o'clockish to record your feedback to the previous day's date. Though Friday's feedback will be recorded straight after the date – you'll understand why when you see the timings. We'll need you for most of Saturday given it's the live finale, and you'll need to travel to London for your big date. The production team have secured an early evening TV slot to show Friday's feedback – it'll help to pull in the audience for the live finale later that night. We've a highlights programme booked for Sunday night – but we don't need you. We'll condense the best bits into a one hour slot. How does that sound?'

I am flabbergasted. I didn't expect such a full timetable.

'It sounds very busy,' I say dubiously. 'I didn't realise the finale would be a live broadcast.'

'Oh, it is, it is. Each afternoon we'll be cutting and creating from that day's footage to create a one-hour programme and, come Saturday night, we'll be airing the double episode and hopefully announce some fantastic news about your new relationship. The Sunday programme simply gives the TV audience a second chance to swoon if they missed the whole week.'

'Oh.'

'Dana ... this was all explained yesterday, right?'

'I can't really say, Tamzin ... there seemed to be so much asked of me yesterday that I have no idea if these details washed over me or not, to be frank.'

'OK, well, shout any time you have questions. We've booked

out a suite of rooms at the Red Lion for you to use each day to get yourself ready. It goes without saying we have a hair stylist and make-up artist so that you'll be camera-ready, and we have a selection of outfits for you to choose from. All transport has been organised and, of course, all expenses for each date will be taken care of by the production team.'

'Make-up artist *and* hairdresser?' I mutter, slowly realising the scale of this arrangement.

'Oh yeah! Of course, if you'd prefer to do your own . . . but the team thought you'd enjoy a bit of pampering throughout the dating experience.'

'It all sounds wonderful, Tamzin.'

'Anything else?'

'Can I ask any details about the male candidates?'

'You'll be given a brief outline before each date. They all live within or close to your county so, should anything develop during the course of the week, it'll be feasible to continue to see each other after the documentary has aired.'

I have nothing else to ask Tamzin.

My only question is for my parents: are they busy next week and could they babysit Luke?

Polly

'As I was saying,' continues my mother, her arm draped awkwardly around my youngest niece, squashing Erica to her aged bosom, 'live and let live – that's my motto.'

I grab my second glass of Merlot and take a deep swig; there is no point arguing over the irony of her remark.

'Then surely you need to start living by that motto, Pauline?' says Fraser, pushing his empty plate aside. 'You've hardly been dignified in your attitude towards Jeff in the past – well, not since I've been around.'

I glance at my sister, who is bristling at the very mention of my mother's social/love life. I wonder if she even knows about the tantric session with Derek. Helen's pursed mouth is working hard to refrain from speaking. My brother-in-law, Marc, glances at her, maintains his quiet composure and simply listens. I imagine that Helen's fingers, interwoven with Marc's beneath the table, are flexing in annoyance, which prompted him to check her expression. Decades together and still they hold hands at every possibility. I was tempted to sit them apart, placing their daughters in between, but who knows what friction that might have caused. In stark contrast, I'd removed our pair of Valentine's cards from the mantelpiece this morning, to prevent my blood relations taking the mickey as much as our son had. I stashed them inside my memory box, kept at the bottom of the lounge bookcase.

'Fraser, live and let live has always been my motto – it may have fallen by the wayside once or twice in the last twenty-three years but I swear that *is* what I live by.'

'Gran, what about the time you slashed Granddad's tyres for—'

'That's enough, Cody,' interjects Fraser, knowing full well the story would quite clearly prove the point that Grandma is lying.

'But she . . .' interjects Cody, eyes wide, pleading to be heard.

'I know. We all know . . . just give it a rest, will you?' I add, appreciating Fraser's tact. I change the subject clumsily. 'Helen, you've hardly touched your roast potatoes.'

'Too much for me, Polly. I'm trying to cut down a little.' I notice she pushes the plate aside as I speak.

'But you've left beef and vegetables too – that's not like you.'

'I know,' says Helen, her widening eyes signalling for me to shut up. Is she OK? Or is she still smarting because of Cody's party invite?

'I'll have your beef if it's going begging,' says Cody, his fork primed to pinch it from my sister's plate.

'Here.' Helen nudges her plate a little closer as Cody launches his attack. Evie and Erica, my two young nieces, sit and stare demurely as their big boy cousin devours yet more food, having already polished off his own substantial portion. They glance at one another, possibly grateful they don't share a house with such a gannet.

'Marc, can I fetch you any more roast potatoes, more beef?' I ask, viewing his empty plate, scraped clean of every morsel.

'No, thanks, Polly that was fine, just enough – I assume there's pudding?'

'Of course, though only if it's defrosted in time, Marc,' offers Fraser, standing to help me clear the dirty dishes. '*Someone* forgot to take it from the freezer last night. Otherwise we'll be fighting over the Viennetta.'

'And who didn't remind me?' I shout over my shoulder, balancing a pile of plates and heading for the adjoining kitchen. 'I'd planned to bake my own pavlova but I ran out of time.'

'I knew I'd get the blame. But we'll let you off, my love – you have been incredibly busy this week. These lovelies keep us on our toes, don't they, Marc?'

'Certainly, you should be grateful you've only got one to contend with. Me, I've got three,' moans Marc, glancing around the table at his wife and two daughters.

'Fair point, though this one has his moments too, I can assure you. Look at him, scoffing for England. Cody must have cost me a thousand pound a square inch in food to achieve his height and size,' says Fraser, following my path towards the kitchen.

I shove the dishes near the sink and turn my thoughts to dessert, grabbing dishes, spoons and an almost-defrosted pavlova from the microwave turntable where I'd carefully stashed it.

'Given the ice crystals still decorating the raspberry pavlova, I suggest ice cream and double cream all round,' jokes Fraser, returning to the dining room. 'Polly's homemade pavlova would have won hands down – her meringue is to die for.'

I hear a polite titter amongst our diners. He's right, I do have a talent for whipping meringues. I haven't a talent for juggling time, though a few less tasks might help.

I wanted pavlova, be it homemade or shop-bought.

I want pavlova.

'Anyone joining me?' I ask, delivering the plated pavlova to the table. Helen and my mother lean forward, peer at it and sit back.

'Viennetta for me, please, Fraser,' says my mother, swiftly followed by Helen.

'OK, anyone else?' I glance around the table as everyone stares at Fraser, who is holding a brick of mint ice cream to share amongst the group, a modern version of feeding the five thousand. 'Bugger you, then.'

As my cake knife swiftly delves into the meringue, I don't lift my eyes, but stare at my dessert.

He's right – you can see the ice crystals amongst the raspberries, but what's a bit of frozen water? I'm about to make my second cut when I decide to swing the knife wider for a larger portion. If I'm having this to myself, I might as well indulge!

Silence descends as we each chew, ooh and aah and seek additional cream from a second opened tub.

I glance around the table at my family.

Cody scrapes his dish clean, Fraser follows suit and the two girls politely pick at their ice cream. My mother heartily consumes hers, and Helen and Marc eat, their hands now conjoined on top of the tablecloth.

Is that really necessary whilst eating your dessert? Can't they be detached from each other for a moment? I'd noticed earlier that their hand-holding continued beneath the table and they only separated when they both needed a fork and serrated knife for the beef!

If I held Fraser's hand right now, he'd stare at me confounded, the entire table would be alerted to his confusion.

Honestly, Helen, the guy's busy trying to scrape the remains of some chocolate swirls from a fluted glass dish. Surely Marc can eat his dessert before the hand-holding resumes under the table and not above for all to see?

Or maybe it's Marc. Is Helen forced to participate in their endeavour to maintain this image of 'being as one' due to his deep-rooted insecurities? Surely after twenty-six years together she can be trusted to eat her ice cream, within his sight, without the risk of abandoning him?

I want to giggle, but take another bite of my pavlova, the edge of which has melted to a puree as it should be while the centre remains solid.

I suddenly get brain freeze but continue to chew as if fighting my own resilient corner.

Maybe my parents' bitter divorce battle – not over the custody of us, given we were sixteen and twenty-three, but rather concerning their possessions – affected Helen and Marc more than I'd realised. Whereas Fraser and I took it in our stride, assuming that they would make their own decisions regardless of having grown-up daughters. Although, if I'm honest, my decision to not get married does relate directly to having witnessed the damage caused by their battles over an elderly dog and a canteen of silver cutlery.

Helen swiftly moves their conjoined hands from the table-cloth, causing me to look up. She stares at me and I shake my head in response; I hadn't realised I'd been staring at their entwined digits whilst lost inside my head.

'How's your dessert, Mum?' asks Cody, scouring the table for unwanted goodies.

'Fine, though slightly cold and crunchy towards the middle – the meringue's gorgeous.'

'Anyone else having any?' asks Cody, pointing towards the remaining pavlova.

After a circle of grimaces, wincing and headshakes, Cody grabs the pavlova plate and cuts himself a huge portion.

Good lad, that's my boy!

Fraser looks on; he's never been outwardly affectionate towards our son, which is probably his male instinct, but as Cody's grown older the bond between them is definitely growing. There's a maturity to their interaction, almost a silent understanding between them that not everything has to be ver-balised, which, in my case, it does. Instead, I've notice my two males have adopted a sequence of fleeting glances, the flicker of a smirk between them as they get each other's meaning. Their bond has strengthened, their relationship deepened. It reminds me of my instinctive ability to know from my baby's cry his current need: food, nappy change, sleep or love, even from the next room. I see such a bond reflected in Fraser's eyes as he watches our son dish himself up pavlova.

I smile, my gaze resting briefly upon Marc, who is also watching Cody hungrily eat his second dessert, but in a dif-ferent manner to Fraser. Marc is studying Cody closely. Did he long for a lad? Want more children? Helen has never said, but Marc's look lingers.

Cody's mobile rings aloud, disturbing the end of our meal.

'I asked you to switch that off,' I say, annoyed that he hadn't bothered.

Down goes his dessertspoon, as out comes my screaming annoyance. I see a flicker of confusion cross his brow before he looks up at me, almost guiltily.

Lola? What she doing calling him?

'I'll just take this,' says Cody, moving from his seat and heading into the hallway.

I stare at Fraser as if I can hold an entire conversation telepathically, informing him in one look about Lola.

'What?' says Fraser, baffled by my expression.

'Nothing,' I mutter, his question and my tone alerting only my mother and sister, who stare in a questioning manner in my direction. I give them each a weak smile and begin clearing the table of dessert dishes. 'Coffee?'

Carmen

I sit with my headphones on watching the 'best of the best' proposal clips on YouTube, while Elliot watches the afternoon's football match. I'm unsure what I'm looking for exactly, so I'm browsing for inspirational ideas from which I can craft my own perfect proposal. For the next thirty minutes, I squirm and cringe at cheesy, word-stuttering proposals, stifle my laugh at a prank proposal and tearfully well up, attempting to hide my unexpected reaction, numerous times to heartfelt declarations of love. After my YouTube stint, I'm still baffled by the down-on-one-knee tradition of some proposals, but I now know what

I'm planning for mine. I want a simple, honest and heartfelt declaration of my love and a short speech proposing marriage.

I feel deceitful hiding behind my laptop, avidly watching all this with my earphones plugged in, but Elliot doesn't seem to notice – he is engrossed in his footie match. I've made a few notes: location, location, location is a priority, closely followed by sentiment and honesty. I'm no nearer writing my own proposal speech but I'm certain of what I don't want my special moment to look like. There is no way I'll be recalling for the rest of my life a bodge-it job, with cheesy lines and no planning. If this proposal-fest session has proved one thing to me, it's that planning is key. I might not have a final list of what I truly want but I have a definite list of what *not* to do come next Saturday evening.

I glance at the clock: 2.30 p.m.

'Is there football on all day?' I ask, interrupting Elliot's zone.

'Pretty much. Why? Is there something you want to watch?'

'Nope. I might nip out for a while and go shopping.' I know he won't argue or offer to join me, so it feels less deceitful. One detail confirmed during my proposal viewings is my need to purchase an engagement ring.

'Can I help you?' asks the young woman, her wide smile filling her face.

Here goes!

I sidle along the front of the glass countertop towards her.

'I'd like to view a ring suitable as a man's engagement ring,' I say, watching for her reaction.

'Have you anything in mind?' she asks automatically, unlocking the counter cabinet from her side and browsing the numerous rings displayed on cushioned pads from above.

'Not really. I'm expecting it to be a band of some description but I can't say I've ever seen anything which I'd class as suitable.'

'In some cultures, men always have an engagement ring which they later use as their actual wedding ring, but it isn't common. If it isn't to be their actual wedding band, quite often they choose a band with a decorative stone inlay or an engraved pattern. Many of these would be suitable.' She withdraws a velvet pad on which an array of gold rings are nestled. 'It does come down to personal preference whether it's gold, silver or platinum.'

'I have no idea what he'd choose: he doesn't do jewellery as such.'

'Oh, a surprise, is it?' Her eyes widen and her smile beams a little wider, if that is at all possible.

'Mm-hmm, I'm planning on proposing next Saturday, so I'll need a ring to present to him.'

'I love that! A leap-year proposal. So few women actually do it though, do they?'

'I'm not certain I'll be able to pull it off with confidence, but I've made my mind up to try, so I'm just going for it.'

I pick up a gold band with a small diamond detail nestled in its middle and bring it closer to my eye for inspection. I select a second, a similar design in platinum, and compare the two. I have absolutely no idea what Elliot will say or do when he sees my offering.

'Do you know his size?' she asks.

Now is my moment to feel utterly foolish.

'I only have this piece of thread, which I measured around his finger and knotted.'

I present the loop as she grabs for a sliding ring measure; she gently rolls the thread along the length and reads off where it settles.

'Size S. I'll go and see what else we have in that size,' she says, catching the eye of her colleague as she departs. I continue to compare the two rings.

I suppose you can never be too careful with customers and jewellery.

It takes minutes but she returns with another velvet pad of rings, each one a band with a slight variation in decoration and pattern.

It takes me a further ten minutes to select what I believe is the safest bet – the first ring I'd inspected. Call it fate, call it whatever, but it fits the brief perfectly.

'I think it's that one,' I say, offering the band back to the sales assistant.

'Super,' she says, replacing all the ring pads back inside the counter display before locking the back section. 'And is there to be anything for you?'

'Me?'

'Well, he'll have his engagement ring . . . will you be having one too?'

I haven't given it a thought and yet I like her suggestion. A smile dawns upon my face.

'Well, it would be rude not to have a little browse, wouldn't it?' I tease, convincing myself that it wouldn't do any harm.

'It certainly would . . . and the added benefit is that you get to choose.'

Within minutes I am manoeuvred across the jewellers towards a different counter inside which the sparkles are much bigger than in the previous display. The price tabs have also increased considerably.

'Do you know your ring size?'

This is the first of twenty questions regarding colour, clarity, caret and cut.

Her twenty-first question, asked as I stand admiring a decent-sized rock on my third finger, left hand, is simple to answer.

'Do you like it?'

'I love it!' I exclaim, moving my hand back and forth under the nearest light to watch the rainbow of refraction sparkle. 'This is the one.'

I am on cloud nine as she totals up the price of two engagement rings, boxes each and ties a bow to secure the neck of my petite jeweller's bag.

'That's a total of three thousand, six hundred and seventy-five pounds to pay'

I wasn't quite expecting to spend that amount today but, hey ho, needs must if I'm going to do the job properly.

I fight the urge to fish my own ring from the beautified bag and wear it on the drive home. I know I'll be cheating myself if I do such a thing. And how bad would it be if I forgot I had it on, entered the house and Elliot noticed it? It would be game over, surprise ruined.

Dana

My back is killing me. All I want to do is collect Luke and have a long snuggle with him on our sofa before it is bath and bedtime for both of us. There are nights when a seven-thirty lights-out feels like luxury in this busy world. Ridiculous for a grown adult but real-life bliss.

As I pull up in front of my parents' house, my head is spinning. I'm bamboozled by the very idea of my week ahead. I visualise our kitchen wall calendar. I have a meeting next Friday to discuss a new venture at the bridal shop, I have a parents' evening booked for Thursday, plus my usual daily flower deliveries . . . but now, I also need to juggle tasks and be available for dating.

I look up to see Luke standing in my parent's lounge bay window, banging the glass and smiling. I imagine he's yelling instructions for me to hurry up. My dad stands behind him, holding him in place on the window ledge. I was never allowed to stand on the window ledge in case I scratched the stained woodwork. How things have changed!

Luke's chubby legs entwine with mine as we lie on the sofa. The TV is showing a Winnie-the-Pooh animation, which I think is a little young for him these days but Luke is transfixed by their colourful antics. Likewise, I am mesmerised by Luke. I gently brush his dark fringe aside. I play with his dimpled fingers as his little body frequently jumps and starts at the excitement of the characters on TV. He's beautiful. Truly beautiful. A squashed button nose, slightly shorter than most. Tiny, slanting, yet sparkling dark eyes. A broad, stocky body, which I know will always need to be exercised and have a tendency towards cuddliness. My hand drops from his temple to his chest. A heart as big as a bucket beats strong within this tiny little being.

A wave of sadness floods over me.

I want to tell his father what a beautiful little boy he's missing out on. To make Andrew see that his little boy is just like every other child who wants to chase wild birds, kick a football around the garden and cries when he scraps his knees. But I know wherever Andrew – the selfish son of a bitch – is, he hasn't the heart or understanding to recognise what he did when he was the first to reject our boy.

I can't let myself think back to those days. The pain, the hurt of his words, crash about my mind if I allow them to. So I won't. I'll block Andrew out for another day.

My mind runs wild with scenarios which Luke may encounter in life – some he might have encountered already when I wasn't there – when others don't accept Luke as he is. When others may be unkind, cruel or rude towards the little boy with a giant heart.

I want to cry.

Cry for the hurt he may encounter.

For the pain he might endure.

Shed tears for those people he'll never get to know, enjoy or love because of their lack of knowledge or acceptance.

And my heart breaks a little more for their loss.

Polly

'Cody, how many of your friends have you mentioned the party to?' I ask, whilst applying my night cream in the bathroom mirror.

'None, why?' calls Cody, coming up the staircase, heading towards his bedroom.

'What did you say?' I say, straining to hear his reply.

'None, I haven't seen anyone to speak to.'

'You've just spent the evening with them! What could have been easier than asking them?'

'I didn't see the crowd actually . . . I haven't been to the pub tonight.'

Someone save me, please. The lad asks for a party, with just one week to go until the event, then fails to invite anyone.

'How can I arrange a party when you have no idea who is coming?'

'Mum, stop panicking. They'll be there, OK? We're not like old people who have to plan everything three weeks in advance.'

'Oi, us "old people", as you rudely call us, have to make arrangements three weeks in advance because we made the foolish decision to fill our lives with offspring like you. Before we say yes to an invite, we have to take into account our kids' every need, foreseeing dramas and it's mayhem if we don't. So please don't knock us for refusing invites because we need to feed you kids – we'd love to swing by the seat of our pants with a carefree attitude but that all ceased once us "old people" had you lot.'

'Okaaaaay!' comes his sarcastic tone from the landing. 'We're meeting up tomorrow so I'll mention it then, but the usual crowd is about twenty or so, if that makes you feel better.'

'You've got a cheek.' Twenty or so! Just hearing a rough amount *has* made me feel slightly better, though I wasn't about to admit it to Cody, given his 'old people' reference. With our immediate family and our close family friends we'll be nearing sixty bodies. Sixty people is more than enough to celebrate and have a good catch-up with. Too many and you never get around the room to chat with everyone. Too few and the party never gets underway. 'I'll pick up a couple of packs of invites tomorrow, address and post them on my way home, then the written invites will arrive by Wednesday at the latest. Though given the short notice, maybe I should send a quick text message first to let people know.'

'Mum, do whatever . . . but without three weeks' notice, I doubt anyone from your generation will be free to make it.'

'Cody, I swear you'll be for it if you carry on!' I tease, knowing he's got a point even if it makes me feel so much older than I want to admit.

I stare at my reflection. I don't look too bad for my age; yes, my skin isn't as bright as it once was and my cheekbones aren't as prominent but I haven't got as many wrinkles as some. I look positively youthful compared to others I know.

Cody crosses the landing and heads towards his room.

A delayed reaction but suddenly my interest is ignited.

'Cody?'

'Yeah.'

'Your crowd always heads for the pub on Sunday nights . . . why didn't you?'

'I . . . I took a date to the cinema, so gave the pub a miss.'

'Oh.'

I can hear the hesitation in his voice.

Dare I ask who?

The floorboard outside his bedroom door creaks; he's waiting, anticipating my next question.

Is that why she called him earlier, forcing him to leave the dinner table? Please don't say he's chancing his luck with Lola again.

Dare I ask and start a row right before bed?

I hear his bedroom door softly close.

Good decision, Cody, especially if *that* young lady is wheedling her way back into your life.

Chapter Five

Monday 24 February

Carmen

'Look what I have!' I announce, rattling a ring box in my palm as Trish makes our morning coffee. I'd intended to do my usual inspection of the boutique before showing her but my excitement got the better of me.

'Let me see, let me see,' cries Trish, abandoning her task and grabbing for the tiny box.

She snaps the lid back and gasps.

'Is this for you?' she asks sternly.

I nod.

'Oooh, you are naughty! Please tell me you've bought Elliot a decent ring too.'

'No fear, he has a classic gold wedding band with small detailing to remove the plainness. But I thought I deserved one too.'

Trish peers at the solitaire diamond, her grin growing as she admires it.

'So you're serious about this?'

'Yep, I'm going for it. It goes against my lifelong dream but why not? We women have fought for and achieved equality in so many areas of our lives, so why not in proposing?'

'Good for you, Carmen. I hope you'll be very happy,' says Trish, returning the box to my palm. 'Are you asking his family beforehand?'

My mouth falls open.

'Haven't you thought about that one?'

'Trish, we're both nearly forty years old. Surely you aren't suggesting that I need to visit his parents and ask their permission?'

'Terry asked my parents before asking me, and I was heading towards forty.'

'I'm not . . . I hadn't thought about it . . . I have so much to do already and that's another task. I doubt Elliot would have given my parents such consideration if he'd been planning to propose.'

Trish raises her eyebrows and returns to making coffee.

'Oh Trish, are you saying I should or I must?'

'I'm not saying anything. You'll do as you please, but I thought it was touching when Terry spoke to my parents first. If nothing else, it included them in the excitement of the occasion.'

'Oh no, don't say I have something else to plan for.'

'Not if you're not doing it, you haven't. Here,' says Trish, offering me a steaming mug of coffee.

'I'll think about it, but don't keep on about it if I decide not to.'

Trish holds her hands aloft.

'It's not my decision, sweetheart – it's yours.'

Dana

'How are we feeling?' calls Jez, as Tamzin leads me from the hotel bedroom where I've had my hair and make-up crafted for the last ninety minutes. I still recognise myself through the fug of hairspray and the glitzy eyeshadow, but only just. Jez performs a little jog and a trot to catch us up as we descend the main stairwell.

'Very nervous but looking forward to the experience,' I lie. I've never been so terrified in my life. From Tamzin's outline of the afternoon, I will be meeting Male A, as they keep referring to him, in a short while and will spend the next few hours getting to know him while two mobile cameramen plus accompanying team move about us taking footage.

How could I have forgotten just how bad I am at first dates?

I'm hoping that Male A is chatty, funny and open to discussion, otherwise this will be the disaster of all disasters – I am not the world's best at making small talk.

'You'll be fine, let us worry about the logistics of the date and you enjoy yourself . . . forget we're even present.'

I stop short.

'That can't happen surely . . .'

'You'll be amazed,' adds Tamzin. 'The cameras will seem like the norm in no time, and you'll be chatting away for England.'

'I'd best watch what I say then,' I quip.

'Oh no, don't. Just relax and go with the flow. The best conversations are spontaneous even if one of you – and I hope this doesn't happen – we've got the legal team on hand if it does – says something which could be libellous,' explains Jez. 'I'm excited about this! Oh, I believe the dating and lifestyle guru wants a word beforehand.'

'Is she a guru?' asks Tamzin, her orange and yellow spiral curls bouncing with each step.

Jez shrugs.

'I haven't a clue. I just know that they are costing us a small fortune so they had better not mess up. Their careers may depend upon it,' he says, peeling off as we reach the bottom of the grand staircase. 'I'll catch you later, Dana – just enjoy!'

'I'll try,' I say, my stomach rolling more than ever as we near the hour.

'So here's how it'll work: you'll be driven to the restaurant where male A is awaiting your arrival, you'll order and chat and get to know each other a bit. Anything that you want, please just ask. Jez'll cut those sections out in the edits to make it seem seamless.'

'What happens if we have nothing in common?' I ask, fearing the worst.

'That won't happen, Dana – they've matched you up with three nice guys. If nothing else, you'll have three enjoyable dates, trust me.'

I'm about to ask more questions when we arrive at the hotel's entrance, where a crowd of the production team are gathered, cameras and mics at the ready.

One guy advances, holding a small microphone towards my lapel. I stand rigidly as he secures it without touching my body.

'Could you say something, please?' he asks, looking up at another guy wearing headphones.

'Such as?'

'Anything.'

I can't think of a single thing to say so I recite the nursery rhyme 'Hickory Dickory Dock'. I see a plethora of lifted eyebrows and failed attempts not to smirk.

'Sorry, my little boy was singing that non-stop at breakfast,' I apologise.

Tamzin nods absentmindedly.

The sound guy gives a thumbs-up and I take it I'm ready.

'Remember to remove that should you nip to the ladies partway through the meal,' says Tamzin, pointing to the mic.

'Of course,' I say. Does she think I'm totally lacking in common sense?

'Are we good to go?' ask Tamzin.

'Yes,' I say.

'Not you, them!' She points to the production crowd.

'The car is outside. Just waiting for Jez,' calls a crew member, circling with a mighty camera.

Why am I doing this? Could I have not searched the dating sites like the chummy-mummies and found a suitable man?

I only have one vow: to introduce my son only when I feel comfortable and I'm sure the requirements of his condition will be respected. The last thing I want to do is to tell a sob story to gain sympathy, which I don't want. I have more respect for my son and myself than allow that to happen.

Polly

'They're nice,' says Stacey, picking up a blue party invite from my desk as I swiftly write another between customers.

'For our Cody's birthday party. You don't think they look a bit babyish?'

'No, not at all. They're quite smart with the foil lettering.'

'They were the only decent ones in the card shop. Actually, we've left it a bit late for a decent turnout but Cody didn't decide he wanted a party until last Friday. These should have been posted days ago but you know what it's like. It was a busy weekend what with trying to book everything last minute.'

'Not enough hours in the day, are there?' says Stacey. 'Our lads have never gone for the party stuff, which is a shame because we rarely get our family together nowadays, apart from funerals.'

'It's the same with ours, we always plan to bring together both sides of the family but it never happens. Our Cody was giving me lip last night about old people needing a minimum of three weeks' notice to say yes to a social drink, and he's not wrong.'

'He's not. Here, do you want me to give you a hand?'

'Would you?' I say, adding, 'If you and Clive are free on Saturday night, you'd be more than welcome to pop along.'

'Nah, we're at a swimming gala all day, but thanks.'

I divide my pile of invites and Stacey settles at the edge of my desk. I've worked alongside her for a couple of years but we remain on the polite acquaintance spectrum; we're like ships in the night most days, with us both being on part-time hours.

'Jill and Tony,' I say, as she sits pen poised above the dotted invitee line. 'The other details are there,' I add, pointing towards a completed invite. Gone are the days when I felt I had a moral motherly duty to do everything relating to my son myself. I would never allow anyone to wrap his presents, not even my mother or sister – not that Helen would ever offer. I refused offers to bake him a birthday cake, or return his unwanted tracksuits in exchange for gift vouchers. *I* was Cody's mum, I would and could do it all and, if the results of my labours weren't appreciated by anyone else, even my son, I took satisfaction in knowing that I'd done it all. Yeah, that kind of martyrdom has faded in recent years. So Stacey is welcome to write as many as she likes, saving me from getting hand ache.

'Is that young woman wanting your attention?' asks Stacey, nodding towards the window.

Standing outside, browsing our display boards, is Lola. She appears to be busy reading the details of the Paris trip but I doubt she's truly interested.

'Maybe. She and our Cody had a thing a while back and now she's suddenly popped up again out of the blue. She already invited herself in for a chat last Friday and I don't really want another, so I'm not falling for a sob story if she does venture inside, OK? Or, give her your spiel on this week's star holiday package if you like.'

'I'm dreading my kids reaching that stage in life. I fear for my own sanity with the amount of worry I'll cause myself.'

'I know what you mean. You can't wait for them to be independent, make their own mistakes and yet . . .'

The shop door swings wide and Lola enters.

My heart sinks.

Really? Is this going to be a weekly routine?

'Polly, could I have a word, please?'

'Sure.' I muster a cheerful tone and a smile, looking up from my half-written invite.

'Next?' says Stacey, putting aside her completed invite.

'Sally and Neil,' I say, waiting for Lola to continue.

'Polly, I wondered if Cody might be wanting a new watch?'

I'm dumbstruck, staring into her wide blue eyes, rimmed with dark kohl – such pale features framed by such heavy make-up.

'Lola, I couldn't say . . . but I don't think you should be spending your money on Cody given the circumstances, do you?'

'I want him to have something nice.'

I sigh.

Can't she read between the lines? I'm trying to be polite, trying to save her wasting her cash and feel dejected afterwards. Why can't she hear what I'm saying?

'Lola, how long has it been since you and Cody were ... dating?' I stumble over the phrase, not wishing to belittle the relationship but, as I saw it, 'hanging out romantically prior to a drama occurring' would have been a more fitting description.

'Eight months,' she says. 'But Polly, I've grown up since then.'

'That might be the case, Lola, but unless Cody chooses to be with you, you can't keep forcing the issue, can you?' There're so many clichés I want to quote: 'Wake up and smell the coffee', 'There's plenty of more fish in the sea, go fishing', 'Please, I beg you, leave my son alone.'

I fall silent and wait.

'Next?' asks Stacey.

'Ann-Marie and Trevor.'

'Are those for Cody's party?'

'Mm-hmm,' I lower my head, unsure if I want to proceed. I'm finding this so difficult. I almost wish there was a series of classes to attend, much like pre and post-natal sessions, to guide me through the process of being the mother of an attractive young man. I would happily study any textbook recommended, consume any offered leaflet and, if suggested by the professionals, make a detailed plan of action detailing my many options. I wanted something like the colour-coded birthing plan I'd swiftly ignored twenty years ago when the pain got too much and I demanded everything I'd previously refused.

'Is the usual crowd going?' she asks, picking up the nearest card. I want her to put it down, to leave but to say so would be rude. I was rude last time and felt awful afterwards for becoming a 'mean older woman'.

'I don't suppose there's a chance ... ?'

Enough!

'Look, Lola, I don't know what you expect me to say. I'm his mother. I saw what you put him through, he was as miserable as sin and, no, I don't relish the idea of that happening again, with you or any other young woman. Reality tells me there may be many more occasions when I have to watch my son go through the wringer until he finally settles down in life, but this . . . this can't continue. I have work to do, you should be at work or college or *something* . . . not here asking me questions about my son.'

Lola's eyes flash with annoyance.

'Fine. Be like that then! You and your family can go screw themselves. I was only asking if you thought he'd like a watch but if it's too much trouble to answer me then I'll speak to Cody myself.'

'But it's simply a smokescreen, a pretence, Lola – you aren't interested in whether Cody wants a watch! Your interest is in getting back into his good books and then you'll begin squeezing yourself back into his daily life. My son might accept that, that's his choice, but I know he deserves better than being treated as you treated him. If that sounds like an overprotective mum, then I'm sorry, but one day, many years from now, you might actually get first-hand experience when another Lola does this to *your* son. Now, I'm sorry to sound so rude, but I have work to do.'

I fall silent.

'Next?' says Stacey, which makes me want to laugh at the comedy timing.

'Esmé and Asa,' I say.

Lola stands staring for a fraction of a second before turning on her heel and leaving the shop.

As the door closes, I sit back and sigh.

'Bloody hell, has the girl no self-respect?' mutters Stacey, looking up at me for the first time throughout the exchange.

'I know this is just another phase of having kids but I'd be happy to bail on this one. Seriously – give me potty training again, it was so much easier than this!'

Carmen

'I can't imagine spending the whole day in the same wedding dress – what's the point, Mum?' says the bride-to-be in a figure-hugging ivory organza gown, complete with flowing veil and sparkling tiara.

Trish and I stand in silence as our mother and daughter appointment hits a sticky situation. I've witnessed numerous family arguments over the years but this particular one is a first.

'But, Persephone, darling, think about the additional arrangements plus the dashing around changing and redoing your hair and make-up each time.'

'Papa said . . .'

I watch the older woman sigh despondently; she's obviously had those words thrown at her on numerous occasions. Her smile is readjusted and brightens before she addresses me calmly.

'Could we see several other dresses, please?'

'Certainly. Are you thinking of gowns that provide a contrast or are similar in style?' I ask, looking from mother to daughter.

'Similar,' says the mother.

'Contrast,' says the bride-to-be.

Another renewed smile is pasted on the mother's face, as she gives a tiny nod in my direction. I can see their silent argument occurring before our eyes. There is no way I am going to please both of these women in the same appointment, on the same day.

It takes a further ninety minutes, a second round of bubbles and half a tin of shortbread before this appointment is complete.

'The total is . . .' I punch the numbers for all three gowns into the calculator and ready myself to take a breath as I press for the total. 'Eleven thousand, six hundred and eighty-five pounds.'

'Thank you,' says the mother, handing over her credit card without a quibble.

Whereas I am quite shocked; I've never charged one family such a price for wedding gowns.

I hand over her receipt, book a date for their next appointment for fittings and bid them both a good day. As I walk the ladies towards the boutique door and Trish tidies the boutique, I try my hardest not to look at my co-worker.

I gently close the door behind them.

We both freeze like mannequins until the pair are a safe distance away from our large bay window.

And then . . .

'Woohoo!' shrieks Trish, clapping her hands to her mouth.

'Boy, oh boy!' I say. 'If that's how much they've paid for wedding gowns, can you imagine how much they're paying for the whole wedding? It must run into tens, if not hundreds, of thousands based on this one appointment.'

'Any chance you'll be ordering three gowns on your return from Paris?' asks Trish, retrieving her tray of used glasses.

'Not a chance, which is ironic given that I own the business,' I say, shaking my head. 'Though the day I book my appointment to choose, we'll be celebrating with bottles of Lanson, that's for sure!' I call after her as she heads towards the kitchenette to fill the dishwasher.

'We'll hold you to that,' shouts Trish over her shoulder.

A lump lifts to my throat. I feel quite emotional as I look around the boutique; in all the years that I have been the owner, assisting so many brides over fourteen years to choose their perfect gown, this is the nearest I have ever been to being in their situation.

I glance at the rails of cellophane-covered gowns. I have imagined myself, on many occasions, wearing every gown I have in stock. Obviously my choice has changed over the years. In my mid-twenties, I went through a phrase of loving a gown styled on a riding habit and topped with a small veiled hat. With the added confidence of my late twenties, I set my heart on a very slinky, sequinned gown which was often referred to as the negligee gown. Now I've matured, I'm sure my choice will be more classic with graceful lines and gorgeous fabrics. It goes without saying I've never tried any of them on; I never wanted to jinx myself or spoil what I hope will be the glorious day when I can officially make an appointment to try on a gown. I've never done a Miss Ingram.

'Coffee?' calls Trish, from the kitchenette.

'Yes, please.' I break away from my daydreaming.

Purely out of curiosity, I check how busy our appointment book is for next Monday. I'm pleased to see there's a quiet afternoon. Impulsively, I pick up the pencil and draw several lines through the afternoon, just to be on the safe side. If I get next weekend's proposal right, I'll be needing all afternoon for my own appointment.

Dana

'Madam, the maître d' will escort you to your table,' says the hostess, smiling brightly whilst beckoning the nearest tailcoat. It feels strange having a dinner date booked for late afternoon and yet the restaurant is busy. I'm usually just arriving home from the school run at this time, but I suppose with TV editing, the candlelight and the other clientele in the foreground, it will make it appear like an evening date.

'Madam, if you please.'

I hot-foot after him, taking in none of the beauty of the high-ceilinged restaurant but just trying to breathe calmly, knowing that when this guy steps aside Male A, my date, will be seated, awaiting my arrival. I am conscious that the cameramen are three steps behind me, and I'm relieved that I allowed the stylist to choose my outfit: a classy jumpsuit and scarf combo in peacock blue with emerald detailing.

'Madam.'

The maître d' steps aside and pulls out my chair. I stare at the man who immediately stands up from the opposing chair. Male A: incredibly slender and willowy with an olive complexion and a heavy brow from under which dark brown eyes stare intently.

'Good evening, Dana . . . I'm Alex, nice to meet you,' he says, shaking my hand. His voice has a sing-songy tone.

'Hi, Alex, have you had far to travel?' I say, as my chair is pushed beneath me and a linen napkin is draped across my lap.

'Just a few miles. And you?'

So begins our relaxed afternoon of wining and dining. I hardly notice the camera roving about our table, though I notice several other diners on the far side of the restaurant craning their necks to guess why we've got a table separate from any others, ensuring an empty backdrop free from staring faces. It was obvious we were getting first-class service from every waiter.

Alex seems nice. I don't correct him when he gets my name wrong, which is slightly annoying. I kick myself each time it happens. You can only correct someone for so long before giving up and answering to Donna, Diana or Deana purely to save their embarrassment.

Our conversation is halted by the delivery of menus and a
wine list. I leave Alex to choose; I know nothing about wine. I
watch as he ponders the selection, drawing his index finger the
length of the page and mmmming a lot. If it were me, I'd go
for the house red – but, as I said, what do I know about wine?

Despite the unusual circumstances and the hovering production team, I feel quite relaxed. I'm hoping that my parents
are having an easy time with Luke; I'd left permission with the
school for my dad to collect him. I know Mum bought chicken
nuggets and mint ice cream as a treat – though what my dad
will think about his 'treat' dinner won't be worth repeating.

'Do you have any children?' asks Alex, staring at me intently
from the other side of the lighted candlesticks.

'Yes, one little boy, Luke – he's five years old, nearly six, in
fact.'

'Oh.'

I'm half expecting another question, but there's nothing, so
I'll be polite.

'And you?'

'Nope. Not that I wouldn't want any, it's just that I've never
had a relationship veer towards serious . . . So, no, no children.'

'I haven't either, but still . . .'

Alex's eyebrows lift slightly.

I suddenly feel scrutinised. That was supposed to sound
lighthearted and yet his eyebrow move made it feel heavier.

'I mean . . . What I mean is . . . we *were* in a committed
relationship – it simply didn't last, so I'm raising my son on
my own.'

Alex gives a bouncy head nod, his gaze fixed on mine. I can
see the cogs of his brain working furiously, trying to assess the
situation.

Was that right? Is that what happened? Or had I found

myself abandoned by a reckless man who chose not to be a father following a test result? Why am I bringing Luke's father into the conversation?

I don't wish to introduce Luke's condition into our conversation, not at this stage, so I keep it simple.

'My son is with my parents this afternoon,' I add, filling the growing silence.

I feel Alex has switched off after just a few minutes. He's still participating in the conversation but he's sitting back in his seat, not as interested or engaged as he was. Is that because I have a son? Or because I wasn't in a committed relationship whilst pregnant? I need to say something … anything … to get the flow back.

'How do you spend your free time, Alex?' I ask, as our starters and the wine are delivered.

I'm waiting for an answer but Alex is busy testing the proffered wine. Alex gives a sharp nod to the maître d, having smelt it, sipped it and slushed it around his mouth before swallowing.

'Thank you,' I say, as the waiter pours me a generous glass. I quickly take a sip: it does taste mellow and fruity, unlike the cheap shudder wine I sometimes pick up at the supermarket.

'I'm quite fussy about my wine, as you can see.'

'It's very nice,' I reply, hoping that a compliment may reignite the conversation.

I'm suddenly aware that the camera is directly behind Alex and obviously pointing straight at me. I'd lost it from my peripheral vision for quite a while, but what are they honing in on now? Have I dribbled my wine down my chin? Has my make-up run, giving me giant panda eyes? I try to focus on Alex and wonder if they'd shot some footage of him over my shoulder, especially when he was testing the wine.

'I also enjoy cycling, some field sports and cookery,' he says, adding, 'And you?'

'Apart from my son, who takes up most of my time, I'm a self-employed florist so I tend to link my free time to my work. We have a tiny garden at home, but still I manage to get planting and sowing when the weather allows. Though, to be fair, my garden takes a bit of a bashing given that Luke loves to kick a football about but has very little control. Maybe I'll have a nicer garden when he's older.'

'Which team does he support?'

'Oh, he doesn't support a team. We just play in the back garden – he has a tiny plastic goal at one end. I appear to be the world's worst goalkeeper – much to his delight!' I giggle. Alex nods but remains straight-faced.

Our date continues pleasantly for a couple of hours. I'm unsure how the experts have come to match us up, but while there's nothing earth-shattering about Alex, he's a nice guy, has decent manners and can hold a conversation whilst eating his meal. Whereas I feel like I'm failing to adapt to being a grown-up for the dinner date. My stomach is still swirling, I can't talk and think at the same time and I've nearly knocked my wine glass over when reaching for it twice. I've come to the conclusion that a dinner date is not really my thing, despite stating to the production team that I love them. I'm really not sophisticated enough to pull them off, like the adults seated at the neighbouring tables. I suppose I'm more comfortable at play dates, surrounded by wipeable surfaces, a ball pit filled with giggling children and some giant foam shapes on which to perch and observe Luke attempting to climb a rope ladder.

By the dessert course, my mind is drifting. I wonder if Luke is missing me.

'Dana, thank you for the delightful conversation, good company and, hopefully, I'll be seeing you very soon.'

I smile politely.

Does Alex think tonight went well?

'Yes, yes . . .' I smile and wait, unsure whether I'm meant to leave the restaurant first or not. I see Tamzin pointing towards the exit, so I give Alex a quick peck on the cheek and swiftly follow her out.

As I walk through the restaurant, other diners look up, inquisitive about who they've had the pleasure of being ignored for. A look of disappointment quickly follows as they can't recognise me or name my co-star. I wish I had the guts to stop and introduce myself.

'Hi, I'm Dana . . . a mum, a florist and no one very special, so please don't waste your evening thinking about me – enjoy your partner's company.' But I don't, I can't . . . I wouldn't have the nerve.

I thank the passing waiters as I walk. I'm dying for the loo but right now my focus is on making it out of the restaurant without a fellow dinner demanding, 'Who the hell are you, love?'

I spot the sign for the ladies.

I'm through the outer doors and into the swish décor with mirrors and fresh flowers before Tamzin can turn about and reach me.

I go into cubicle one, lock the door and sigh with relief.

Relief that date one is over. Relief that my stomach can relax now I've undone my wide buckled belt. Relief that I can pause for a moment without seeming to be rude.

Sheer relief.

I sit and ponder for a second.

He's nice, polite and charming . . . though there was nothing which clicked or drew me to him. I didn't like his eyebrow raise when I first mentioned my situation but he settled into the conversation and was kind enough to ask about Luke's love of football.

I finish, flush and wash my hands.

I fix my mascara, which has smudged a little but nothing to worry about.

I leave the ladies toilet, expecting the sea of faces awaiting me in the foyer but not their look of horror.

'Microphone!' shouts Tamzin, as Jez stands by shaking his head, while the others struggle to keep from smirking.

Carmen

I sit on the edge of their three-piece suite, surrounded by Coalport figurines of ladies wearing wide-brimmed hats in various elegant poses, and fiddle with my china cup and saucer. Elliot's parents, Jim and Sally, sit and stare at me.

I'm not sure if I should remain silent to allow my words to sink in or break the silence and explain myself. Whichever I chose, there'll be no going back. So I choose to remain silent.

I sip my cooling tea. And wait a little longer.

I wish now that I'd waited to eat the single ginger nut which had been resting in my china saucer. Sadly, I was greedy. I would like to ask for a second, but I don't.

'Sorry . . . say that again,' asks Jim, leaning forward in his fireside armchair.

'I said, I've come to ask for your consent to ask your son to marry me.'

'Why are *you* asking *him*?' asks Sally, fidgeting with her own china teacup.

'Now there's a question, Sally. I'm really not sure, if I'm honest ... we've been together for eight years, we've bought a house, we've created a joint life and yet he has never asked me, and so I'm going to use the tradition of a leap year to ask him instead.'

Sally draws her chin in, and blinks uncontrollably. I can see her confusion. I know she's wondering what the world has come to and is probably grateful that she received a proposal from her man over four decades ago.

I sense her disappointment, and I completely share it. But what am I supposed to do?

'Are your own parents aware of this plan?' asks Jim.

I shake my head. Given I am the only daughter amongst their five offspring, they've no doubt been dreaming of a moment such as this when Elliot might arrive, alone, nervous and unannounced, on their doorstep. Sadly he has kept them waiting too.

'Oh,' says she.

'Oh,' repeats he.

'I know the modern world is confusing, my parents say that all the time, but I do truly love Elliot. I don't believe I'm wrong in wanting what I want. I feel I've waited patiently but now, needs must. I want a legal commitment so we can begin the next chapter as man and wife,' I explain, adding, 'None of us are getting any younger, are we?' As the words leave my lips, I want to kick my own arse for using Haughty Hannah's bloody line.

They both stare at me; the silence is deafening.

There is a definite lack of enthusiasm flowing and I wholeheartedly wish Elliot had got his act together before now and had endured such an occasion with my parents. Though, to be fair, I can imagine his attempt at gaining parental consent would have gone a whole lot smoother than this. In fact, I could guarantee it, knowing how desperate my parents are to see me, their only daughter, settled. My mum would have subtly disappeared into the kitchen, only to listen intently to the men's conversation through the crack in the serving hatch. My dad would have done his silence-is-golden bit whilst Elliot outlined his request, but inside he would have been thrilled to bits, jumping at the chance to congratulate Elliot before calling in my mother, who would have done the entire 'I know nothing as I was absent, please inform me' routine, which she never quite pulls off given that her eyes sparkle uncontrollably when she's excited. There would have been backslapping from my dad and embraces from my tearful mum, who'd produce a round of tea and a plate of sliced malt loaf, thickly buttered. There would be excitement, warm welcomes to the family, despite our eight-year relationship, and this would have been enhanced further if any of my four married brothers had happened to be there during Elliot's visit. I can't imagine that any one of my relatives would not have encouraged Elliot in his quest. But me, here and now ... wow! I've dropped a bloody big clanger on this one!

I look down at my cup and saucer: it's a tiny china cup but I can see there is plenty more tea left to drink before I can escape with a goodbye and a peck on the cheek. The next fifteen minutes may be filled with polite conversation, but unknowingly they have given me their answer with their muted 'ohs'.

'Has Elliot ever discussed marriage with you?' asks Jim.

'Of course, we've been together for eight years, Jim,' I lie, chuckling as I speak. 'We've discussed everything but he just hasn't asked me. All I'm doing is playing my part and speeding our commitment along.'

'Not really – you are asking my son to get married ... Have you not wondered why he's never asked?' asks Jim.

I fall silent and stare hard at Jim. My heart rate is rapid.

My palms are sweaty. Does Jim know something I don't? Have Father Cole and devoted second son been having honest life talks without my knowledge in Jim's potting shed whilst Sally washed the Sunday dishes and I dried? I'd never suspected their relationship to be so close, or open.

I wait, anticipating a revelation.

'Marriage might not be something he wants in life,' says Jim, his voice lowering as he reaches the end of the sentence.

'Has he told you that?' I prompt, vowing never to be sidelined with a tea towel during future Sunday visits.

'No, but when a man decides what he wants in life, he doesn't drag his feet, Carmen.'

I'm taken aback by his honesty. Eight years of knowing Elliot's father and *this* is the moment he chooses to be frank. Cheers, Jim! The last time was when I'd proudly showed off my homemade hanging baskets, which I'd planted and nurtured myself rather than buy them; his only remark of 'trailing lobelia would have enhanced the overall shape' was not what I was wanting to hear. Especially as my cascading geraniums overflowed with vibrant colour and I had remembered to water each basket every day and not just the first three days, unlike every other summer basket I'd ever had.

I sip my tea to gain vital thinking space after such a remark.

'Carmen, dear . . . I'm sure he has his reasons,' soothes Sally. 'I'd suggest waiting a little longer.'

Deep inside, I feel a switch flick. This was a bad suggestion by Trish; I shouldn't have come. I shouldn't have entertained the idea of involving his parents, just to be polite or respectful; I certainly shouldn't have been the least bit confiding.

'Well, I wanted to ask you, but I now realise that you have your own expectations for our future. All I ask is that we might keep this conversation to ourselves. I would like my proposal to be a surprise for Elliot. I feel that, in time, you may come to respect my decision.'

Within five minutes, I have politely kissed them each goodbye and said my farewells.

As I unlock my car, I notice that their front door is firmly closed. Their habit is usually to wave from the doorstep until we've driven partway along the road. But not today. Or rather, not for me.

Dana

'Honestly, Dad, I can't stay,' I protest, as my parents settle to watch TV for the remainder of their evening. 'I've been on the go all day, I'm fit to drop.'

A bathed and pyjama-clad Luke is affectionately plastering my face with sleepy wet kisses, his two-handed hug around my neck is unrelenting. If I were to stand up straight, I predict his Paddington Bear slippers would lift from the carpet – that's how much he has missed me.

'There's a new programme starting, they've been advertising it all week. I saw the producer chatting with Eamonn and Ruth this morning, he was explaining it's a social experiment . . . one of those documentary type things about dating. He seemed most excited to see if social science and the experts can predict true love between strangers. Dana, you'll love it,' enthuses my mum, though what she'll be thinking in less than ten minutes is anyone's business.

I can't bring myself to explain, or confess. I'm dumbstruck it's going to be aired at a prime time. This is my cue to deliver a round of kisses, thank them for looking after Luke without query or complaint and leave, before the credits for *Taking a Chance on Love* begin to roll.

'Anyway, watch your programme . . . and I'll phone you in an hour.' I collect my sleepy child and his bag and hastily take my leave.

My mum presses a pair of school trousers, freshly washed, dried and folded, into my hands as she kisses me on the doorstep.

'He had a little accident earlier.'

I drive home with a sense of doom bearing down on me.

Why couldn't I just be honest with the two people who have always supported me? They've never judged me or scolded me; they've played such vital roles in my life. Regardless of my situation or my decisions, they've always had my back. They've only ever wanted what was best for me. And Luke.

I should have stayed, watched the opening episode sitting beside them. Even if I couldn't bring myself to explain prior to appearing on the screen, I should have stayed. I giggle, thinking that it would make rather a hilarious *Gogglebox* moment in their lounge. I imagine their jaws dropping, their eyes widening and their simultaneous stares in my direction, as I cringe, a decorative cushion held up to my face. My other viewing position might have been peering through the hinged crack of the lounge door, ensuring that I could only see a sliver of the TV screen. Such a childish act, last used to protect me from Dr Who and the invading Daleks, as if that would ease my embarrassment.

I feel like a chicken.

A scaredy-cat who should face her fears.

I glance at Luke in the rear-view mirror; he's hugging his elephant contentedly and drowsily watching the passing traffic through lopsided glasses. His eyes are half closed and he's struggling to stay awake given the rocking motion of the car.

My dad has obviously played with him and run him ragged non-stop in an effort to entertain him after school, which has wiped my little soldier out. I suspect Luke will be fast asleep by the time we reach home – my dad may well be asleep in his armchair soon too. Though he'll get a shock when my mother wakes him to see my image on their TV screen.

On arriving home, I'm reminded how different my life could be as I lift Luke from the car, attempting not to wake him, always a job and a half given his stocky frame. I'm not asking any new partner to completely devote themselves to my child. He'd be incapable of loving him like I do. I'd be happy to accept a partner who could befriend Luke, care for him, correct him when necessary and comfort him tenderly in my absence. I imagine that loving someone else's child is difficult enough, fraught with issues and, at times, simply damned hard work. But I'm not prepared to share my life with any man alive who would stand by and watch me struggle with this particular task. I have to nip from the parked car to open the front door in preparation, then sneak back to the car, unlock the rear doors, undo his safety buckles, ease his legs from the moulded seat, tease the soft elephant ear from Luke's tight grip. Every stage is another job to perform and triumphantly celebrate when I don't wake the sleeping child. Then there's the lift, cradle and manoeuvre whilst preventing his head bumping against the doorframe and the stagger towards our doorstep like a marathon runner bent double crossing the finish line. The only prize being a still slumbering child and not a gold medal.

The finale is a frantic dash up the staircase and a gentle plop on to his bed before dashing downstairs to retrieve my handbag, lock the car and secure the front door. Could I imagine Alex standing back to watch me perform this intricate task? Or could I imagine my sleeping boy cradled in Alex's arms, his head lolling and his feet dangling?

Yes . . . ?

No.

I can imagine Alex being gallant enough to half-heartedly offer. He's polite enough to feel uncomfortable whilst watching a mother struggle with the dead weight of a sleeping child. But could I see Alex having the innate instinct to simply act – nah! Which is a shame, he seemed a nice chap at first.

Having laid Luke on his bed, I traipse downstairs to lock the car and close the front door. I hesitate as the final sliver of our neighbourhood remains in view, and pause to look outside, up and down the quiet street.

By now, any one of my neighbours might be staring at their TV screen, pointing frantically and shouting, 'That's the woman next door!' Further afield the chummy-mummies could be doing the same with a slight alteration: 'That's Luke's mum!' No doubt they'll critically analyse my conversation, my body language and my lack of flirting skills. They'll watch me devour my three-course meal and I hope to God that the production team have edited out the toilet sound effects.

I slowly withdraw behind the solid front door and await my parent's verdict.

'Mummy?' says Luke groggily as I carefully remove his hoodie. His eyes remain firmly closed.

'Yes, sweetie?'

'Grandpops's mad –' he slaps his lips together before continuing – 'paper shop man . . .'

My ears prick up, tuning in to Luke's sloppy speech.

My dad argues with nobody, ever. He sees it as a lack of decorum, control and a waste of breath.

Stay calm, stay blasé and listen carefully.

I peer at Luke's relaxed features, willing him to continue, but his eyes are closed, his button nose snuffling and his breathing working its way back towards a deep sleep.

I sigh. He'll say no more. A wave of sadness envelopes me, because I know the only reason my dad would ever argue or be angry is because of this little boy. He will defend to the death Luke's rights to a good life and . . .

'He's just a little boy,' mutters Luke, in his sleep.

I bite my lip as Luke's brow furrows and then relaxes as a fleeting memory of today is hopefully erased.

Instantly I want to hug my dad. I have no details, no proof, but I sense that sometime today in the paper shop my dad reacted to someone. Was it a cruel remark? An intense stare? But he's been a proud grandfather standing up for my son. Not what my dad expected to have to do when I announced I was pregnant, or even when I made my second announcement declaring I'd be a single mum. I received nothing but tight hugs and kisses on my third and final announcement. I'd waited ten days to say, readying myself and getting my own head around the final test result before sharing it with the family.

My eyes well up, realising my dad has endured a moment today justifying my decision of six years ago. I want to squeeze him. I wish he'd said earlier. I wish Dad had shared, but he's swallowed it like I do, most days, for fear of it ruining the other twenty-three hours and fifty-eight minutes of our precious day.

'My God, you could have said . . . your father nearly had a coronary!' screeches my mother, at 10:03 when she phones straight after the programme airs.

'Sorry, I just didn't know what to say and then I got all

embarrassed about choosing that path and then ... oh well ... what did you think anyway?'

'You came over bloody brilliant ... but we didn't like the guy!' she says, instantly talking over her shoulder to my dad in the background. 'I'm just telling Dana – we didn't like him, did we? Nothing against him but he didn't seem very child-friendly.'

I'm about to ask why but she continues anyway.

'I can't see how the so-called experts put you pair together. What on earth did you have in common? Your father reckons that he's probably the worst of the three and that the other two will be better matches. The first episode is all about warming up the audience for the week ahead, isn't it? Viewing figures and all that.'

'I'm not sure, Mum. Alex was quite nice to talk to. I sensed he wasn't overly interested in me but he was pretty intelligent and attentive. Did that come across?'

'Oh no, I wouldn't have said that. Hang on a minute, I'll ask your dad. Did you think that guy came across as attentive and intelligent?' I don't answer because although it sounds as if she's talking to me, she isn't, she is in fact asking my dad, who will instinctively know it's him she's speaking to purely by her manner. That's how my mum works on the telephone; it can be confusing for her friends or PPI callers, though it's hilarious if observed from in her lounge. 'Your dad agrees with me. He reckons he called you Diana several times during the episode – which is simply rude in my opinion.'

'Maybe they've edited it to make it appear a certain way, which isn't funny if they portray him as uncaring or unin-terested,' I say, suddenly concerned by how Alex might be perceived by the chummy-mummies.

'Don't fuss, Dana – you came across very well. I said to your dad, "You can tell we raised her to have manners" – they cost nothing yet are worth a fortune!'

Cheers, Mum! Of all things she homes in on my bloody manners. Not my hair, styled by a professional, my perfectly applied make-up, which I could never replicate in a month of Sundays, or even my polite conversation. I don't know whether to laugh or cry that my nerves held out to portray my manners to the nation. Let's just hope that the chummy-mummies at the school gate appreciate the finer things in life. Somehow I doubt it.

'Hang on a minute, your dad is pointing to the TV screen and telling me to watch. Dana, they're showing a brand-new advert ready for tomorrow night's viewing – oh Dana, they clipped together some lovely pictures of you from tonight's episode. They've even added some glitzy writing which floats about the screen showing the title. I might phone your aunty and make sure she's watching tomorrow night – she won't want to miss it, love.'

My nerves suddenly kick in and I need the toilet, quick.

'Mum, I'll see you tomorrow. Thanks for having Luke and I take it you'll be tuning in for episode two?'

'You bet, we wouldn't miss it for the world. I've already said to your dad, if tonight's guy was the worst I might need to buy a new wedding hat by Saturday!'

'Mum!'

'You never know, Dana ... they'll no doubt have saved the best till last!'

I arrange to drop Luke off tomorrow morning, bid Mum goodbye and hang up before dashing up the stairs two at a time for the loo. My mind is racing with visions of people I know all tuning in, dissecting and pawing over every detail witnessed on their TV screen. Didn't Mum say earlier that she'd already watched Eamonn and Ruth conduct an interview? I have no doubt that by Friday the world and his wife will have an opinion, which they won't hold back from airing at the school gate. I need to do what is right for me and my Luke. I can't afford to be swayed by other people's flippant opinions. I must maintain a clear head and focus on my values – even if that means disappointing my parents and a few thousand viewers.

I stop dead on reaching the top stair.

Would it be a few thousand viewers? The prime-time slot would make a huge difference to the audience size. I won't be a pawn in a TV ratings war for Jez's production team to score points against a rival. I won't be remembered as some airhead from a dating programme who upturned her life to be a one-week wonder for the cameras purely to entertain the nation's chummy-mummies.

A sudden attack of nerves overwhelms me – this could be much bigger than I'd first imagined. The production team might have a website, discussion forum or a Twitter feed with hashtags!

The question is dare I nip online to see?

Polly

'Polly, it's Marc.'

I sit bolt upright in bed before he can say another word. It's 11.22 and I was asleep, but now I am awake. Wide awake, alerted by Marc's sombre tone.

'Polly, there's been a situation . . .'

'Is everything all right?' Instantly I feel stupid; he wouldn't be phoning if everything was all right. Is it Dad? Mum?

I'm out of bed, grabbing my dressing gown and dashing around our bed towards the door. I need Fraser, who is still downstairs with Cody. I'm on the landing before I know where I am.

'Polly, Helen has been taken to hospital . . . She's . . .'

I stumble down the stairs and burst into the lounge, to stand wide-eyed and staring at Fraser and Cody, slumped on either sofa. Both jump up on seeing me, my mobile clutched to my ear.

'Marc!'

'She's taken some tablets, Polly . . . lots of tablets.'

'How many? What type? How? Why? *Marc?*' I don't give him chance to answer; my mind is racing. My sister. Helen, no!

Fraser calmly mutes the TV and stands in front of me, both hands reaching for my shoulders to gently rub them.

'They've taken her to the Royal . . .'

I repeat Marc's words mainly for Fraser's benefit.

'And you, where are you?' I interrupt his calm voice.

'I'm at home, the girls are in bed . . . I called an ambulance and they came and they've taken Helen in.'

You're at home! Why aren't you with my sister?

'Polly, can I ask you to go and . . .'

I don't need to be asked.

'Marc . . . speak to Fraser.' I thrust my mobile at Fraser. I'm flying back up the staircase faster than I have ever moved. My sister needs me.

'Hi Marc, it's Fraser . . . is there anything else we can do? Would you prefer to go too and I'll sit at yours in case the girls wake up?'

Silence.

'OK, no, that's fine, mate – if you think that's best . . .'

I stop on the landing hearing Fraser's calm voice. Did Marc just say 'no' to Fraser's kind offer? Why wouldn't he want to be with her? What's going on?

It takes me twenty-seven minutes to reach the Royal. I park hurriedly, pumping into the machine the entire handful of change

that Fraser kindly gave me as I left, after I'd refused his offer
to drive me. I have no idea where to go, what ward to ask for,
who to report to, but I need to see my sister.

I stride across the vast car park with an array of lights and
alien signs filling my view. These places are huge, no one truly
knows where they are heading, everyone must have to ask for
directions. I dash towards a large painted sign offering a selection of arrows and destinations. A&E jumps out at me, so I
follow without knowing whether this is the right place to go.

The large glass doors automatically open and I burst through
straight to a reception desk where a young woman smiles and
asks if she can help.

I quickly explain, give Helen's details and I finally breathe.
I stand watching as the young woman taps her computer keyboard and locates my sister.

'If you'd like to take a seat, someone will be with you
shortly . . .' The empathy in her manner makes me want to cry.

She knows. She read the details. She can see my panic. She
knows all about it and relayed that in her tone and look.

I turn and go to sit where she's indicated, row after row
of blue seats arranged like an airport lounge but without the
duty-free. A handful of people sit and wait, staring at me. A
large plasma screen is muted whilst displaying Sky News. I
watch the yellow info band crawl along the bottom of Anna
Botting's talking image. Forget the rest of the world, what about
my sister, our Helen – why are her details not urgent enough
to replace tonight's football results?

I take a seat and wait. My gaze follows everybody as they
walk the stretch of tiled floor, regardless of uniform, lanyard,
pace or haste – I'm alert and ready to respond to the first flicker
of interest in me, Helen's younger sister.

*   *   *

I don't know what to say, so I remain silent and hastily follow the quick-paced step of the nurse leading me through a succession of corridors, left, right, left; there are signs overhead – I'm not even looking at them. I'm simply being led through this sterile maze by my companion. She tried to communicate but, not to be rude, I don't want polite small talk, just my sister.

I'd waited for ages and finally Anil had introduced himself.

He led me into a tiny family room, sat me down and explained gently. Whilst her two girls were safe and sound tucked up in bed, someone called Helen, who I don't think can be my sister, had taken lots of tablets. Lots of paracetamol. Planned purchases, apparently, given the numbers involved. The same woman had also drunk several large whiskies. Combined the two poisons, then went upstairs to lie down. Her husband arrived home late and called 999.

Anil's voice was soothing and patient, his eyes kind, as he talked about this stranger called Helen. I didn't interrupt him, I just waited patiently to hear his news about my sister, also called Helen.

'We found this . . . inside her trouser pocket.' He'd offered me a folded piece of paper, at which I'd stared, not wanting to take it from his grasp. It wasn't for me.

Now, the quick-stepping nurse indicates right and we enter the double doors of a small side ward with just four beds. There is only one occupant.

'Thank you,' I say most gratefully, as she returns to her post.

I near the bed, half expecting to see the face of that stranger, Anil's patient, above the yellow cotton blanket.

It's my sister, Helen.

I stand beside the bed and stare at her sallow features, her brown hair falling back from her forehead, splayed out upon the white pillow. Without saying a word, she slowly opens her eyes and takes in my presence.

'I can't pretend to understand where you are right now. But sometimes all we need is for someone to hold our hand during our darkest nights ... I promise you, I won't let go until the sun returns, OK?'

I reach for her hand and squeeze it tight. I'm her sister and this is what loving siblings do for each other.

Her blue eyes glisten and well up before her tears flow.

There is nothing else to say, so I gently stroke her hair with my free hand.

Chapter Six

Tuesday 25 February

Carmen

Our kitchen wall clock reads ten minutes to three in the morning as I drain my second mug of chamomile tea. My mind swirls with suggestions and unforgivable reasons for why Elliot has never asked me. Does he not love me? Does he love another woman? Doesn't he want children? The stream of questions laps my mind in a never-ending loop, thanks to Mr Cole senior. Eight years, living as a couple for six of those years – how could this not end in a proposal? I've been patient. I've been hopeful and yet there's nothing to secure our happiness. Have I missed some vital sign? Has Elliot alluded to an unhappiness which I refused to see or hear?

The chamomile tea hasn't worked. I am neither relaxed nor in peaceful slumber, so I search the kitchen cupboard for a tot of something a little stronger. I don't usually do whisky, but needs must tonight if I'm to cease this incessant questioning, set free by Jim's direct query.

I accidently find a half-empty bottle of Elliot's favourite

tipple, Jameson Bow Street, his poison of choice to end any celebration or birthday, under the sink unit.

'Let's see,' I whisper, uncorking the bottle and pouring a generous helping. A helping larger than any I've seen Elliot ever pour for a third party, even when aiming to be sociable. Elliot is rarely heavy-handed with his Jameson Bow Street.

I lean against the countertop and cautiously sip the amber liquid.

I've seen Elliot do likewise on so many occasions and yet I'd refused to taste it, for fear of waste – I'm not keen on shorts.

The amber liquid is smooth, rich in sherry spice and oak, laced with sweet toffee – the warmth glides down my throat and a wave of guilt lifts from my innards. I inspect the glass tumbler before taking a second sip and enjoy the slow expectation of a soothing sensation.

Nice. Elliot will be pleased.

He offered enough times, in the early years. I recall numerous occasions when we'd arrive home from a wedding or christening and he'd sink into the armchair for a final drink to end the day. He'd lazily hold his tumbler aloft and offer, 'A sip?' and I always refused. He'd smile, eyes heavy and sleepy, and shake his glass, a second silent offer before my repeated refusal. His mellow gaze would linger on mine, then the tumbler would return to being his, rather than ours, shared.

Why had I never taken a sip before?

Scared of not liking it?

Simply because it was his?

Instantly I see my error.

Eight years in and finally I'm trying something which Elliot loves.

Has he ever refused to try anything I've offered him, be it smelly cheeses, extra dry wines or a foot spa?

Nope. Never. 'I'll try anything once!' is his immediate reply.

How many other things, experiences, interests or places has he tried to introduce me to – and I've refused?

My chest suddenly feels heavy with regret. Have I sailed through eight years without grasping opportunities to connect with Elliot along the way? A montage of memories rush much like endorphins – this weekend in Paris has to be the very best weekend we have ever experienced together. No refusals to his suggestions. From Friday night onwards, I need to prove to Elliot that I am the right woman for him. I won't ignore any attempt to share the life he loves with me.

I down the remainder of the Jameson's in one gulp and gasp as the spices give an extra kick to the back of my throat.

Dana

I'm as nervous as hell as I sit upon the large red studio couch and stare directly into the eye of the camera. Jez keeps indicating for me to look away but I'm fascinated by what's happening behind the cameraman and just at the number of people involved. If the truth be told, I'm also slightly frightened by the presenter sitting opposite.

I feel like a million dollars, having once again had my hair and make-up crafted by professionals, though the straight-legged slacks and blouse are from my own wardrobe.

Presenter Cain Marsh sits before me, though, his whiter-than-white teeth and perfectly tanned skin are making me feel slightly inferior. He's definitely a metrosexual who's groomed to within an inch of his life. His left eyebrow has more definition and shape than my entire body. According to Tamzin, he's very nice but, so far, Cain seems more bothered about his profile shot than talking to me. Which is one reason I keep looking towards Jez for some guidance.

'Dana, so tell me, what are your initial thoughts on Alex, date number one?'

I don't know whether to be honest, polite or lie. I remember that I have nice manners and I can't let my parents down.

'Cain, I think he was very polite, easy to talk to and paid attention to what I had to say . . .'

'But would you? Seriously, if the urge took you?'

I'm not quite sure what he means, as he doesn't appear to be talking in full sentences. 'But would I?' – what's that supposed to mean?

Oh!

I blush.

'Oh, ladies and gentleman, it appears my question has caught Dana on the hop . . . well, we've news for you, Dana. We've already spoken to Alex and he's more than happy to join you on another dinner date, spend an afternoon enjoying the sun together or something a little raunchier, if you get my drift!' Cain turns to camera and begins winking in an unsavoury manner.

I cringe.

I look away from the interviewer, searching for Jez and the experts who are swarming around behind the circle of cameras. Tamzin is shaking her head, Jennifer the relationship guru has a hand clasped across her mouth and seems totally embarrassed, and even Jez looks slightly taken aback by Cain's crude interview style.

'I'm not so sure after one dinner date, Cain . . . I think Alex was lovely, and I wouldn't mind getting to know him a little better, but if you're asking me was there an "instant sexual connection" between us, then I would have to say I don't think so.' I'm hoping my beautiful manners are coming across well in correcting this fool.

'Oooooh, honesty, ouch!' croons Cain, licking his right index finger to gesture being burnt.

Polly

I replace the telephone handset and burst out crying in the middle of our lounge before I've even made breakfast.

Fraser quickly bundles me into his arms and hugs me tight whilst I sob into his clean work shirt.

I feel lost, helpless, confused about what to do in this situation. Do I collect my parents so that we can spend the day here comforting each other? Despite their rift, they would make an effort to be pleasant, given the situation. Or is it a case of keep calm and carry on?

'I don't understand!' I wail, having held it together long enough to explain to both my elderly parents why their eldest daughter is in hospital. I'd waited until seven o'clock before rocking their world with such news. 'Mum says she must have made a mistake, thought they were—' I stop. It sounds fanciful to say 'vitamins', as my mother had suggested.

Helen has never taken vitamins in her life.

'Shhhh, now. Until she's well enough to explain, you can only be there and support her, Polly – don't try and twist your head around this.'

Dad had taken the news much harder; he had understood straight away. No excuses. No fairy tale.

'It's because of Marc, isn't it?' I ask, drying my eyes and seeing Fraser's concerned expression.

'You don't know that, just wait.'

'I know it . . . he was late home. Where had he been? Why so late arriving back from work on a Monday evening? Did you pick up on anything on Sunday?'

'Nope. They seemed exactly the same as every other time I've seen them, holding hands and being Helen and Marc.'

What had I missed? Had she tried to talk to me, make me understand the situation, but I'd selfishly been wrapped up in my own world of Fraser and Cody. Why hadn't she confided in me? Tell me what was happening? Hadn't they sat holding hands on Sunday, as they typically did? Had something happened since Sunday lunch?

Fraser slowly releases me and I stand on my own two slippered feet, raking my fingers through my hair and planning my next task. I need to act. Do what is necessary to ensure that Helen doesn't have any worries or concerns regarding her girls, then she can focus on herself and getting back on her feet.

'I'll phone in sick, say it's a family emergency. Stacey might be able to cover for me. I can do extra on another day.'

'Polly, let's see what's arranged for Helen first. Marc will need to organise the two girls and decide what's happening.'

'She's my sister.'

'She's his wife.'

I stare at him, knowing he's right, but surely Marc's claim is lessened if this is all because of him.

'Do you want me to phone and ask him what plans he's made for the girls? His mum might—' asks Fraser.

'*His* mum?'

'Yep, his mother might have stepped in to support her son.'

I reach for the phone's handset, which Fraser deftly beats me to in order to phone his brother-in-law on my behalf.

*   *   *

I arrive at half ten, a whole hour later than I should start but understandable in the circumstances. I'd explained everything to my boss; I cried as soon as I mentioned Helen – I was totally fine until I had to outline the reason. Family emergency didn't seem to cut the mustard, but as soon as I mentioned attempted suicide he stuttered and stammered towards an agreement. So the travel agents would open late and I was given an hour to check that all was well with my loved ones before heading in.

So I am here for another shift. My emotional armour is in place, my mind is set to 'focused' and hopefully the customers are few while the clock will be swift and kind.

Part of me keeps wondering why I'm here. Yet, in reality, I know there's nothing I can do right now. I've spoken to Marc, who'd phoned the hospital early and was told that Helen was staying in for further blood tests and close observation. He didn't know if she'd be having a psychological review with a professional or not.

But surely she won't be sent home without talking to someone?

I could barely speak to him. I wanted to question him. Fraser said I mustn't. So I listened as Marc explained how he'd taken the day off from work and was taking the two girls to see their mummy, who'd got a 'nasty tummy bug', during afternoon visiting.

I'm not needed.

I feel sidelined. I felt useful in last night's drama, and yet now I'm redundant.

'And tonight?' was my only comeback. 'Can I help by having the girls overnight to free you up?'

'That would be perfect, Polly – thank you,' said Marc instantly. 'If I pack them each an overnight case, will that be OK?'

I wanted to wail, yell and scream; only Fraser's presence – he had handed over the phone to me after his initial enquiries – prevented me from demanding answers.

'You all right, Polly? You seem a bit distracted,' says Stacey, calling over from the next desk.

'I'm not feeling it today. I wish I was elsewhere.'

'Oh, what a thought – where would you choose?' Stacey's smile brightens and she scours the nearest shelf of travel brochures. 'I'd pick somewhere in Dubai.'

This isn't what I need. But I play along, purely to avoid an emotional discussion with my co-worker. She's nice enough, always pleasant, but I want my business kept as mine.

I follow suit and my gaze drifts aimlessly along the shelf of colourful brochures: New York, the Maldives, Florida, Russia or Paris? I couldn't care less. I don't want to be visiting any right now. If I could snap my fingers and be at my sister's bedside, I would be – minus her husband.

'New York,' I say, to satisfy Stacey's interest, though I give no explanation.

'What I wouldn't give . . .' coos Stacey, grabbing a brochure and flipping through.

The door chime sounds and the stylish lady from the wedding boutique next door enters, her handbag clutched in front of her as if she's unsure of herself.

She heads straight for my desk, because Stacey has her nose in a glossy brochure, daydreaming.

'Hi . . . I'm looking for some details about the all-inclusive trips to Paris advertised in the window.'

'Hello, please take a seat.' I automatically switch on my professional persona, smiling and attentive. She settles in the chair, drops her handbag to the floor and leans her elbows on my desk, trying to view my screen. She seems uptight, nervous, slightly overeager compared to our usual customers. 'It's Carmen, isn't it?'

A brief nod and her smile confirms that my memory hasn't let me down. I bring my computer screen to life.

'A former colleague of ours bought her wedding dress from you a couple of years ago,' I add, purely to provide context. 'Beautiful dress . . . an unusual design.'

'I remember . . . like a waterfall effect in tulle.'

'Yes, the very one . . .' I pause, knowing the impression of the dress has lasted far longer than the marriage did. I steer the conversation away with another question, to be on the safe side. 'How's business next door?' I'm unsure whether February is a good month for bridal gowns or not, but still, it helps to build a rapport with my customers.

'Very busy . . . I've nipped out between appointments. I wasn't sure how long this might take.'

'Well . . .' I do my usual holiday-booking spiel. 'It can take as long as you wish, depending on your needs and requirements. Do you know exactly what you'd like or are there add-ons to the package which you'd like to make to personalise it for yourself and . . . ?'

'My boyfr– I mean fiancé,' she says, blushing. 'Hopefully fiancé, once I've proposed.'

I notice her flush disappears as quickly as it arrived. Her skin is perfect, a true peaches and cream complexion, and what I wouldn't give for that hair, fire red and flowing like a mane.

'OK, any specific dates you were thinking of?'

'Friday.'

'*This* Friday?' I ask, a little surprised. Most customers, apart from our regular pensioners who jet off with very little notice, have little opportunity to just up and off.

'Yes, this Friday . . . for a weekend stay.'

'Coming back Monday or Sunday?' I ask, tapping her details into the computer.

Carmen

I watch as her computer comes to life. My nerves are jittering and my throat is dry, confirming a slight fear about what I'm about to do.

I'd clocked the poster offering a holiday of a lifetime to Paris when I walked by yesterday. Some may say I'm stupid – obviously my potential in-laws think so, and Anna clearly thought so too when I mentioned it earlier as we unpacked our weekly delivery. Trish had sighed deeply, adding: 'Be careful – you want genuine sentiment not some flashy city break which doesn't represent you as a couple.' She's got a point. I trust Trish's judgement; I've known her long enough to know she has my back. Though I hope she's not suggesting that Elliot and I aren't romantic. Because we are. We might not splash out on Valentine's Day, which is partly my fault for not saying anything over the years, but we *are* romantic. We have our moments. I can name numerous occasions when he's arrived home with flowers for absolutely no reason – not lately, of course, but he has done in the past. I once ordered a whole box of Love Hearts with our names printed on them, though it was slightly ruined when we opened them to discover they'd misspelt 'Elliot' as 'Leliot' – we still ate them, it didn't affect the flavour. Plus there was the occasion when we considered getting matching tattoos for our fifth anniversary, though we couldn't decide on a design. I didn't like his Celtic warrior symbol whilst he didn't care for my peacock feathers. Merging the two would have been entirely ridiculous, so we scrapped the idea.

But still. It's the thought that counts in a relationship; you can't expect everything to work every time.

I am planning to propose marriage only once in my lifetime and so, after this morning's epiphany, I've decided to go the whole hog. In my mind's eye, I see us dashing about Paris, having the time of our lives, with my proposal the defining moment of our perfect weekend.

I've transferred some money from my own savings account to ensure I can plan as I like. What's the point in working hard, saving hard and not spending it to make memories? You can't take it with you, can you?

'So, you are interested in Paris, flying out on Friday and returning on Sunday evening?' she repeats, typing quickly.

I nod eagerly. I want her to press buttons and create the best honeymoon package without it being an actual honeymoon.

We spend the next twenty minutes browsing classy hotels and direct flights, eventually securing a luxury suite at the Hotel Splendide Royal, near the Champs-Elysées. I feel quite spoilt – this is a first for me; usually I leave such planning to Elliot or hastily opt for cheap offers on the internet. I never use travel agents.

'Anything else you'd like to do on your visit?' asks Polly, her fingers poised over the keyboard, once we have the basic bookings in place. 'I can book a multitude of tickets or events before your arrival.'

I reel off a list of ideas. I want each day to be filled with sight-seeing, culinary delights and an unmistakable air of romance which will lead up to my big moment.

Her eyebrows lift into her fringe and her eyes widen as she jots down my extensive list of ideas.

'Not that I've given it that much thought,' I mutter, more to myself than to her.

It's at this point I'm grateful to Trish for insisting I 'nip next door to the travel agents and book properly'.

'That's quite a list. How about I have a browse through the necessary details and current offers . . . I'll come back to you with a definitive list of possibilities and prices. Then you can choose which to book as a package. Does that sound OK?'

'That sounds great, you've been really helpful,' I say, collecting my handbag. 'Nip round, or give me a call, if that's easier.'

'Perfect, see you in a short one.'

My mood is as high as a kite as I enter the boutique.

'That couldn't have been easier,' I say, adding, 'I couldn't have wished for better service or choice.'

'What did I tell you?' says Trish, neatly packaging a pair of satin shoes for collection later.

'In fact, shouldn't they be included in Friday's business meeting? How easy would it be for couples to nip next door and get an exclusive deal on a honeymoon package after planning and booking their wedding through us?'

'It's short notice but the owners may be interested. Your meeting is Friday, isn't it?'

'Yep, I'll mention it when I speak to her later on,' I say.

Dana

I've been home for a matter of minutes, but I'm not entirely happy with today's interview session with Cain Marsh. My hands might be busy wrapping floristry wires around individual tiger-lily stems to meet an online order but my mind keeps replaying Cain's question: 'Would you?'

Is this not an example of what's wrong in today's society?

Or have I been away from the dating scene for so long that I'm slightly naïve about such crude remarks? Surely people are allowed to meet and get to know each other, enjoy each other's company before diving into bed?

I quickly look at my computer to check the details of the flower order before continuing; the last thing I need is to mis-read the requirements and create an arrangement which doesn't delight my customers. I'm surprised to see an influx of visitors perusing my website in the last forty-eight hours – surely that's not linked to the TV programme? With a floristry business as small as mine, I can't afford to lose sales or get a sloppy rep-utation in the local area. Likewise, I can't afford to appear on national TV and be used or humiliated. Such an outcome would be disastrous for me and the business, and I'd never forgive myself for embarrassing my boy.

A lump leaps to my throat at the very thought of disap-pointing Luke.

It's the one thing I vowed I would never do. From the moment that midwife told me I was expecting a child with Down's syndrome, I vowed that every breath I took would go to making my baby's life the best it could be. Down's syn-drome or not, my baby would have every chance to do what he wanted in life, whether he showed an aptitude towards a specific talent, a desire to strive and achieve a particular goal, even those dreams which others deemed unreachable ... my vow was to help my child reach his full potential as a human being, come what may.

I dismissed the boundaries that others appeared to be laying down for my son to comply with. There was no way I would follow the restrictive routines of yesteryear when children with this condition or other so-called disabilities led a shel-tered, unfulfilled life due to society's misperceptions and lack of understanding. There would be no cotton wool wrapped around my boy; he'd be allowed to be a child and I would support every choice he ever makes.

My Luke's little extra within chromosome 21 simply gives me a little extra determination to play my part as his mum.

Likewise, I'm not asking for much in life, just a decent man who's willing to share my days. I'm not searching for wealth or fame, I don't really care about finding some hot-looking stud who believes he is God's gift to women and who everyone else thinks is drop-dead gorgeous . . . just a decent guy, an ordinary bloke. A guy who knows how to work, how to enjoy life and who can commit to someone so we can build a life together. There'll be good times and bad times, there'll be big issues and small annoyances but still, whatever comes our way, we'll cope, together.

My hands fall still partway through cutting greenery and ferns.

Someone who can appreciate and share Luke's interests would be perfect.

Should I have outlined those desires during this morning's feedback session?

I resume pushing fern fronds into the rear of the arrangement as a backdrop.

I doubt Cain would have understood a word I'd said if I had. All he seemed to want was a rundown on Alex's chances of getting some. And that is one thing I won't be talking about on national TV because I have manners.

I jump down from my work stool and switch on the radio. I need to clear my head and chase away Cain Marsh's innuendos, so I turn the volume control to loud, and then give it a little extra turn just like Luke does before returning to my work bench.

Twenty minutes later, I sit back to admire the beautiful arrangement of tiger lilies. I've gone a little over the top, more flowers than I'd usually use for the price charged, but today I needed to enjoy my work. I needed to return to my base and get lost in my world to combat the negativity that Cain Marsh brought me.

Carmen

In no time, Polly gently taps on the door of the boutique. Anna opens it and I instantly become nervous at the prospect of seeing the list of options she's holding.

'Hello, that was quick,' I say.

'Not my first time,' she teases, waving her list.

We huddle on the chaise longue as I read her suggestions.

'I think that's a logical order in which to get around Paris in three days. I've tried to plan for Friday night, all day Saturday, though you might wish to leave Sunday free for a more leisurely day to spend celebrating. How does that sound?'

I am quite overcome on reading her itinerary.

'That ... sounds ... wonderful ... thank ... you ...' I manage, trying to hold back the tears. When I succumb to the emotion, I snatch at the nearest box of tissues much like a mother of the bride on seeing her daughter's gown.

'I've enquired at several of our reputable contacts and have noted the prices next to each event or tour ... the total amount is in addition to your earlier payment.' Polly hands me the paper. I simply look at the bottom line, nothing else matters; I'm not about to quibble over individual fees. Through the blur of my tears, I see the stated figure of nine hundred pounds.

I'll be proposing just once, so what the hell, blow the expense.

'Perfect. I'm happy to go with the itinerary, and you're right about leaving Sunday free. We can spend the day relaxing before the flight home. I'll pop round to pay just before closing up here, if that's OK with you?'

I hand the itinerary to Trish, who is lingering – it was her suggestion to try next door rather than booking on the internet, after all.

'Polly, before you go, any chance I could have the contact details for your owners? I'm launching a new business venture that they might be interested in.'

'Sure, I'll have that ready for when you come in to pay ... Right, I'll skedaddle and get these tickets booked and confirmed. Bye now.'

I watch a grin dawn upon Trish's face.

'She's done a good job, hasn't she?' I say, as the travel agent dashes past our front window.

Trish nods. 'Told you – you should always use professionals when it matters in life.'

'Have you been watching that dating programme that's just started?' asks Anna, interrupting our conversation. 'It's following this woman's first dates with three different guys.'

'Nope,' says Trish, confused how Anna's question links to our conversation.

'They're using professionals to see if they can determine true love between strangers ... me and my mum are loving it. Social media has gone crazy predicting who her dates will be. Some are suggesting they've got an A-list celebrity lined up as the third guy and he's the one she'll choose for the final date on Saturday.'

'Oh, to be young and so naïve,' says Trish teasingly. 'You know it's all hype to boost the viewing figures, don't you?'

Anna ignores her and carries on. 'I'm still going to tune in every night. I'm surprised you pair haven't been glued to the screen. It's worth watching because the woman's local, or so my mum reckons.'

I listen to her excited babble before interrupting. 'Did you not have a first date experience last Saturday, for which you left work early?' I ask, glancing at Trish, who doesn't disappoint in her reaction.

'Oooooh, yes, she did! Come on, spill the beans . . . Pretend you're on this new dating programme and we're interviewing you,' squeals Trish.

'Stop it, the pair of you. Cody was lovely, we had a nice drink, went to the cinema and we've arranged to meet up on Thursday night . . . I might even go to his birthday party on Saturday. Though, I'll need to record the finale of the dating programme if I do attend – I can't miss seeing who she chooses.'

'Not shy about getting an invite, are you?' asks Trish.

'Stop it, you're as bad as my mum,' says Anna, flouncing off into the back room, leaving the two of us to giggle at our childish behaviour.

Polly

'Hello, my darlings,' I call cheerily, as my two nieces dash up the driveway and run into my waiting arms. I'd driven straight from work to collect them. 'Are we thinking films and cookies or films and pizza for our sleepover treat?'

A chorus of films and pizza fills the air, as I stare beyond the girls at my brother-in-law, adorning his doorstep, with two holdalls stuffed to the zips with their belongings.

'Pizza it is, and we don't care if Cody complains!' I usher the two to wait by the car whilst I collect their overnight gear from their father. 'How is she?'

'Not good. She's suffering from severe stomach spasms and they're concerned about her liver function as the blood tests aren't good, but she's in the best place.'

'Has she said . . . ?'

Marc shakes his head, slightly too quick a response for my liking.

'Really? Any chance of me visiting tomorrow – I'm free to do the evening.'

'I'd prefer to go then . . . It's best you look after . . .' He nods towards his daughters leaning against my car.

'OK, but if you change your mind, just let me know – Fraser will happily look after the girls at ours while I visit Helen.' I take hold of the offered bags and lug them back to the car, a fake smile plastered on my face for the benefit of my two nieces.

'Can I sit in the front?' asks Evie, once Erica has climbed into the rear seats.

'No, because the seat catch isn't locking properly . . . Uncle Fraser's got to look at it,' I explain, for the umpteenth week. 'If I brake harshly, the catch releases, which is dangerous.'

I'm surprised when she accepts my explanation and joins her sister on the back seat.

I turn the key in the ignition, check the girls have their seat-belts fastened and indicate. Their doorstep is empty; their father has gone inside without so much as a wave goodbye.

Bastard.

Carmen

'What are you doing?' asks Trish, as I sit behind the reception counter, doodling on my notepad.

'I'm trying to figure out what I'm actually going to *say* come Saturday evening.'

Trish gives me a sympathetic smile. 'Harder than you thought?'

'You bet. I've watched so many proposals online . . . there's funny ones, ones linked to happy memories and their shared experiences, some tearful, emotional proposals . . . but none of them seem right for us. Elliot isn't one for showing emotion and I couldn't carry off a humorous proposal.'

'Which leaves you with the theme of memories you've built together.'

'I just don't want it to seem like I'm giving him a lecture, trying to prove how great we've been together or harping on about how good we'll be in the future.'

'Do you have to write a proposal speech?'

'Yeah, it won't be the moment for me to wing it – I'd waffle for England and ruin a week's worth of planning by messing it up. Can you imagine me coming back on Monday and saying I bailed?' I laugh.

'That wouldn't be funny, Carmen.'

'What did Terry say when he proposed?'

Trish purses her lips, her cheeks colour and gives me a little smile. 'I can't remember exactly . . . it was lovely, just as I'd dreamed, but it happened so fast. He told me he loved me dearly, said how much joy I'd brought into his life, but then my memory goes a bit blurry until the "will you marry me" bit.'

'Oh great, here's me sweating the small stuff when really it won't matter.'

'It will. I just got carried away when Terry produced the ring box, that's all.'

'So the lesson is don't produce the ring until after the speech . . . OK, noted.'

'I can't imagine Elliot reacting like I did . . . I jumped about on the spot for ten minutes.'

She has a point. How am I expecting Elliot to react? He's not the emotional type. Not the overly affectionate, huggy type either. I can't imagine him jumping about for ten minutes unless he won the lottery.

'I'm expecting a shocked silence and a lengthy pause, if I'm honest. I think he'll be taken aback – he'll never anticipate me organising all this, he knows me too well.'

'If he's silent, you can't take that to heart, Carmen . . . he'll be so surprised, but that's half the thrill. I wasn't expecting it either, but I said "yes" straightaway.'

'I feel nervous just thinking about it, let alone doing it, Trish.'

'You'll be fine . . . just make sure you enjoy it too.'

I suddenly grab the notepad and stuff it under the counter and on to my lap; Trish looks shocked by my sudden move as the boutique door opens.

'Elliot . . . what a nice surprise!' I holler in an overly cheerful voice.

'Hi,' says Trish, instantly understanding my lightning-speed reaction.

'Hi, babe, hi, Trish, I'm not disturbing an appointment, am I?' he asks, looking around the empty boutique.

'Oh no, we have another twenty minutes until our next bride-to-be arrives.'

Trish smiles politely but I notice she drifts away from the counter as Elliot approaches. He's out of breath, his suit jacket gaping, his tie slightly skewed from the collar, his name badge proudly in place: Elliot Cole, Assistant Bank Manager. I didn't think I'd see him to say goodbye, given that Monty's stag do officially starts at five o'clock. I'd lay in bed and chatted while Elliot packed his overnight bag late last night, to enable him to leave for Cardiff straight from the bank. I fully understand that the stag and his boys can't lose a minute in their efforts to get ahead of the rush-hour traffic.

So this unexpected visit is a bonus.

'I thought I'd best drop by as soon as I knew. Martin reckons no one's volunteered to cover my Saturday morning shift so it looks like I won't be—'

He doesn't finish his sentence before I interrupt, hitting hysterical in record time.

'Elliot, I've booked it!'

'What?' His brown eyes nearly pop from his head.

'I booked it this morning! We fly to Paris on Friday at half five.'

'You didn't say!'

'I wanted it to be a surprise! You agreed last Sunday morning . . . your boss will just have to find someone, Elliot. Go back and tell him!'

'Carmen, I can't demand that my line manager finds someone to open the branch.'

'He'll have to work a Saturday morning then – it'll be quite a novelty for him as manager.'

'He'll think I'm shirking if I go back and say you've booked it.'

'Tough. Elliot, you're off work for the next three days so this needs sorting today . . . Please, go and speak to him.'

'How bad will that look?'

'Tell him you'll work double when you're free on another weekend. There's no way you can work *this* weekend!'

Elliot stands raking his hand through his hair. He can't look at me, but stares around the boutique as his brain works overtime trying to figure out what to say to his line manager at the bank.

This is all I need. I roll my eyes and give a headshake towards Trish, whose eyebrows are signalling shock.

'Sorry, but I did explain on Sunday . . . Why didn't you listen?'

'I did . . . I told him first thing on Monday morning and he's just come back to me . . . it happens, Carmen.'

'You said you'd get the shift covered . . . I thought a surprise would be nice,' I mutter, though my heart rate remains sky high. My chest tightens. If I develop a tingling sensation in my left arm, I'll be shouting for an ambulance.

'Surprises are great but I wish you'd said you'd booked it already. I'll go back and tell him – see what he says.'

'See what he says? No, Elliot, he needs to know you definitely can't be on the rota for this weekend's Saturday shift.'

Elliot straightens his tie and gives me a fleeting smile before pecking me on the cheek.

'I'll call you later to let you know we've arrived, OK?' he says.

'Speak to you later, drive safely,' I call after him as he turns and strides through the boutique.

'See you, Trish,' says Elliot, as he passes Trish straightening the gown rails.

'Oh my God!' I screech, as soon as the door closes fully. 'It's a bloody disaster.'

'Keep calm, Carmen. He'll sort it. I'm sure his boss will understand and pull something from the bag to cover Elliot's shift.'

I grab the notepad from my lap and throw it down on to the reception counter, causing my pen to bounce from the surface on to the floor.

'Until he confirms he's definitely off work, it's a waste of time me even writing a speech!'

'Carmen . . . don't lose it now,' soothes Trish, crossing the boutique to stand in front of me calmly.

I hold my hands up in frustration. I'm trying my hardest to make this the perfect proposal, going against all my childhood dreams, and the fiancé-to-be won't be present!

'This is just a blip ... Elliot will get this sorted in no time and then you can return to your speech writing.'

'Until then, my proposal is up the swanny and on hold.'

'No, until then we'll focus on another bride ... Come on, let's grab a coffee and biscuits before she arrives.'

Trish gently leads me from my seat towards the kitchenette.

My chest feels tight, my heart is racing. I can't speak, I just want to cry.

Polly

'The Red Lion called earlier, Mum,' shouts Cody, as soon as I enter the house amidst the unfamiliar buzz of young girls and their belongings.

'I can't hear you, Cody – just give me a minute to get my coat off,' I answer, hurriedly packing the girls upstairs with their bags.

I go into the lounge to find him sprawled on the sofa, flicking through the channels.

'The Red Lion called, they said they have a cancellation for Saturday but you'll need to phone back and confirm and pay the deposit by midday tomorrow.'

'Oh, fabulous! That's my first choice, though I'm awaiting a call from the Blue Lion too. Which would you prefer?'

'The Red Lion. It's in town, parking would be easy and the train station is only up the road if anyone wants to head to a nightclub afterwards.'

I peer at him.

'Are you saying that our celebration isn't really enough? That everyone will want to head off afterwards for more drinking?'

'Yeah, that's what we normally do.'

'Oh Cody, really! Can't we just enjoy a decent night as a family – especially given *this* ...' I indicate up above where the sound of excited footsteps can be heard dashing about our spare bedroom. 'Without half the guests twitching to leave early to get a decent entrance price.'

'Mum.'

'Cody, please. There's a chance she might not be out of hospital, Marc won't come then, will he? Your nan and granddad are worried sick about the implications this has for Helen – please don't let something that could bring us all together be the thing that doesn't happen just because a handful of your mates wish to dash off.'

'Hello, do I hear little ... oh, it's you two. I thought the girls were in here,' says Fraser, entering the lounge, on arriving home from work. 'Are they OK?'

'Yep, as far as I can tell ... Mum's tummy bug is getting better is what they told me, so we'll stick to the story, right?' I say, nudging Cody's leg to ensure he's listening.

'Yeah, I get you.' He resumes flicking through the TV channels, and I hope all talk of nightclubs has been banished.

Fraser nods, planting a kiss on my forehead before removing his jacket and tie.

'Thank you,' I say, touching his cheek.

'For what? Having the girls here?'

I nod.

'No worries, I wouldn't want them anywhere else if we can help out. I know Marc's family are close but the girls don't see them that often, do they?'

'Nope. Which is why I was shocked when you suggested his family might lay claim.'

'Lay claim?'

'You know what I mean.'

'Listen to you getting all possessive regarding your sister's girls ... Are you OK?' he asks, following me through to the kitchen as I prepare to make a cuppa.

'I am, but I don't see why his side – they've never taken an interest in Helen, never treated her like one of their family, yet now they want to be all hands-on with the girls. Well, no thanks! I'm here. I'm prepared to do what is needed for my sister and ...' I stop, grab the kettle and fill it with cold water. I can feel my heart racing, my stomach churning; my mind is a complete whiz – just as it has been all day. 'I'm sick of folks picking and choosing what they do, when they do it and how much interest they pay to others on a daily basis but perking up like meerkats when there's a drama.'

'Polly, the kettle,' says Fraser, indicating I should turn the tap off now the upper filling limit has been reached.

I dash out half the contents and snap down the lid ready to boil.

'And you think they're only interested now because she's in hospital?'

'Yeah! They're probably more concerned about their precious son than my sister.'

Fraser nods and takes the kettle from my hands, as I appear to be clutching it instead of making my much-needed cuppa.

'Surely my parents have more need to be with the girls at the moment, given that it's their daughter who's in hospital and they can't spend all day there, as they'd like. The girls would at least keep them busy – take their mind off things.'

'Can I ask why they're here then?' says Fraser, preparing mugs with teabags and sugar.

'Because Marc wants them both at school from tomorrow and not off. Dad's driving is a bit ... you know, and Mum hasn't got a car so how could she get them back and forth?'

'And we can?'

I settle at the breakfast bar now that my task has been withdrawn from me.

'Yes, I'll drive them both across town each morning ... I can't imagine Helen will be kept in for much longer.'

Fraser pulls a face.

'Do you think?'

'It depends on their observations, Polly ... you know that.'

'She'll be fine,' I say. 'This will have been a mistake, a misunderstanding caused by ...' I stop speaking on seeing Fraser's face. His expression is quizzical, eyebrows raised, and he's looking at me much like my father used to do when questioning my theories as a child ... one of those 'really now' faces that makes you rethink your words and come up with the true answer.

'I wouldn't be so sure. How many times have you accidently popped four blister packs of tablets by accident and then ...'

'Don't!'

'Exactly.'

I suddenly remember what Anil gave me at the hospital. I jump down from my stool, rush into the hallway and rummage in my coat pocket for the piece of paper. My fingers trace the folded edges as if collecting Helen's fingerprints.

Did she write this before or afterwards?

For me or Marc?

I turn it over: there's no indication – it looks innocent enough, simply a folded piece of white paper.

I return to the kitchen as Fraser places my steaming mug on the breakfast bar.

'They gave me this the other night,' I say, offering up the paper.

Fraser's comprehension is swift and sudden, seeing what's in my outstretched hand.

'You read it,' I tell him.

'Polly, surely this should be given to Marc unread ... It's private.'

I shake my head.

My hands unfold the paper. I lay it flat beside my mug.

I'm sorry. Look after my girls, tell them I love them so much. Helen x

I read her words in silence, crumpling the note into my palm before I begin to sob.

Fraser's hands prise my fingers apart to remove the note before cradling me in his arms. I can feel his strength wrapped around my shoulders like a protective blanket. I know he's right with his logical manner and yet I want him to be wrong about this situation. Wrong about my sister. Her efforts and the possible outcome, which I know won't be a quick fix for any of us, least of all Helen and her girls.

A thunder of feet is heard crashing down the staircase; I pull away and prepare to pull a smile from my metaphorical bag of tricks.

'Hey, girls,' calls Fraser, as the kitchen door bursts wide open revealing two excited nieces. 'What's it to be, pepperoni or Hawaiian?' His excited tone diverts their attention from me, as I quickly wipe my eyes and grab for the crumpled paper, stuffing it into my pocket.

*   *   *

'Shit!' I launch myself off the sofa at just gone ten o'clock and search for my handbag in the hallway, shouting through to Fraser, 'When did Cody say the Red Lion wanted the deposit to be paid by?'

We'd ordered and eaten pizza, and watched nonsense TV with the two girls before bidding them sweet dreams, and had spent the last hour lazing on the sofa staring at a drama.

'By midday tomorrow,' comes his reply, as I return to the lounge, handbag in hand, to search for details and contact names.

'The Blue Lion haven't got back to me, so it's a good job the Red Lion have, though if I lose the booking, we won't look pretty partying in their car park,' I say, finding my to-do list. 'Monica, that's the name.' I grab my mobile and begin dialling.

'At this time of night?' asks Fraser, pausing the TV drama. 'You're hoping.'

I shrug, simply relieved to have remembered before the morning.

'Hello, is it possible to speak to Monica, please?' I give a wide smile, as the young woman puts me on hold to tinny lift music. Fraser nods and returns to his drama. I've lost the plotline so there's no point him waiting for me. 'Yes, hello, Monica . . . Polly Willis here . . . yes, yes, I know. Sorry I have left it a little late to call and secure the booking . . . yes, I don't blame you for thinking I wasn't interested. Oh, please, don't offer it to anyone else. I did get the message but we've had a family situation . . . anyway, am I still able to confirm the booking and possibly pay the deposit over the phone?'

I can hear the frustration in her voice: dealing with the general public isn't always the easiest of jobs. I can tell she now thinks I'm a total time-waster and a good-for-nothing mother who's blagging an excuse. To be fair, I don't really care, given the previous two days I've had. But I will sleep better tonight if this job is sorted and the venue confirmed.

I spend another five minutes on the phone, reiterating our requirements and making an appointment for tomorrow morning to view the conference suite, which I appear to be booking, given that our credit card is pinched between my fingers.

'Thank you, yes, I'll sign the paperwork tomorrow,' I say dubiously, knowing full well I should have dropped by on my way home from work tonight but, hey, family comes first in my book.

I end the call, relieved that I've paid for the room hire … one less task to mither me.

'Are we sorted about his present? I ask, unsure whether Fraser has finalised the details.

'Of course! Do you think I'd leave something like that to chance?'

'No, but given the week we seem to be having, I thought I'd ask.'

'All sorted. Five thirty appointment on Friday.'

I return to the sofa. My mind is now a scramble of party ideas. Venue booked, catering nearly sorted. The DJ needs chasing, text invites need monitoring and a quick dash around the local card shop should provide me with all the decorations and balloons that I'll need – unless the venue can offer me a package deal on that tomorrow. Though it might be cheaper if we do it ourselves.

'Are you going to switch off any time soon?' asks Fraser, stroking my head as I snuggle under his arm.

'Doesn't look like it. I'll get through this week, then take some time for myself next week.'

'Mmmm.'

I don't bother trying to convince him. He knows I'm lying. He knows my weekly routine off by heart. Monday, Tuesday and Friday working at the travel agents and the rest of the week dashing, running, hustling and being wherever I'm needed for the older and younger generations.

My phone bleeps. A text from my dad.

Fido booked in for 2pm tomorrow x

'OMG!' I yell, knowing perfectly well Fido's appointment will clash with collecting my mother from her class.

Fraser stares, awaiting my explanation.

'Dad didn't call to confirm before booking the dog groomers ... and the appointment's tomorrow. How am I supposed to drive Mum home *and* take Fido?'

'Really? Since when have you been the taxi for that job?'

I peel myself from under his protective wing to stare at him for full effect.

'For the last eight years with Fido and the previous ten years with that mongrel he used to have!'

Fraser watches as I sit staring at my phone.

'What time does your mum need picking up from The Bed Shop?'

'Two o'clock.'

'I'll take a late lunch and drive her home.'

'Thank you,' I sigh, snuggling back into position and breathing in his comforting warmth. 'I chose a good 'un.'

Fraser murmurs his gratitude before kissing my temple.

Dana

'Seriously, this is how you portray yourself, Dana?' asks the instantly recognisable voice.

'Andrew … nice to hear from you after so long!' I reply without flinching.

'I turn on the TV and there you are filling the screen … what are you playing at?'

'How dare you! You chose to walk out on my life the minute Down's syndrome was confirmed – so, go figure! I've spent five years looking after my son … our son and yes, now, having spent five years alone, I have a right to begin having a tiny slice of a life of my own. You've got a bloody cheek!'

'Dana, everyone we know saw you.'

'Er, yeah! Likewise everyone we know witnessed your hasty decision to abandon ship – but that didn't stop you doing as you wished six years ago!'

'Dana!'

'Andrew!'

'Could you have not informed me?'

'I don't have to ask for your permission! Could you have not informed me prior to a major life decision just how shallow you actually were, or was that too much to ask?'

'Dana!'

Breathe, I tell myself. It amazes me how quickly Andrew's voice can ignite my emotions.

'Our son is very well, by the way; he's doing well at school. I thought I'd say since you haven't asked. I can also confirm that since starting school he does frequently ask, "Have I got a daddy?" Though I am trying to play it down, so that should ease your guilt,' I say calmly, trying to regain control of my rising anger.

'Dana, you didn't even mention his condition during your dinner date last night, so don't lecture me about the moral high ground!'

'Why should I? It was a first date. When you met Hannah, did you immediately discuss your son's condition or did you chat about the weather first?' I snarl, hurt that he would hurl such a remark at me.

'Hannah has never had an issue with Luke's condition.'

'Hannah has never met Luke! And why's that, Andrew? Because you've never made arrangements for access or visiting. You've seen him three times in five years! Luke hasn't even met his two half-brothers, so don't try that crap with me.'

Andrew falls silent. He can't argue with fact.

'Dana, you know I can't . . .'

'Andrew, you could if you wanted to. I've been telling you for nearly six years, you are welcome to visit him here for as little as an hour – simply name a date and time.' I'm happy to stomach Andrew visiting my home if it means my son gets to see his father. I know my parents don't harbour such forgiving feelings but I'd do anything for my boy to have a proper relationship with his dad, despite the events of the past.

I wait for him to speak but Andrew's conversation stalls, probably due to the dam of guilt over which his words must climb before flowing. A dramatic pause follows . . . which would mean so much more if we hadn't been here before but, sadly, such a pause means absolutely nothing.

'Dana, I can't.'

'Can't or won't?'

I know it's difficult for him. I get that we are each made of different stuff, have different views and opinions on life. Andrew made his choice and I made mine. So why keep interrupting our life if he can't or won't participate?

'Luke's beginning to ask questions and so far I have very little to tell him . . . it would be great if you could play a part. If not, then leave us alone to get on with our lives. I've never asked you for anything, Andrew. I've never even asked you for money. So I don't appreciate you popping up every eighteen months or so when you're rattled by something you've heard or seen.'

'You're appearing on the bloody TV! What am I supposed to do?'

'Nothing, Andrew. Pretend you've never met me or simply ignore the programme – there are plenty of other channels to watch.'

'Ha bloody ha, as if that's easy when my wife's hooked on the first two episodes!'

'That's your business, not mine.'

'Everyone is talking about it . . . I think I have a right—'

He doesn't get to finish his sentence.

'Right? You want to discuss rights, Andrew? I'll tell you what rights you have . . . none! You walked away from your rights on the day we visited the midwife. Since that day I have fought for my boy's right to do all the things any other child does, including your other two sons . . . and now, after nearly six years, I have the right to a private life, to get to know someone who the experts think might be a true match for me. Someone who won't let us down, someone who might enjoy the life we have and someone who might be able to show both Luke and I love and affection.'

'Dana . . .'

'Goodbye, Andrew.'

I end the call with as much animosity as if we'd been present in the same room – funny how emotions can flare in one phone call. I haven't heard from him in eighteen months and yet still his attitude angers me every time we speak.

I imagine him ending the call and instantly returning to his family life, blasé and carefree. Me, I sit for thirty minutes on the bottom stair, clutching my mobile and crying. My memory relives our most important conversation, the one that began this sparring match to which we've just added another round:

'What?' I'd said, puzzled by his response.

'I mean . . . I'm not sure I'm up to . . . you know.'

I'd instinctively cradled my swelling bump.

'Andrew . . . what are you suggesting?'

'Dana, I can't . . . I couldn't possibly . . .'

'Andrew?'

He'd fallen silent, lowered his head and I had tried taking my cue from the top of his dark hair, sitting in the midwife's tiny office. She had sat behind her incredibly tidy desk, offered a pre-printed list of counselling options and support groups but provided no immediate support to either of us during this difficult discussion.

Can you request another midwife partway through an appointment? Do midwives specialise like doctors do? I suppose being professional can sometimes come across as cold if you're to appear unbiased and factual.

I was on my own.

Correction: baba and I were on our own.

After a six-year relationship, in which Andrew and I had been totally committed, *that* was day one of fighting my own corner.

'You've read the leaflet, Dana. It suggests the baby might never be potty-trained and probably have difficulty speaking. I don't think it'll be able to attend a mainstream school and possibly need specialist help all its life. The result is positive, Dana . . . she's just confirmed it. If we have this child, we'll have a full-grown baby on our hands for a lifetime,' said Andrew.

He'd finally looked up on finishing his sentence, but his gaze couldn't meet mine.

'That's your interpretation of the leaflet, Andrew. Not mine. It looks as if I'll be finding a way to cope alone,' I'd said, my eyes welling with tears.

'He might not be capable of leading an independent life,' said the midwife. 'But he could still have a valuable and unique life.'

We'd both stopped talking, and turned to stare at her.

'He?' I repeated, my hand stroking my stomach.

'He?' asked Andrew, his voice lifting to a jubilant tone. 'It's a boy?'

The midwife glanced at each of us, then quickly flicked through the notes in our file.

'It says here you were told the gender during your last visit,' she said, panic entering her voice.

'Not us. No,' I said curtly. How come they could spill the beans on one detail and yet be unable or unwilling to fully outline our baby's prospects?

'I am so sorry ...' Her words faded, and Andrew's smirk faded too. I'm still not entirely sure whether her 'sorry' related to her error or to Andrew's reaction to the news that his son had Down's syndrome.

Would it have made a difference if Luke had been a girl?

Not to me it wouldn't. My baby was my baby in every possible form.

I suspect it would have made that moment slightly easier for Andrew if Luke had been a girl. After that appointment, Andrew was no longer walking away from a bundle of cells but a fully-formed 'boy', a potential mini-Andrew. Sadly, chromosome 21 had totally buggered up Andrew's dream. And our relationship.

It's what I call a kaleidoscope moment. As a young child, I

loved playing with one. I used to stand for ages staring at the pretty colours and snowflake patterns made by the beads before twisting the lens one notch to gain a new pattern. I loved how everything in the pattern changed in a second. Yet sometimes you ruined your own fun by turning the lens and losing a snowflake pattern you really liked. Everything you could see changed because of one twist. And the worst thing was there was no going back to the pattern you had previously enjoyed before moving the lens. It was gone, erased forever. That midwife appointment was like my childhood kaleidoscope. I was enjoying my world: I had a partner, was expecting a new baby and had a bright future. Then, with one positive test result, someone moved the lens and nothing in my world was the same again. The patterns, people and circumstances changed in a second and I couldn't get it back to how it was before that one appointment.

I knew there and then it would be just me and him.

Him. My baby boy.

Andrew proved me right within three days, when he moved out of our tiny two-bedroomed house to stay with his mum.

I've relived that scene a million times. I've tried to forget it a million times too, but that one scene puts such a fire in my belly that I draw on it whenever I need a little extra push to overcome the absurdity of others. That one scene paved the way for so many of the unfairnesses my son has to endure both in society and even within his own family. Luke has never met Andrew's parents or his two aunties. There's an entire side of the family from which Luke's genes derive – and yet nothing. How can any family not coo over a newborn, a grandson or nephew? Sadly, Andrew's family couldn't open their hearts to Luke. They saved their emotional bonding for the two babies which Hannah bore him, forgetting about my Luke.

Chapter Seven

Wednesday 26 February

Dana

I'm determined to walk Luke to school today, despite the interest about the TV programme. I don't have to interact with those who don't usually talk to me. I can politely walk on by.

It feels ridiculous even to me that I appear to be walking with my head down, chin resting on my jacket zipper and my gaze held low, so low that it doesn't lift from the pavement. I clutch Luke's hand as we pass the usual groups near the school's metal railings. I've prepped Luke that Nanny and Grandpops will collect him later as Mummy is elsewhere, he has no idea where. I suspect I'll be having my hair restyled, make-up applied and another lovely outfit being pinned to me to ensure that it fits for my second date – whatever that turns out to be, and with whoever.

As I pass each small group I notice people staring in our direction, their heads together as if whispering as they watch us go by. I tighten my grip on Luke's hand; he appears to think it's an ordinary Wednesday morning walk to school. I'm so self-conscious it is surreal. Being the centre of attention feels alien, so intrusive, and yet you'd think I would be used to being singled out – I'm rudely but frequently referred to as 'the mother of the little boy with . . . you know'. From day one of primary school, every parent knew my child, while it took me weeks to distinguish Libby from Molly or Tyler from Max. But now, probably because I've created the attention rather than had it sprung upon me by Mother Nature, I can't raise my gaze from the grey pavement. To others, I must look as if I'm scrutinising the white blobs of aged chewing gum for a crazy local council initiative group.

Finally, we reach the school gate. I don't care now, I'm occupied with my boy; all thoughts about other adults staring at me drift away. They don't matter. Luke matters most. I check he has his rucksack, reinforce my repeated request to show his teacher the note written in his diary stating that his grandfather will collect him at home time and tell him that I love him.

'Love you, Mama,' slurs Luke, walking backwards to wave goodbye at me. My heart melts a million times over. I stand fixated until Luke stops waving and turns to walk in the correct manner into the small playground. I watch as the playground teacher acknowledges him and he does likewise before running off towards a group of friends.

Good boy, Luke.

'Dana,' says a gentle voice, a hand reaching to touch my forearm.

I look up to see Bethany's mum rocking her pram; I assume her newborn daughter is cosy inside.

'Hi,' I say, my smile oversized and a little frightening for 8.45 a.m.

'Well done, I loved it,' she whispers to me, giving me a wink. 'I hope the week is filled with lots of surprises and enjoyment.'

'Thank you,' I mutter, blushing profusely.

Instantly I feel awful. She's had the decency to put herself out to speak to me and I couldn't even spare a few words of congratulations last week for fear of catching baby fever from her newborn.

That was wrong of me.

I peer inside the pram hood to view a tuft of brown hair snuggled within a white crocheted blanket.

'Is she doing OK?' I ask, trying to backpedal from my self-ishness last week. 'You look really well after just two weeks.'

'She's not sleeping too well but she's got a nice routine as far as feeding is concerned, so I'm grateful for that,' she says, giving me a wide smile.

Why couldn't I have been more forthcoming last week? Now it looks like I've only taken an interest because she was nice to me.

'And her name?'

'Hetty . . . Our Bethany chose it.'

'That's a lovely name,' I say, cooing over the sleeping baby. I linger for a second more than is necessary and a wave of memories stirs in my heart. This was the moment I used to dread when I'd push Luke out in his pram. Those first few weeks when people wanted to fuss over him, to see him for the first time but were unsure what they would see or how they should react. I wanted them to react as they would to any baby, but for some people it was simply too much. My news had quickly done the rounds, my decision had been discussed and analysed from every point of view and now they were actually staring at the sleeping baby with Down's syndrome. I longed for them to smile, pinch Luke's chubby cheek, stroke his dark hair; on a few occasions I got my wish, but only from very precious people. Those people who secretly walk amongst us understanding the power of life, who can selflessly deliver a few genuine words to a new mum who desperately needs their support. Others couldn't even pretend. They showed utter embarrassment on seeing my baby and gave apologetic looks. Offered their sadness and condolence. Once or twice, folk shed tears. One person was so stuck for words they complimented me on my choice of pram – seriously, a Silver Cross pram is not as unique as my first born!

I saw nothing more than my perfect baby fast asleep.

I simply aww and step away from sleeping Hetty. She's a newborn – there is nothing more to do.

'I was frightened that that new baby smell would set me off,' I say, in a feeble attempt to explain last week's behaviour.

'That's how I am ... it gets me every time,' chuckles Bethany's mum. 'Newborns should have a warning sign attached!'

'Sorry, I know you as Bethany's mum – I've forgotten your name,' I say apologetically.

'Sam.'

'Sam, yes ... She's beautiful but being broody wouldn't do me any good, so ...'

'You never know – after this week the world could be your oyster.'

'Oh don't ... I couldn't bring myself to watch either episode.'

'Full marks to you,' says Sam turning to view the line of chummy-mummies watching us from ten feet away. 'You've given them something to talk about, if nothing else. I've heard that they're bragging on Twitter that you're a friend of theirs.'

I laugh.

'That wasn't my intention, Sam. And how ridiculous is it that they care so much about their perceived status on social media?'

'Good luck anyway ... I'll be watching and cheering you on. I reckon they're probably saving the best until last, do you?'

'That's exactly what my parents said.' I feel encouraged that someone other than family wishes me luck, though I doubt I'll get much support from the chummy-mummies. 'Anyway, I must dash ... got a date tonight, as you know!'

We both giggle as I hot-foot it from the school gate heading for home.

Polly

'So the room hire includes the use of the room and clearing up after us?' I say, pacing around the edge of an empty dance floor at ten o'clock in the morning, followed by a suited young man.

'It does.'

'And what time do we need to be out by?'

'Midnight.'

I notice he straightens his face on answering. I can imagine that much like Cody he thinks the night is just beginning at that time and not that it's bedtime, which I have no doubt is what I'll be feeling come Saturday.

'The bar is staffed from what time?'

'Fully stocked prior to your arrival and manned from thirty minutes before your designated hire time.'

'From seven o'clock then?'

It is perfect. I can't knock the décor, the cleanliness, the arrangement of bar, dance floor and DJ corner ... I can visualise Saturday night in full swing before my eyes. It might even be suitable for my fortieth birthday next year, if we choose not to go away on a holiday of a lifetime or book a thrill-seeking experience like a hot-air balloon ride.

I exhale, the knot within my chest loosening.

I'm relieved that my biggest hurdle is sorted but if I'm to get this party swinging by Saturday, I still have much to do.

'Is there anything else we can organise?' he asks smoothly.

Well trained by the management, I see.

'I realise how short notice this is but ... can you give me some options and prices for a selection of nibbles and savouries.'

My events manager disappears to fetch a large folder of options, complete with pictures and prices. Though, given my mindset this week, having pictures might make my selection easier. He outlines numerous packages; I feel as if I'm in uncharted territory here but listen all the same as he lists specific menus, serving options, a variety of cold and hot delicacies. By the time he stops talking, I am baffled as to what I'd like to eat come Saturday evening. But it's February, so it needs to be warm and satisfying. The hot buffet alone made a serious dent in our budget. But I won't sleep if I fear that our guests have gone home hungry; I'd much rather they leave the party with an individual doggy bag to chomp on the journey home.

I finally settle for a selection of hot filled baps: pork, lamb or steak with accompanying condiments and sauces. Plus an array of desserts and a cheese board.

He then asks the question which I have no idea how to answer.

'And that'll be for how many guests?'

'How many does the room comfortably hold?' I ask, forgetting the details mentioned earlier.

'Seventy with ease, eighty at a push ... Our fire certificate dictates the numbers.'

I quickly calculate in my head; if everyone I sent the text to arrives, even if they haven't answered, then we'll be fine with sixty. If those that have answered are the only ones attending, then our small party of twelve will have enough food to last us into the middle of next week.

I need to chase the RSVPs.

And the DJ.

'Can I book for sixty guests please?'

I watch as he pulls a calculator from his inside pockets and begins punching in numbers.

'And you're happy to pay that in full today?' he asks, as I mentally tick off another task from my busy week.

Dana

'Nervous?' asks Tamzin, as she leads me from the hotel room where once again the experts have performed wonders with my hair and make-up. Today's outfit is more my style: casual yet everyday smart in designer jeans, a sheer floaty top with camisole underneath and my ankle boots.

'I'm dying inside. I'm more nervous than I was on the last date,' I confess, rubbing a hand across my stomach. I'm not about to be sick but it's pretty close.

'You've got nothing to worry about. Jez was delighted with the feedback from last night's programme, though he wasn't too happy with Cain's interviewing.'

'Really?'

'Yep. Jez felt he was a little crude at times, which isn't what Jez is trying to portray with this show. The experts explained their spiel about how they'd selected your three matches very professionally and then Cain blows it like a cheap barrel of beer smuggled into a posh wedding. No, you'll have a new interviewer for this second date – and maybe we can get to the bottom of what you really think of Male B.'

I stop walking and stare after her as she continues.

'I *was* honest.'

Tamzin turns around to look at me.

'I know that, but Jez wants you to be a little more open with your reasons . . . don't stick to clichés – tell it like it is. Feedback from our audience suggests they thought you were very relatable in the dating experience, you came across as honest and a decent everyday kind of person, which appeals to the masses. They almost sided with you, which is what Jez wants. By the end of the week, he wants the TV audience to view you as a close friend or even relative – so much so they'll forget you're a total stranger on the TV.'

I listen intently as we resume our walk.

'And today's date?'

'Not a dinner date today. I believe this guy has opted for a very different venue . . . I think you'll love it. The panel of experts were delighted with his choice.' She gives me a wink as we reach the foyer, which is filled to bursting with production crew and equipment boxes.

'How are we?' calls Jez, breaking off his conversation with one of the many experts, I forget who's who.

'Fine, thank you. I was just saying I'm more nervous than last time, which has surprised me.'

'Good, good. A quick question before we get going . . . You did bring your passport with you, as we asked?'

I rummage in my handbag and offer him my passport, though I hope he doesn't open it and view my horrific photograph.

'Excellent, we're good to go then. Onwards, crew!' shouts Jez, handing me the passport and, turning on his heel, leading the way towards the hotel exit.

Carmen

Rings
Hotel
Flights
Restaurants
Sight-seeing tours
Restaurant bookings
Boutique work
Elliot's work?!?!?!

'Trish, apologies, but I've taken it as a given that you're OK to take Saturday's appointments while I'm away. Are you?' I say, my pen hovering above my to-do list.

'Mmmm, I wondered when that little detail was going to cross your mind,' she teases.

'Sorry! I've checked the appointment book and it is a fairly quiet day, but even so, that was rude of me to assume. Are you sure it's OK?'

'I'm sure. Anna will be here to help.'

I cross off another item.

'I'm officially ready, planned and paid-up in full for our mini break – the only detail unconfirmed is the attendance of the fiancé-to-be! How ridiculous is that?'

'I can believe it, Carmen. You haven't stopped this week ... you've juggled the boutique, the proposal planning and the preparation for the meeting about the new venture,' says Trish. 'But stop worrying – it'll come together, sweetheart, so don't panic.'

'But what if it doesn't?'

'But it will, trust me.'

'What if he doesn't get the time off work? I can hardly go it alone come Friday evening and leave Elliot behind . . . he might be able to catch a flight on Saturday afternoon, I suppose, but it wouldn't be the same, would it?'

'Hardly appropriate to attend a couple's mini break alone on night one.'

'Can you imagine it!'

'Carmen, please stop it!' Trish's voice has edge; she's serious.

'Tell me how, Trish.'

'Stop thinking so negatively, focus on the fabulous weekend ahead. You'll ruin the experience for yourself if you carry on as you are. Everything is going to be just perfect, I can feel it.'

'I wish I could,' I mutter, feeling calmer but still very concerned that my weekend dream might fade.

'You need to calm down, take some time out for yourself. Can't you book a massage or something while Elliot's away?'

'I could do with some quality "me" time but with so much going on . . .'

'Oh, who's this?' interrupts Trish, as an adult male leans against our bay window, shading his eyes with his hands to peer inside. I can just make out his actions beyond the bridal gowns in our window display.

'We've an hour before our next appointment is due,' I say, watching the figure make his way to the entrance.

As soon as the door opens, my heart sinks. It's Adrian, Elliot's older brother.

'Hello, what brings you to these parts?' I call as cheerfully as I can. My heart races – which seems to be normal for this week.

'I was passing and thought I'd drop by,' he mutters, looking awkward and very uncomfortable as he walks through the bridal wear towards the reception counter where I am perched, staring and shocked. I turn my to-do notepad over and push it aside.

'Really?'

Eight years I've been dating his brother and I've never had this pleasure before. I know where this is going. I imagine he's spoken to his parents, who have told him of my intentions, and he's here playing the big-brother role and acting as official spokesman for the Cole clan.

'Mmmm.' Adrian surveys the boutique in an inquisitive manner.

'Have you never been in here before?' I ask, unsure how to proceed but wishing he'd just say what he wants to say.

'Nope. Never. I've passed it many times but I don't think this was here when we got married so . . . Tara went elsewhere for her wedding dress.'

He gives a polite smile, as if I might be offended by her choice of bridal boutique despite my company not existing at the time. I'm not sure whether he's impressed or not by his little brother's partner's tiny empire, but I daren't ask.

'Pity . . . but should you ever renew your vows or if Tara ever gets married again, she can drop in, I'll help her choose something special,' I tease, trying my hardest to remain calm and light-hearted.

'Phew! Chance would be a fine thing,' retorts Adrian.

Come on, man, say what you've been sent to say. I'll take it on the chin, I'll explain the best I can and when you've finally gone, I'll probably burst out crying at the lack of support I'm getting from the Cole family after eight years. We don't see Adrian and Tara much these days; we did when Elliot and I first met, but they were already married, settled and planning babies so drunken nights out as couples soon fell off their social agenda. They had more important nights to consider. Within a year of us starting dating they had baby number one; baby number two followed quickly, but not as swiftly as babies three and four arriving in the same pregnancy. So we've had plenty of christenings and soft-play birthday parties to attend but very few opportunities for the couples' nights out to resume.

'Anyway . . .' he says.

'Yes, *anyway*.'

'How's Elliot?'

'He should be harassed at the moment; he needs to get out of working this weekend, but yesterday he and the guys headed off to Cardiff for some rough-terrain mountain-biking experience, part of Monty's stag do.'

'Wow, that's come around quickly.'

'Yeah, just the five guys are going. Monty didn't want a big bash kind of a night,' I add.

Adrian nods. I can see he's struggling, stalling the conversation, almost laying the foundations on which to proceed. I have a gnawing feeling in the pit of my stomach that this conversation isn't going to go well.

'My mum phoned to say you'd popped around.'

Finally.

I nod, my eyes fixed on his, though his gaze flutters about my face and the nearby tiara display that Trish is dusting. For a moment the silence feels icy cold and uncomfortable, until he resumes speaking.

'She mentioned that you intend to propose at the weekend, and she said that Dad had been a little . . . aggressive in his remarks and that maybe you got the impression that his ideas . . . remarks represented both of them.'

I nod again, not wishing to interrupt his flow.

'Well, they don't. Mum thinks our Elliot should have done the decent thing by marrying you before now, so she's quite

happy with your intentions. My dad's probably feeling somewhat patriarchal – you know what he's like with his idea of
gender-assigned roles. He doesn't mean to sound so gruff, but
he's old-fashioned through and through.'

I'm instantly relieved. Sally's never been overly friendly
towards me but she's always been fair and treated me like one
of the family, even if it's a tad stifled. Bless her for taking the
time out to call her eldest and ask him to come round. She
obviously gets where I'm coming from about the whole marriage time-window, which gives me a warm flush of emotion
towards her, as if she's got my back too.

'I get it. I wasn't offended by his remarks, more taken
aback that he seemed to suggest that he knew Elliot had a
reason for not proposing to me. That did make me feel a
little uneasy. I know Elliot is close to your father but he's
never explained to me why we've not got married yet and
so, yes, I was upset by Jim's suggestion. It was as if he knew
something I don't.'

'Mum did mention that. Look, Carmen, Elliot has never
spoken to me about marriage . . . we haven't got that kind of
brotherly relationship, have we? We were close as youngsters
and teenagers – as thick as thieves back then. I suppose we've
drifted over the years, what with me being with Tara and the
kids, Elliot focusing on his career and you – but, believe me,
he's never suggested to Mum that he's no intention of marrying
you, OK?'

'Thanks, Adrian, I appreciate you dropping by and please let
your mum know I'm grateful for her concern too.'

'Does that alter your plans? Are you happy to wait a little
longer for Elliot to propose or are you still hell-bent on doing
the leap-year thing?'

'Oh, I'm doing it. I heard what your father said, and I respect his opinion, but, no, I've planned it all. Come Saturday, I'll be asking Elliot to marry me . . . Let's just hope your father hasn't ruined my moment and told him about it.'

'I don't think he will – he'd see that as interfering, which is probably why Mum phoned me rather than speak to you herself,' says Adrian.

'And you?'

'Me? Carmen, does it matter what I think?'

'Kind of . . . you're his big brother, after all,' I tease, hoping I might have another supporter alongside Sally.

Adrian shuffles from foot to foot, scratches his head.

'If the truth be known, I was a little shocked when Mum said. I proposed to Tara after two years – there was never a doubt in my mind that I'd marry her. Would I have accepted if she'd asked me first? Yes, I suppose I would have.' He pauses and smiles. 'But, and here's the father in me coming out, I want my two daughters to receive proposals . . . which seems like double standard, doesn't it?'

I laugh heartily.

'I like your honesty, Adrian, if nothing else.'

'See, us men, we want it all our own way, don't we?'

'You certainly do, that's true enough.'

'Anyway, I'd best be going. But I'm sure we'll be seeing you soon.'

'Say hi to Tara and the children for me; it seems ages since we got together.'

'We'll make a date in the coming weeks, eh?'

Within seconds, he's planted a gentle kiss on my cheek and left.

Trish and Anna peer at me from across the boutique.

'Adrian, Elliot's older brother, come to smooth the waters,' I say.

'He doesn't look a bit like Elliot, does he?' says Trish, shaking her head.

'He looks like their dad, Elliot looks more like his mum,' I say. 'Well, at least I know where everyone stands in relation to my plans.'

'That's funny, because their opinions don't actually count!' teases Trish, shaking her head at Anna.

'But it's nice to know his mother understands where I'm coming from.'

'Sure, and it's better to have her on your side than not, in my opinion.'

Dana

'Flight attendants, please prepare for gate departure, doors on automatic, cross-check and report ... thank you,' comes the nasal announcement over the tannoy system.

I am bewildered beyond belief. I find myself sitting in seat D3 of an aeroplane, waiting on the tarmac and preparing for take-off – all within an hour of Jez hailing, 'Onwards, crew!'

Everything has happened so fast.

A procession of sleek executive cars and transit vans met up outside the hotel's plush entrance and flew along the motorway. Before I knew it, we were checking-in, handing over passports and being escorted across a windy runway to this plane, of which we have filled the first seven rows. I've fastened my seat belt and am watching an attractive brunette wildly gesturing towards the exit doors at the front, sides and rear of the plane.

Someone pinch me. Surely this can't be happening?

I sit back and prepare for take-off. My mind buzzes with

excitement as I'm informed that we have just forty-five minutes until we land. Where are we heading?

'How are you finding the experience?' asks Jennifer, the relationship and dating expert, leaning across the aisle to speak to me.

'Oh, I'm fine. It only hit me last night that other people have watched how I behave on a first date, which feels weird.'

'And your family, how did they react?' she asks in her deep Aussie drawl, peering at me over her specs.

'Oh, I didn't tell them. I chickened out,' I blurt, due to my nerves.

Instantly her face falls. 'Why did you feel the need to do that? Haven't you a strong bond with your family?'

'Yes, but I simply couldn't find the words to explain what I'd applied for. They both loved the idea once they'd watched the episode, but they didn't know beforehand.'

'They weren't upset or disappointed?'

'Not in the slightest. They tend to respect my decisions in life and so . . .' My words fade as the memory of my announcement of the Down's syndrome test result fills my mind. 'I knew they wouldn't have an issue.'

I didn't doubt for one minute that my parents would go along with whatever I decided on hearing my baby news. They knew that I'd had the result and knew that I would share the details when I chose to. I'm lucky. So very lucky to have the support of a strong loving family, unlike others I know whose parents still treat them like children despite their fortieth birthdays dawning. I might be their child, even be seen as their baby still, but my parents fully respect my choices as an adult; this is the kind of relationship we've nurtured since I was a teenager. I'm hoping it's the template for my relationship with Luke when he's older too.

A sense of pride wells inside as I remember my announcement in their front lounge.

'I've received another positive result and I'm delighted to announce I'm having a beautiful baby boy.' I didn't even mention his condition because it was of little consequence to me. Instantly, I had been swamped with hugs and kisses of congratulations.

I return to reality to find Jennifer staring at me across the aisle, the beginnings of a smile on her red painted lips. I know she witnessed my regression into a beautiful memory.

'Oh no, I can assure you I have the best of family support . . . They can't wait for Saturday . . . my mum's already joking about buying a new hat!'

Her wide smile breaks across her face.

'That is good news, great to hear,' she adds, before the force of the aeroplane's take-off pushes us both into our seats.

'Welcome to Edinburgh! The temperature is eight degrees centigrade – an unusually warm afternoon for this time of year.

'Edinburgh!' I look around the neighbouring seats; various crew members stare back as if surprised that I hadn't been told.

'Male B requested the location as part of his interview process,' calls Tamzin, once a crew member points in my direction.

'Is he Scottish?' I ask, intrigued to find out as much as I can beforehand.

'Ooooh, now that would be telling,' teases Tamzin.

I secretly watch her for the next five minutes, hoping to pick something up from her body language, spying on any details she might leak to the passenger seated beside her. My Tamzin-watch doesn't provide me with any new information, just a few uncomfortable smiles when she spotted me staring.

Scottish.

Male.

I envisage fiery red hair, a wiry unruly beard and a Fair Isle knitted jumper. I immediately chastise myself for such stereotypical thinking; it irks me so much when others make assumptions about Luke and his abilities.

My Luke. Mum says he's being such a good boy about this week's arrangements. Though he has demanded fishfingers and beans for tea tonight; this week's lack of fruit and vegetables might play havoc with his digestive system, which doesn't bode well for little accidents at school. My heart feels heavy. I've missed out on some bath times, a few farewell kisses at the school gate and story times because of this dating adventure. I promise myself I'll make it up to him with extra cuddles next week and maybe a trip to the zoo the following weekend.

Parents' evening! My brain screams at me. I haven't given Mum the specific questions I wanted answers to.

I grab my mobile, open my notes app and begin compiling a list.

Parents' evening questions for Mrs Salter –

Thursday, 27 Feb, appointment time: 3:10 p.m.

What strengths have been observed in his learning?
What weaknesses have been observed in his learning?
I've noticed his confidence growing when interacting with other children. Have you witnessed this in the classroom?
Is he still being a little too boisterous in the dining room when it comes to food?
Is there any improvement in his acknowledgement of needing the toilet?

I quickly read through the list; if I can't attend, I'll at least have the answers to my most important questions. The school offered me a telephone appointment with Mrs Salter, but I declined. I'm happy enough for my parents to attend and view Luke's work on my behalf. I want to add a sixth point to the list but I don't want to be seen as being pushy, especially as I have sent a couple of stand-ins to parents' evening. But the mistake or rather the oversight in the classroom's weekly rota won't be addressed until I confront it.

I add the extra item.

> Please add Luke to the daily tidy-up rota as he is a very
>   capable child.

I'll message the note to my mum as soon as I land, then they'll be prepared for tomorrow afternoon's meeting. Plus I'll email it to the school office for the attention of Mrs Salter, giving her notice of the questions before the appointment.

It takes seconds for the production crew to be whisked through the airport and baggage collection, after which we are escorted towards another line of executive cars and transit vans to whiz into Edinburgh. I'm not remotely aware of who is who any more, the crew and the experts have merged into a mass of bodies which move as one, like a football crowd.

I stare from the tinted window at the passing sights: Murrayfield Stadium, the zoo and, finally, Princes Street. I've never been to Scotland before so the twenty-minute journey feels special despite my pre-date nerves. I wasn't this nervous meeting Alex so maybe it's a good sign. Maybe not. Maybe I'm simply talking myself into a fairyland to make myself feel better, but surely a positive mental attitude is a good thing.

'Where's Dana?' calls Jez, marching frantically up and down the line of parked cars when we eventually stop.

'She's in here,' calls Tamzin, opening the automatic window. The car door swings wide and Jez's smiling face appears.

'You good to go?'

'Of course.' I grab my coat and handbag, then attempt to shuffle out of the car but the heavy door takes some opening so I fall rather than step out of the executive vehicle. I look up to see the camera crew capturing every moment. I must look like a right sight if my date is watching from a hiding place.

'Can we do that again, please?' shouts Jez. 'Maybe the driver can assist her?'

I'm quickly ushered back into the car and the door is slammed shut.

Take two captures the driver elegantly opening the door for me and supporting my hand as I step from the vehicle, and unceremoniously trip over my own bloody feet, dropping my handbag and its contents on to the pavement. I crouch down to scramble about the driver's feet for my belongings – lipstick, mascara and tampons – before they roll into the gutter.

'Again!' cries Jez.

It's late afternoon, there are curious tourists milling around and I'm being filmed getting out of a plush car – the whole scenario is totally ridiculous.

Take three: the door didn't open as smoothly so I crack my forehead on the inside window.

Take four: I sneezed as I stepped from the vehicle.

Finally, take five: I exit the car and walk several steps before Jez shouts, 'Cut!'

'Bloody hell, Dana – you made hard work of that!' mutters Tamzin, shaking her head and causing her zingy curls to dance.

I feel like an utter fool. How did I think I was ever swish

enough to pull off a dating documentary when I can't even get out of a car? Someone please call for a responsible adult to help raise my dear boy. I hope that Jez doesn't create an outtakes section at the end of the week showing my car exits and toilet sound effects. I'd never be able to face the chummy-mummies again and Luke would have to be home-schooled on my limited knowledge, which would be the biggest downfall of his life!

I'm so consumed by analysing my lack of life skills I haven't clocked where we are.

'Dana, simply walk in a straight line from this stone pillar to the end one . . . and please stay on your feet,' instructs Jez, gesturing to the camera man to record my walk.

Ha bloody ha, Jez.

I focus on my task. I concentrate and manage to walk, one uneventful step after another, along the required route for the camera angle Jez wants before noticing the colourful banner strung up on the red sandstone building announcing the Scottish National Portrait Gallery.

I adore portraits and art.

My excitement overflows and I can't hold back my smile.

'That would have been a better shot, Jez,' shouts the cameraman, pointing out my expression.

Jez pops up from nowhere.

'Walk it again, Dana . . . but smile like you were just doing,' shouts Jez.

For the life of me, I'm no actor; I've only just mastered the art of walking on command, let alone a retake of a genuine smile.

I redo the walk with the additional smile with the camera in front of me, which is slightly distracting, but Jez doesn't complain when I reach the end pillar so I assume he's happy.

Tamzin rushes towards me as I await my next instruction.

'Remember, if you nip to the toilet . . .' she says, fixing the tiny microphone next to my collarbone.

'I'll remember.'

'Mmmm, you said that on date one,' she mutters, titivating my hair. I get the feeling Tamzin is tired of being my minder. She's obviously disappointed by their selection having spent some time with me. Maybe she expected me to be chummier, more feminine or slightly less naïve, but surely I'm supposed to be me. Isn't that the whole point? It was me who answered the isometric test questions, my face that was photographed from every conceivable angle and my backside that was filmed walking along before they decided my smile was slightly more pleasing.

'Now, Dana, your date is standing at the top of the main staircase . . . We're going to enter the gallery and position ourselves at the top and bottom of the staircase so, as you go in, please don't look at us. Focus on him, OK?' explains Jez, holding my gaze as he speaks before turning to Tamzin. 'Give us five minutes, then send her in.'

I watch her orange curls perform a lively dance. Jez runs inside with his camera crew. The experts file in after them; none of them look at me as they pass.

'Your hair must take ages to do,' I say, admiring her look.

Tamzin frowns.

'It's not real,' she mutters, her brow furrowing further.

This is going to be a long five minutes.

I enter the foyer of the portrait gallery, where every surface is pristine and gleaming – there isn't a soul around. I was expecting the buzz of visitors, the stare of security staff or gallery staff manning the ticket desk. But there's nobody apart from Tamzin, leaning against the open doorway, frantically gesturing for me to walk through the foyer towards the staircase.

I do as I'm told.

The staircase sweeps up and curves slightly in the most elegant of fashions. One camera crew captures my arrival and continues to roll as I walk, which I feel I've mastered now.

I climb the stairs and it's only when I'm halfway up that I can see there is a man standing at the top, awaiting my arrival, and he's definitely not Jez or his camera crew.

Polly

'Mum, I'm here! Don't worry, you won't be late,' I call my mother from the curbside, knowing I'm later than I had planned. 'Come out to the car, we'll head straight off.'

I put my phone in my handbag as my mother exits her front door, checks the door is locked and then checks she has her door key. Typical Mum – why doesn't she check before the door is well and truly shut?

I watch as she walks towards me. Sporting bright white trainers and dressed in her new velour burgundy tracksuit from M&S, she takes tiny shuffling steps, her head lowered, watching where she steps on her gravelled pathway.

She looks older this week.

I glance in my rear-view mirror. I see the dark circles under my own eyes, the tiny splash of make-up which I've used purely to detract the viewer and a slick of lip gloss.

We all look tired this week.

'Hello, Polly, I thought you weren't coming,' says Mum, climbing into the passenger seat, and securing her seatbelt.

I give her quick peck on the cheek. It feels like tissue under my lips.

'Just delayed. I had to view the venue for Saturday's party, organise a buffet and then cut through the traffic – not easy given the snarl-up on the ring road. But I'm here now.'

'Is this seat catch mended yet?'

'No, though I'm not sure if it's the catch or the springs – it hasn't lurched forward for a week or so.'

'It doesn't feel secure. Look – it rocks back and forth.' She demonstrates by rocking the seat's backrest violently, just as she did last week.

'I know, I'll get it sorted, Mum. Or you can discuss it with Fraser when he collects you after the class if you prefer.'

'Will he meet me outside The Bed Shop?'

'Yes, that's what we arranged.'

I start the engine and away we go, heading back into town, but at least I know now that the ring road is a nightmare and can avoid it, ensuring she's on time.

'So, how have you been?'

'Worried sick. I keep saying to Derek – where does this leave us?'

'Derek?'

'Oh yes, he's been most helpful about Helen. Very supportive . . . he's a caring man at heart, though I know you don't know him well enough to judge.'

'Are you sure Helen would want you discussing her situation with Derek, Mum? I've hardly even said much in front of our Cody; it's very much her business and she probably won't want it discussed by everyone.'

'Phew! You're just like your father, you are! I bet he's all "let's brush this under the carpet, everything will be all right by next week".'

'Mum! That's not fair. Dad is beside himself to think we could have lost her but he's ready to support her in any way he can.'

'Mmmm.'

'Please don't, it's tough enough without the bickering between you two. She comes home tonight. The girls are staying an extra night at ours to make sure Helen gets some rest and then we'll see what she wants to do. There's no point us arguing amongst ourselves about this one.'

'Now that sounds like Fraser,' she says.

'It probably does, given my daily interaction with him, Mum.'

'Are his parents coming on Saturday?'

'Oh yes, they'll be picking you up at just gone seven o'clock, so if you can be ready and waiting, that'd be great.'

'Are you not collecting me?'

'No, Mum, I can't collect everyone.'

'Who's driving your father then?'

'We are but . . .'

She clicks her tongue in that annoying manner which has haunted me since childhood.

'Mum, we live on the same side of town as Dad. What's the point in us driving past his place to get to yours, knowing he can't get there either? This way you both get collected and delivered home safely without hassle or fuss.'

'Olive doesn't like me. You know that, don't you? It'll be all politeness and fake smiles. "Hi, Pauline, how are you?" she'll ask. I'll answer and then there'll be total silence for the rest of the journey unless Fraser's father is in one of his chatty moods. I'll sit in the back, counting the streetlights passing the window.'

'His name's Malcolm, Mum. Would you prefer a taxi then? Let me book you a taxi.'

'Mmmm, like your dad's having a taxi.'

'Actually, he did ask for a taxi but Fraser refused to consider it when I mentioned it.'

'Won't Fraser be drinking?'

'No, not now he's promised to collect Dad to save him getting a taxi.'

'If anyone should be getting a taxi, it's you . . . you should be celebrating your son's birthday, not ferrying everyone else around.'

'Absolutely, but life isn't like that, Mum. Fraser's happy to drive.'

Silence descends as my mother squirrels away the details. I can't keep everyone happy, but I'm busting a gut keeping all the balls in the air without dropping one. Which has become the main aim of this week. Come Sunday, I can have a quiet day at home and forget juggling for a day or so.

'Come in with me,' says Mum, when we can't see hide nor hair of Derek outside The Bed Shop, their designated meeting place.

'Do I have to?'

'Polly, he's probably waiting just inside; he'll have forgotten our arrangement and gone straight up. It'll only mean you walking me in, and then you can leave.'

How can my mother sign up for a tantric intimacy class and yet be unable to enter the double doors and meet her fellow tantric learners?

'I'm parked on double yellows, Mum,' I say, hoping that's enough of an excuse. In truth, I don't want to see any of the participants for fear of bumping into the same crowd whilst shopping in Waitrose.

'Polly, please.'

'All right.' I put my hazard lights on and climb from the car, locking the doors. I'll only be a minute: a quick nip over the road, in through the double doors, deliver my mother and back out.

Funny how you never notice certain things without actually

looking. Beside the entrance to The Bed Shop, which we've visited many times, I'd never noticed the glass door situated to the left. As we enter, a steep set of steps ascends directly before us; there's very little room to even close the door behind us before we begin to climb. At the top, I hold the banister rail for a moment to get my breath back, and I'm taken back to find an entire new world which I didn't know existed. The first floor is decked out as a series of workout rooms – wooden flooring and mirrors, and glass frontages putting participants on show throughout each session. An absurdly healthy-looking lady sits behind the reception desk, amidst a promotional display about juicing, beaming an over-welcoming smile at us.

There is no sign of Derek.

'OK, Mum, I'll be off then. Fraser will meet you at two o'clock. Remember, he'll be waiting outside for you.'

'Polly, don't go.'

A flashback from nursery days occurs, though the demanding individual isn't two foot tall.

'Mum, I need to . . . You're here now . . . sign in at reception and take it from there,' I say, indicating the lady behind the reception desk.

'What if he doesn't show up?'

I shrug. Good. That would be perfect.

'You'll still have a wonderful time learning whatever it is you're going to learn, Mum. Now, I really must go. They look a friendly bunch,' I say, pointing towards the glass wall of a workout studio where mats are being unrolled, and seeing a range of ages, mainly my mother's generation, wearing an assortment of dressing gowns and kaftans. I give her a quick peck on the cheek and dash down the stairs, fighting the momentum created by the steepness of the flight.

As I leave through the main door, I see it stuck to my windscreen in a plastic bloody envelope.

Bastards!

I dash across to my car and yank the offending parking ticket from the windscreen, whilst scouting for the cheeky git who'd signed it. In the distance, as far as the travel agents and the bridal boutique, I can just make out his patrolling uniform. He might look as if he's plodding along but I know for a fact he must have broken an Olympic speed record to have achieved that distance between me and him given the time recorded on my ticket.

Seventy quid wasted.

I unlock my car and throw the ticket on to the passenger seat before manoeuvring into the afternoon traffic.

Dana

'Hello, I'm Brett Fallon. Nice to meet you,' says Brett, extending his hand as I climb the final stair. His accent is deep Scots, his colouring not quite as I'd imagined. His thick hair is a tumble of auburn curls, a contrast to the neatly trimmed beard which covers half his pale complexion, but it's his piercing grey eyes, which instantly dilate on meeting my gaze, that hold my attention.

'Thank you, Brett . . . I'm happy to meet you,' I say, blushing profusely as my nerves are reignited.

'I can only apologise if you'd hoped for a dinner date but I tend to show myself up in social situations like that so I thought an art gallery would be more pleasant . . . though I didn't expect them to close it to the general public just for us.' Brett laughs.

'They haven't?'

'Yep . . . there's no one here but us. It feels selfish in some respects.'

I stupidly look around, knowing perfectly well there was no one downstairs, but I refrain from looking at the camera crew – Jez will want us to pretend they aren't present either.

'I thought they only favoured the rich and famous with private viewings. And, believe me, I'm no one special.'

His brows crease before his wide smile reappears.

'Neither am I, but given that we've got my favourite gallery to ourselves, we'll pretend –' Brett leans in close to whisper, his aftershave permeating my next breath – 'for one night.'

There's no point him whispering to avoid the microphones – I know how much they can hear.

I nod in agreement.

My gaze lingers on his grey eyes, framed with such long lashes.

I like Brett. In an instant, I sense he's not flash, not super-suave but ordinary like me. He's a decent sort, like the hundreds of good eggs that I see driving around town, shopping alone in the supermarket or doing the school run most days. The ones I can never pluck up the courage to speak to.

I can't keep staring at his beautiful eyes, so I shift my gaze and am instantly distracted by the sight over his left shoulder.

An enticing sight which I've known and loved for a lifetime.

I gasp in surprise, my hands lifting to my mouth in childlike delight, acting a lot like Luke in a sweet shop.

'Shall we?' Brett indicates to his right towards the first archway, intent on starting our tour, but I'm stuck fast to the spot and staring.

'Could we?' I say, pointing towards the portrait displayed to our left.

'Sure.'

'Do you come here often?' I ask, as we stroll towards the camera crew. Jez obviously hadn't expected us to take this route, given the amount of hand-flapping and hasty instructing he does as we slowly approach.

'Many times during my childhood and now every time I come home to see the family. And you?'

'Never ... which is why I didn't expect to see her.' I nod towards the Singer Sargent painting staring down at me.

'Lady Agnew of Lochnaw ... You like her portrait?'

'I love it. She's breathtaking,' I stammer, staring open-mouthed at the vast canvas. 'Look at her gaze ... it's so alluring!'

'A definite beauty of her time,' says Brett, staring up at her delicate features.

'Such an informal feminine pose and yet that look,' I say, sounding as if I knew something about art. 'I wonder what she was thinking?'

'Mmmm, I wonder. I'm sure her husband asked the same question,' mutters Brett. His tone is suggestive and we both begin to giggle.

'Her name was Gertrude – hardly regal, is it?'

'It probably was back then ...' Brett pauses before adding, 'If it wasn't, then maybe she was just a tad closer to being "no one special", a bit like us.'

'No one special ... she was the granddaughter of a baronet who just happened to marry another baronet?'

'A valid point. I stand corrected; she's obviously someone *very* special.' Brett's laughter resonates deeply and his smile reaches his eyes.

I like his humour.

'Come on, let's go through,' I say, bravely linking my arm in his, which he allows without hesitation, gently patting my hand into place upon his sleeve.

'Don't you want to admire your painting for a little longer?'

'*My* painting?' I giggle at his phrase.

'Sorry, the way you were talking, I assumed ...' Brett gives a broad smile.

I stare at my painting and ponder.

'Mmmm, I think I'm going to allow the gallery to borrow her for just a little while longer ... until I've had my lounge redecorated anyway.'

Brett laughs as we head back towards the staircase.

As we stroll past the camera crew, trying to ignore them, I spot Jez giving the thumbs-up to a bemused Tamzin.

Polly

I open the passenger's door and draw the seat forward to try to take hold of Fido's lead, attempting to coax the poodle from the confines of the back seat. He's huddled in the corner, inches out of my grasp. With the driver's side wedged close to the neighbouring car, I daren't risk trying from my side.

'Fido, baby ... Come on, sweetie ... you know we have to go,' I urge, through gritted teeth; we have just minutes to spare to get to his grooming appointment on time. The dog bares his teeth and growls deeply. At home he's the sweetest thing, but not today, not inside my car.

I should have brought treats to entice him. I should have brought Dad; he wouldn't have done this if Dad were here.

He's not an aggressive animal but how do you explain to a dog that he's going to the groomers and not the vets? Both tend to focus on his rear end but with rather different emphasis.

It's been fifteen-odd years since I've needed to drag anything from the rear seats – namely Cody – and I'm not sure if I can squeeze back there without getting stuck . . .

I pull the seat's back forward, easing my hips past the upholstery as I step into the rear foot well, half bent, head low and reaching for Fido.

'Here, Fido, I know, I know . . .' I reach for the tiniest bit of looped leather lead which the dog has cleverly hidden beneath himself.

Clunk!

The passenger door closes on its own.

Thump!

The back of the passenger seat springs bolt upright, bumping me on the arse.

Great!

I try to turn around: nope. I manage to sink down to reach between the seat and the doorframe for the door handle.

Bloody great! Today of all days the seat catch decides to jam.

If Fraser has to come and rescue me from my own car, he will not be impressed, Cody even less so. Though given that he is only at the end of the High Street, he might be a better shout.

I begin to wiggle backwards over the front seats, pushing myself off the rear upholstery, much to the dog's surprise.

'I'm not doing this again,' I rant to myself, awkwardly bending my body to avoid the gearstick. 'Right now I'm supposed to be enjoying a nice relaxing coffee while Fido is being beautified and yet, here I am . . .'

That's when I suddenly remember that I have windows in my car, and they aren't tinted.

Lola is standing stock still, staring open-mouthed at her ex-boyfriend's mother crawling all over the upholstery of her own car seats in the middle of the multi-storey car park.

Doesn't she have anything to do other than wander around town every day?

I cease struggling and give a little wave, as if this my normal activity on Wednesday afternoons. Instantly I regret it, seeing the surprised look on her face. I never wave as she saunters past the travel agents, and yet when I'm in a compromising position I do so warmly.

How ridiculous am I?

Lola continues to stare. I freeze, like a tableaux from my school drama days, with a fake smile in place.

Go away, Lola! Ah, my usual sentiment returns within a heartbeat.

I remain in situ and smile.

Lola's big-booted feet turn and she slowly continues on her way across the car park. I resume my frantic struggle to ease my hips between the bulky headrests and twist flopping into the passenger seat as gracefully as a woman can with her boots in the air. My temple hits the door, my eye missing the handle by inches.

My passenger door is suddenly wrenched open and fresh air breezes down my collar.

'Polly, are you OK?'

I view Lola's smudged kohl eyeliner and frizzy dyed hair from upside down.

'Fine, fine, and you?' What else can I say, given the situation and our relationship?

'I was helping my mum with her weekly errands and just happened to see you . . . Are you sure?'

'Thank you, Lola.' I swing my feet around and sit upright in my own passenger seat, a place I wouldn't usually sit. 'Come on, Fido – we've got a date to keep.' I reach between the gap in the seats and take hold of his lead. And he lets me. I climb from the seat, spring the passenger seat forward and Fido trots from my car like a dream.

Little bugger!

I nonchalantly collect my handbag, slam the door and lock my car – return of the 'ordinary woman' being the act I am aiming for. I can see the confusion etched on Lola's face. She's probably wondering if she's helped in any way or debating whether my antics need to be posted on her social media at the earliest opportunity.

She stares, not sure what she has just witnessed, and I bid her goodbye, not sure what the hell I just did.

'Must dash, we're slightly late,' I say cheerily. As I speed along the pavement I silently promise to perform an act of kindness towards a stranger in the next twenty-four hours as a thank you to the gods.

I scurry along towards the car park's exit, Fido running to keep pace. We've cut it fine, too fine for my liking. I've been present when they've refused a latecomer and demanded part payment for a lost booking, which seems fair compensation for lost income, but not when it's potentially me.

'I'm sorry, so sorry . . . we had problems . . . parking,' I say, as we dash into the dog groomers, to be met with a tired smile from the young man. 'Fido Willis, for a shampoo and trim.'

'No worries, you've just made it,' he says, ticking us off in the appointment book.

I sigh with relief.

'This way, Fido, we'll see Mummy in a while,' he says, taking the lead from my hand. I want to laugh and correct him but decide not to – he can call me what he likes as long as he honours the appointment to shampoo and trim Fido's overgrown coat.

'Do you mind if I wait?' I ask, indicating the sofa area.

'Sure, take a seat . . . He'll be the whole hour.'

I quickly settle, fishing my mobile and my to-do list from my handbag.

'Hello, I'm calling about a DJ booking for Saturday night. I was told that someone would call me back but that hasn't happened yet, and I'm getting slightly concerned,' I explain in one garbled breath.

'Ah yeah, Saturday . . . I need to check. If you could hold the line a minute . . .'

I don't answer, given that I'd called earlier in the week, but the line goes silent. All I seem to do concerning this party is hold the line and wait. I should be grateful that I haven't got 'Greensleeves' being played to soothe my nerves.

'Hello?'

'Yes.'

'Yeah, we can't do that.'

'Sorry?'

'I said, we can't do that . . . we're already booked.'

'I asked the question several days ago and was told someone would get back to me and now I'm being told it's definitely "no" with just three full days to go to find a DJ,' I say, my nerves instantly fraught.

'Yeah.'

I don't know what to say. I feel like wrenching someone's head from up their own arse and giving them a lesson on manners and business etiquette, regardless of whether they're a multimillion-pound enterprise or a solo DJ.

Why can't people get their act together when showcasing their services?

If I'd been them, I'd have called me back the same day to confirm Saturday wasn't possible. But no, instead, the customer – me – has to chase about when that's really is the last thing I need to be doing.

'Can you suggest any other DJs that I could phone?' seems the only sensible thing to ask.

'Mmmm, there's Milo, or maybe Trev's available . . .'

My mind instantly makes defining judgements about the age and possible talent of each of them, based on the names alone.

'Milo? Have you got his number?'

'Hang on a minute.'

The line goes silent.

Within a few minutes, she returns with a mobile number and I'm back on a mission in search of a DJ.

'Hi, is that Milo?' I ask tentatively, fingers crossed that the guy is talented, an expert in his field and yet also available for this coming Saturday. It doesn't bode well if he is, because it suggests that he isn't either of the former.

'That's me, Milo of Musicland. How can I help?'

'Milo, I've been given your number about DJing. I was wondering if you're available on Saturday from seven thirty onwards?'

'Yep, I can do that . . . what kind of gig is it?'

Gig?

'My son's twentieth birthday at the Red Lion,' I explain.

'In the wedding room?'

'Yes, the events room at the rear . . .'

'I know it.'

I exhale deeply, unaware that I'm so uptight over such a detail.

Within five minutes, we've agreed a price, a time for him to come to set up his equipment and even 'yes, of course you can help yourself to a plate of buffet food' before I end the call, relieved that another task is complete.

*   *   *

'Here we are . . .' I hear the young man as he comes through the stable-door gateway before I see the dog.

'That's Fido?' I point in horror at the pom-pommed cream poodle that stares up at me. He wouldn't look out of place at Cruft's.

'Doesn't he look lovely?'

'Oh no! My dad will go spare . . . Fido usually has that fluffy, cuddly . . .' My hands billow and circle before me.

'Oh, the teddy-bear cut . . . Oh!'

'Exactly – oh!'

'Nobody said,' he mutters, staring dolefully at the dog.

'Surely my dad said when he booked the appointment?'

The groomer checks the appointment book, his index finger running down the details.

'No, it just says name and mobile number . . . I'm sorry, I should have checked, but when you were late and . . . I assumed . . . Can we come to an arrangement on the price?'

'He's my father's dog . . . I don't know what to say, but I know what he'll say when I take Fido back home looking like this.'

'I can only apologise.'

The door opens, admitting a large Saint Bernard and a harassed owner, doing battle with the door and his dog.

'Can we say a fifty per cent discount?'

'Deal.' I haven't time to haggle. I know my biggest argument will be with my father so I may as well save my energy for that conversation.

Carmen

I leave my car parked behind the boutique and hastily make my way along the High Street to Skin and Tonic, the beauty salon.

My fraught nerves are instantly soothed on entering: the tranquil atmosphere and the heady smell of essential oils is a welcoming delight.

'Hi, I have an appointment with Hollie for six o'clock,' I quietly announce to the reception lady, who indicates that I should take a seat for a moment.

My aching body sinks into the plush leather sofa; I rest my head back and close my eyes. I'm happy to just stay here in such comfort – never mind my session. I have nothing to think about, nothing to plan – nothing that's within my control anyway – so I can simply sit here and . . .

My drifting thoughts are interrupted by a gentle tap on the shoulder.

I snap my eyes open, startled to see a kindly face with a glowing complexion peering at me.

'Hi, I'm Hollie . . . Would you like to come this way?'

Did I fall asleep? How long was I there for?

I daren't ask, but instead jump up and trot after the slender figure dressed in a pastel grey and pink tunic. I watch as her pretty feet flip-flop in front of me in sparkly mules.

We weave our way through the salon, amidst nail stations with ladies busily chatting to their clients, whose nails are being sealed under strange lights, past a spectrum of nail varnishes challenging any rainbow to sparkle brighter, and finally we enter a tiny room, where the warmth and muted lighting envelops my tired body. The hypnotic sound of raindrops gently falling fills the air and a sense of calm washes over me.

'If you undress down to your briefs, lie face down upon the couch and cover yourself with both towels, I'll be back in a little while,' says Hollie, indicating the door as she speaks.

Hollie exits, closing the door tightly behind her.

I don't need telling twice.

I whip off my clothing, my boots and am down to my briefs in seconds. I carefully fold my clothes and place them on the nearest chair.

I spy the large brown bottles of carrier oils, to which I've requested that bergamot and lavender be added to aid my relaxation. I clamber on to the massage table, lie face down and cover myself with the large white fluffy towels, as instructed. My forehead presses against the padded hole in the base of the table, and my shoulders naturally fall forward and sink into the towel and paper lining sheet beneath me.

This is exactly what I need. Tomorrow, I will thank Trish for the suggestion – or nagging – which she gave me. This type of self-care has fallen by the wayside for me in recent years. I've allowed my 'me' time to be lost to an extra hour of boutique admin or an extra hour in front of the TV watching something which I don't care for but which interests Elliot's inquisitive mind.

I should stop those negative habits, allow him space to enjoy what he likes and for me to take time out for the things I need, such as this. It would be a more productive and positive way to use our spare time, rather than me wasting time following his pursuits and neglecting myself. Working in the evening needs to stop too – that isn't a smart move in anyone's world: all work and no, or very little, play makes Carmen a bore.

Knock, knock. I look up towards the door.

'Can I come in?' asks Hollie, returning to the massage room.

'I'm ready,' I whisper.

She manoeuvres the towel covering my upper body away from my shoulder blades and positions it below my waist, exposing my entire back. I reposition my forehead into the face hole and watch her feet move about the room. I can hear the gulp of the oil into the bowl, and imagine her adding my essential oils, drop by drop, to the mix.

The gentle rain continues to pitter-patter as Hollie's pretty feet return to the table and her warm hands smooth my back in long delicious strokes.

'How does that feel?' asks Hollie after the hour-long massage.

'Thank you so much,' I answer dreamily, as my mind floods with positive and re-energised thoughts. My eyes remain closed, but I'm sure my contented smile reinforces my answer. It had taken a whole hour but it's been time well spent, given my instant feeling of wellbeing.

'I've left a glass of cold water on the side. Please be careful as you get up, in case you feel light headed. I'll be waiting at the desk when you are ready.' She quickly exits and leaves me to dress.

I lie in situ for another few minutes, enjoying my relaxed state until I feel it would be rude for me to linger any longer. I'd hate to cause Hollie to run late for the next client in need of her healing hands.

A gentle aroma of lavender wafts as I lift each limb to dress. I quickly drink my glass of water, vowing to drink a second as soon as I arrive home to flush my lymphatic system.

I switch my mobile back on and instantly six missed calls from Elliot buzz on to the screen.

My heart stops.

I find my way back to reception, thank Hollie and pay before dashing back along the High Street. All sense of tranquillity is snatched from my world as I clutch my mobile to my ear, willing Elliot to pick up.

'Hello,' hollers a male voice; it's not Elliot's.

'Hi ... who's that?'

I stop dead on the High Street, unable to move.

'Monty ... Elliot can't speak at the minute; he's talking to a doctor ... The prat has done his knee in by falling off his sodding bike so we're all sitting in A&E awaiting his grand entrance wearing one of those bloody knee-brace things. Carmen, are you still there?'

'Yes, I'm here . . . just taking in the details. Can he walk?'

'Who knows? The idiot shot down a track without checking what was at the end of it.'

'And what *was* at the end?'

'A sodding twenty-foot drop . . . which he plunged over, and then he landed badly because he tried to hold on to the bike!'

'But he's OK, apart from his knee?'

'Mmmm, his front tooth is slightly wobbly but nothing major – bloody lucky, if you ask me. But he won't be if we have to spend all night sitting around this place. We're supposed to have had a skinful of scotch in the middle of Cardiff by now.'

Oh great!

'That's a relief. Can you tell him to call me when he is done? I'll be at home.'

'Sure will, see ya.'

In an instant, Monty is gone.

I slowly make my way to my car, unlock it and settle in before turning the key in the ignition.

Another day done. One day less before we head to our weekend in Paris. Which in all likelihood will now include Elliot hobbling around and swallowing painkillers every four hours.

I sigh.

Not quite the romantic mini-break I'd imagined.

Dana

My lounge clock reads 8.30 p.m. as I flop on to the sofa, clutching the TV remote control. After his busy day at school and after-school fun with Grandpops, Luke swiftly fell asleep just three pages into his bedtime story and so I snuck from his room to take up my position here on the couch.

I survey the silent room. Nothing has changed since breakfast time: the pile of clean folded washing still needs putting away, the large cobweb hanging from the light fitting survives another day and an invite to a parental networking session with the Down's Syndrome Research Foundation still awaits my acceptance on the mantelpiece.

And yet something *has* changed.

Something inside me may have changed. I sense that today I am slightly different from yesterday. Different from breakfast time even.

I lie back and stare at the wafting cobweb, which I really must get down – but I've been saying that each night for a month.

I daren't allow myself to pinpoint the true reason for the change, though I might allow myself to believe it has something to do with Edinburgh. My fleeting visit? The gallery visit? Viewing my painting of Lady Agnew of Lochnaw?

Perhaps.

Maybe.

Possibly I'd experienced another kaleidoscope moment in life. Had I twisted the mirrors and tubing to create a new pattern which was better than the old one?

I must stop thinking before I fool myself. Watch some TV, take the folded washing upstairs . . . get that bloody cobweb!

I daren't move. I'm suddenly aware of everything surrounding me, as if I've turned the kaleidoscope barrel and unknowingly created a new snowflake pattern but with fresher brighter colours than previously ever seen.

I mustn't continue with these thoughts. I can't allow my brain to twist and connect the minuscule shapes to form new patterns that I'll fall in love with. I know from experience that one tiny twist and everything will be lost. Irretrievably changed and lost forever. And the memory of what is lost will cause me endless pain by remaining in my head. And my heart.

I can't. I won't. I mustn't allow my thoughts to wander, grow or connect to form pretty patterns because it might pinpoint the reason for my kaleidoscope twist . . . and there's a definite chance that the name Brett might feature in that pattern.

Part of me wonders if the camera crew captured anything which links to my current thoughts. I'm tempted to tune in to watch tonight's episode, purely to make sure I didn't make a fool of myself. They say a camera never lies but I doubt they capture everything, or least I'm hoping not.

I clutch a small cushion to my face and cautiously peer over the top at the TV screen. I don't know if I can face watching myself appear in the opening credits, let alone watch the entire episode of *Taking a Chance on Love*.

I've switched my mobile off, knowing my mother may ring mid-programme to ask what I thought about Brett. Or maybe she won't need to. Maybe I gave myself away so anyone and everyone watching tonight's episode will instantly know.

I cringe a little more and lift the cushion to cover my lower lashes.

How embarrassing. Thirty-nine years of age and acting like a lovesick teenager.

It's only date two and I'm already singling out one guy from the two I've met. Alex was nice, polite, well-mannered but . . . he wasn't Brett.

Stop it, Dana, stop it now.

I close my eyes and all I can see is Jez doing a geeky thumbs-up to Tamzin, who is beaming and nodding back to him across the gallery landing as we walk by.

Where were the experts at that specific moment? Were they jubilantly high-fiving each other and congratulating themselves on picking a winner for their dating match experiment?

On hearing the theme tune, my eyes snap open.

Decision time.

I watch. I can't help myself. In fact, I can't stop watching. I watch the hour-long episode through again from beginning to end, immediately after it has finished airing to the nation.

My mobile phone records five missed calls from my mother. I daren't speak to her because I know exactly what she'll say and it will either relate to the colour of her wedding hat or will focus upon the final closing moments!

I throw the remote down beside my seat as I pause the TV screen for the umpteenth time at a particular shot. A specific moment which I have now watched more than thirty times in every possible TV playback mode: slow motion, normal speed and even fast forward – simply to convince myself that I'm seeing things. I was present in the moment, so I know exactly how it felt from my side, but seeing is believing. How might it appear to others? Better or worse than I remembered?

I know my faults in life. I understand and appreciate exactly why I react, behave and respond in the way that I do. I'm not perfect – none of us are – but even I can see that this particular image, now static on my TV screen, tells only one tale. The close-up is dominated by two faces: mine and Brett's. Those faces are inches away from each other, our gaze locked, and I definitely remember bated breath ... The TV image doesn't portray such sensory involvement for the audience, but I'm certain they get a clear picture.

I reach for the small cushion and bring it high before my face to watch for the final time. This time I'll imagine it's not me, it's some other thirty-nine year old on a date in the art gallery.

I press play on the remote control: slow motion.

I peer from behind the cushion as both faces move closer, automatically tilt and their lips connect. Eyes close. I watch his hand gently come into shot, sliding up and around her neck before disappearing into her hairline. I watch their noses bump and their eyes remain firmly closed as their mouths passionately enjoy each other.

After fifty-six seconds of kissing, I hit the pause button.

I don't need to witness the next ten seconds. I've seen it enough times.

If I saw that couple together kissing in real life, I know what I'd be thinking, assuming and predicting. And yeah, if I were my mum, I'd probably be buying a wedding hat too!

I hastily depress the remote's off button and the TV screen goes black.

It's late and I'm tired.

I need sleep.

I need to think what I'll say tomorrow during the feedback session. I want to be honest. I need to be true to myself but I don't want to jump the gun and assume anything. I need to plan my answer carefully, play it coy, if necessary, because tomorrow I can pretty much guarantee that the new presenter – and I pray they'll be kind to me – is going to demand I answer one important question. Having experienced the best date of my life with a great guy, who was interesting, humorous and my version of gorgeous, I will be asked what I thought when Brett dramatically and unceremoniously pulled away from our romantic clinch.

There is no avoiding the question: Jez's camera crew captured every second of my bewildered look, my utter confusion and aftershock in close-up. I don't need to see that clip ever again to confirm it looked as bad on the screen as it felt for me in real time.

Carmen

I wait up until eleven o'clock. I've cleaned the kitchen, vacuumed the lounge and am dressed in my pjs, awaiting Elliot's call.

I don't know whether to be angry or not, given that I spoke to Monty at seven o'clock; couldn't Elliot have phoned or texted me from the car as they drove to Cardiff? Wouldn't that have been the sensible option, especially as he couldn't drive, and then he'd be free all evening to down a skinful of scotch?

Whilst cleaning the kitchen, I'd spied Elliot's favourite tipple for the second time this week and refrained from pouring myself a large glass – just because he was having a skinful didn't mean I had to. Anyway, one sip of whisky would undo all my good work drinking three pints of water to aid the benefits of my earlier massage.

Finally, at 11.23, my mobile rings.

Elliot.

I wish I could ignore it. Wish I was out enjoying myself and surrounded by noisy friends, but I'm not. I'm sitting on the sofa staring at my mobile screen.

'Yes?' My voice has an edge that I can't hide.

'Babe!'

He's drunk.

'Hi, Elliot, how are you?'

'Fine. Fine.'

'Fine? How can you be fine with a knackered ligament?'

'Torn, that's all. Six weeks in a knee brace and maybe some physio sessions but I'll be fine. Just fine. Fine.'

He's definitely had a skinful.

'Can you walk on it?'

'Yeah, I've got crutches. I'm a bit slow but walking is no problem.'

'What about Paris?'

'I'll be fine.'

'Did they give you painkillers?'

'Oh yeah, I've had two lots of those.'

'You've had two lots did you say?'

'Yes. Two. Lots. It doesn't hurt. I'm fine.'

I bet you are, mixing four painkillers and a belly full of scotch.

'Elliot, have you eaten?'

'We're just going for a curry now . . . then bed.'

It gets better and better.

'Can you put Monty on, please?'

'Monty . . . Carmen wants to speak to you. No, I'm not bloody joking. Here she is.'

'Hello?'

'Monty . . . can you make sure—'

'No, no, no, no, no, no way, lady . . . I'm not his babysitter. Bye, Carmen!'

The line goes silent.

Then I hear the noisy handover of the mobile.

'Hello . . . Monty said he's not doing anything you say, so I'm back.'

'Elliot, will you make sure you drink plenty of water and eat some food before bed, please?'

'Yep. I'll do that. Monty's calling me, I need to go now. Bye. Bye. Love ya. Bye.'

He ends the call before I say 'bye'.

I cradle my mobile to my chest and whisper 'bye', for all the good it does. Then I dowse the lounge lights and make my way up to bed, with Maisy, our border collie, lying on top of the duvet for company.

Chapter Eight

Thursday 27 February

Dana

'Hi, Mum . . . I know, I know . . . I wasn't ignoring you but, yeah, I was,' I say, as I drag an unwilling Luke over their doorstep.

'I couldn't believe what I was watching . . . One minute he was laughing and joking about the artwork, being so tender towards you . . . and I just knew he was going to kiss you at the end of the date, but I'm shocked that he pulled away like that. Your father's not impressed either.'

Oh great! That's one conversation I can't wait to have.

I drop Luke's school rucksack and bundle him out of his coat, draping it on the bottom stair.

'Grandpops?' slurs Luke, pointing upstairs.

'Yes, Grandpops is upstairs having a shower,' answers Mum, as I make my way through to their lounge.

'Up?' asks Luke of his nana.

I settle in the armchair as Luke nosily bolts up the stairs to hammer on the bathroom door.

'I wonder what he'll say in his feedback . . . He'll have to explain himself,' says Mum, entering the lounge.

'Not necessarily, Mum ... he might choose not to. I don't know how to play it. Should I be honest and explain that I was really enjoying myself all evening? Or do I act a bit coy until someone hints to me what Brett has said? I'll look a fool if I wear my heart on my sleeve and he says he didn't like me.'

Mum shakes her head and settles on the sofa with her morning tea.

'He seemed so lovely too ... I kept saying to your dad, "The experts have got it right this time, that's for sure."'

I envisage her remarks as the programme aired, my dad nodding along or keeping schtum as he saw fit. I bet her voice hit that high-speed, shrill tone; it always does when she gets excited. And last night, I bet she was on top form watching us move around the empty gallery enjoying the art, viewing the sculptures and mosaic pottery. Watching her now, despite the early-morning start, I can see remnants of excitement still lingering under the surface, just wanting good news for the couple she watched last night on TV. She's bubbling, she's alive and I know she's willing that, somewhere, not so far from here, a certain young man is feeling slightly annoyed by his own actions and has a decent explanation for his unceremonious end to what started as a delightfully engaging kiss.

'Sorry that I've had to ask you to take him in today, but I need to get a flower order out by ten o'clock and if I had to do the school run in between making up the arrangement and its delivery, I'd be cutting it fine for my feedback slot,' I say apologetically. 'Plus I've a small table arrangement to make for a meeting I have tomorrow.' I feel I've overstepped the mark this week. I know my parents are happy to have Luke every minute of the day, and Luke loves being here just as much as they love having him, but even I can see how some might call me a poor excuse for a mother. I can almost hear the chummy-mummies slating me at the school gate and even on social media: 'I don't know who she thinks she is!', 'Fancy gallivanting off to Edinburgh for a date and leaving your son behind!' and even 'I can't see what's so special about her anyway, she's a plain Jane in all respects!'

I sink into my mother's three-piece suite at the very thought of their comments.

Maybe I should walk Luke to school purely to save face with the school-gate crowd.

'Dana?'

Dad's voice makes me jump. I look up to see him in a coordinated outfit of claret M&S sweater and trousers, his hair slightly wet but combed back. Luke is hanging on to his right hand.

'Sorry, did you say something, Dad?'

'Just be careful . . . You don't know how the production team are cutting and editing and what story they are weaving, OK?'

I nod.

He's got a point. I can imagine if last night's heroine hadn't been me, I would have been tuned in and hanging on to every word as the couple got closer and closer in the reality of four hours rather than the fleeting TV experience edited to perfection and timed to precisely one hour. I also know that I'd have jumped from the sofa screaming in frustration as Brett pulled away from that final clinch.

I sink lower into their sofa.

Dad sits in his armchair, pulls Luke on to his lap and they settle to watch the morning news.

And today I'd be at the office water-cooler analysing every move he had made and she had made in last night's episode. I can imagine coffee breaks up and down the nation filled with comments about last night's events. Are you supporting Team

Brett or Team Alex? Which is exactly what TV producers want for good ratings: audience chatter, forum discussion and drama sells TV.

The very thought makes me cringe just a little bit more.

'Right, I've got work to do so I need to dash. Luke, come and give me a two-hand love.' I bend down as Luke dashes from Grandpops's lap to swing both his hands around my neck and snuggle into my cheek before delivering a wet kiss. I squeeze his little body tightly into mine, slightly tighter than usual if that's possible.

'Bye, my darling. Be a good boy and I'll be back before bedtime,' I say, reluctantly releasing him and straightening his glasses.

Luke hastily nods before returning to my dad's lap. My guilt about leaving him this week means very little to Luke, whilst weighing heavy in my heart. I'm probably trying to convince myself that I'm doing the right thing, that I'm not a negligent parent for desiring change and an additional adult to join our life. Maybe my guilt relates purely to the intrusive method chosen on a lonely Friday Valentine's night after one too many glasses of cheap wine.

'Good morning. I have a flower delivery for Mrs Edith Regis,' I announce, placing the freshly made arrangement on to the reception desk at the Golden Years Retirement Home.

'She'll love those ... She's ninety-seven today,' says the matron-like woman manning reception.

I smile. This is when my job brings true satisfaction, knowing that I've brightened someone's day with my handiwork – and provided her granddaughter with as much delight, knowing that her birthday idea came to fruition after just one phone call.

'Could you sign here please?' I offer my clipboard and pen

to the receptionist and she duly delivers a scribble. It isn't much proof should I ever get a complaint about non-delivery, but it's good enough for me and my reputation. She returns the clipboard and pen to me and then stares.

'Oh, it's you!'

'Sorry?'

'You, Dana from off the telly . . . I thought it was going very well last night, and then he pulled away so horribly at the end of the kiss . . . What was all that about?'

I am lost for words.

This is the last thing I expected on my deliveries. Was that totally naïve? Have I unknowingly opened Pandora's box? I've browsed the net and squirmed whilst viewing the hashtag #TeamAlex and #TeamBrett. Surely the audience can separate the show from my daily life? It's only Thursday; how much bigger can this get by finale night?

'Would you be interested in seeing Brett again if he could explain himself?' she asks quickly before I have chance to gather my thoughts together.

'I, errr, well . . . I'm not . . . Oh, I haven't even thought about it,' I stammer, knowing full well I'd thought of little else since I left the gallery. En-route to the airport, Tamzin had tried to coax an answer from me. During the gate check-in, Jez had wandered about looking mournful and scowling; gone was the thumbs-up sign which he'd so eagerly given. And now a total stranger is asking for an update and I don't have one to give.

'Never mind, lovey . . . there's plenty more fish in the sea,' she says, patting my hand.

'Thank you, I think. Bye.' I beat a retreat from the retirement home, knowing I'll be facing similar questions in my feedback session in the studio.

Polly

'I'll do it,' I say, taking the kettle from her. 'Sit down, tell me how you are.'

For the first time in her life, Helen acquiesces to my request and goes to sit at her kitchen table. I fuss about the familiar yet unfamiliar kitchen, caring for my sister, doing the only thing I can: making her tea. Helen sits in her towelling housecoat, her hair unwashed and her face bare of the basic make-up which she applies every day of her life. Not today.

She's silent. Watching. Mindful that'll I jump on every detail she offers and question everything she doesn't mention.

For the first time, there's a vast expanse of silence between us. Every other occasion of our lives, our family bond, our memories, our sisterhood has paved the way to here, but right now she looks like a stranger, whilst I feel like one.

As I stir her tea, I notice the grime around the mixer tap, the speckles of grease layered on the cooker top and the tacky rings inside the fridge door. This isn't the kitchen of my sister but the kitchen of a woman whose focus has been elsewhere for some time.

Helen doesn't answer me.

Not until I settle opposite her.

'Lost. I don't expect anyone to have the answers or to able to make it right for me, but it's as you said, I just need people to hold my hand while this darkness lingers.'

'Oh, Helen.' My hand reaches across the table for hers. She has such slender hands, pale and fragile – so different to mine. I've never noticed before.

I wait.

'He's having an affair . . . She turned up on our doorstep on the Sunday night and had the gall to announce his intention of leaving me . . . I feel so stupid. So damned stupid for not seeing, not suspecting what he was up to . . . for so fecking long.'

My innards twist with anger on her behalf. It's a good job Marc is out food shopping.

'Four years!' Her faces grimaces, forcing home her pain and disbelief. 'Four fecking years of lies, deceit and going behind my back with some slip of a thing from work . . . What a fool I've been.'

'I always saw you two being so happy, so close; you're always so tactile with each other . . .'

'Oh yeah, he kept up the pretence despite his dalliance elsewhere . . . making a mockery of our marriage. Erica was just three when they started seeing each other.'

I'm lost. I have no advice to give. All I can do is listen and make tea.

'You had the right idea in never getting married, Polly. What's the bloody point when one person decides to throw it all away for the sake of a cheap affair?'

'Helen, I'm no expert, believe me. We've had our ups and downs over the years but I know Fraser would never stray – we both know the expectations of the other and what would break us.'

'*Trust*, that's what you and Fraser's relationship is built upon – ours obviously isn't. Did we think that a day in church was enough to cement us as one? Yet it's slipped away, despite our vows.' She sips her tea and looks at me over the rim of the mug.

'And now?'

She shrugs. 'Who knows . . . I don't. It's a twisted waiting game while Marc decides what he's going to do . . . Apparently he's "not sure".'

'Even after ... ?' I can't bring myself to say it, yet I can't ignore the elephant in the room.

'Exactly.' Her eyes well and hot angry tears begin to flow. 'He was with her on Monday night – that's been their routine – and I was left here alone but for the girls and I just thought, what's the point? He wants her, she wants him, so why not do what you want ...'

'But the girls?'

'I've let them down, Polly ... I've told them I'm unhappy and have stomach ache but they're not stupid. Evie's already asking questions and Erica's become so clingy – and I've caused that, Polly. Me, their mother, the one person they should be able to rely upon tried to bail out on life because ...' She falters. 'For what ... I couldn't take the hurt? The upset? I didn't love them enough?'

'Helen, stop ... In that moment you had no answers, you weren't thinking straight and your pain simply overwhelmed you ... you did what you did, as I see it, as a cry for help. And whatever Marc decides to do, we're all here for you and your girls. Deep down, you know that; you don't need me to remind you. You're my sister, my only sister, and we've only got each other, Helen.'

I see my words reflected in her eyes, as she continues to cry and stare helplessly across the table.

Carmen

'You look beautiful, Michelle,' I say to her full-length reflection as I zip up her bridal gown. 'Monty's going to be knocked sideways when he sees you walking down the aisle.'

'I hope so ... The year and a half of wedding planning flew

by but these last few weeks are definitely dragging. And there's still nine days to go!'

'But you're under the double-digit countdown,' I reply, stepping away to allow her to view her gown to its full effect without me hovering in the background.

Michelle chose well at her initial appointment twelve months ago – she knew exactly what she wanted. A simple, figure-hugging gown, which skims her waist and hips before floating gently into an A-line skirt to flick at the hemline as she walks. She refused any bling detailing on the bodice, ignored the crystal droplet option, which she rightly believed would distract from her deep blue eyes. Instead, her wedding gown focuses upon her as a woman and a bride. She looks breathtaking. I feel honoured she chose my shop for her appointments and, ultimately, her purchase. I did remove the majority of my mark-up – mates' rates.

'Are you ready?' I ask, knowing her mother, sisters and matron of honour, Nicole, are patiently waiting on or around our chaise longue.

'Yep, let's show them.'

'Walk over towards the large gilt mirror and I'll help you to step up on to the platform,' I instruct, ensuring she knows her route through the boutique to present her gown in the best possible manner.

I position my hand high upon the edge of the curtain and quickly draw it back.

A gasp of excitement fills the boutique, quickly followed by a gush of happy tears and a motherly offer of tissues from Trish.

Michelle gracefully glides across the floor, her hemline flicking with each step. I dart ahead to be at the gilt mirror and platform ahead of her to offer her a helping hand.

Once in position, I crouch down to smooth her hemline and step back to admire our bride-to-be.

Stunning. Simply stunning.

Everybody in her party is in tears, some grapple with camera phones, capturing the moment under the boutique's spotlights, which highlight and enhance every shimmer in the fabric.

'Thank you,' she mouths to me, admiring her gown.

'My pleasure,' I mouth in reply.

And I truly mean it. It will feel strange attending her wedding after she's purchased the dress from my boutique; I never get invited usually, but this is somewhat different given that Monty and Elliot are such close friends.

I am truly delighted for her. Michelle's gown and overall look matches her dreams and that is visible to everyone present. This is the moment she's been waiting for and of which she deserves to enjoy every moment.

'Shall we crack open another bottle?' I say cheerily to the gathered crowd. I don't wait for an answer but leave Trish and Anna to hold the fort while I escape to the kitchenette.

I don't usually open the best; I have a policy that the bubbles are Prosecco unless there is a very special occasion, when I have been known to ask for the champagne to be opened. This is one such occasion. I am not prepared to skimp on my friends. It's not in my nature and I hope it never will be.

I open the chiller cabinet, ignore the nearest bottle of Moet and grab the Bollinger.

My fingers nimbly remove the gold foil, release the cork's wire cage and deftly twist the bottom of the bottle to release the steadfast cork. I wrap a white cloth around the neck and re-enter the boutique.

The excitement has calmed a little, the tears are dry and the ladies give a little cheer at the new arrival. I hastily usher Trish to collect three additional clean glasses for us staff, there's no reason why we can't enjoy a small one with our guests.

'Say when,' I say, pouring Michelle a glass carefully: the last thing I want is a disaster while she's still wearing her gown. I tip the bottle gingerly, the bubbles flow as Michelle indicates enough as I near the lip of the glass flute. I quickly pour for each of her ladies and then a small amount for each of us.

'Michelle, it has been an honour to source your dream gown and we all wish you the very, very best of luck and future happiness in your marriage. To Michelle and Monty!' I say, and the gathering chorus, 'Michelle and Monty!' before we each smile and take a sip.

The bubbles dance on my tongue. It seems an age since we shared a celebration in the boutique but how could I not, given the closeness of our connection?

Anna grimaces at her second sip and passes on drinking any more of her bubbles. Trish swallows hers as if there is no tomorrow. I stand and sip, savouring the moment. This time next week, this could be me celebrating my engagement to Elliot. I can't imagine what it will feel like having that ring on my finger twenty-four hours a day, seven days a week, and knowing that our next job will be to decide on a date, book a local church, choose bridesmaids and groomsmen, write the order of service, reserve a horse and carriage, invites, flowers, groomsmen's suits, bridesmaids' dresses, wedding cake and decorations, reception music, favours, honeymoon destinations – wow, so much to organise!

Suddenly I feel a little overwhelmed.

I give a small giggle at myself. Here I am feeling overwhelmed at the thought of organising all that and yet I'm part of the industry. How must another bride-to-be feel as an outsider? Though this just adds more weight to my new wedding centre venture, bringing all the necessary services together to aid a couple's planning.

I exhale.

The champagne tastes good, the company look so happy and I am on the verge of my own exciting adventure, well ... as soon as Saturday comes and I pop the big question.

I watch Michelle. She's radiant, the happiest I have ever seen her.

Inside my heart quietly aches. This is what *I* want. I want that glow at the prospect of marrying Elliot, I want the excitement of knowing our day is around the corner, just waiting to happen.

I have never been jealous in my life before, but in this moment, watching Michelle in her stunning gown, I can admit ... I'm a tad jealous of her situation.

'Doesn't she look gorgeous?' sighs Nicole, handing me her empty glass once all the champagne has gone.

'So elegant and so divine,' I say, placing the empty flute glass on the tray. 'Just nine days to go and Monty will know he's such a lucky guy.'

Nicole doesn't answer but looks at me sharply.

Not a word is said but something just happened. Something changed in her demeanour. Does she think that by praising Monty I'm knocking her Steve? Or even Elliot?

'Not that I'm saying Steve wasn't a lucky man when he married you,' I add quickly, just in case I've caused offence.

Nicole smiles, but I can see it is a forced, unnatural smile which goes no higher than her lips.

What the hell?

Nicole continues to watch me. I quickly replay the conversation in my head. I can't see what I've said to instantly quieten her spirit.

'Are you OK?' I ask, unsure whether I should apologise or quit the conversation.

'Me?' She seems shocked by my question.

'Yeah.'

'Fine. You?'

'Yeah.'

Silence.

I want to move away, take the tray back to the kitchenette where I know Trish is waiting to load the dishwasher, but I'm fixed to the spot.

Something is wrong. Very wrong. I can sense it in Nicole's face. I can almost read it in her eyes.

'Carmen!'

Michelle's voice brings me from my moment.

'Can I take this off now?' she asks, indicating the changing area.

'Of course, yes ... Anna, could you take this tray through to Trish, please?'

I take one swift glance in Nicole's direction, she's dropped her head and is staring at the floor. She doesn't look comfortable.

I follow Michelle to the changing area and assist in unzipping her gown.

What the hell is wrong with Nicole?

'I can't wait now; the wedding seems so real now that I've seen the actual dress in which I'll be married.'

'Is Nicole OK?' I ask carelessly, rudely interrupting her moment.

'Nicole? Yeah! She's fine.'

I give a smile to acknowledge her answer but I'm not convinced.

I can sense Michelle watching me, so I try to hold my smile in place until I have her gown removed and safely stashed into its protective cover, and then I can leave her to dress in peace while I rejoin the family group.

I carry the dress in the billowing protective cover in both arms, like a bride being carried high over the threshold, and exit into the boutique area. My smile is firmly in place as I pass the females readying themselves to leave as soon as their bride-to-be joins them, and carry the bridal gown over to lay it upon the chaise longue.

I'm so conscious that all eyes are on me. I avoid glancing towards Nicole.

'Ladies, it has been an absolute pleasure and I can't wait to see you all on the seventh of March – we will have such a fabulous day. Let's hope the weather is kind for the photographs,' I say, giving my voice a giggly undertone.

Trish and Anna are still in the kitchenette, loading the dishwasher.

For the next five minutes, I brightly bid them all goodbye, repeat my sentiments that the bride-to-be looked fabulous and eventually herd them towards the door. I notice that Nicole's energy is muted.

We linger uncomfortably at a goodbye peck. We don't hug, as Michelle and I did.

I wave and smile as the door closes and, as soon as they've walked the length of the bay window, my mask falls.

I'm confused. What just happened? Did I say something wrong? Did she say something wrong but I didn't catch what she'd said? Was she embarrassed by a remark? Where was our hug and why did kissing Nicole's cheek feel awkward?

'Carmen?'

Her voice catches me off-guard.

Nicole's standing inside the closed door, her hand clutching the handle, her expression pained, brow crumpled, eyes peering at me.

'Nicole!' Instantly my smile returns on seeing her direct gaze.

'Carmen ... I'm sorry but ... well, just ... Carmen, can I have a word?'

'With me?' I'm apprehensive; I can hear it in my voice. My smile disappears.

Nicole walks to the chaise longue and slowly sits down, her handbag cradled upon her lap like a barrier to hide behind.

I don't hesitate, but sit down on the platform in front of the large gilt mirror used just moments ago to showcase our friend's bridal gown.

I wait.

Nicole can't meet my gaze.

'I'm so sorry. I don't know how to say this but I think it needs to be said ...'

I nod, oblivious to her intentions or meaning but, yes, whatever needs saying needs to be said. And said as soon as possible, given the heightened rate of my heartbeat.

My eyes must be pleading in expression.

My body is wound like a tight spring, held static for fear of what the next few minutes may bring.

'Carmen ... you've known me for a fair while now and I hate to be the one to say – Steve is going to kill me for even mentioning it. I promised I wouldn't but, hey, I would want to be told ...'

'Nicole, please,' I urge, unable to bear her commentary as it delays whatever is to follow.

Nicole straightens her back as she continues, 'Carmen, Steve and the boys think that Elliot is seeing someone.'

I burst out laughing. A deep, throaty laugh that uses every muscle in my body from the abdominals up to my face.

'Yes, me!' I stupidly retort, laughing wide-mouthed and with eyes shut tight.

I suddenly hear my own words lift into the air around

me. I snap open my eyes and see the look of horror on Nicole's face.

She slowly wets her lip, swallows and lowers her head.

I cease laughing.

The boutique air has become thick, rancid and heavy.

I can't breathe. I can't speak. I can't sit here staring at the top of her lowered head. Waiting for the next line, another snippet of information. The name. The reasons. The theory. The guys' remarks whispered in confidence to wives. Their unspoken fears that their guy will follow suit. Their promise not to tell. Their promise to quash any remark made to them. Their startled look of horror when discussing it with another female on Saturday night in the Cross Keys, especially when the woman in question rushes to join their secret conversation and neither of you knows what to say, do or how to smooth over the awkward situation.

I am proposing on Saturday, he is away for three days, I have a speech to write, a new business venture to launch tomorrow morning and now, this.

'Is Steve away on the stag do?' I ask softly.

Nicole nods.

'So *that* is actually happening . . . for a minute there I thought I'd been duped by a late-night phone from a couple of drunken men about a torn ligament and some painkillers,' I say. 'Nicole, I'm sorry but you're going to have to explain why the guys think as they do. I want to know – you can tell Steve I dragged it from you.'

Nicole swallows deeply and nods.

She spends the next ten minutes explaining that Monty, Andrew and Steve have noticed comments he's made about other woman during nights out in bars. The guys are taken back as he never used to comment, never openly stared. In recent months he's ventured over for a chat, despite the other three advising him not to.

I realign my expression from shock to a noncommittal smile.

I listen carefully, absorbing every detail and trying to remain calm.

'Has anyone seen him go off with any of these women?'

Nicole shakes her head.

'Witnessed any uncompromising acts?'

'No.'

'But you all know?'

Nicole nods.

'Even Hannah?'

Nicole gives another nod.

'Well, that's bloody great news! And, what am I expected to do with such information while they enjoy their bloody stag do in Cardiff?'

'Carmen, I am so sorry. When you said about Monty being such a lucky guy . . . it reminded me of a comment Steve made about Elliot being lucky to have you. I guess I reacted and you spotted it . . . I'm so very sorry to be the one.'

'Steve thinks Elliot is lucky?'

Nicole nods, closing her eyes as if pained.

'So, let me get this straight before . . . well, before I lose the plot. There's been lot of smutty offhand comments, lots of flirting, shall we call it? But no actual evidence?'

'None.'

'And Monty, Andrew and Steve all think the same?'

'Yep, Magoo's been kept busy with the baby so hasn't caught up with them lately.'

I wasn't about to show my ignorance and state that the guys hadn't met up in ages, months, in fact, because clearly that wasn't true. Elliot had lied to me.

I lean back, stretching my arms behind me to support my weight. I look at the ceiling filled with tiny halogen bulbs, then lower my eyes to take in the rich burgundy of the chaise longue, the tiara display sparkling under the intense lights, rail upon rail of designer wedding gowns, each in its protective cover, awaiting a newly engaged woman and her dream man.

I want to cry.

I want to scream.

I want to disappear.

I don't want a mini-break to Paris.

I don't want two engagements rings sitting inside my bedside cabinet drawer.

I have no idea when Elliott could be having an affair; to my knowledge he goes to the gym every Thursday night and Saturday when he's not on bank duty. The rest of the week he's home watching the football, cricket, quiz shows, and asking how my day has been.

I stand, causing Nicole to flinch.

'Thank you, now I know what you and Michelle were discussing in the Cross Keys when I inadvertently walked up and joined you, having escaped Hannah,' I say as cheerily as I can.

'I just didn't want to be the one to say.'

'No worries, no one need know . . . it's OK, Nicole.'

'Are you OK?'

'I am absolutely fine,' I say, walking towards the boutique's door.

Nicole scurries to join me; the relief etched on her face is clear.

'See you soon, Carmen.'

'In nine days, I believe.'

Nicole's mouth twitches in surprise but she decides against saying anything as the door closes.

I stand staring at the busy street through the door's glazed panel. My hands are shaking, nerves twitching me towards nausea and my mind is spinning with a montage of city sight-seeing. Outside, the world and his wife simply carry on as before, mothers with pushchairs, elderly ladies with tartan shopping trolleys and gentlemen with worn walking canes – everyone looks so happy and content whilst I've taken delivery of bad news. Part of me wants to step outside, into the chilly but bright day, amidst the cream-coloured stonework, and ask what they're playing at, passing this way when I feel as I feel. Could they possibly take a detour along a neighbouring street while I get my act together.

'Are you OK?' comes a gentle voice.

I daren't turn round. I can't face Trish.

I cough.

'Could you give Anna some petty cash and send her out to buy milk, sugar and coffee . . . I could do with a chat,' I say calmly.

'Did you hear?' I ask, slumping into my chair in the rear office as soon as Anna is safely out on her errand.

Trish settles on the edge of the desk and nods.

'Now what am I to do?'

'Do you believe them?'

I shrug.

'Carmen, you need to address this before anything else . . . Do you believe them?'

'My head is saying no way, he's always at home with me. Yes, he's out at the gym a few times a week but, more importantly, when does he meet up with the guys?'

'So it's not a regular haunt they drink at every week?'

'No! In fact, that was a reason we all went the pub on

Saturday night, because it had allegedly been such a long time since the guys had been together.'

'Unless that was a total lie.'

'Yep, exactly.'

'Does he definitely go the gym on Thursdays?'

'I'd say yes. I see him wash a sweaty-smelling kit when he arrives home, unless he goes drinking in shorts and a T-shirt.'

'Gym bag.'

'Yeah.'

Trish raises her eyebrows.

'Nah. He's not a fifteen-year-old girl heading for school with a change of shoes and a shorter skirt safely hidden in her bag.'

'Just saying.'

'He has days off when he's worked a Saturday shift ... to balance his hours on the rota system but the other guys aren't off on those days.'

'So what it boils down to is a few too many comments about other females?'

'Yes, from what Nicole said. She reckons that nobody has seen him go home with someone else, or gone off with them in the pub, club, wherever they've been ...'

'It's just irresponsible comments then, Carmen ... men say all sorts of shite when they're drunk.'

'I bet your Terry doesn't!'

Trish smiles ruefully.

'See. I bet your Terry could get as drunk as a skunk and not eye up another female ...'

Trish sighs.

'That's what I want, Trish, that security in a relationship. I'm here, after eight years of emotion, time and effort being ploughed into a relationship with a guy who I was about to propose to and now I'm not sure if what Nicole's said is true.

Whereas you – you instantly have that secure knowledge that your Terry would never disrespect you in that way. You are his number one, his first and last thought of each day. Me, I don't have that ... because if I did, I wouldn't be questioning his actions.'

'Oh, Carmen.'

'Trish, focus on what she actually said: he's commenting about other women! That's why he hasn't committed to me after eight years, isn't it? Elliot is metaphorically still out there fishing for the right one. He's not sure it's me he wants to be with even after all we've built together. It makes sense.'

'I wouldn't listen to them, chick,' says Trish.

'How can I not? The guys have known him for a lifetime. Nicole said they're concerned, that he hasn't acted like this for years but now ...' I say, adding, 'Even the wives, including Michelle, are obviously shocked by it because I caught them discussing it in the pub last Saturday night. And today I made one comment and there was a flicker of something across Nicole's face. I saw her thoughts register in her expression and then it was gone ... but she'd changed. She couldn't hide that something was wrong.'

'And now?'

'I don't know. I can hardly call him and have it out. He's probably halfway down another bottle of whisky in the middle of Wales. For all I know he might not even be with the guys anymore – Elliot might have cancelled his plans now he's damaged his knee and made off elsewhere for a couple of nights. Oh, Trish, what the hell do I do?'

'Nothing.'

I stare at her.

'Seriously, if I were you, I'd do nothing.'

'And make a right prat of myself come Saturday?'

'You won't make a prat of yourself, Carmen. Somewhere along the line there is a big misunderstanding waiting to be uncovered whether it be from the guys who claim what they've noticed or their wives who've repeated some light-hearted banter as something much more. But you, you've done nothing wrong and I suspect neither has Elliot, given what you've said.'

The boutique door flies wide open, Anna dashes in clutching a bulging shopping bag and holding a newspaper.

'Looks who's made the front page of the local paper!' squeals Anna staring in delight at the full-page image.

Dana

I'm as nervous as hell. Despite the professionals giving me the onceover in hair and make-up, I feel an absolute wreck as I perch on the studio couch.

'Dana, tell me . . . how did that kiss feel?' asks Jennifer, who has been hastily promoted from relationship and dating coach to replacement presenter for *Taking a Chance on Love*.

I hesitate and glance at the camera, which I know is zooming in on my expression, much as it had done during yesterday's final shot.

I sigh deeply.

'Oh dear, that bad?' she asks, her brow puckering slightly. 'And how did that make you feel?'

I glance from the cameraman back to Jennifer.

I really don't want to talk about this, but how do I say that without being unkind to her or appearing defensive about what happened with Brett? I'll look a right cow on national TV if I speak openly.

'You seem lost for words, honey,' she says, glancing around

for off-camera support. I notice Tamzin has moved into my peripheral line of vision. I'm not sure whether that's for my benefit or Jennifer's.

'Can I be frank?' I ask, adjusting my hemline and sitting back on the large red couch.

'Of course, of course ... that's what we always encourage when discussing relationships ... focus on being honest and building trust. There's nothing that can't be discussed, simply choose your words carefully so as not to upset or offend.'

It's two minutes into the feedback interview and already I'm bored by her textbook speak.

'Go on,' she urges, leaning forward as if that's going to ease my nerves.

'I'd prefer not to discuss the situation or Brett before I've had a chance to chat with him. I have to be honest and say I had a lovely evening, he was easy to talk to, good fun to be with and we ... well, I think we were on the same wavelength in many respects. That goodnight kiss was a little unexpected but it felt right, it felt ...'

'It looked passionate from where I was standing,' interrupts Jennifer, her eyes sparkling.

I glance up to be met with her overactive reaction to anything romantic, but I suppose that could an occupational hazard for these experts. Do they understand their chosen topic so much that it ruins their chance of finding it in life or maybe enjoying it?

'Engaging is how I'd describe it ... I know we are appearing on a TV programme but if that kiss had occurred at the end of a normal date, I'd have gone home a happy girl.'

'But the manner in which it ended, surely you can't excuse that?'

'No, I agree ... it wasn't a satisfying ending to a goodnight kiss. One minute we were kissing, Brett's hand was cradling my head, and the next moment it was fresh air on my face and a look of shock on his features. I have no explanation for why it ended that way.'

'Then he was off dashing down the staircase.'

I nod; she'd described it exactly.

'And have you spoken to Brett since?'

'No. I was told we weren't allowed to contact each other – I've followed the rules.' I keep it simple. I keep it real.

'Ah, well, here on *Taking a Chance on Love* we have spoken to Brett and . . .'

My heart is about to burst from my chest. Jennifer pulls a card from beneath her papers and begins wafting it about as she talks between me and the camera lens.

'Sadly, he expressed a desire not to comment. We did ask for an explanation of his behaviour last night. He said, and I quote, "you seemed a very lovely lady, he enjoyed his time touring the portrait gallery with you and found you very humorous and down to earth. Just the kind of woman he wishes to meet".' Jennifer reads the details from the card and then watches me intently, wanting a reaction, I guess.

I'm lost. Brett enjoyed himself. He liked me. We had a good laugh together. We had plenty of things in common and he went in for the goodnight kiss – yet he broke it off as if my skin had scalded him.

I stare into space, my mind whirring with the details.

'Now, we're very sorry, Dana, but we can't force Brett to discuss his behaviour. It would be very interesting to find out why he did what he did but we aren't at liberty to dig deeper or demand an explanation. Is there anything you'd like to say on hearing his statement?'

I can see Tamzin and Jez dashing around behind the camera

crew. Are they annoyed that I'm not dishing the dirt for their TV audience or have they truly got my best interests at heart? I'm really not sure. They seem genuine enough, but do good people make for high ratings? I fear not.

'I'm not bitter. He seems a nice guy. I don't understand why last night didn't end on a more conventional note but none of us are perfect. We each have our issues, don't we?'

'Dana, that is very kind of you to try to see it from his point of view, it really is, because it was clear for us all to see you were shocked. Let's take another look . . .'

I don't have time to catch my breath before a rerun shows our passionate kiss and the awful ending. In the studio, I look away just in time and watch the production team's faces as Brett swiftly pulls away with lightning speed and the clip freezes on a close-up of my shocked expression.

Jennifer leans forward and strokes my knee, as if that helps my situation.

'My heart goes out to you, Dana – it really does. Last night, we all thought today's feedback session would be filled with lots of juicy talk about potential second dates on Saturday night. But Brett's behaviour and subsequent "no comment" has really dampened the mood in the studio. So, my question for you is, is there any chance that you and Brett will be seeing each other again?'

'I doubt it. I haven't any contact details so unless the programme supply them off-air, I have no means of contacting Brett.'

'He might be watching right now. Is there anything you'd like to say on-air?'

I shake my head.

I see the disappoint dawn upon her face. It isn't the answer she wants.

'OK, let's put that sad subject to bed . . . So, Dana, how are you feeling about tomorrow's date, date number three?'

I sit up straight; maybe talking about tomorrow is a safer topic.

'I'm looking forward to meeting Male C. I know nothing about him and hope that we can spend an enjoyable date in each other's company without any disasters.'

'Absolutely. This is what dating is all about, Dana. I tell my clients all the time . . . dating isn't easy but focus on having fun, being positive and, above all, stay safe!'

I smile and nod. There doesn't seem much else for me to do but sit this one out. This studio session will be over before I know it and then I'll be speeding my way back to my little boy.

'Any thoughts about the kind of date you're hoping for? So far this week you've had a dinner date and the unfortunate date in a gallery . . . what's next, I wonder?'

'The gallery night was as enjoyable as the dinner date, it was only the ending that went badly . . . but I'm happy to go along with his choice of date.'

'Would skydiving be OK?'

I shrug.

'Deep-sea diving?'

'I'm not so keen on water but I'll play along.'

'OK, Dana, we are going to have to call it a day there and we all wait with bated breath for your third and final date tomorrow night with Male C. Thank you for joining me on the sofa of *Taking a Chance on Love* and let's hope that when I next speak to you, Dana, you too could be taking a chance on love!'

I give a weak smile, aware that the camera must be focused upon my reaction to her cheesy lines and eagerness for a romance to blossom.

I remain seated and smiling until Jez signals that the camera has stopped rolling.

'Nice one, Dana. You were more open and honest during that session. I wish you all the best for tomorrow night. Personally, I think this guy is the one for you!' whispers Jennifer, as the techies remove the microphone from my blouse.

I give her a polite smile. I'm not holding my breath that the outcome of this date will be any different from the previous two. Alex was nice, Brett was gorgeous, but still I'm no further forward in taking a chance on love.

Polly

'And?' asks Fraser, stirring the gravy while I dish up the cooked vegetables.

'She's not sure if he'll be coming because he can't make up his bloody mind what he wants to do! Can you believe it?'

'No, I can't. What's wrong with the man? He nearly lost his wife and he's "thinking it over"? He needs a kick up the arse.'

I pile sweetcorn on to Cody's plate and the words spill out without thinking.

'Have you ever thought of ... you know ... having an affair?'

'Polly, no! I bloody haven't ... Don't you start questioning our life. We're solid, love.'

I glance around, giving him a smile. He knows me well enough. It would kill me to lose him to another woman, the man I've grown up with, the man I have created everything with, shared my son with, and ...

I swallow quickly, as the second spoon of sweetcorn blurs amidst my tears and I spill it across the countertop.

'Hey, hey, hey ... don't you start upsetting yourself,' says Fraser, his arms circling my shoulders. 'You've always said that a marriage certificate is a piece of paper and, as proven, it hasn't kept them together. We are just fine. Always have been, always will be.'

'But if they split up, it makes a mockery of everything.'

'Hang on, who says their marriage is the blueprint for everyone else on this planet? Look at your parents ... twenty-six years together and they still divorced ... people change, people choose different paths ... decide on different futures. Us ... we want the same so, here we are.'

'And what if one day we want different things?'

'When that day comes, we'll decide what to do,' he says hugging me tight, resting his chin on my shoulder. 'But until then, my lovely, you are stuck with me.'

'I wouldn't want it any other way.' I wipe my face on my sleeve before turning back to the sweetcorn.

'Good to hear it ... now, you finish dishing up and I'll call Cody from upstairs.' Fraser roughly plants a kiss on the back of my head before peeling himself away from my frame to call Cody.

'I said, Dad, what can I do?' I tell them both, as Fraser and Cody sit open-mouthed, staring at me across the dinner table. 'I can't collect Fido's shorn hair and glue it back into place, can I?'

'You could but he'd look ridiculous and the RSPCA would be in touch,' laughs Fraser.

'I swear he thinks I can mend this mistake. Dad's said he's not going to walk the dog until his coat grows back!'

'I hope he doesn't think you're going to do the daily honours whilst that happens,' says Fraser in disgust.

'He'll have to buy Fido a little tartan coat and cover him up, or take him out after dark,' laughs Cody.

'Or you can offer to do it so your mother doesn't end up lapping the estate.'

'Dad! I haven't got time to walk Fido ... but I'll shave all the bobbles off if he wants with my electric shaver.'

'Good, go and offer your services to please your grandad,' says Fraser, thumbing for Cody to go and do. 'Go on!'

Cody saunters off into the lounge to phone.

'If you think that was bad, you should have collected your mother,' he says, as soon as we're alone.

I close my eyes; I'd forgotten to ask.

'I waited for ten minutes outside on the street before venturing up the staircase. I thought it best I go and find her in case she'd forgotten and had already left. Oh, how I wish she had.'

I stare as his face cracks into a smirk.

'Never before have I seen an entire room of older people all stroking and hugging each other in such an intense way. It was quite a sight.'

'In the large workout room?'

'Oh yeah, they were all lying down, arms and legs entwined, hands reaching out in every direction, stroking ...'

'Stop it! I don't want to know.'

'Derek was there, his hair slicked back and his dressing gown untied and falling open,' says Fraser, taking my hand and gently pawing it in a distinct and awkward manner. '"Pauline, tell me, Pauline, do you like my touching you like that?"'

'Oh no! Stop it, stop!' I yell, snatching my hand from his.

'I kid you not. He was puckering and wetting his lips, adjusting his ...'

'La la la la la la la!' I shove my fingers in my ears and pretend I can't hear a thing. The last thing I need this week is my mother and her 'friend' defining their relationship.

Fraser pulls my fingers away from my ears.

'I'm quite looking forward to old age if that's what you can get away with – as a young lad I'd have had my face slapped for much less.' Fraser laughs at my expression. 'I wouldn't encourage our Cody to try such moves, I'll tell you that much.'

'Tell me what?' asks Cody, rejoining us from the lounge.

'Devious Derek and your gran were busy . . . being intimate today in a class full of people – your mother would have lectured him if she'd seen his behaviour.'

'Eww!' says Cody.

'Exactly. Now, can we all stop imagining it and get on with our evening? I booked the venue earlier today, and a DJ too.'

Carmen

Trish kindly offered to conduct the current bridal appointment, supported by Anna, giving me an hour of freedom. From the back room, I can hear Trish wrapping up the appointment, having sold a chic little gown by a talented French designer, Pierre. A beautiful gown which some might say is a little plain or understated, but the cut and flow of the fabric highlight the very essence of femininity.

I am present physically but working on autopilot after this morning's news. On the outside I resemble Carmen – I've checked in the mirror several times – but on the inside I am a gibbering wreck. My mind is swimming with comments and distorted looks as my inner self does battle with itself. Questions spill and tumble about my head: do I cancel? Should I believe his mates? We've gone eight years without any solid commitment! What's Elliot said to his father? We have a twenty-five-year mortgage but no engagement ring! As one questions ends another begins and so I simply can't focus.

I pour myself a glass of Prosecco, finishing off the bottle opened for the current bride-to-be. I really shouldn't be drinking alcohol: I should be hydrating my body after last night's massage. The stress of all the planning and juggling of this week had been gently eased away last night, but this morning's remarks have put me in dire need of a second massage. I roll my aching shoulders as I stand, sipping bubbles. Was I twenty-four hours too early in attending that pampering session?

My only interruption is the bleep of my mobile phone.

Automatically reaching for my handbag, I'm instantly annoyed that a modern gadget has so much control over me. It's probably Nicole apologising for this morning and telling me not to worry. Which is a little late, given my plan for the weekend, though she doesn't know that. My mind is working overtime. Have the crowd been speculating that our relationship might not make the additional nine days to join them at Michelle and Monty's wedding service? How embarrassing is that going to be come 7 March?

I unlock the screen: a text from Elliot.

Oh my God – has Steve told him that Nicole's told me? Has Nicole told Michelle, and Michelle's confessed to Monty?'

I tap the screen to read:

I am def off on Sat – just confirmed by boss ☺

'Thank you, thank you, thank you,' I squeal, my voice cracking with emotion.

There's no kiss.

Why is there no kiss?

I take another sip of the bubbles as I ponder.

'News?" asks Trish, entering the kitchenette with a tray of dirty glasses and crumb-covered plates.

'Elliot is off on Saturday – his boss has just confirmed.'

Trish puts down her tray and begins clapping wildly.

'I'm just as excited for you, that's all,' she says in a comedic tone.

'Why didn't he phone me to say?' I mutter, my spark of instant relief fading fast.

'Because you've been as tetchy as hell all week and he won't want to hear any more of it,' suggests Trish. 'He knows you better than you think, and that was before his boss caused the complication . . . but that is all in the past now. See, I told you didn't need to worry.'

'Mmmm.'

'Carmen, this is what you've wanted all week; don't allow one remark to undermine everything you and Elliot have.'

'What's that?' asks Anna, bustling through with a handful of scrunched-up paper napkins.

'Carmen was just saying Elliot's off work on Saturday . . . so it's full steam ahead,' says Trish, loading the dishwasher.

'Phew! How good does that feel!' says Anna, wiping my forehead like a drama diva.

'Yep, phew indeed!' I say, handing my empty flute glass to Trish.

'Though now you're probably back to worrying . . . what if he says no?' continues Anna.

I stare in horror. Why would she say that? Why would she spoil my day any further? Why would another female choose to openly air the worst possible scenario while the Universe was still aligning and configuring my future? Why, oh why does the sisterhood never stick together on matters of the heart?

'Anna!' screeches Trish, picking up on my body language. 'Why would Elliot say no?'

'Well . . . he might not want . . .'

'No, no, no, no, no, no, no!' bleats Trish, her hands waving in front of Anna's face to stop the free-flowing words from pouring forth as they seem to be doing. 'She's just sorted the issue of Saturday, we don't need another drama to focus on, thank you.'

'I'm just saying that . . .'

'I hear you, sister, cheers!' I retort with attitude, suddenly unable to speak politely.

'Anna, Anna, Anna! Elliot is going to be so blown away by the magnificent wave of love and emotion felt and understood this weekend, so much so that he is going to be shouting "yes" from the Parisian rooftops before Carmen has finished giving her proposal speech. That's how I imagine it!' says Trish, as sternly as I've ever heard her talk to anyone.

Anna stares at Trish as if she has lost the plot.

'And you, Anna – how do you imagine Elliot reacting?' Trish is wearing a grimacing smile which is veering between creepy and that scary-mother 'you're in trouble when I get you home' look.

'Oh yeah, right, of course, yeah, Elliot will totally accept . . . he won't be able to wait to say yes and, yeah, will defo be saying it before you manage to finish asking him. In fact, he might say it before you even start to ask him . . . in fact, I think there's chance he might even be planning his own marriage proposal as we speak, not realising that you are about to ask him instead. Yeah, right, yeah, that!'

'You don't even know Elliot, so why would you think that?' I ask. My voice has hit ultra-flat monotone, with a defiant edge, purely for effect. I stare at Anna, without blinking, as my weekend dreams slide toward the nearest toilet.

Anna shrugs.

Trish is breathing slowly. Heavily. Nervously.

'Anna, weren't you wanting to get the satin shoe display finished before going home tonight?' she says, her eyes wide, motioning wildly for Anna to get the hell out of here.

'Oh yeah, that's right, it was my goal for today . . . Thanks for reminding me, Trish – I owe you one.' Anna quickly hurries from my presence.

The silence lingers after she's left.

When did Elliot stop putting a kiss at the end of his text messages? Did Elliot ever put a kiss on his texts? Just like last night – since when did I not say goodbye before he cut me off?

Trish gives me a weak smile as she drops the washing tablet into the dispenser.

I return her smile, though my eyes fail to engage, just my mouth.

'What if she's right?' I ask.

Trish obliges by giving me a big false smile.

'Seriously, what if he says no?'

'He won't.'

'He might.'

'He bloody well won't.'

'He could.'

'I'll kick his fecking arse for him if he does!' she says.

'Trish . . .'

'Carmen, don't go there!'

'It'll go one of two ways and I can't not talk about it.'

'Please don't. You'll ruin everything you've planned and then, come Monday, when you're dancing around this place and we're planning appointments for your gown fittings and tiaras . . . you'll be like, "what a fecking saddo was I harping on about what I'd do if . . ." Why do it to yourself?'

'Because it might happen.'

'It won't.'

'But it might!' I spit, not wanting to face reality but knowing I must. 'If he says no, will it be the end of our relationship or could we continue as we are?'

Trish lowers her eyes and purses her lips.

'Trish?'

'I can't answer that, Carmen . . . only you know what his reply will mean for your relationship.'

'But that's it . . . I don't!'

Trish rubs my forearm and gives it a squeeze.

'What would you do?'

'Carmen, you can't ask me that.'

'I bloody can!'

Trish shrugs.

'I think it would depend upon why he'd said no.'

I wait for her to explain further, but she remains silent, so I prod, 'Such as?'

'If it was because he couldn't ever see us getting married, then it would be the end. I don't think you can live with staying as you are forever. But if it was because he wasn't quite ready . . .'

'After eight years?'

'Yes, after eight years he might feel it's in your future but not right now, that's a feasible reason. Then I could continue as was before the weekend . . . but I'm not you, honey. You need to know what you want before you ask, just in case . . . though I am sure he is going to snatch your hand off at the suggestion of getting married.'

'I'm not suggesting, Trish – I'm actually asking to get married. There's no grey area here, there'll be no "if you want" or "maybe we could", not for me anyway.'

'Oh Carmen . . . I'll have my fingers crossed for you, you know that,' she replies, her eyes going all sparkly with tears.

'I know you're right. I have to think it through, and I have, sort of, but I do want to be married to Elliot. So I need to tell him that.'

Trish gives my forearm another gentle rub and a squeeze. I know she has my interests at heart. I also know that Anna is in for it when they get a quiet moment together out of my earshot.

Dana

'Mmmm, you're not going to be happy,' says Mum as she opens the front door to me just after five o'clock. Luke runs up behind her and launches himself into my open arms.

'Hello, my darling. Did you show Grandpops your practice book?'

'Noooooo,' cries Luke, his face crumpling.

Mum's shaking her head and pulling a 'leave it' expression.

'Oh, never mind. Maybe Mrs Salter was using it to show other parents how your beautiful class work is,' I say, soothing my son's disappointment.

'Don't ask,' mouths Mum.

'OK.' I pick Luke up and carry him, clinging to me koala-bear style, into the lounge. He's far too big for such a move but my back can take it – just. 'Hi, Dad, have you had a good day?'

'Oh yes, the boy's doing well at school. He's third in the class on their sticker star chart,' he says, grinning from ear to ear.

I glance at Mum. What's going on?

'Luke, down we go,' I say, depositing his chubby frame on the nearest empty sofa seat. 'Remember, little piggies have very big ears so please be careful, but can someone explain?'

'The teacher said that she wasn't happy not to have seen you in person. She said, and I quote, "Now would be a good time to discuss the situation about his learning."' My mum changes her voice to impersonate Mrs Salter, but she sounds nothing like the primary school teacher.

'What does that mean?'

'People's speech.'

'Are you joking?' I spit, flopping down on the far end of their sofa, as Luke busies himself with his cuddly elephant. 'How many times have I chased them about weekly speech therapy sessions? Four times? Five?'

'At least five from what I know; it could be more,' says Dad, changing the TV channel. 'They still aren't using the visual timetable you asked for either.'

'And did she say when those could begin?' I can't keep asking for the same things over and over and being ignored. Anyone would think I was trying to make their job harder, not easier.

'She's not sure, but they want another little girl to attend the same sessions because they feel he won't respond well to being taken out of the classroom. The little girl has a stutter – her parents are asking for weekly sessions too.'

I can't believe my ears. 'How many times do I need to explain that Luke is fairly happy with any change in routine as long as he is talked through the changes before they occur. How come they can follow this rule when it suits them, to deal with a minor disruption such as a change of seats or a new teaching assistant, but forget when it's important to his development?'

Mum pulls a face, stares at Luke, then she continues, 'Anyway, she feels that if they share the sessions then the speech therapist will have an easier time.'

'And Luke?'

Mum shrugs.

'She seems more concerned about how he'll react to being alone in the session than the advantage it'll have for his communication skills. I told her, it's his lack of control over his tongue which causes the difficulties with articulating words but he's getting better with practice, even the little bits you do at home,' explains Dad.

I'm now wondering how Dad's day could be described as good or Luke as doing well at school?

My dad is very biased with regards to his only grandchild.

'Anyway, she wants you to call her . . .'

'Call her? Why has she waited until now to ask me to call? I'll happily call Mrs Salter any day she likes, not just for parents' evening, she knows that. I've told her many, many times.'

I want to scream. Why can't people simply contact me when necessary rather than leave me bobbing along thinking everything is going well because I don't hear anything from the school? There's nothing written in his little diary: I check it every day. My security and confidence in others is suddenly stripped away. Do I need to go back to delivering him to the reception area every day purely to ensure I have contact with school staff on a daily basis? I don't want to as it singles Luke out as being different, but if I can't trust them to call me, what else can I do?

'She sent this too.' Mum hands me a brown envelope. 'It's the answers to your questions.'

I'm puzzled why Mrs Salter didn't simply discuss them with my parents. I had phoned to make them aware my email had been sent, rather than give Luke the job of handing in a letter.

Dear Ms Jones,
Thank you for your email outlining your concerns regarding Luke's progress in Year 1. Below are details which I hope answer your queries.
  What strengths have been observed in his learning?

I have noticed that Luke has grown particularly fond of painting over the last term and a half. He is able to hold the paintbrush correctly and mix colours when directed. He often has little accidents with his water pot which can cause situations in lessons with other children's work being ruined.

What weaknesses have been observed in his learning?

Luke needs practice forming his words. Some days are better than others, but sometimes I don't understand what he is saying or asking for. This can result in little accidents relating to his toileting.

I've noticed his confidence growing when interacting with other children. Have you witnessed this in the classroom?

Luke loves being with the other children. He shows an aptitude for kindness towards others and is very loving.

Is he still being a little too boisterous in the dining room when it comes to food?

Luke does have a tendency to want second or thirds at dinner time. The dinner ladies do offer him a little extra but frequently refrain as maintaining a healthy wellbeing is essential at such a tender age.

Is there any improvement in his acknowledgement of needing the toilet?

Luke will take himself to the toilet when necessary but leaves it a little late regarding passing water, which has resulted in accidents in the classroom.

Should you have any concerns, please don't hesitate to contact me.

Kindest regards,

Mrs Richards

I read the letter and have two questions to ask.

'Who is Mrs Richards?' I ask. 'And why isn't Luke's name being added to the classroom cleaning-up rota?'

'She's new to the school,' says my mum. 'She joined last term.'

Both my parents shrug and then seem astonished when I burst into tears.

'I don't bloody believe this! The answers haven't even come from the woman who teaches him every day and who I speak to regularly . . . Why haven't I been introduced to Mrs Richards?'

Luke looks at me from under his brow, his big eyes staring woefully at my tear-stained face. My tears have made him uncomfortable. I quickly wipe my eyes and bundle my son on to my lap, jiggling him up and down awkwardly.

Do the school think I don't notice when Luke returns home wearing his spare joggers with two pairs of wet school trousers wrapped in black bin liners?

'This doesn't help anyone,' I say, staring between my parents. 'What a waste of time. I am so sorry – you must feel as if I've sent you into a situation which was never going to be informative or productive in finding out about his academic progress. I might as well not have bothered.'

I reread the letter over the top of Luke's bobbing head.

'Basically, her answers outline that I am raising a very lovable child who is happy when painting, eating or playing. Though he needs to focus on handling water, whether it be his toilet habits or his painting skills. And – surprise, surprise – he needs to practise his speech with a professional speech therapist, which I've been chasing them to organise since last September! What about his lovely handwriting, which is coming along so well despite his poor dexterity skills, or his love of music or his subtraction and addition work?'

I hug my boy.

I feel fooled yet again by the school. I had thought they'd been listening to my requests and looking after Luke's needs appropriately. It now feels as if every day is a little hit and miss.

I silently vow, yet again, to demand another meeting with the school about the speech therapy.

Polly

'No way, Mum! Please say you're joking!' snaps Cody, across the dining table.

'Milo of Musicland . . . do you know him?'

'Know him! He's Lola's older brother.'

My knife and fork go down, mimicking my mood.

'Look, I had a choice of two DJs: Milo or Trev. I assumed that Trev sounds . . . well, years older than you'd have chosen, so I went with the other guy. He sounded so enthusiastic and upbeat. I'm out of my comfort zone here, Cody, and beggars can't be choosers, eh?'

'But it does mean that Lola will expect to come,' says Fraser.

'Not necessarily,' I retort.

'Oh, I bet so too,' adds Cody. 'She'll use it as an excuse, even if it's just to carry his speaker cables.'

'Do I chance him then?' I ask, looking from one to the other. 'Or contact Trev?'

'But what if the other guy isn't available?' says Fraser.

I nod smugly.

It's amazing how those who haven't done any of the booking or deciding can knock those who are left doing the donkey work for his party.

'Just leave it . . .'

'Are you sure? She's your ex, so I'll expect you to speak to her if she proves to be difficult,' says Fraser. 'Lola is not your mother's concern but yours.'

'I know.'

I'm not convinced and sense that neither is Fraser.

I snuggle up to Fraser's back once he climbs into bed and turns out the lamp.

'Thank you,' I whisper into his warm skin.

'What for?' comes the reply in the darkness.

'For everything ... for today, yesterday and possibly tomorrow.' I swallow as the enormity of my words wedge in my throat.

'Polly?'

'I mean it, Fraser ... I was watching you both today and I was so proud of the man you are, the way you conduct yourself with Cody, and your compassion for Helen, Marc and the girls ... and even my parents. You certainly do things right in life, whereas me ... I bumble along making mistakes every day and somehow get through, only to begin again the following week.'

Fraser swiftly turns within the confines of my arms, his face inches from mine, his sweet breath tickling my cheek.

'I do what I do for us, Polly. We made a deal in life; we complement each other. You amaze me each day with your endless love for others – it's you who fetches, carries and organises us all. Not me. Are you OK?'

'I'm fine, honest ... just, listening to Helen today, it makes me wonder what the future holds, that's all.'

'Come here,' he says, putting his arms around me and stroking my back. I imagine his eyes staring intently into mine as we face each other in the dark. His hands gently lift and lower, the length of stroke increasing to move from my shoulder to hip and back up. I feel the pressure intensity with each stroke, his breath quickens against my cheek and, finally, his hold draws me nearer into his chest. My hands unlink from around his torso and lift towards his jawline, as my mouth finds his.

Chapter Nine

Friday 28 February

Carmen

I arrive at the boutique an hour earlier than usual. I didn't sleep well last night, tossing and turning, for hours, mulling over everything. Lying alone in the darkness, I felt an overwhelming sadness. I missed Elliot's warmth beside me. The dog is being boarded with Trish and Terry so, I even missed Maisy snoring as she had throughout the previous night. My mind played awful tricks on me, throwing up negative dreams of Elliot hobbling around Cardiff, cheating with numerous beauties. This time in my life should be joyous; I should be creating memories which will last for a lifetime. Instead, I'm churning over suspicious comments which have no feasible evidence, worrying about in-laws and trying my hardest to create a proposal speech which is worthy of his answer without being mushy, overly sentimental or sounding a tad desperate.

And now I'm here at the boutique, dragging tables left, right and centre to create one decent-sized meeting table. I feel increasingly guilty and annoyed with myself for wasting last night by staring at the TV and not running through my speech for today one last time. Instead, I filled my time waiting for Elliot's second late-night call from Cardiff, which didn't come through until 11.17 p.m. He was drunk but sounded as if he was trying his hardest to cover it up by talking non-stop and pronouncing each word very slowly.

From past experience, I'd wager Elliot was legless, which is ironic given his injured knee.

When will I learn my lesson?

Finally, I have the tables in a formation that I'm happy with, and throw a freshly laundered linen tablecloth over them to hide the mismatched surfaces. I run about snatching wedding paraphernalia from around the boutique to decorate said table, to create something resembling a top table at a wedding without the cutlery. My attending florist is bringing a fresh centrepiece to help me and to support her home-grown business, so I need to leave plenty of room for it to be admired.

'Hello! Ohhhh, we are a busy bee!' exclaims Trish, arriving in a spritely manner.

'You can say that again,' I say, pushing chairs into place. 'I want it perfect for when they arrive. First impressions and all that.'

'Carmen, it'll be fine . . . Believe me, if I were a local business owner in this industry I'd be wanting a slice of whatever you are planning.'

'Thank you,' I say, grateful as always for her support.

'Secondly, Anna and I have the cushiest day ever without any appointments, so we have no reason to complain, my lovely. We'll be on hand if you need anything fetching at the last minute.'

'I'm as nervous as hell.'

'Why don't you let me finish off out here and you take some time to prepare – practise your spiel or whatever you've planned?'

'Would you? You are a sweetie, Trish,' I say, not waiting a second before accepting her offer.

'I know,' teases Trish, arranging the next chair whilst still wearing her coat.

'And Maisy?' I ask, eager to hear about my fur-baby.

'She wolfed her breakfast down, much to Terry's delight – they were heading out for a walk as I left,' says Trish, manoeuvring the chairs.

'Thank you so much. I'll put the kettle on first, then settle to read my notes,' I say disappearing towards the back office.

I've made coffee and delivered biscuits by the time Anna arrives, flustered and blustered by the horrible weather we've been granted today. Trish has begun polishing and tidying the display cabinets and instructs Anna to begin cleaning the many mirrors in the boutique. Trish knows I want perfection today. I have one chance to explain my new business venture and persuade others to join me.

'Is there any way I can have my laptop and extension cord set up at the far end?' I ask, thinking that I'd like to sit in front of a backdrop of beautiful wedding gowns. 'I've written tiny name cards and a seating plan, if you could lay those out too.' I disappear to practise a little more.

By eleven o'clock, I'm still nervous but ready to go. Thankfully, the majority of the invited business owners have arrived and are already clutching a glass of champagne generously poured by Trish, while Anna, eager to meet our new local celebrity, darts about collecting coats and umbrellas.

'Hi, nice to meet you ... Welcome to The Wedding Boutique ... Please help yourself,' I say over and over again to the many familiar faces. I eye my closest critic warily. Mr Knightley of Knightley's Limousines once had a similar dream of a joint venture but following a spate of unexpected issues with his chauffeur service and numerous reports of vehicle breakdowns during bookings, his reputation has plummeted. His misfortune has bolstered bookings for the horse-and-carriage lady. I've learnt from experience that in this industry everything moves in phases and fashions: you need to keep your finger on the pulse and move with the times – which is the road to success on which my proposal rides.

By ten past we are all seated and it's down to business. I hate to stand and speak before the gathered group but needs must.

'Thank you so much for coming here today. As you all know, I'm Carmen, proprietor of The Wedding Boutique. For fourteen years, I have focused all my efforts on my boutique and have taken delight in helping many brides-to-be choose their dream gown. For years, I have been just one part in a couple's wedding day, and have frequently heard complaints about the difficulties of trying to book so many specific services. Today, I'm launching a new venture to bring those services together into one place ... my hope is to be able to cater for all areas of a wedding rather than expecting couples to go in search of suppliers and goods offered in various locations,' I explain, holding my hands together to stop them from shaking. Whilst I talk I keep glancing at Trish, who is offering moral support from the sidelines – she's smiling so I must be sounding OK despite my nerves.

I continue.

'Each one of us around this table provides the services required by the majority of our couples. We each bring a wealth of expertise in our fields and endless possibilities for those seeking our services. I propose that together under one roof we could support each other in securing more bookings, creating more memories and strengthening our local industry for years to come.'

I quickly provide them with a wealth of information about costs, proposed rental space and outline how my venture can be manned and bookings arranged in their absence.

When I finally fall silent and ask for questions, there is a flurry of interest and positive reactions to my proposal.

Dana

I can't believe Carmen remembered me. I'm quite humbled that she would go out of her way to invite me to her meeting when she hasn't seen me for years; she's a nice person. I bet Andrew knows nothing about this; he wouldn't be too happy.

'How's Luke doing?' was her first question on greeting me. No mention of anything else, she simply asked how my boy was doing – how lovely. I'm hardly ever asked about Luke's welfare; people usually just want to delve into his difficulties, but not Carmen. That was really sweet of her.

Not that I knew her that well when Andrew and I were together, but still, I suppose I could have made more of an effort when we did see each other in the Cross Keys.

I look round the boutique as others arrive, gather their brochures and grab a coffee. My display was easy. I created a table centrepiece of white lilies, roses and shamrock; the colour contrast is stunning, the overall effect fetching and yet classy from all directions. I simply had to position the arrangement on the table, where it sits in pride of place for all the vendors to see. I don't need flash leaflets, plastic banners or glossy postcards to sell my wedding wares – flowers speak for themselves.

I stare around the table. I know several people, such as Kevin

Knightley with his limousines, and I recognise other folk from around town but my networking circle isn't as big as it could be, so this meeting might drum up some business. I'm the only florist so far, which is good news, but still I'm flabbergasted that Carmen should be so generous as to invite me to hear about her new business venture.

I'm conscious that people keep looking at me and doing a double-take. The youngest woman from the boutique keeps smiling at me, so I take it she's recognised me from this week's TV. I'd hate to guess what she thinks of my behaviour. Though at her age, I'd probably think that a thirty-nine year old still seeking love was a bit strange – the years fly by so fast and suddenly you go from her tender age to mine.

I sink a little lower in my seat as others join the table and settle down with their business portfolios, I bet they all have an opinion on reality TV and the so-called professional experts. Though funnily enough, I haven't required their help much this week. Jez probably feels it's been a waste of time hauling them around for the week after the initial selection process. In hindsight, the travelling crew could have been as small as just Jez, Tamzin, the camera guy and one or two extras ... I don't know what's the point of all the rest, though I bet they are charging a small fortune for their services.

Polly

I'm nervous. I wouldn't usually go to this type of meeting, so I have no idea what to expect. I'm excellent at my job, with many years of experience, but even so, why I've been trusted to attend this meeting is beyond me.

Clutching an armful of glossy brochures, I'd entered The

Wedding Boutique with a flurry of nerves gathering in the pit of my stomach. I can't believe I've entered this establishment for the second time in one week. I feel out of my depth representing our company amidst a group of other industry specialties. And I know for a fact that Stacey isn't impressed by having to do additional hours to man the agency while I'm at this meeting.

'Hello, I'm so pleased you could come, Polly,' said Carmen, welcoming me into a throng of other individuals. 'Please take a seat and we'll do the introductions once everyone is settled. And please help yourself to a hot drink from the reception counter.'

Within minutes, I was seated at a beautifully decorated linen table in the middle of the boutique and am sipping aromatic coffee with eight energetic people each expressing their delight to be here representing their offered services or talents: chauffeured cars, cake design, beauty services, men's tailoring and Monica, the events manager from the Red Lion. I'm dreading saying anything, but with only one more woman to give her introduction I know it's a must.

'Hello, I'm Dana ... I'm a local florist who works from home. I can cater for everything from a few simple buttonholes, table decorations, bridal party bouquets, church decorations and even reception locations and bridal suites – I can create flower designs for pretty much any area where the couple wish to incorporate flowers into their special day. I created the centrepiece for today's meeting.' She points to the arrangement of fresh flowers decorating the table, an arrangement of lilies, roses and blue-green leaves.

Then it's my turn.

I want to hide. I feel such a hypocrite being here, given my thoughts on marriage.

All eyes turn to me.

'Hi, I'm Polly. I work part-time in the travel agents next door where we're able to provide information and book any package holiday for honeymoons, whether it be a short getaway or a luxurious all-inclusive trip to a long-haul destination ... whatever the couple desire.'

I fall silent – my introduction was a little short compared to the others – then Carmen takes the floor to explain her idea further.

'It would be so much easier if we could work together to enhance the services offered in one location,' explains Carmen, gesturing around the table as she speaks. 'We all know how quickly our diaries fill when the wedding season begins, and we can each appreciate how much time and effort goes into attending appointments, making enquiries, comparing services when it could be so much easier for our clients.'

Carmen continues to outline her vision and I relax, knowing I'm not selling myself but the travel agents' services and expertise. Carmen's idea sounds perfectly feasible and I can see it working. I'm slightly different – my wage doesn't depend upon engaging with the group – but if the travel agents can get additional bookings ...

I listen in awe as Carmen explains the details of her plan, knowing that deep down she is probably nervous about her own personal adventure, which will start later today. Wow, such focus to remain in the moment knowing what an exciting and life-changing weekend lies ahead of her!

'Thanks,' I say absentmindedly as the brochure of laminated pages is passed to me. It's not that I'm not interested in the discussion, more that my mind is swimming with family tasks and concerns for others. I've played my part, said my bit about the travel agents and I've lost interest. I've never been one for all things wedding related, but I appreciate that that's my quirky issue, not theirs.

I flip the cover of the brochure to reveal exquisite wedding cakes in all shapes, sizes and colours. The detail and craftsmanship is highlighted by each photograph, skilfully showcasing the talent of the baker. I'm impressed.

That's when a niggle forms at the back of my brain and begins to work its way forward.

A worry.

A forgotten task.

An unknown concern brought to light by . . . Oh my God, I haven't thought about a birthday cake for Cody!

A wave of panic overwhelms me as I snap the brochure shut, causing several people to look in my direction and give a polite smile to my panic-stricken expression.

'How long does it take you to make a one-tiered fruit cake?' I ask, interrupting numerous conversations.

The wedding cake lady looks up and grimaces.

'Well, it really depends on how long I have and what the requirements are . . .'

I can hear myself saying something similar in the travel agents when people ask how long it takes to book a holiday.

'Usually?' I prompt.

'One tier, marzipan with royal icing and intricate decoration takes a fair amount of time.'

'Mmmm, any chance that a one-tier birthday cake could be done by tomorrow?' I ask, adopting a comic yet desperate tone.

'Tomorrow?' several people repeat.

'Yep, that's right. Sadly, you heard me correctly . . . tomorrow.'

I point a finger towards my own chest and whisper, 'Sorry, distracted mother . . . just remembered a forgotten item.'

'I don't usually ask favours, but it completely slipped my mind,' I explain, as we gather together at the end of the meeting. I pray that the cake lady is as dedicated to her talent as she's just convinced us. Fingers crossed she can deliver by tomorrow evening.

'We do have a local wedding cake delivery booked for tomorrow, so I can't create, bake and deliver you a fruit cake at such short notice – but I could get one of my girls to rustle up a nice sponge cake with iced decoration for tomorrow. How's that sound?'

'*Deal*. Anything will be better than a tiddly shop-bought cake with my wobbly icing scrawled across it, that's for certain.'

I watch as she scribbles down the message details on the back of an envelope.

'I owe you one,' I say in relief, as if I could deliver a two-week package holiday in return, which I can't.

'No worries. I'll deliver it to the Red Lion too, OK?'

'You are a life-saver,' I say, peeling numerous ten-pound notes from my purse, once she'd named her price.

In no time, I'm back in my comfort zone at the travel agents.

'I've been rushed off my feet,' says Stacey the minute I walk through the door. 'I've taken three bookings . . . one for a honeymooning couple plus two all-inclusive family package holidays.'

I don't say it, but welcome to my world, Stacey – I man the desk every Friday morning and, yep, that's a usual morning for me.

Carmen

'You did so well, Carmen . . . very professional,' whispers Trish, as she hands me a coffee cup.

'Was it OK?'

'More than OK, extremely impressive,' Trish replies.

I finally get to breathe, as my guests mingle and flip through the supplied literature whilst enjoying their coffee.

'Can we all be accommodated in the available space next door?' asks Kevin Knightley as soon as I am available to chat.

'Absolutely. Have you ever seen inside? The ground floor alone is huge, then there are three more floors which could accommodate us all if needs be. I realise that it's been boarded up for years, but the owner has given me a tour and inside is structurally sound. You have to remember it was the nearest thing we had to a department store in this area, so the floor space is vast.'

Mr Knightley nods encouragingly, which is a surprise, given his reputation.

'Granted, you might need more promotional material than most as you couldn't have your vehicles parked inside.'

'But it might enable me to move premises and garage the limousines elsewhere, which would be a financial saving.'

'Exactly. I for one wouldn't need accommodating, given that I'm next door, and neither would the travel agents, for instance, but the florist, the cake designer, the milliner and the photographer could all have individual space within a combined property.'

I feel encouraged by each question, each conversation and the interest received before my guests leave, taking my proposal literature with them.

'Phew! Am I glad that's over,' I sigh to Trish and Anna as I close the boutique door on my final guest.

'And now you can focus upon your main proposal!' says Trish, with an air of excitement.

'Oh, bloody hell, I'd forgotten about that one! Though I have piled our suitcases into the car ready for an effective and swift departure once Elliot arrives home.'

'What time are they expected back from Cardiff?' asks Anna, looking at her watch.

'Two o'clock, so we'll be heading straight to the airport as soon as he gets back.'

I breathe in deeply and exhale just as strongly.

'You've had a week and a half, lovey,' says Trish, slipping her arm about my shoulders for a hug.

'I know and it's not over yet, is it?'

'Nope, but this is where the fun starts!' she says, releasing me from her bear-like grip. 'Why don't you leave now, and we'll get this place looking shipshape ready for tomorrow?'

'Would you?'

They both nod enthusiastically, causing a knot of emotion to rush to my throat.

'Thank you, you are the best,' I gush, blinking rapidly.

'We know,' sings Trish, as she rolls her sleeves up to begin dismantling the decorative meeting table.

I give them both strict orders to just tidy up and then go home for an early finish, to 'phone me if you need me' and 'wish me luck' as I stride from the boutique.

As I dash through the door a thought suddenly hits me.

Next time I enter the boutique, I'll be engaged!

Dana

'Sorry I'm late,' I apologise to the school receptionist as she signs me in for my meeting with Mrs Richards and Mrs Salter just before one o'clock. I've snuck into school, avoiding passing Luke's classroom window for fear of disrupting his daily routines.

'No worries, we understand that you're busy . . .' She lowers her head rather than finish her sentence. But it confirms that even the school office staff know which is Luke's mother; I bet she couldn't pick Tyler's mother out in a line-up! 'If you'll take a seat, I'll tell them that you are waiting.'

I perch on one of the low chairs outside the head teacher's office. I dearly wish my meeting was with the head, Mrs Huggins; she's an old-school sort who believes in the abilities of every child. I get the impression that whoever Mrs Richards is she's lacking in that department.

I'm surprised they agreed to a meeting when I called first thing this morning, I thought I would need to wait a few days for a suitable time when both ladies were free.

Within minutes, I spy Mrs Salter approaching along the corridor and, at her side, a stern-looking woman who I've never had the pleasure of meeting before.

'Mrs Salter, so nice to see you again,' I say warmly, shaking her by the hand.

The teacher returns the sentiment, gives a weak smile and lowers her kind eyes. I have a feeling she's here purely for decoration and not by choice.

'Miss Jones, I'm Mrs Richards. I organise the SEND department with the school and I'll be leading this meeting so we can discuss Luke's needs and his development within mainstream education.' I note she doesn't offer her hand to shake so I don't offer mine. I hate that my son is linked to the school's Special Educational Needs and Disabilities department but needs must, given his condition.

We walk in silence towards an empty office at the end of the corridor, which I've been shown into many times for private discussions about Luke.

I take the offered seat around the meeting table; suddenly today's little discussion feels very different. Is it Mrs Richards' presence or my attitude?

'How can we help you, Miss Jones?' asks Mrs Richards, her pen poised above a writing pad which she's produced from nowhere. Mrs Salter stares at the polished table.

'I was unable to attend parents' evening, but my parents relayed a message regarding speech therapy, but only if the session is shared with another pupil due to concerns about Luke's reaction to being alone . . . I'm a little lost, that's all.'

'We feel the session would benefit both pupils. It is a one-hour slot and we know how long it takes for Luke to settle with new people—'

I interrupt Mrs Richards, I can't help myself.

'Not if the change is explained to him beforehand. I keep asking that the school start using visual timetables with him to help him to navigate his day in pictures. He uses one at home, and he is happy to trot back and forth to see his next task: brush teeth, get dressed, clean glasses, tidy toys away – he's very good at following it, plus it gives him some independence.'

'All our children have a large timetable pinned on the class-room wall . . . every child benefits from knowing what is coming next in their day,' says Mrs Richards. There is an edge to her tone. I expected this woman to be more understanding about disabilities and behavioural issues, or at least to be open-minded about finding ways to help inclusive education.

'I appreciate that, but if Luke had a pictorial timetable pinned alongside the class one, he would cope much better. You could even put a toilet reminder on there to help him avoid little accidents. He'll soon get used to a new routine as long as he is introduced to each image. Honestly, the system works for him. And as for poor reactions to attending a speech session . . . this is the first I'm hearing of it. I haven't had any messages in his diary, not one.'

A heavy silence lingers after I finish speaking. I continue to look at each woman; neither one speaks.

They don't want him here – the thought suddenly pulls me up sharp.

'Is the speech therapy session the only concern or is there something else the school would like to address but . . . ?' I can't bring myself to ask out right. Suddenly this feels like a kaleidoscope moment. I daren't twist the mirrored tube in case the current pattern changes. Luke loves this little school. I can't risk gambling my son's current snowflake pattern for one that is a fraction different but which will change his world forever.

My breath snags in my throat.

I wait.

Mrs Salter continues to stare at the table's wood grain and coffee rings.

Mrs Richards looks everywhere but refuses to meet my gaze.

Oh my god! What kind of discussions have they been having behind my back, whilst I've been happily standing at the school gate thinking everything was harmonious? And only now they bring it to my attention, when I've asked for a meeting. How dare they? Are they having similar meetings with the parents whose children have ADHD, autism, epilepsy?

I can feel the panic rising in my chest. I want to rant, scream, shout but mainly beg – please don't close your hearts and mind to my little boy. He's just a little boy! A little boy like any other, who simply has extras. Luke's extras are no more disruptive than Tyler being naughty in every lesson, no different to Max running off at every opportunity, than Ryan wetting himself, Jack fighting during story time and Harry, who still cries each morning when his mum drops him off. My Luke is the third from the top of the sticker star chart so how can you imply he's not welcome in your classroom?

I have simple solutions to support his daily needs but you're not listening to me. No one has answers to Tyler's behavioural issues, Harry's crying or Max's repeated attempts to escape yet you're happy to accommodate their education.

I say the only thing that I can.

'Could you ask Mrs Huggins to call me, please? I'd like to arrange a meeting with her instead.' I stand, calmly return my chair under the table and head for the exit. As I reach the door, one last request jumps to mind. 'Oh, and from today, Mrs Salter, if Luke has a little accident, I'd appreciate the school office texting me and I will collect the bin liner myself. Please don't send him to the school gate carrying it. Thank you, both, for your time.'

I sign out, politely say goodbye to the school office lady and just make it through the reception's security doors before hot angry tears spill down my face.

Despite my prayers, I sense a kaleidoscope moment has just occurred; the school's driveway seems entirely different as I traipse towards the metal railings.

Polly

'I told him not to be late,' mutters Fraser, pacing the hallway, waiting for Cody to arrive home. We both stand ready in our coats, eager to leave the house the minute Cody steps through the front door.

'Have you called to remind him?'

Fraser throws me a disgruntled look.

'I'm not his nursemaid.'

'He's probably been waylaid, or he misinterpreted your instructions, that's all.'

Fraser opens the front door, as if that'll speed our son's arrival. This has always been our usual day of celebration but still, with the party tomorrow, maybe Cody doesn't think his father's instruction about tonight is important.

'I told him, "Come home immediately from work, we need to dash out" – how can that be misinterpreted as anything other than you are needed at home urgently?'

I'm not helping matters, so I remain quiet. I know how long he's been waiting for this evening to arrive. Months . . . actually years isn't an over estimation.

'Here he is, *finally*.'

I'm bustled out of the door and along the driveway towards a startled Cody; we've never greeted him on the drive on his arrival from work before. Not even on his first day.

'What's up, guys?'

'You're late. Quick, get in,' says Fraser, zapping his own key fob and settling into the driver's seat.

'Jump in,' I say, heading for the rear door, knowing my leggy son can't cope in the back seats any longer.

'Is anyone going to explain or am I supposed to guess?' asks Cody, as Fraser cuts through the town's traffic, navigating busy roads and heading along side streets in a manner befitting a spy.

My gaze meets Fraser's in the rear-view mirror, urging him to explain.

'We're about to collect your birthday present . . .'

'*Seriously?*'

'Seriously,' I mimic from the back. 'Though your father was on the verge of cancelling as you took so long to arrive home.'

'I told him . . .'

'I know, you said a million times in the hallway . . .'

'Anyway, we ordered it a few weeks ago, before you'd decided on a party . . . but we're certain you'll like it.'

Cody turns round in his seat to look at me.

I nod, eagerly watching his expression.

I'm expecting him to be shocked, a little taken aback – our son might not be expecting a big present but we didn't get to have the eighteenth like other families so we've waited the extra two years to make this one special.

A lump leaps to my throat.

We need to make the most of such moments – our days as a threesome may be drawing to a close if he continues to mature and the pace of life continues as it is.

Fraser keeps glancing at me in the tiny mirror. His eyes are flashing with sheer joy. I really do love this man, he tries so hard to provide everything we need in whatever way he can. And yet, even on the brink of realising another joyous moment, I can see Fraser becoming nervous as we get near.

I chose well: the best and right man for me.

'What the hell!' exclaims Cody, as Fraser pulls in to the garage forecourt. I watch as he does a double-take out of the window before glancing between me and his father for confirmation that his initial thought is actually correct and not a dream that will be dashed any second.

'Happy birthday, son,' says Fraser, drawing up alongside a brand-new Audi A3.

'Are you joking?'

'Nope, it's yours, Cody,' I add, as a warm flush of excitement drifts to my stomach, knowing another milestone moment has been reached. It always seemed like a wild present whenever Fraser mentioned it, but I knew he'd planned it for years, wanting the gesture to be significant for our only child.

The two men dive from our car and are greeted by the sales team, all smiles and arm-pumping handshakes. I stand back and watch. The memory lodges in my heart, like the other milestone birthdays when Cody's excitement overflowed: his first true birthday, the big bike birthday, the first football match birthday, and now today. Emotionally, I hold on tight to scenes such as this because I expect that one day soon my only part in his birthday day will be a hasty phone call, a hasty invite to share a meal with his family and a tiny slither of his birthday experience every four years. Right now, Cody remains ours – Fraser's and mine.

Carmen

As the concierge unlocks the door of our Parisian suite, I'm struck by an attack of nerves *again*. At every stage of our journey, my stomach has been jittery, then settled only to be reignited in a short time. Elliot arrived home from Cardiff slightly later than expected, cutting our dash to Heathrow Airport incredibly fine, arriving with just moments to spare before the gate closed, Elliot struggling along due to the knee brace and crutches. I hadn't thought to phone ahead and request assistance. When we eventually got on the plane, the lack of legroom proved uncomfortable for him, but thankfully the crew were obliging, stashing his crutches in the overhead storage. Thankfully, the flight left on time and was incredibly short.

I'd envisaged our hotel suite from the computer images I browsed whilst booking but when we step inside and I'm met with the reality of the vast amount of space, tastefully decorated in calming cream and beige, for just two people, I am overwhelmed and feel slightly greedy. And I'm slightly embarrassed that a uniformed man is carrying our baggage.

Elliot hobbles inside, does a double-take and simply stares at me before addressing the concierge.

'Cheers, mate,' he says, tipping him with a folded note.

I dump my handbag on the nearest chair and survey our beautiful rooms, following Elliot's lead. It's a three-roomed suite, consisting of lounge, bedroom and bathroom; every piece of furniture is larger than life, made for two bodies with room to spare, and is tastefully angled denoting areas within each room. Plush lighting and huge mirrors highlight and reflect every view from every angle. In brief, it meets all my expectations of a honeymoon suite for those not on honeymoon.

'Are you going to tell me what the plans are, or is that a surprise too?' asks Elliot, throwing down his crutches and flopping on to the ginormous bed, disrupting the plethora of tiny satin cushions. 'This bed is huge!'

'Tonight, we have a city tour by limousine and a late dinner booking at a seafood restaurant. On Saturday, I've booked a visit to the Louvre, a guided tour of the Arc de Triomphe, a wine-and-dine river cruise along the Seine . . . then a hosted tour of the Eiffel Tower before we go to the Moulin Rouge. I've left Sunday free for chilling. How does that sound?'

'Carmen, it sounds bloody amazing but what's the occasion? It's not our anniversary, is it?' He eyes me suspiciously.

'Don't worry, you haven't forgotten anything. I just thought we needed a break from the normal routine and when I visited the travel agents . . . *this* was my choice.'

'I'm impressed. But you usually opt for long haul.'

I shrug. Having got this far this week, I don't trust myself to fake an answer. I need to stay safe from this point on, no dramas, no issues and no false answers.

'OK, keep your little secrets ... but thank you – I appreciate the treat. Cardiff with the guys was fun, despite doing this.' He points to his knee. 'But now we've got an entire weekend to focus on us without distractions. How fabulous!'

'What distractions?' I leap on his comment, my insecurities instantly resurfacing.

'The daily running of the boutique, your new wedding venture, Monty's wedding, then there was Christmas before that, and before that your parents moving house ... There is constantly something going on in the background that gets in the way of us just being us.' He counts each item on his fingers, reinforcing his point. 'Next weekend is Monty's wedding and then we're free of any obligations.'

He's right. Elliot has just summed up the last eight months of our lives and I know that if he wanted to he could recall the previous eight months, which were similarly incredibly busy, filled with other events and other family members.

'We need to start saying no a little more often and making time for us, don't we?' I say, feeling slightly guilty that I've judged him so badly since Nicole's remarks when he's totally right about our busy lifestyle ... which may explain why we are where we are in our relationship.

'We need to let others pick up the slack for a while – your four brothers do very little for your parents, my older brother does even less for mine. Everyone stands back and relies on us jumping in and offering before they even think about putting themselves forward with an offer. That needs to stop.'

'I agree. Can we make a pact that we'll address the issue once we get back home?'

'We sure can, Carmen ... It'll sound selfish to others but still, they can start sharing the load a little more.'

'And we can spend more time together enjoying ourselves – like we did in the beginning.'

'Exactly.'

'Deal?' I ask, a sense of relief washing over me.

'Deal,' repeats Elliot, before whispering, 'Come here.'

He beckons me towards the bed.

'*What?*' I say coyly.

'You know what!'

I'm contentedly dozing in Elliot's arms when the suite's phone rings beside the bed. Slowly opening my eyes, I see Elliot leisurely stretching over me to answer it.

'Hello?'

Silence as he listens. I stare at his bare torso and dark chest hair as my brain sluggishly catches up with the time, date and location.

'Thank you, tell them we'll be down in ten minutes,' mutters Elliot, smirking at me beneath his tousled fringe.

'The limo is here.'

My brain suddenly registers what's happening and I leap from beneath the duvet.

'Bloody hell, Elliot,' I scream, frantically collecting my strewn clothes from the carpet. 'And now we're late!'

'Shush, the car can wait. What's the rush?'

'You can hardly walk and ... *we* need to shower.'

'Yeah, like walking's my issue given the tumble we've just had ... are you serious?' he says, pulling a face. 'I think I've just proved my mobility is fine.'

I stop mid-clothes collection and laugh out loud.

He has a valid point. If anything, his spontaneous request for me to join him has proven a torn ligament is going to be the least of my worries this weekend.

'And a shower?'

'Mmmm, well, as polite as that might be towards our fellow diners, I'm actually not that fussed about a shower.'

'*Elliot!*' I screech, taken aback by his slovenly ways.

'Like we always showered afterwards when we first met! I don't think so . . . how many times did we just head down to the corner café for coffee and croissants afterwards?'

'Stop! Stop! Stop! Fair point, in the beginning we did, but . . .' I giggle; I can't argue with him. 'At least have a cat-lick wash, if nothing else.'

He flings back the duvet and heads for the bathroom.

Naked, he dashes past me, albeit with a newly attained hobble, and I stand and admire his arse before it disappears behind a closed door. He does make me laugh when he recalls our early days. We couldn't get enough of each other; we showed respect towards other people, of course we did, but we didn't care if we spent all afternoon in bed and then, as Elliot said, nipped down to the corner café for coffee.

I swiftly dump my pile of spent clothes and unlock my suitcase, searching for a suitable outfit whilst the bathroom is in use.

When did those days stop? When did we go from lounging about in bed to living our life at ninety miles an hour to please family and friends and meet work commitments? Is that where we went wrong? Should we have spent more time doing the things we did in the very beginning? Those days when I was obsessed with the size of his hands and would sit tenderly outlining the shape of each finger with mine, pressing palm to palm to measure the difference and taking delight in everything which was Elliot.

I smile at the memories.

The bathroom door opens and Elliot reappears, a towel wrapped about his waist. He knows very well what reaction 'that look' provokes in me, but ignore him I must – we have a limo waiting.

'I'll be two minutes,' I say, scurrying with my armful of fresh clothing into the bathroom.

'You've paid for a set duration; he'll wait, if only for an additional tip,' comes Elliot's voice.

He's right, but I wanted everything to be perfect this weekend. Though I can't complain about our antics during the last hour.

Dana

'I can't believe you're late! Of all the days, Dana!' snaps Tamzin. Jez is stomping around, spitting feathers. He wanted you dressed and done thirty minutes ago; now the whole crew are hanging around waiting.'

I daren't speak, because I know I'll rant at the first person who upsets me after my meeting at the school. I wanted to phone my parents for moral support but daren't because I knew once I started crying the floodgates wouldn't close. I am livid at the injustice in this world. Disgusted that some adults can be so small-minded towards others. That . . .

'Dana!' shouts Jez, striding through the hotel foyer. 'We're running late and this is supposed to be—' He stops, peering at my fixed expression before asking, 'Are you OK?'

'Fine!'

He stares intently at me.

'Good to go?'

'Yep.'

'OK, let's do it.' He leads the way through the hotel exit to our waiting vehicles. I climb in, belt up and sit back. I'm happy to go along with whatever plans Male C has requested but everyone needs to step back and give me space because I'm not in the mood for being messed about. Not today.

'Quads Are Us?' I whisper, as the car turns from the main road down a winding mud track. Tamzin gives a weak smile; she's got the measure of me today so has remained silent throughout the short journey. 'Am I dressed appropriately?' I gesture down at my cream blouse, skinny jeans and sturdy boots.

'Apparently they're providing you with a boilersuit because of the amount of mud that splatters up.'

'Great,' is all I muster.

Instantly I feel bad for Male C. He's obviously requested a fun date and I'm turning up as miserable as hell. I need to change my face and mood quickly, otherwise the camera crew will capture it and no amount of editing will alter the image he'll be greeted with.

I need to leave my troubles behind, mentally stash them on a shelf inside my head and enjoy the next three hours. Before I know it, I'll be home cuddling my one true love as I read him a bedtime story.

The orange boilersuit does nothing for my figure. It billows around my body like a deflated balloon joined in the middle with a large zipper. I'm given a crash hat and plastic goggles to enhance my appearance even further.

'This way, please,' instructs Jez, his faithful cameraman chasing his leggy strides. 'Now, Dana, we need you to climb on to this quad bike. The man will give you a few brief instructions and then you're to head on out over that hill there, and just on the other side you'll see we've positioned Male C.'

'Also on a quad bike?' I ask, unsure about the first impression this stranger will have of me zooming across the muddy landscape.

'Of course,' replies Jez, frowning at my idiotic question.

I struggle to climb up, and I struggle to master the controls after detailed instruction, even though it appears to be a simple lever mechanism, like a lawn mower.

'You ready?' asks Jez, pulling my goggles into place.

I nod.

'Go!' Jez slaps my back as I depress the lever and shoot forward at a fairly rapid pace. An arc of mud splashes up from each wheel as the quad bike makes easy work of the terrain and I find myself climbing up and over the nearest hill as instructed by Jez. I see that a single cameraman is alongside me, piggy-backed on another quad bike. But I instantly forget the camera; I'm past caring if the truth be known.

Having completed my mission of up and over, I spy the red boilersuit astride another quad bike on the far side; he also has an accompanying cameraman on another chauffeured quad bike to capture his every move. I head over and attempt to pull up alongside Male C. I fail miserably to stop in time but still, we are within speaking distance.

I remove my goggles, which are speckled with mud, so I assume my face and hair are too – a waste of the beauty professionals' time and effort back at the hotel.

Male C jumps down from his quad bike, extends a huge hand and delivers a firm handshake.

'Hi, Dana, I'm Connor ... Sorry about all this but I'm a

thrill-and-chill kind of guy, so I'm hoping we can have a laugh together.'

'Nice to meet you, Connor. Wow, thrill and chill – that sounds interesting,' I stammer. I can't make out much of his appearance: his crash helmet covers most of his blonde hair and his face is mud splattered too, but he does have a wide smile, which eases my nerves.

'OK, follow me.' He jumps back on to his quad and away he shoots. I try my hardest to keep up with him but Connor nips up and over all the obstacles littered about the landscape. Muddy water is flying everywhere, my body is bumping up and down on the wide seat at regular intervals and my face is collecting the purest of mud packs that I've ever used as I pursue my date.

Carmen

'To us,' whispers Elliot, as we snuggle up on the back seat of the limousine, each with a glass of chilled champagne in hand. As the limousine smoothly pulls away from the hotel, we clink glasses and passionately kiss before sipping our drinks.

Despite the familiarity of the bubbles dancing upon my tongue, the moment is perfect. This is what I've been dreaming of. Just the two of us together, with time on our hands to be us. A weekend of simply laughing, talking and enjoying each other's company. I'm hoping that by tomorrow night we'll feel reconnected and reenergised so when I pop the question, we can enter the next phase of our relationship together having been reminded of our foundations as a couple.

Our driver ignores us behind his screen of glass. I watch his peaked cap bob this way and that as he navigates the busy traffic, avoiding the nimble motorcycles cutting through the traffic, the stream of pedestrians on the numerous zebra crossings and the wayward traffic that appears from every angle to join the flow.

I snuggle beneath the crook of Elliot's arm, my head resting back, as the beautiful city flashes past the car window. In every direction, a festoon of fairy lights in red, neon blue and yellow decorates the skyline and I pretend they were hung earlier today and illuminated especially for us. The traffic lights, the brilliant billboards and the street lamps all shine with an additional twinkle, creating a star-like effect for me and Elliot. The vehicle drives along the Champs-Elysées towards the Arc de Triomphe; we decline the offer to park, get out and mingle with the milling crowds taking photographs as we have a tour booked for tomorrow, so the driver circles several times, enabling us to view the mighty structure illuminated in gold spotlights up close.

'Elliot,' I say, looking up into the underneath of his chin. 'Thank you.'

'For what?'

'For agreeing to come along. We've been busy, and you're right to complain and bring it to my attention, but I wouldn't want to be here, right now, with anyone but you!'

He gently kisses the top of my head and I relax into his body, realising that my last sentence is probably the most honest moment I've shared with Elliot in a while. So often I hide what I feel, swallow the emotion as something that he wouldn't understand or want to share, when the reality is that that could actually be something very special which I should be sharing with him. And if I can't share my feelings with him, what's the bloody point in us being together? Surely life isn't supposed to be about self-censorship when it comes to the ones that we love?

Our car drifts back along the Champs-Elysées towards the Place de la Concorde with its huddle of street artists beneath the watchful gaze of the statues of the Fontaine des Mers. In the background, the Eiffel Tower dominates the Parisian skyline and my stomach flips at the very thought of tomorrow evening. I've written two proposals: one is slightly more serious than the other. I've learnt both off by heart, so I won't need a prompt card.

'Can you imagine the view from up there?' whispers Elliot, his mouth gaping open.

'We've a tour booked for tomorrow.'

'OK, let's do it.'

His voice has an excited buzz and I know I have done the right thing. It might have taken me all week to get my head around my plans but it was the right decision.

'London is busy but Paris seems so alive in comparison,' says Elliot, gawping through the tinted window. 'There's a different vibe amongst the crowds. Do you get what I mean?'

'I do,' I say, grateful that he seems to be in the same headspace as me. I don't care if it's the champagne working on our empty stomachs or the wonder of the city, being on the same page is all that matters.

Finally, our limousine glides along a boulevard towards the Eiffel Tower. It looms ahead of us, like a Christmas tree covered in yellow-gold lights, or a lighthouse for the city with its blue-white strobe light sweeping back and forth through the darkness, keeping us safe and secure until morning.

'How beautiful is that?' I exclaim, as my stomach continues to somersault.

'Pretty nobby for an aerial mast though, isn't it?' teases Elliot.

'You don't have to go on the tour tomorrow; you can always stay on the ground and I'll hike up to the observation deck.'

'No way! If you're going, I'm going.' He squeezes me tighter into the side of his chest, and a flood of laughter fills the rear seats. I watch his Adam's apple bob as he gives a throaty laugh.

This is my Elliot, full of life, teasing me to high heaven and enjoying himself. This is the Elliot who's been absent for a while, sitting alongside his Carmen, the busy boutique owner – who has also been absent from their partnership, with her head full of business plans for more years than I care to mention.

As we glide along, our eight-year relationship seems to unfold like a giant map before me, much like the Parisian sights, and everything on our journey seems so clear, so specific, as if I can see every event and memory we've shared together. Each memory has its history, a specific time and purpose in bringing us together, in building what we have. We've had drama, fun, excitement, our ups and downs, thrills and reflections, all of which have paved the way for where we are right now, here tonight . . . in Paris.

I need to stop thinking, as my emotions well inside my chest. I need to enjoy the moment, acknowledge our journey and look forward to tomorrow. If I continue this internal monologue, I'll be crying before we arrive at the Avenue des Ternes restaurant.

Dana

I breathe in the lavender oil and my mind drifts elsewhere as I wait for Connor to join me. This is more my thing, though I'm very conscious that I'm lying on a massage table with only two huge fluffy towels covering my totally naked body. I would much prefer a complete outfit at this stage of the dating game, but after the quad bike 'thrill', this is Connor's choice of 'chill'.

The splattering of mud which evenly covered every inch of my boilersuit and exposed skin has been washed away, thanks to the power shower which I was able to indulge in alone. Though our arrival at the spa complex was cause for a few strange looks as clients dressed in white waffle dressing gowns peered at us striding through the lobby. If I'd been rolled in mud, I would probably have been cleaner than my actual state after quad biking.

The gentle sound of falling raindrops fills the double therapy suite; it sounds as if we are on a veranda in a refreshing tropical storm.

I raise my head to see if Connor has entered. The room has mellow lighting and two massage therapists standing on the sidelines awaiting our male, who will occupy the other massage table for this joint session.

This is a first for me.

The camera crew are circling the room, their reflections eerily picked out in the tinted mirrors. Their presence disturbs each flickering candle, causing the light to dance and throw strange shadows against the walls.

'Dana, can you look away please? I'm not as bolshie as I make out on a first date,' calls Connor from the adjoining dressing room.

I oblige him by turning my face towards the blank wall.

I can hear the other massage table creak relentlessly as mine did when I climbed up.

Did he bravely drop his robe beforehand? I had struggled to remove it once in place, needing the assistance of the kindly massage therapist.

'Ready.'

I turn my head to view a semi-naked male lying face down under fluffy towels identical to mine.

'Hello, I'm Connor, and I probably pick the most inappropriate date nights ever,' he says, giving a wide smile.

'Hi, Connor, I'm Dana and this is a first for me.'

'Relax and enjoy it, and we can chat while these ladies work their magic on our tired muscles,' says Connor, his face resting on the flat table. 'You're supposed to put your face in the hole but I can't chat properly that way.'

I relax my cheek down into the towel beneath me and smile.

'What made you choose a massage session?' I ask, repositioning my chest and shoulder on the towelling sheet. As I speak, the two therapists step forward and begin rearranging the white towels on each of us revealing our bare backs and shoulders, before filling their hands with warm oil.

'Phew, now, there's a question. Years ago, and I literally mean years ago, I dated a woman who swore by them. Every few weeks she used to take herself off for an aromatherapy massage to ease her back and shoulders. Over time she dragged me along; I didn't want to go initially but I had to be honest and say it was working wonders for the footballing injuries I'd picked up playing for my local team.'

The therapist's hands gently touch my lower back in long, firm movements lifting towards my shoulder blades. It feels wonderful. I exhale slowly, then deeply inhale, enjoying the soothing strokes.

I listen as Connor calmly explains. He's honest, he didn't flinch at mentioning another woman, even on a first date, which I think is pretty mature. We all have previous relationships and friendships which we've left behind on our journey through life.

I'd be blind in not seeing the very obvious before me: a masculine frame with defined biceps and triceps – I have no complaints about how today has ended.

Polly

'Are you still awake?' comes Fraser's voice through the darkness.

'Yep.' I don't want to admit it to myself and definitely not to Fraser but I'm waiting for my son to return home.

'If you're worrying about the party, well, don't – everything will be fine. You can't micromanage everything, you know?'

'I know. I've done all I can and what will be will be.'

'So?'

'So, what?'

'Why can't you sleep?'

'I don't know.' I can't admit that I'm frightened that my son might be sharing his night with Lola. I can envisage them driving around the local area in his new car. I'm hoping he's not showing off, getting into trouble and restarting what I see as a disastrous relationship. How do I turn a blind eye to her previous behaviour? I know she may well have grown and matured since they split but still, why my son? How can she claim an attraction to someone she treated so badly?

So I've lain awake listening to next door's cat whine for thirty minutes only to be ignored on their doorstep; I've heard the bickering couple across the road arrive back from the local and the spluttering engine of their neighbour arriving home from a late shift.

I'm listening for a brand-new noise, one to which I'll become accustomed: the purr of an Audi engine, the clunk of a closing door and the tread of his footsteps.

If I say one word on the subject, Fraser will correct me. He's far more objective than I am. He doesn't get the concern I have about that particular girl. If the truth be known, I'd prefer my son to be out with any other female, in any situation, to him being with Lola.

'Come here.' Fraser wraps an arm over my warm body and snuggles into my back. I can feel his breath tickling my neck, his thighs resting behind mine. *This* is how we have always been. Us. Me and Fraser, Fraser and I. We're not a demonstrative couple, we've never felt the need to lavish each other with compliments, bouquets or public displays of affection. This, right here, has been us for the last twenty-three years.

Within minutes, his breathing softens and lengthens as he dozes back off to sleep without a care in the world. Fraser never worries about Cody in the way I do. His concerns revolve around the kind of man we've raised rather than the interactions he encounters, be it with his friends or with girls. I know Fraser's sleepless night would be caused by negative behaviour towards others, a lack of respect towards me, say, but never by a late-night drive with an ex.

We took many late-night drives when we were dating. At the time I never imagined that anyone would be lying awake awaiting my return. Who does when you're young, adventurous and curious? Since then we've had good times and bad along the way, but for the majority of our time together this has been us. Together. United, despite not being married.

It was a shock to find we were expecting Cody, but there was never any question about our next steps: finding a house, securing a deposit and beginning our lives as a family. Fraser had wanted to make it official but it wasn't necessary, not to me. It almost felt like we'd be doing it to please everyone else but us. And it was us that mattered.

I get why the likes of Helen and my mother sometimes question the decision we've made, but still, each to their own. Isn't that the rule? What's right for them isn't necessarily right for me, for us. And despite their remarks over the years, Helen's done what she's done. My mother divorced my father after twenty-six years together. And yet here we are, snuggled up and content after twenty-three years together.

I wonder if we'd have stayed the course if we'd chosen to get married once we had Cody? I know it was what my parents had wanted but, having witnessed their Third World War, there was no way I was prepared to follow suit.

We've stayed together, through thick and thin, in sickness and in health, because we wanted to.

Wow!

If Helen's proved anything this week, it's that a marriage certificate is nothing more than a piece of paper which you can use when you need to paper over the cracks. Though even then, maybe it wasn't the most suitable fix-it. How is she to trust Marc ever again, knowing he can ride roughshod everything she has believed in for all of these years? How can he make amends knowing he's stepped outside of their marriage and caused such hurt to his wife and both his daughters? He cheated on them as much as Helen. How would I have felt if my father had cheated on our family?

I hear a car engine outside, see the reflection of the headlights move slowly over a section of wall by the window. The engine dies. A car door slams beneath our window.

This is Cody.

I hear the key in the door.

The heavy tread on the bottom stair.

He's home.

I glance at my bedside clock: twenty past one.

How's he ever going to get up for work tomorrow?

Carmen

'Stop squeezing me! I'll burst if you hold me too tight,' I giggle, as we enter the hotel lift, heading back to our suite.

Elliot presses the button, then playfully squeezes me tighter, despite my request. We've had the best evening together, and have laughed more than we have in months.

'Please don't, otherwise my marinated bream, chilled langoustines and citrus pavlova will be wasted, and such divine food cannot be wasted, Elliot!'

He releases me quickly, and we stand openly staring at each other. I can see a wanton desire burning in his eyes, a slightly squiffy expression but the desire is there, alive and burning bright.

'What?' he asks, frowning in a boyish manner, wobbling on his crutches.

'Nothing.'

'Don't lie!'

I give a seductive shrug. I'm heartily full, slightly more than tipsy and very much in love.

'Tell me,' he demands playfully, moving closer despite his crutches.

Dare I?

I dare.

'You have approximately five minutes to brush your teeth before I ravish you senseless,' I giggle, hoping that an air of confidence featured somewhere in that proposition.

'*Really?* Now there's an offer a guy can't refuse!'

The lift comes to a halt and the doors glide apart.

'Five minutes, did you say?' says Elliot, awkwardly grabbing my hand and hobbling as fast as he can along the corridor towards our suite, dragging me behind him.

Chapter Ten

Saturday 29 February

Carmen

Despite his crutches, Elliot and I hold hands like lovestruck teenagers for the entire morning as we walk around the Louvre, refusing to let go even for scratching noses, undoing coat zips or attempting to walk in opposite directions. It feels stupid, juvenile and yet so bloody wonderful! When did it become important that I use both hands to obtain change from my purse? When and why did this stage ever stop? Did we lose this goofy-yet-romantic 'teenage' stage once sex entered our partnership? Wasn't it possible to combine that rather than lose the previous stage altogether?

'So, what's it to be?' asks Elliot, staring at signs defining the eight curatorial areas, with miles and miles of floor space to cover and only 35,000 artefacts on display.

'*Mona Lisa* . . . please, please, please.' There's no chance we'll visit everything in the tiny time frame we have, so I must see the one piece I've longed to view.

Elliot pulls a face.

'That's not a very good impression,' I tease, knowing *La Joconde* is last on his culture list.

He doesn't argue, doesn't try to change my mind, because he knows I've been waiting years to view her enigmatic smile. He unfolds the museum map, locates our position in relation to her position and we're off on a mission. No doubt Elliot's calculating that once we've seen her he'll never need to hear my request again. Ever. Little does he suspect that my second request will be the Venus de Milo, but too much information at once is never good for Elliot, so I allow him to lead me, hobbling through the crowds.

'How's your knee?' I ask, as we wait our turn.

'Tired and aching but it's the crutches that are giving me gyp. Kids at school made it looks so easy, but my aching back and shoulders are killing me.'

'Say if you need a chair,' I urge, knowing he'll be in agony once the painkillers wear off.

'Could you imagine attempting to push a wheelchair around this place?' he asks, thinking of the countless staircases feeding the flow of bodies through the building on the upper and lower floors.

Finally, we arrive.

Before us, placed behind a double-glazed unit of bulletproof glass which mimics any cashier's bank window, minus the chained biro for customer use, sits my *Mona Lisa*, staring back at the sea of gawping faces.

She's much smaller than I'd imagined, and given the exclamations of surprise in an array of languages from the jostling crowd surrounding me, we are in total agreement.

'Why's she so small?' I ask Elliot, puzzled that this fact had been hidden from me.

'Why is she so bloody popular is more the question?' he retorts.

I frown and go back to staring aimlessly at the portrait. I can't see the brushstroke detail I'd like to, or the stone damage by her left elbow or the split landscape depicting bridges and a winding road.

'Happy now?' asks Elliot, failing to feign any interest and instead openly scrutinising the ginormous painting *The Wedding Feast at Cana* on the opposite wall.

'I am, but . . .' I can't put into words how I feel. I'm thrilled that I am looking at Leonardo's painting, that I've finally made a journey I've waited years to make, and yet I'm disappointed by the end result. How can I have built this moment up to be so great an experience when the reality is actually quite underwhelming – not what I was expecting.

'Now, that's a painting! And, boy, it must get overlooked because of her!' he laughs, as he drags me away through the crowds to stare at the other picture.

I stare, twist my head from side to side and stare some more, while Elliot raves about the size, the brushstrokes and the talent of Veronese. I'm jealous. Elliot is having the art experience I wanted not five minutes ago.

'Are you ready?' I say, feeling as flat as uncapped lemonade.

'What's next?'

'You choose. I'm not much fussed now.' I lead the way towards the room's exit.

'Are you serious?'

Elliot hobbles behind, catching me as I saunter back, retracing our steps.

'Venus de Milo?'

'If you want.'

'Carmen!'

I stop, turn and see his confused face.

'What?'

'"What?" she says ... We came here just for you to view the portrait and now you've got a face like a bulldog chewing a thistle ... What's up?'

'Have you ever waited years and years, since childhood, to do a certain thing and it simply doesn't live up to your expectations?'

'Er, yeah!'

'So you know how I'm feeling ... Come on, where to next?'

'I didn't ruin that for you, did I?' he asks sheepishly, peering at me.

'Nah, I ruined it for myself by bigging it up in my head. Serves me right really.'

I indicate the folded map clutched in his hand, and Elliot busies himself balancing on crutches and unfurling the map to find our next point of interest.

'Happy?' asks Elliot, three hours later as we exit the museum.

'Yeah, if slightly mind-boggled and overstimulated by all the artefacts ... but I've seen more than I imagined given how vast it is, despite your injured knee.'

'At least we've seen what we came to see.'

'Let's grab a cab and make for our next stop, the Arc de Triomphe.'

Dana

I curl up on the rear seat of the executive car, plugging my headphones into my mobile – the screen might be tiny but I can still watch the *Taking a Chance on Love* final feedback show as we journey to our final destination: London.

Tamzin smiles as she watches me settle to my choice of early evening TV viewing; I'm sure I must appear narcissistic but I don't care any more. If the rest of the nation are enjoying it, then so can I.

Within seconds I'm lost in watching a woman dressed in a white robe, her damp hair hidden under a turban-wrapped towel, happily chatting to Jennifer in a spare room at the spa. I don't listen to her words, instead I watch her bright smile, her clear vibrant complexion, as she explains what a lovely third date she's had with Connor.

I was pleased that Jennifer didn't stick to her textbook questions. She missed out the waffle of the previous interview this time and kept it real. It meant I could do the same and I answered every question she asked openly and honestly. After just twenty minutes, she'd bid me a good night and that's how my third feedback date interview ended: with me feeling deeply relaxed, full of renewed spirit and energised in my journey towards finding true love. I left for home feeling delighted that maybe the social science experts had chosen well.

For the nation's audience there was only one question left to ask: who was I going to choose for a second date? And then there's the finale night question, which Tamzin hasn't mentioned for a few days. Is Jez really expecting me to pose the big question live on air?

I spend the rest of our journey on the phone, describing my school visit to my parents and afterwards chatting to my boy about our plans for next week, some quality mum-and-son time watching elephants at the zoo.

There is a growing excitement deep within me as we near London. I don't want to get my hopes up but I sense that tonight's second date will be the thrill of the week.

Polly

The events room didn't look huge until I decided that a pack of twenty colour-coordinated balloons and two carrier bags of tinsel decorations was enough to jazz it up for our party. I step back to view my handiwork but Fraser's face says it all.

'Does it still look bare to you?'

'Yep . . . for the effect I think you're after you'll need much more. Do you want me to . . . ?'

He doesn't even finish his sentence before I give a resounding yes.

'The same as these,' I say pointing to the trio of blue balloons, complete with curled silver ribbon and a weight, bobbing over each linen-covered table.

Fraser grabs his keys and heads out.

'And remember to buy more of the weights too,' I shout after his retreating figure.

He reaches the door, halts and I hear him say, 'Hi, there, didn't expect to see you here.' A quick look over his shoulder at me suggests concern. Fraser leaves and Lola enters.

'Hi, Polly . . . How are things?'

I'm standing with a length of silver foiled ribbon in my hand, curling it against the open blade of a pair of scissors.

Now is not the time.

Gone are her oversized boots, her fake-fur coat and the thick smudge of kohl under each eye. She's wearing a woollen dress, and her eyebrows appear to be different in size, shape and colour.

It's rude of me but I don't answer. I simply look.

Before she even opens her mouth to explain I want to ask her to leave.

Why does this girl get under my skin so much? I don't class myself as rude or unpleasant and yet Lola brings out every negative vibe in my body. I never thought I would develop an older-woman syndrome towards young women. I always imagined that I'd mature gracefully without feeling the need for spiteful actions towards the younger generation, and yet here I am at thirty-nine feeling so venomous towards one female.

Am I jealous of her youth?

Intimidated by her surly manner?

No. None of the above, and yet she only has to say my name and my innards are raging – urgh!

'Polly, I was wondering if there's any chance I could come tonight?'

I watch as she enters the room and walks across the wooden dance floor to stand in front of me.

Am I hearing this right?

'I've mentioned it to Cody . . . he was noncommittal but he did say that he thought you'd have an issue with me being here, so I thought it best to speak to you.'

Couldn't he simply have said no?

I clear my throat, putting the scissors down on the nearest table.

'The thing is, Lola, I feel we've been here before. You dated my son, we welcomed you into our family for that time and yet you behaved in a manner that I didn't think was the right way to treat my son. Now that might sound as if I'm overprotective, almost smothering him in a way, but from where I stand, I didn't think you were the right person for him to be dating. And so when it was over, I was relieved. Then there were all the silly games that you played afterwards, when my son couldn't venture into town without being harassed by you, called names in the street and forced to desert his mates for the evening and return home just to silence you . . . I felt that was a little unfair too. Do you see what I mean?'

She nods.

'After which, our household endured many weeks of phone calls, unexpected pizza deliveries, unwanted taxi cabs and, correct me if I'm wrong, those were all initiated by you as a means of getting back at my son for calling it a day and not dating you.'

Lola nods again.

I am on a roll.

'I see the situation very differently to you, Lola. You might wish just to attend his party tonight, join in with the celebrations and enjoy a good night amongst a group of friends, but to me you spell danger. And not just danger for my son, but for me and Fraser too. Cody's no angel, I know that. He's got a lot of growing up to do too, but I can assure you he didn't deserve half of the stuff you dished out as revenge. I don't want to be condescending towards you, or rude, but I want my son to be with a girl who makes him happy, who makes him proud to be with her, whose company he enjoys – with you, my son was miserable, drained of life and on occasions upset. He didn't show it, as I might have done, but as his mum I could see it.'

'I get where you're coming from.'

'Do you? Do you really?'

She nods yet again.

'Well, given that I'm being so honest, maybe I could just continue and finish this conversation. I might be his mother, I might seem really old in your eyes, but potentially the girl that my son dates could end up being his partner in life and even the mother of his child . . . both of which will determine how many years of his life will be spent being happy. I have absolutely no choice in who my son wishes to date but I fear for his happiness and my small family if he chooses the wrong one, Lola.'

She stares.

I fall silent. I've said it all: every doubt I have about her and every concern I have for my son's future happiness.

'Sorry, but I've got nothing else to add.'

That speech has been rattling around my head for many months. I thought I'd feel calm if it were ever delivered, but I don't. I feel like an utter bitch. I'm thirty-nine and she's eighteen.

'See you, Polly.'

I watch as Lola retraces her steps towards the exit. She's gone in a flash.

I stand there, replaying the scene in my head.

Should I have been so honest?

'Are you all right?'

Fraser breaks into my thoughts, as he re-enters with three carrier bags from the card shop.

'I'm such a bitch!'

He plonks the goods on to the nearest table and begins unpacking the decorations. He's done me proud, purchasing the exact ones I'd chosen earlier.

'Difficult conversation, was it?'

'Not really, she didn't say much apart from ask politely to come to the party, and I basically told her no.'

'OK. She knows now. Let's hope she'll stay away and allow Cody to enjoy his party with his friends and family.'

'Hope?' I glance up at him.

'Yeah, hope . . . Lola's not one for taking advice now, is she?'

Carmen

Within minutes, we're deposited on to the busy traffic island, home of the great archway, amongst a fresh crowd of tourists.

We take the obligatory selfies with the monument as a back-drop before making our way, tickets in hand, to the kiosk to be swiftly directed to the entrance.

'A last-minute DIY job, would you say?' mutters Elliot, pointing at the undercoat of gunmetal grey paint and the moulded aluminium handle, which look so out of place amongst the elaborate Neoclassicism stonework. I laugh at his humour, but my face falls once he opens the door.

I had imagined a plush visitors' foyer behind the grey door, with informative staff wearing bright smiles and offering two options: the stairs or the lift.

Nope. Behind the grey door is three feet of tiled floor leading to step one of a very long spiral staircase, with a metal banister and a wall-mounted handrail. This installation provides a fascinating swirl above our heads, which simply keeps turning for 284 stone steps.

I stare around, which takes all of two seconds.

There is no foyer, no smiling staff and, more importantly, no lift!

I have a boyfriend with a tour ticket, a knee brace and a set of NHS crutches!

As Elliot looks at me, his eyebrows lifting, a female tourist walks into my back. She also seems surprised to find nothing behind the grey door apart from an English couple frozen like statues.

'Now what?' I ask.

'I can't do stairs with these, can I?' he groans, as the woman sighs impatiently down my neck for blocking her way.

'We'll leave it,' I say, turning around and coming face to face with the miffed female; behind her stand three children and an adult male. I can't understand a word she's muttering, but her body language speaks volumes. She's annoyed at me for blocking her way to the first step.

'Don't be daft. You've bought tickets.'

'But you can't climb,' I moan.

'You go . . . I'll wait down here.'

I'm torn. Go. Stay. Yeah, go – that way only one ticket will be wasted.

The stranger and her brood impatiently push past, causing me to make full bodily contact with each one as they squeeze by. Not something I choose to do in life.

'Carmen, go on.'

'All right, as long as you'll be OK waiting down here.'

'I'll be fine.'

'Try and give your ticket away if you can. Someone outside might as well use it.'

In a split second, Elliot has hobbled past me and through the underwhelming door, back into the sunlight.

I take the first step.

One, two, three . . .

By the time I've taken forty-six steps, my thighs are burning, my hands are clutching on to the metal rails on both sides and my lungs are about to burst forth from my chest. I wish I'd stayed with Elliot. Damn my thrifty attitude of 'We have tickets – we can't waste both of them!'

I look down and see a backlog of bodies behind me, most of them irritated by the slow woman blocking the staircase, so I release one hand from the rail and move to the side, like I do on the Tube or the Metro. The crowd race past, showing off their energy and springy young thighs, while I clamber on as if climbing Mount Everest, wondering when my trusted Sherpa will bring me an oxygen tank. Partway through, I pray there is a base camp nearby in which I can spend a night before continuing my ascent the next day or, given my lightheadedness and wheezing, next week! Sadly, that's in my dreams too.

Finally, I reach the plateau and make an undignified scramble for the row of benches kindly provided for those dying of exercise. I feel ill. Joking aside, if I develop a pain in my chest that moves to my left arm and a sense of doom, I will be cruelly demanding that an ambulance crew sprint up those stairs to attend me. Though my current sense of doom is probably due to my subconscious knowledge that what goes up must stagger down eventually.

I hope Elliot isn't cold and hungry outside, wondering why I haven't rejoined him yet.

After a considerable time watching the passing crowds, many of whom wear the same desperate expression that I must have had, I gently ease myself from the bench and take a look at the exhibition pinned up on the walls. I don't read everything as I'm conscious that Elliot is waiting.

I groan on realising that I have a second small climb to reach the summit, the observation platform.

That's when I see it.

A set of metal double doors with a polite notice taped across announcing 'out of order'.

I bloody knew it! How could there not be a sodding lift given today's modern amenities?

I begin the final ascent.

A brilliant blue sky greets me as I emerge into the open air of the observation platform. People are swarming in every direction, cameras and mobile phones snapping images as mementos. There are silver spikes creating a fitting yet scary boundary, and I'm amazed that some tourists are attempting to lean out beyond them, despite the potential consequences fifty metres down. The majority of visitors line the boundary, taking crazy-faced selfies. I find a section of free space at the barrier and simply stare down at the beautiful star shape created by the surrounding incoming roads. From up here, Paris seems incredibly neat and tidy, organised into geometric sections giving a vibe that life is sweet, in every way possible.

To my right the Eiffel Tower stands proudly, under which tomorrow I will pop my question. From that moment on, for the rest of my days, the gigantic tower will hold different memories each time I see it. Today, it's simply an icon amongst icons; from tomorrow it will represent the next chapter in my life. Our life.

The more I think about the prospect of proposing, the better it feels that I have ventured along this path. I know my initial reaction was one of horror, which has been diluted into acceptance and now I've finally arrived at exhilarated. I would never have imagined myself proposing to a man, let alone Elliot, but standing here with the Eiffel Tower in the distance it feels like the most natural thing in the world.

I take a few snaps with my mobile, walk the perimeter boundary, peering through to locate Elliot far below. He isn't easy to spot amongst the crowds, his dark hair blends in.

My eyes search the masses. It looks like an ant farm; everyone is busily going about their day, and yet each one has a life, desires, fears and, sadly, losses. No two people down there are the same, have the same, or want the same ... and yet, somehow, we are supposed to go through life and find the one who best fits with us. How impossible that seems right now, viewing a mass of bodies moving back and forth below me.

How do two people ever find their match?

Or do we each have several plausible matches wandering about the world?

I suddenly spot Elliot.

He's sitting beside the right-hand pillar of the arched monument, his head bowed, knee brace in place, his crutches laid upon the paving stones, watching the passing tourists. I watch as a lone woman walks by him, short skirt, long legs and a flowing mane of hair, and his head follows her stride.

Elliot, don't!

Seconds later, another woman walks by and his head twists in her direction to watch and admire.

Bloody thanks! I'm not the jealous type but of all the moments to witness my boyfriend window shopping the passing parade – this doesn't leave me feeling good. I know he's not blind, and we all do it. Us females know window shopping is great; you can admire from afar, drool a little and dream without having to venture inside the shop, try on or even purchase. Nicole's comment flashes through my mind.

Is this what Elliot's doing whilst out with his mates?

No wonder they've noticed, he hardly bloody hides it. I watch his head, and suppose his gaze to be moving continually to watch every lone woman who walks by him.

Thanks a bloody bunch, just what I needed to see!

I lift my mobile clear of the railing and snap a photo of the ant farm below.

Not that I want one. This unexpected image of Elliot is seared upon my memory.

I pull back from the boundary, for fear he might see me spying, which is ridiculous, but still . . .

My legs carry me down the spiralled staircase faster than I could ever imagine. I am now the one frustrated by the slow tourists blocking my path, holding both rails and not allowing me to pass.

Two hundred and eighty-four steps is nothing when the motivation to get down them has suddenly been given to you.

My breathing is heavy, my hamstrings tight but I do not need to sit down once I arrive at the bottom stair. I need to speak to Elliot. Ask him what the hell he is playing at?

Mmmm, maybe not. I'd probably sound like some crazed bunny boiler and for what . . . him happily watching the traffic?

'Hi,' I call, approaching the spot where he's leaning against the neoclassical stonework. 'Sorry I took so long. It was a bugger to climb to the top and then getting back down was so frustrating.'

'No worries, I've just been sitting here.'

I wait for him to add further details but he doesn't.

I smile at him, waiting. Lord knows what I expect him to say or confess too.

'What?'

'Nothing . . . Do you not want to know what you can see at the very top?' I ask, playing for time.

'Sure.'

I unlock my mobile, and begin flipping through the images, brilliant blue skies, landmarks and history fill each frame. I can feel a dividing wall between us, as we stand side by side. I glance up to see if Elliot's viewing my snaps but he's elsewhere.

'Fantastic. See, I told you it would be worth it,' he mutters. 'Now where?'

'We have a dinner cruise on the Seine booked later, so what would you like to do now?'

'I fancy grabbing a kip back at the hotel . . . yeah?'

A kip? Is he serious?

'Are you tired?'

He yawns an extended fake yawn, almost childlike in its lack of authenticity.

'Wow, that tired!' I exclaim.

'Yeah, really tired . . .'

'OK. Let's head back.'

Elliot leads the way on crutches in search of a taxi, and I follow.

Dana

I wait patiently as instructed in the foyer of the Shard. I am nervous as hell and conscious that passing guests are staring at me and yet again wondering why I have a TV cameraman circling me. I simply smile. I'm starting to get used to being stared at; I don't have the urge to explain that I'm no one special.

Jez and Tamzin left me here some twenty minutes ago in order to capture for the audience the big moment when they learn who I've chosen to go on a second date with. Jez briefly outlined that they'd hired yet another executive car with tinted windows and that my chosen date would be driven through London to appear as if by magic at the foyer doors. To heighten audience anticipation and the drama, I've been asked not to share my choice with anyone. I haven't, not even with my parents, despite my mother asking constantly all day. I know the woman is keen but why ruin the fun at the final hurdle?

'Sorry, love, these things take ages,' mutters the remaining cameraman who's been left to babysit me in the foyer. 'There's ages left until we're live on air – but we all have to be ready and waiting.'

'No worries, I'm getting used to it.'

It wasn't really a difficult decision based on how I'd enjoyed myself on my previous dates. Three dates, with three different men, each one very different in terms of location, enjoyment and connection.

'Oh, Dana, now I'm not trying to sway your decision – you know your own mind – but he was absolutely lovely,' was my mother's poor attempt to influence my future happiness.

I'm not visibly shaking, which is a good sign as I was incredibly nervous on our first date. I've already asked what the format is for tonight. Apparently, we're having pre-dinner cocktails, then wining and dining overlooking the cityscape, which all sounds very plush.

Despite the live nature of this show, I'm not too nervous. Apparently, Jennifer is undertaking to present a running commentary while the camera pans back and forth between our conversation. I've been asked not to swear on live TV. I'll definitely have to remember my mic if I nip to the loo this time. I check my reflection in the nearest polished surface; the professionals have once again given me a makeover worthy of royalty. Hair, make-up and this time a long flowing gown for the finale evening, giving me the feeling of Cinderella going to the ball. Though it appears, given the time I've been standing here, that Prince Charming may have lost his way en route.

Carmen

I stare across the linen-covered table. It's a perfect setting – I couldn't have asked for a more beautiful ambiance, even if the conversation is a little stilted. That's my fault for being het-up by an internal monologue which I can't openly vent.

I'm mad at him.

I've been silently mad at Elliot all afternoon, since leaving the Arc de Triomphe, because I'm stuck. I desperately want to ask what he's up to. Ask him what he's playing at. But how do I ask such questions knowing I have two engagement rings secretly stashed in my suitcase and a proposal planned for tonight?

I have two choices: keep schtum or ask . . . and I daren't ask, which frustrates me.

'How's the seabass?' asks Elliot, breaking into my thoughts.

'Lovely, and yours?'

'Good, yeah, good.'

Silence descends as we continue to eat, I sporadically take a sip of wine and notice that Elliot's glass remains virtually untouched.

'Have you taken your painkillers?'

'Yep, three lots today, though my knee feels a bit better than yesterday.'

'And from when you'd initially injured it?'

'Totally different . . . each day it's getting a little better.'

I nod. I'm pleased. I don't like to think he's in pain or uncomfortable and yet, deep inside my loving heart, a flicker of evil ignites; if the bastard is playing away or planning to, I hope his pain registers off the Richter scale.

I attempt to dowse my negative thoughts with a blanket of love, trust and honesty.

I continue to eat, my mind playing out the scenarios before me.

'So, Elliot, let's be honest. Having climbed to the top of the Arc de Triomphe, I saw you openly admiring the ladies walking by – what's all that about?'

It's honest, it's frank and, given my current pre-proposal position in life, bloody ballsy. One wrong move or question and my entire plan will come tumbling down around my love-struck soul.

But can I possibly propose when I suspect he might be trying his luck elsewhere?

My second option develops with pace.

'So, Elliot, let's be honest and open here. Nicole happened to mention that your entire crew of friends are concerned that you're checking out other woman during nights out. I hadn't even realised that gym night had been ditched in favour of boys' nights out, so my question is what the hell are you up to?'

I can imagine the shock registering on his face if either scenario became reality.

I can almost hear the excuses, the 'hey, Carmen babe's alongside the 'what are you suggesting?'s. I can almost feel the negative vibes, the sullen silence which would follow, the caustic undertone that would accompany us to the Eiffel Tower, ruining my moment.

I have two choices. Actually, I have three.

I choose the third: to keep schtum.

On Friday afternoon, I chose to come to Paris to be with the man I love and spend an unforgettable weekend reconnecting before my big moment.

And that is what I want to focus on: reconnection.

I sit back, having finished my succulent seabass presented on a bed of spinach, decorated with cherry tomatoes. I have cleared my plate, except for a discarded sliver of fried skin, which doesn't appeal to me. Elliot's meal, much like his wine, remains half finished, and he puts his cutlery together and sits back.

I reach for his hand across the table between our plates and wine glasses.

His fingers are long, his nails clean and clipped, and I play with them, tracing and stroking each digit. Elliot smiles as I move from fingers to thumb and back again, slowly lingering before moving on to the next.

'Hey, look,' he says, interrupting my game, pointing to his left outside the cruiser.

I turn to see the gothic towers of Notre Dame with its central rose window watching us stealthily from beside the Seine. The fire damage is still visible on the ancient stonework but the beauty remains beneath the criss-cross of scaffolding.

'It's bloody massive,' mutters Elliot, staring intently. 'It makes you wonder how they managed to create such a structure in the first place. The original was built by hand ... but it'll be repaired using today's technology.'

'I can't imagine it,' I say, taken aback by his intense interest.

I can admire its beauty, its presence and yet Elliot's seeing something far deeper, much like I had hoped from the *Mona Lisa* earlier.

'Look at you getting into it,' I say, squeezing his hand.

'Don't you think it's amazing how little by little, piece by piece, humans can create something that outlives their physical life?'

'I felt that earlier about the painting but you weren't interested.'

'A painting is quite different. I know artists don't complete their works in a single day but that ... that took centuries to build, far longer than any painting, Carmen. You wait – it'll take years to rebuild given the damage to the roof. Rebuilding will be no easy task, despite what the experts might say.'

I take instant satisfaction from hearing Elliot suggest that the duration of time equates to worth – a suitable note for later. Though, given my favoured speech, there won't be room for me to reinforce anything: it's short, sharp and very much to the point.

'Do you see those rib-like sections? I know they're called flying buttresses – they take the weight of the walls and what was once the roof, allowing for the expanse of elaborate windows ... I bet you didn't know that?'

'No, but more disconcertingly I didn't imagine you'd know such facts, Elliot.' I laugh, seeing his beaming face.

'You forget, I'm more than a pretty face,' he says, squeezing my hand lightly.

'So, no relation to Quasimodo then?'

'Sadly not, Esmeralda,' teases Elliot, playing with my fingers just as I had played with his minutes before. 'Though should you need rescuing from the gallows any day soon, I'll be sure to leap into action.'

It isn't his pledge which makes me smile but the sentiment behind them. He's never been one to be open about his feelings but still, if I read between the lines, I get where he's coming from.

I sigh, grateful that I have maintained a dignified silence about Nicole's comments. How ridiculous am I, allowing negative thoughts or suggestions to cloud my judgement?

I blush, relieved that only I know the true extent to which I have fought down the urge to confront him.

'What's the smile for?' asks Elliot, leaning forward across the table.

'Nothing.'

'It doesn't look like nothing from where I'm sitting.'

'Shush!'

I'm saved from further embarrassment and teasing by the waiter arriving to collect our plates. Our hands snap apart, like typical English tourists, not willing to show affection in front of a third party.

Dana

From where I stand, I can't see the limousine draw up to the curb. I don't witness the uniformed chauffer step from the vehicle to open the rear door.

What I do witness is Tamzin's reaction as she stands with bated breath watching the proceedings from a vantage point that I was denied. It's my date and yet I'm not allowed to watch – go figure. Tamzin's zingy curls bob back and forth as she tries to peer around Jez and his camera crew to see the secret occupant of the limousine.

I imagine she thinks I'm mean for not sharing but my word is my word, and even Tamzin's bribe to stay friends afterwards wasn't enough to tempt me. I have no doubt she'll probably sweet-talk Jez into adding a bloopers section to the closing credits for Sunday's highlights show, in which case my toilet visit will be aired for sure.

Polly

'Mum, come and meet Anna,' says Cody, walking me through the crowd towards his table of mates.

A sea of faces politely murmur hello, the lads I recognise from frequent visits to our house over the years, the young ladies not so much, given that most look much older than their years. Funny how you lose track of the opposing gender when your household revolves around just one.

'Hello, nice to meet you,' says Anna, smiling broadly as Cody takes her hand.

I settle into the vacant seat bedside her. I wasn't expecting this.

This is the Valentine's flower girl then, is it? She's petite with an elf-like face, and her fringe has a dramatic asymmetrical cut which accentuates her large eyes.

'Nice to meet you, Anna. Though I wasn't expecting to be introduced to anyone tonight ... he's kept this secret to himself.'

'Mum, you're embarrassing her. Stop it,' says Cody, to cover his own embarrassment. 'Ignore her, Anna, she's pulling your leg.'

'Pulling her leg about what? You?' I ask, noting the same adoring expression in Cody's eyes that I saw in Fraser's when we were young.

'Well, it's very nice to meet you, Polly – I believe you work in the travel agents,' says Anna.

'I do.'

'I work in the bridal boutique next door. I saw you briefly at Friday's meeting. I know you've organised things for Carmen, my boss.'

'Sorry, yes, Friday's meeting – I thought I recognised you. Yes, Carmen. I wonder how that's going.' I quickly glance at my wristwatch: 9 p.m. 'I bet that's all sorted by now.'

'Yeah, she'd arranged everything for early evening ... so I bet she's dead happy by now, and relieved. Did you see the matching rings she'd bought?'

I shake my head and listen as Anna excitedly describes what I'd call a 'diamond rock' with an accompanying gold band designed for a man.

Cody sits watching her speak, his eyes never leaving her face. It's clear there is something different about this girl. She's definitely not like Lola.

I keep it short for fear of outstaying my welcome and return to circulating around the room.

The music is playing, the dance floor is full, the bar is busy, the buffet virtually gone. I couldn't be happier. Yes, it's been a hell of a week but we've done it. We got through it and next week I can relax a little and recuperate.

'Would you like to dance?'

I'm startled by the question but how can I refuse Fraser's

polite request and extended hand? This isn't our style but, hey, how better to show your son up at his own birthday party than by taking the floor and slow-dancing to a number that is not a slow dance? I know that's all that's in Fraser repertoire, given his lack of rhythm.

He leads me to the corner of the dance floor, currently the emptiest space, and wraps his arm about my waist. I don't care that everyone else is bouncing up and down to the latest rave music, we're doing it our way, like always.

'I love you,' whispers Fraser, as I rest my head on his shoulder and look up.

'I know. And I love you.'

'That's never wavered for us, has it?' he says, as we begin to slowly rock from side to side.

'No, from that first moment you walked into the college refectory, I knew. Even though you were chatting to Denise Bradley at the time.'

'I wasn't. You've got your crushes mixed up. I was talking to you.'

'You weren't, you didn't even notice me. You were mooning over Denise . . .'

'If I was mooning over Denise, how come I asked you out that afternoon to the pictures, eh? Explain that one . . . yeah, you can't.'

'And now you're going to say that Denise was just an excuse to stop by our table because you knew her,' I tease, having joked about this moment for so long.

'Exactly! You girls don't know the half of it,' says Fraser, squeezing me tight.

'Has Cody introduced you to Anna?'

'Yes, a few minutes ago. She seems nice.'

'She does, and he seems smitten.'

'I'd say.'

Everything is going well.

The dance floor is full of lively movers. Cody's mates have bagged numerous tables near the bar and it appears a huge group of them have actually turned up, despite not answering my text invite. Cody's birthday cake sits centre stage, with the remnants of hot rolls and half-eaten desserts scattered the length of the buffet table, which help to dissolve my fears of loads of leftovers whilst proving that I'd catered for plenty.

'Lola's here,' whispers Fraser into my ear as I enjoy my wine. It's the first chance I've had to sit down all night, to actually have a decent conversation with a friend. How long has it been since I saw Jill and Tony – our friends from school? Ages, yet before I even begin, I'm pulled out of the conversation. 'Can't you speak to her, Fraser?'

'I can but . . .'

Yep, he's too kind. Such a conversation isn't one that Fraser will handle well, given that, firstly, she's female and most females can get around Fraser, and, secondly, he won't want to appear brutish by asking her to leave.

'Where?' I ask, apologising to my friends and promising to return in a second.

'Over by the bar.' Fraser nods to the swarm of bodies waiting to be served.

I cross the room, eyes on Lola as she queues for food. From the back, I can see her short skirt curving upwards from the outer thigh, leaving little to the imagination. She's side-stepping from one foot to the other as she waits to be served, her clutch bag thrust beneath her left arm, a note being waved in her right hand.

Who is she with?

The rest of the people in the queue are busy chatting with one another as they wait. Not Lola. She is alone. Which heightens my annoyance.

I spy Cody and make a beeline.

'Cody . . . Lola's here. What do you want me to do?'

'Ah, Mum, don't say that.'

'She is . . . look,' I point towards the bar. 'Are you going to speak to her, or shall I?'

'I will. She's probably here to hang around with her brother, Milo.'

I watch as Cody strolls over and taps her on the shoulder. Lola's face ignites into a beaming smile as she turns and gazes adoringly up at him. She shoulders begin to sway, her eyes study his face as he speaks and her giggling begins. It's plain to see how much she likes him but, oh dear, can we go through that again? I couldn't. I wish Cody would turn a little so I can see his expression, witness for myself his true feelings – hers are obvious, but maybe he's encouraging her slightly. Flattered by the attention . . .

I'm suddenly aware that, yes, I am standing in the middle of the floor, staring at my son chatting to a young lady, which will look slightly obsessive from a third party's point of view. But I need this resolved. Lola needs to leave.

Cody finishes talking and returns to me.

'She's staying but she isn't going to cause a fuss or a scene, Mum.'

'Really, Cody?'

'Mum, please just leave it . . . She'll be fine, I'm sure.'

'Cody!' I'm exasperated. This is precisely why I feel as I do.

Cody touches my forearm before walking back to his table of friends and Anna.

I give a heavy sigh, take a final look at the gatecrasher and return to chat with Jill and Tony.

Carmen

'Finally,' says Elliot, as we slowly approach the Eiffel Tower, illuminated as darkness falls, his crutches clunking on the paved walkway. 'It's been in my eyeline from the second we arrived.'

We'd disembarked from the river cruise, both fit to burst due to the fabulous food we'd consumed, and hailed a taxi for the short journey.

My stomach is tumbling like a circus performer with stage fright. Having a beautiful meal before proposing is a definite mistake, which I'm sure many males have realised over the centuries.

'Isn't it beautiful though?' I say, linking arms and wanting to swoon as much as possible as we walk through the flood-lit gardens approaching the tower, despite the clunky manner in which he moves thanks to his bloody crutches.

'Mmmm, though I'm not really up for the actual tour,' says Elliot, giving me a dubious look.

'I gathered that . . . Never mind, we can still walk the avenue and take a look, can't we?'

'Sure, as long as you haven't set your heart on seeing the view from the top.'

I smile and shake my head.

I want to burst out and tell him there and then: no, Elliot, the view isn't what I have my heart set on. Climbing 1,665 steps of the Eiffel Tower to view the sights of Paris for the second time in one day, but from a slightly different angle, is not something I could do anyway: my thighs are cramping from my earlier efforts at the Arc de Triomphe.

Every step I take nearer, I get warmer.

I'm getting flushed.

My palms are sticky.

I'm getting flustered.

I'm beginning to sweat. Not a gentle, feminine, glistening glow across my temple but a full-blown, is-this-an-early-meno-pause-meltdown? flush.

'Carmen, you've gone a bit red. Are you all right?' asks Elliot, stopping to stare at me. 'Do you need to sit down?'

'I'm fine.'

Elliot peers at me. 'Maybe it's food poisoning?'

'Elliot, I'm fine, honestly . . . it's nothing.'

He eyes me suspiciously.

'Honestly, can we just enjoy the view and the glorious gardens? When we get to the Eiffel Tower, we can take a few pictures.'

We fall silent.

Tourists mill around, posing in groups and positioning their hands to create the illusion of holding the illuminated tower, pushing it over or wearing it as a hat.

I'm desperately hoping that Elliot won't request such a pose when we arrive. I'd like the next fifteen minutes to be a stylish affair, with two mature adults being sophisticated and debonair and focusing on their binding love, rather than trying to create a funny picture which will lodge in my memory, forever distracting from my carefully planned proposal. A distraction which Elliot will then refer to constantly throughout our life together whenever any social outing requires a funny anecdote. And I will get used to smiling politely whilst wanting to kill him for keeping the eternal spotlight on his immature behaviour and not my heartfelt declaration of love upon which our family will be built. From which our children will spring forth, from which our grandchildren and every future generation of the Cole family will spring, long after we have become worm food and are a distant memory.

In my head, I want this iconic tower to stay alive within us both as a magical reminder of the love we share on this day and every day to come. I imagine that in the years ahead we'll be changing nappies, feeding children and arguing with teenagers but the moment a TV clip of Paris flashes upon the screen and we see the Eiffel Tower, we'll both soften, reminisce and sigh heavily, this special day grounding us within our busy family life. This memory. This hour. On 29 February ... when I proposed to him. I can almost hear our enjoyment recalling our proposal story, amongst friends and family for years to come.

I hear myself speaking to an eager group of friends, anyone new coming into our lives from this point. 'Yes, yes, really, I proposed to Elliot ... yes, a slight twist on tradition but you know how it is when men drag their feet a little, us women sometimes need to take the plunge, don't we?' And 'Don't be silly, of course you won't mess it up.' And 'Honestly, I thought that, I was as nervous as hell, but given all the preparation that I'd done beforehand ... I simply wanted to savour the moment and ask him to marry me. I would encourage any woman to take matters into her own hands and propose ... Don't wait for him to do it – make it yours.'

Make it mine! That is exactly what I intend to do in the next fifteen minutes, if Elliot could quicken his hobbling pace and actually move a little faster on these bloody crutches. Doesn't he know I've got a beautiful diamond ring hidden in my coat and it's burning a hole in my pocket?

'Come on, Elliot, I'll race you!' I holler, releasing my grip on his hand and playfully jogging off.

'Carmen, I can't!' he shouts, as I turn around to jog backwards, beckoning for him to speed up. 'These crutches are killing my hands and shoulders.' I ignore his complaint.

'Come on, slowcoach, we've got things to do and people to see!'

I watch as Elliot tries an awkward hop, skip and larger 'push off' from his crutches which lengthens his stride and definitely propels him faster.

'Yay! And it's Elliot going for gold!' I encourage, as I continue to move backwards. I feel awful – if his shoulders and back are aching from the constant strain of the crutches, it can't be pleasant – but I have more important things to think about. 'If you make it across the finish line in record time, then I'll give you a back massage later. How's that sound?'

'A naked massage ... sounds wonderful.'

'Naked ... who mentioned naked?'

Elliot gives me a wry smile, his eyes squinting, as he closes the distance between us. This is the face I love, the grin I treasure and the eyes that I want to wake up to see for the rest of my life.

'Beat ya!' I call, my outstretched hand touching the rusty metal of the Eiffel Tower.

'Well, that isn't bloody difficult given these buggers,' puffs Elliot, bringing up the rear.

'Well, touch it then. You aren't finished until you've left your fingerprints on it,' I add, breathing heavily but not due to the exertion, more nerves at the task ahead.

Elliot smiles, his hand reaching for the almighty metal structure, and pats it.

'There, happy now?'

He leans heavily on his crutches, resting his injured knee, whilst I pace about on the spot, looking up and around at the sheer size of the tower. I ignore the three hamburger and ice-cream trailers complete with chalkboards – everyone needs to make a living but I don't want them as part of my memory. Instead I focus on the intricate way that the neon lights appear through the intricate lattice work, how the night's ghostly clouds provide a continually moving backdrop for this giant and how couples lovingly hold hands whilst strolling beneath the four giant feet.

I quite like the shade of olive green it's painted, though dealing with such a quantity of rust must take some dedicated elbow grease and a sturdy wire brush! Amidst the pretty flower displays and the numerous concrete blocks used as posing pedestals for selfies, the ticket office and sovereign gift shop, I feel as if I'm standing beneath the world biggest cake topper, on which a bride and groom are probably standing at the very top.

Elliot stays near a giant foot, leaning against the iconic structure and the concrete building which encases each corner. He looks relaxed, recovered from his short dash on the crutches, but I think I'll give it another five minutes or so before I invite him for a slow walk around.

My eyes follow the tiny caged lift gliding its way up a leg strut – funny how you never notice it in pictures or on film yet there it is, never ceasing but working constantly day after day. Much like me with our relationship, quietly caring for Elliot the best way I know how on the good days and the not-so-good, shall we call them?

I slowly walk in circles, staring intently at the metal structure above my head, but really I'm buying time. I'm trying to focus, to meditate and calm down before embarking on my big proposal. I'm not bothered by the crowds of tourists milling about; I'll never see these people again in my life. All I care about is getting it right for me and Elliot.

I want it to be perfect.

I want it to be a natural step.

I want it to be unique.

I need it to be memorable.

Everything I've planned and prepped in my head and heart meets my goals.

I take a huge breath and slowly exhale.

This is it. After eight years of loving, my moment has arrived.

I stride back towards Elliot, who is leaning heavily on his supports, a confident smile on my lips. I manoeuvre him and his wretched metal crutches a little way away from a group of arguing tourists, before throwing the crutches to the gravel floor.

I stand facing him.

'Give me your hands,' I instruct, taking control and looking deep into his quizzical face. His gaze is darting about my features as if unsure where to focus.

'What?'

'Shush!'

His eyes widen at such a command.

I squeeze his hands in mine and stretch up to kiss him. His warm lips react to mine. This feels right, we feel right. This is it.

'Elliot, don't utter a word and please let me finish, I've been practising for days how to say this properly and I would like to get it right first time.'

Elliot's eyes widen further in surprise and he nods, as if scared to answer – which isn't quite as I'd imagined.

'We both know that we, you and I, have been together for eight years, living together for several of those. We've had some good times, bad times and once or twice some ugly moments but, hey, I'm not counting or including those unfortunate days. Despite everything, the good, bad or ugly, I have loved you. When we've laughed, cried and shouted at each other ... I have loved you. When I've seen you every day or whenever we've been apart . . . I have loved you. The bottom line to my existence for the last eight years is that you, Elliot Oliver Cole, are the one I have loved from the first day until this moment here today and so I would like to ask you a simple question . . . *Veux-tu m'épouser?'*

The words spill from my mouth in a logical, orderly manner. I can hear that my speech made sense. I didn't race. I didn't rattle. I didn't splutter or stammer. I didn't cry. I actually held it together, which is more than I have done when repeatedly practising the speech each time I've been to the toilet in the last twenty-four hours, the only alone time I have had.

I stare into his eyes.

There is total silence. Everyone else seems to be listening to our conversation; the entire universe has stopped to earwig.

His eyelids flicker rapidly as my words register.

He's better at French than I am, I've heard him conversing with the waiting staff during our weekend.

His fingers twitch in mine.

He gulps deeply.

His lips part slightly . . . hesitate, and then continue to separate.

His eyes close as he whispers, '*Non.*'

Polly

'Polly, can I have a word?'

I turn from the hand basin in the ladies to behold Lola before me, drink in hand.

'Hi, Lola, enjoying yourself? I didn't realise your brother was a DJ.'

I feel relaxed, and I can't be bothered to take issue with her, given that the night's nearly over, everyone has enjoyed themselves and I've had more than my fair share of white wine.

'Well, I would be, but I see that Cody's with someone . . . He didn't say that at the bar.'

'He doesn't have to explain to anyone, Lola, least of all to you. He didn't tell me either, he doesn't need to.'

'How long's he been seeing her?'

'I'm not sure, it's recent but . . .'

'So you weren't joking about the flower delivery last week?' She doesn't give me time to answer before continuing. 'My mum said you were just being a mean cow towards me, when actually you were telling the truth.'

My mouth drops open.

I cringe that her mother saw straight through my mean comment. To actually hear their view of me cuts deep.

'Lola, I wasn't joking. It probably sounded very mean but . . .' I can't lie but I can't excuse myself either.

'And she's what . . . eighteen?'

I shrug. 'I haven't a clue . . .'

With perfect timing the ladies' door opens and in walks Anna, all smiles.

'Hi, I'm Lola.' Lola immediately thrusts a hand in Anna's direction.

'Anna, nice to meet you.'

'I'm the ex.'

I watch the sneer dawn upon Lola's face as she watches for the other young woman's reaction.

Anna doesn't react.

'I know, Cody pointed you out earlier. I've heard a lot about you from his mates. I think it's good when people can remain friends after a relationship breaks down.'

Touché!

Lola is silenced. Her mouth works like a goldfish's but nothing comes out.

'Lola was just being polite, Anna . . . I wouldn't want you to think the two of us are close. Are we, Lola?' I add.

Lola's eyes narrow before she spins on her heel and leaves the ladies.

Anna doesn't say a word. Neither do I.

'I'd better go and mingle,' I say eventually.

'Mmmm, I need to go.' She points to the lavatory cubicle. 'I was desperate when I walked in, but somehow lost focus. See you later.'

I leave the ladies, humbled that Anna handled Lola with more maturity than I can usually muster. But as soon as I walk outside, I enter a new drama.

Lola is dragging Cody across the dance floor towards the exit, parting the lively dancing like Moses parting the Red Sea.

Cody is trying to wrestle his hand and wrist back without being forceful, his head shaking vigorously.

'Hang on, where are you two going?' I ask, glancing between them. Cody looks annoyed, Lola furious.

'Outside.'

'Cody?' I call in earnest, knowing that any second now Anna will emerge from the ladies' toilets.

'We're not,' answers Cody, despite his body being pulled towards the exit.

'We are!' Lola's voice has edge, her grip is vice-like.

'Lola, this is exactly why I didn't think it was right for you to stay,' I say, placing my hand on theirs in an attempt to pacify her into releasing her grip.

'No, you just don't want me to ask him. That's your problem, you're jealous,' she rants, turning her focus to me.

'Lola, don't speak to my mum like that!'

'Why not? She says what she wants to me. Cody, we need to go outside – I have something to ask you.'

'Ask me here.'

'No, it's embarrassing.'

'Lola, no!' My heart leaps into my mouth. This can't be happening. Has that been her intention all along – to ask him a question during his own birthday party, in front of his friends, family and now a new date?

Cody stares at me, trying to understand why my reaction appears so stricken.

'Lola, no, you can't do that. It's not fair on Cody. Tonight of all nights.'

'Traditionally, I can *only* do it tonight of all nights, Polly . . . Cody, will you marry me?'

Our hands remain entwined in a complicated knot of digits and palms.

Cody's mouth drops wide.

I gasp.

Lola beams in delight.

The silence lengthens.

'Well?'

Cody shakes his head and starts to wrench his hand from the knot.

'Cody?' she stammers, her eyes big, her beaming smile fading. 'You said you loved me.'

'When did I say that?' snaps Cody.

'You always said . . .'

'I said nothing of the sort. And this – this is not what I was expecting you to ask me. No, if that's what you need me to say, you've heard it from me!' He gives a final yank of his arm and his hand is freed. Mine too. I want to die with embarrassment. I had joined them in her proposal. The moment she has probably been planning all week. The moment when she thought all her dreams would come true if he said yes. I had stood there holding their hands like a conjoined triplet. How embarrassing! Or is now the embarrassing moment – the fact that having heard what she'd asked and his answer I am still standing here, dumbstruck at the situation unfolding at my son's birthday party.

'I think you need to leave, Lola,' I say quietly, not wanting her to make more drama which everyone else is alerted to.

'Cody?'

'No. Not now, not ever!' says Cody.

Please be quiet, Cody, please don't upset her further. You know what she can dish out – it'll be all over social media in ten minutes, she'll be slating you to anyone who will listen. Be firm. Be polite. Be kind.

'Cody?'

'No.' Cody walks back to his table of friends.

'Polly?'

I hold my hands up and back away.

'Lola, you shouldn't have done that to him. He's been patient with you, very polite given how miserable you made him in recent months, but to think that he would ever say yes to such a proposal is ludicrous. It really is.'

'I thought you'd understand.'

'Me?'

'Yes, given that you and his dad never married, I thought you'd understand why it was so important for me to ask him, to try and show how much I cared . . . Fraser's obviously never bothered asking you.'

'Excuse me! Whatever you think you know about mine and his father's relationship, you are way out of line, young lady. It is no business of yours how we decide to live but it was me who didn't want to get married, not Fraser.'

I watch as her eyes widen. She might have heard my mean comments but she's never before seen me this angry. Never.

'But, Polly . . .'

'You don't truly know us, Lola, so please don't assume you understand the decisions I've made in my life. Now, please, I would like you to leave. And I believe my son would like that to happen too.'

'Polly, can I just explain how I feel . . .'

'I think you just did!'

I place a firm hand on her shoulder and steer her towards the exit. I walk her through the double doors and out into the car park.

I want to turn and walk away. I'd like to, but I can't.

'How are you getting home?' I ask. I can't leave a young woman alone to find her way home, despite being so angry with her.

'I'll walk.'

'Oh no you won't. You stay there. I'll ask reception to call you a cab.' I leave her perched on the wall and head towards reception.

I'm fuming.

Fuming on two counts. First, because of her stunt with Cody. Second, because she had the audacity to call me out on misinformation which she thinks defines our relationship. Cheeky minx!

'Polly!'

I turn back to look at Lola. She's standing where I left her: alone. She looks incredibly sad for one so young.

'I just wanted to say I'm sorry,' she says, her head tilted and staring at me. 'That's all.'

I watch as she turns away and settles herself down on the car park's low wall to await the taxi I'm about to order.

I regress in years: Lola looks how I felt, still feel, every time Olive ignores me. A flicker of guilt ignites. Am I Lola's Olive? Do I make her feel incomplete as a person? Inferior to our family?

'Lola.'

She looks up.

'I'm sorry too,' I say, adding, 'I could have been kinder. I simply want Cody to be the happiest he can be. I'm probably a little too protective. That's my issue, not yours.'

Lola gives a brief smile before turning away.

Carmen

Did Elliot say '*non*'?

Did I mix up my French and inadvertently ask him something entirely different? To which '*non*' is a sensible and fitting answer!

I am frozen in time, holding hands with a man who just answered '*non*' to the biggest question of my life.

I'm rubbish with languages. Totally useless, but even I know that '*non*' is not 'yes' in French . . . he's supposed to say '*oui*'!

My brain is stuck in a loop.

Oui to marrying me.

Oui to spending the rest of his life with me.

Oui to creating babies.

Oui to sharing my life.

Oui to . . . oh my god, he didn't say '*oui*'!

I drop both his hands as if burnt by his skin and step back from him.

'Carmen . . . please.'

I raise both my hands to signal for him to stop talking. I can't hear anything at the moment other than the single syllable which is marching about my head, much like I'd confidently paced around the base of the Eifel tower some ten minutes ago before asking a ridiculously stupid question in French of my lover of eight years.

I turn my back and walk away.

Instantly my iconic Eiffel Tower blessed with memories of love crumbles to dust; it exists no more. From this moment forth, I know I will cringe each time it is mentioned.

I don't care that he can't bend down to retrieve his crutches, I need to focus on me at this moment in time. I need to breathe. I need to walk. I need to cry. I need to holler and scream into the night sky and ask why, oh why and somehow delete the word 'non' which is circling my mind like a Formula one racing car from my memories.

He said 'non'.

Why?

Does he not love me?

Doesn't he want me?

Doesn't he want children with me?

I walk. I'm blind to the people around me – suddenly everyone is a backdrop of actors and we are the only couple in Paris. God forbid that I should bump into another couple proposing at this very moment. Please save me the humiliation of seeing a traditional proposal where she says 'yes' or 'oui', worse still if he accepts her proposal! I won't be able to hold back the tears. And I, Carmen Smith, can't lose the plot by wailing and retching my insides out beside the Eiffel Tower on a crisp Parisian night. This was not my plan. In my plan, Elliot answered 'oui'.

I look up to stare blankly at the expanse of gardens in front of me. I have no idea in which direction I should walk. I didn't wait for Elliot so have no idea where I am. Or where he is for that matter.

'Carmen!' I hear the emotion in his voice before I actually spot him way behind me, amongst the crowd. He's frantically hobbling along in an awkward yet rhythmical manner, smooth-clunk, smooth-clunk, as his weight falls heavily on his lame side.

I wait. I can't bear to look at him as he approaches but stare about me, fighting back the fresh flood of tears that threatens to burst forth at any second.

He said no to my proposal.

Why would he do that to me? To us?

'Carmen . . .' He finally reaches me. I lower my head unable to look into his face, for fear that he'll see how upset I truly am. 'Carmen, please stop and listen to me.'

'I'm listening.' My voice has edge, my eyes have more tears.

'Look, I get that you're upset, and rightly so . . . but I can't agree to marry you just to make you happy, Carmen . . . I just can't.'

'But why?' I look up to see him sigh, look around and return his gaze to my staring face. I'm waiting. However hurtful his next few sentences, I want to know. I need to know why.

'Look, we can't talk here . . . Can't we go somewhere?'

Getting away from here is what I want.

'The hotel?'

I wince at his suggestion.

'OK, point taken.'

'Can't we just walk until we find a café bar?'

We walk like the blind leading the lame. There's no touching, no eye contact, no direction, no consolation; we simply walk through the park, hoping that a suitable venue will appear.

Dana

Seeing his face approaching the large glass doors, accompanied by Jennifer and the cameras presenting live, my face breaks into a huge smile. Initially I had my doubts – he wasn't my first choice, my gut reaction choice – but still I'm delighted that he agreed to attend our second date live on air.

'Good evening, Dana – you look utterly fabulous,' says Connor, his hand reaching for mine before he masterfully kisses the back of my hand.

'Thank you, Connor – I'm so glad you agreed to join me. Shall we?'

Tamzin's mouth is agape, her eyes wide and staring as we enter the lift, heading for pre-dinner cocktails.

Jennifer and the roving camera crew squeeze in beside us too.

'Were you surprised when they contacted you?' I ask, once we're settled before a panoramic view of the city skyline, sipping an espresso martini and a whisky on the rocks.

'Not really. I figured we'd had a good night and enjoyed ourselves, but . . .' He pauses, then continues after taking a sip of his drink, 'I wasn't convinced that you were going to contact me.'

'Why not?'

Connor hesitates and pulls a comedic face. The camera crew circle our table but I ignore their intrusion and focus on Connor.

'You can be honest . . . Jennifer says that honesty and trust is the best policy when discussing relationships, so please feel free to say.' I notice Jennifer quickly delivers a piece to camera.

Connor gives a huge sigh. 'I've watched your previous dates – I was told not to but I did. Look, you are beautiful, and I had a really great time doing the quad bikes and then enjoying such a relaxing massage but, well, it got me thinking . . . sometimes there's an instant connection, isn't there?'

I take a sip of my drink; I'm watching his every move and listening intently. It's so refreshing that he talks so openly, that there's no trickery. He appears to speak from the heart.

'Go on.'

'Do you remember that I mentioned a previous partner when you asked me about the massage? Well, I hadn't thought about her for years, a decade maybe, and yet since last night . . . well, she's all I can think about. Sorry, I know that's not what you wanted to hear, sitting here on our second date, but I now realise I might have made a mistake in letting her go from my life.'

'Are you serious?'

He smiles and slowly nods his head.

I begin to laugh.

Jennifer turns white in horror, Jez begins frantically gesturing off screen, while Tamzin has both hands clapsed across her mouth. This is going to bugger up the live finale, for sure.

'Can you believe it? How ridiculous am I?' he asks, raking a hand through his hair.

'You've been chosen by me to come on a second date and yet you actually want to be elsewhere with a woman you broke up with a decade ago?'

'Yep, utterly stupid, isn't it? I don't even know where she is or what her circumstances are now, but there you have it. I'm Connor and in the last twenty-four hours I do believe I might have matured!'

I continue to giggle – the situation is completely absurd.

Jez is about to have a coronary. Jennifer is deep breathing at the thought of adlibing until the close of the finale's live feed.

'Connor?'

'Yep?'

The camera crew descend upon or tiny table. The silence is deafening. You could hear a pin drop.

'What the hell are we doing here? You need to find your lady and I, well . . . I should really have asked for Brett to join me, but I was so frightened of him rejecting my offer of a second date that I bailed.'

'You're kidding!'

I shake my head. 'No. I enjoyed my date with you, honestly I did, but I felt something special when I was with Brett . . . before he dashed off during our kiss.'

Connor can't stop laughing now.

'Connor, would you be offended if I leave our date? I think I need to talk to Jez and find out where Brett is!'

'No offence taken, Dana – maybe I could get my act together and find out where my ex is, maybe even give her a call.'

'Jez,' I say into my mic, 'I'm about to disconnect my microphone but first can I ask if you could get your horde of experts to locate Brett? I need to ask him a question about the other night.'

In one swipe, my microphone is separated from my gown. I give Connor a peck on the cheek and go. As I take my leave, Connor reaches for his mobile and begins swiping through his contacts.

Polly

I watch as Fraser takes the microphone offered by the DJ and the lights are raised a little, allowing our guests to see him clearly.

Fraser taps the mic head twice to check it's working and then begins.

'In a moment, I'd like to say a few words but first, I believe my son has a gift of appreciation for his mum. Cody?'

I gasp as Cody strides across the dance floor carrying a huge bouquet of white roses, wrapped in cellophane and completed with a satin bow.

'Cheers, Mum, thanks for this and . . . for everything,' he says, handing me the bouquet and delivering a hasty kiss to my cheek.

I blush profusely as our guests clap and cheer.

'You're welcome, son,' is all I can muster before I'm too choked to speak. I know Cody appreciates everything, the entire family do, but to have it acknowledged so publicly is a little overwhelming for me. I do what I do through love.

'Can I thank you all for your company this evening, helping me and Polly celebrate our son's birthday. It's not every year we get to enjoy his celebrations, given that Polly ignored my coaching talk on how to push an eight-pounder down a birth canal. But, hey, she managed it eleven minutes later, didn't you, sweet?'

There's a titter of laughter around the room as all eyes rest on me. I smile, unable to think of a fitting retort in front of such an audience.

Fraser continues.

'We've done what we felt was best by him, made him go to Scouts when he wanted to play computer games, talked him into being a striker when he'd have happily been in goal and steered him away from motorbikes when he was too eager to gain his independence. We've given him Calpol whether it was needed or not, made him believe in Santa Claus, the Easter Bunny and the Tooth Fairy but then lectured him on stranger danger about everyone else. I've stayed quiet when he's worn bright pink shirts, aired my opinion on some very dodgy hair-cuts and opened all the windows once he's gone out in an effort to rid the house of the stink of so-called designer aftershaves, which smell no better than my good old Hai Karate.'

I look over at Cody as our guests begin to laugh. His face is reddening, his head is lowered, but he's laughing too, taking it in the good spirit in which it's meant.

'So it only goes to show that, with love, care and lots of attention, which are the three things we promised him as a tiny baby . . . I suppose what I'm trying to say is I think we've pulled off a decent job.'

Fraser falls silent, and our guests acknowledge his honesty with a huge round of applause and unexpected wolf-whistling.

I'm walking towards him without a thought for anyone other than Fraser. I've never heard him speak so eloquently in public. I suppose I remember the shy teenager he used to be. At home he's comical, but only when sentiment surfaces and he needs to cover his emotions. But now, here tonight, in front of everyone we know and care about, Fraser's just summed up the last twenty years of our life, dedicated to each other and raising our boy.

I proudly stand beside him, smiling up at his expression. He's choked, but rightly so; he's just done our Cody and me proud by showing how much he loves our life.

I need to do the same.

I take the microphone from his hand, which he duly relinquishes, thinking I'm leading him from the spotlight.

'Fraser, thank you . . . from both Cody and me – I couldn't have put it better myself in summing up the years we have spent nurturing and loving our boy. We've proved we can work as a team, share each other's daily lives and still laugh, despite the dramas. Which gives me even more reason to ask . . . Fraser, will you marry me?'

Our guests fall silent; not a sound is heard as I watch my proposal hit home for Fraser.

'I'd be honoured to marry you, Polly.'

Our guests erupt into applause, and a cry of 'How embarrassing!' lifts above the cheers – which I assume is our son hiding his delight with a wayward comment.

We, Fraser and I, are lost in a kiss.

Someone takes the microphone from my hands but I'm oblivious as to who.

'My parents, ladies and gentlemen! Finally we'll all share the same surname!'

Our guests titter some more, as we ignore the dimming lights, ignore our son's quip and sink into an embrace and slowly dance.

'Thank you,' whispers Fraser, holding me to his chest.

'What?'

'Thank you for asking me . . . I've never truly lost that desire I had to make it official all those years ago. But I knew how adamant you were not to have history repeat itself. I knew our relationship would be different to your parents', but I understood your worries too. I'm delighted that you're happy enough with our little lot to put old fears aside and get married.'

'Oh Fraser . . . I don't deserve you, I really don't.'

Carmen

I feel such a fool standing in the hotel reception asking to be let into my own room. Elliot still has the plastic door key in his pocket and I had more important things to think about than remembering to ask for it. We were a couple so why should we not share?

'Madam will just need to wait two moments . . . we will create a spare,' says the smiley young woman, oblivious to my struggle to maintain my public face as she tap-tap-taps at her computer keyboard.

As I wait, I plan the next thirty minutes of my life – it is all I can do. It is all I can plan ahead for, having been refused the possibility of a marriage or children. The next thirty minutes is all I can manage, given the knot of tears threatening to overflow from my chest.

In no time I have a brand-new plastic door key and am stepping from the lift beside our room, number 668.

I unceremoniously wiggle and waggle the key to gain entry, which proves to me how useless my basic life skills are. Once inside, I flick on every lamp to illuminate the darkened hotel room. I want to do anything that will eliminate the last hour from my memory – if it's a Parisian night outside my window, I want Italian daylight to lift my mood.

Would reception switch my room if I ask? I'd be happy with a downgrade; it would be better than staying in a room that had started the weekend as a pre-honeymoon suite. Now it is simply heartbreak hotel, or rather it will be, once I'm undressed and sobbing neck-deep in a bubble bath.

I run around the three-roomed suite, gathering my toiletries, focusing on running a bath and trying to prevent my mind from slipping off-task and remembering the word '*non*' before I break down uncontrollably. If I let myself cry before the bubbles form, I'll no doubt drop to the bathroom floor and be found by the maid tomorrow morning in the exact same spot, dehydrated, swollen-eyed and surrounded by crumpled tissues.

I survive the thirty minutes in the bath accompanied by tears. I manage to dry myself and don the large fluffy white towel with the hotel logo emblazoned on the breast pocket. I even unwrap and wear the flimsy matching towelling slippers they provide.

I lie on the bed.

The bed in which hours ago we made love.

The bed to which we were supposed to return, wearing our engagement rings, in order to make more love.

The bed in which we were due to wake up tomorrow morning and smile at each other, blush and begin our new chapter, planning for becoming man and wife.

I crawl into its centre and stare around the room.

It really is a honeymooners' room.

Did I jinx myself by booking such a suite?

I grab my mobile from the bedside cabinet and speed dial.

'How's Maisy?' I ask.

'Sod Maisy ... how are you?' asks Trish, bursting with excitement.

'Elliot said no.'

'What?' screams Trish, her voice rising ten decibels.

'He said no,' I repeat.

I grab a small satin pillow and hug it to my chest as I tell my friend every last detail. I describe how we sat opposite each other in a café bar. I twiddled with the stem of wine glass, he traced the edge of his pint glass. I cried, he looked embarrassed. He spoke and I cried some more. The candle on the table burnt out and the waiter didn't know what to do except bring me more tissues.

Trish mmmms and ahhhhs as I speak; there's nothing she can say. I tell her how he'd explained his reasons.

'Look, Carmen, this isn't easy ... for either of us ... but you deserve an honest answer,' he'd said.

I'd pulled a 'do you think?' face.

'I probably should have talked this through with you before now, but I've shied away from doing so because I knew how upset you'd be ... and I truly don't wish to hurt you. But I already know that marriage is never going to be a goer for me. Ever.'

'Never?'

'Never. I knew this conversation would come up one day, so it was wrong of me not to have addressed it before, but you seemed OK as we were, plodding along with the life we have.'

'*Had*.'

His eyebrows lifted on hearing my correction.

'I see.'

'Do you? Do you really, Elliot?'

He shrugged.

'Because sitting where I am and hearing your answer of "*non*", I don't think you do.'

'I know you're gutted, and I didn't mean for this to happen. If it had entered my head for one minute that we were coming to Paris for you to do . . . to do that . . . then I would have said.'

Silence descended, and we'd stared at each other as if daring the other to speak.

Had he never heard of leap-year proposals? Had he been so oblivious to my intention all weekend?

I wouldn't want to be him explaining this to me. But then, if the situation was reversed, I wouldn't be explaining this to him. If I were him, I'd have said yes to a marriage proposal. And there lay the difference: he didn't propose marriage, did he? He'd never wanted to!

'All I'm saying is that I know I'm happy as I am. We're together, we live together, our life works together – why change it?'

'Because I want commitment, Elliot,' I'd said.

'We have commitment: the house, the mortgage and our life together – isn't that enough?'

'No.' My answer sounded as harsh and as hurtful as his had been.

I'd sipped my wine, staring around the café bar at the other couples. I'd imagined each one as loved up and happy as we were not thirty minutes ago.

'Can't we stay as we are?'

I'd breathed deeply, the air filling my lungs to a conscious capacity, before I'd slowly exhaled. I needed to stay calm. I needed to explain my values and desires in a rational manner, otherwise he'll relay my performance during the next boys' night out and I'll be a laughing stock amongst the social group. *His* social group.

'I have what I want in life, Carmen.'

'And children?'

He'd given the tiniest of shrugs.

'Don't you want children?'

I'd waited while he swigged his beer, before he gave me a tiny headshake.

'Was that a no?'

'Yep.'

'And when were you going to share that gem with me?' I'd said to him.

'Carmen, you've hardly been forthcoming on your plans for the future so what am I supposed to think?'

'Sod you, Elliot! You know I want marriage and kids ... children. You've always known, and now you think you can tell me your plans have changed and I'm supposed to not be upset.'

'I haven't changed my mind, I've never planned on ...'

'So what was all the crap the other night about Judy breast-feeding in the pub. Why bother asking me what I'll be doing?'

'It seemed a reasonable question, given her behaviour.'

'When I'm nursing another man's child, what will you care what I do?'

'Carmen.' His hand reached for mine, but I snatched it back. Touching Elliot was the last thing I wanted to do right then.

'And don't you "Carmen" me, right? I never said I didn't want marriage. I've never said I didn't want children. I've simply been the silly bint waiting for you to get round to it in your own sweet time without me twisting your arm up your back. I didn't want to be the kind of girlfriend who constantly drops hints, sulks at the news of other engagements and then coerces a proposal and pretends it was his choice. Instead, I'm the live-in girlfriend waiting for the things she wants in life to be delivered by a guy who didn't want the same things in the first place. What a fool I am!'

I suddenly become aware that Trish hasn't said anything for ages.

'Trish?'

'Yeah, still here . . .'

'So I'm back in our room, correction, *my* room, chatting to you.'

'And there's no chance he'll change his mind?'

'Nope. Though I wouldn't want him to, Trish. Elliot knows what he wants. I know what I want.' I pause before continuing. 'So it's over.'

'Oh, Carmen.'

I break down and floods of tears drench my cheeks. 'Trish, I never expected this.'

'I know, my love, I know. You did what you felt was right and this is the end result,' she soothes.

'I do love him, Trish . . . I love him with all my heart but I know I can't carry on as we were before given that he can't . . . won't commit to me or my future.'

'Oh, Carmen, my heart breaks for you.'

'And mine. But I suppose what I'm saying is that my life's

ambition means more to me, however dearly I love Elliot. This break-up will hurt me but not as much as saying goodbye to my ideas about marriage and children will.'

'How did you leave it?'

'I'd heard enough so I willed my body to follow every instruction that my brain gave and I did something I've never done before. I stood up, collected my handbag and swiftly, without any tears, exited stage left.'

'Where is he now?' she asks.

'Gone. He collected his things whilst I was in the bath and he's checked in elsewhere, I guess.'

'OK, I'm sure he's safe and sound for one night. Now, you get some sleep and I will call you first thing tomorrow, you hear me?'

'Yep, thank you, Trish. I do appreciate everything you do for me.'

'My pleasure ... Get yourself into bed and you'll drop off in no time.'

'I hope so. Thank you.'

'Bye, Carmen.'

'Bye, Trish.'

I listen until Trish puts down the phone at her end, unwilling to cut the connection with home. She's been an absolute rock to me and, when I spy the right gift, I will treat her as a thank you.

I roll over on the bed amongst the piles of cushions, stare at the decorative ceiling rose and wonder how many guests have suffered such a turnabout of situation whilst staying in this suite.

Who comes to Paris to propose marriage and goes home as a singleton?

I guess very few. Boy, I belong to a select group.

I'm not tired. And there's no chance of feigning sleep when my mind is whirring with questions.

I look around the stylish room. I have no idea what I'm doing here now. I've no desire to venture out before morning; at least here I am safe and sound. I'll probably watch a bit of TV. I suppose I might find some comfort reading the Gideon's Bible that's kept in every hotel room drawer – though I'll struggle here, given that it will be written in French.

My mobile begins to ring. I snatch it up without looking at the screen.

Bless her, Trish has obviously remembered some wise words of comfort which she thinks are vital to my wellbeing.

'Hello, Trish!' I say, half expecting her to say, 'Carmen, this too will pass,' or, 'Remember, wherever there is sunshine, shadow must fall.'

'Hello . . . Carmen?' says a man's voice.

I instantly sit up.

It's certainly not Trish. And it's definitely not Elliot.

Dana

'What are you playing at?' asks Jez, his hands gesturing wildly as we stand in the foyer, his redundant crew staring from the sidelines. 'You've just buggered up our live finale!'

'I thought it best that I said – surely that's better than playing along with something that felt fake? You heard what Connor said – he hasn't stopped thinking about a distant ex, and I had my doubts about my choice.'

'So why didn't you say earlier in the day? The way this is panning out, the final shot that my audience have seen in tonight's live finale episode was a second limousine pulling to the curb and another man's trouser leg stepping from the car. You're damned lucky that we can hold them in suspense until tomorrow night's highlights show – making it look like a finale night tease – otherwise this documentary would be ruined!'

I don't know what to say other than keep apologising profusely. I can feel Tamzin's wrath from here, but surely Jennifer is right: honesty and trust are what relationships are about. I wasn't being very honest with myself when I chose Connor, and how can I build trust with him when deep down I know my true choice was always Brett. In one evening, in Edinburgh, something had clicked between us; some kind of connection occurred whether Brett wants to admit that or not.

'Jez . . . I need to speak to Brett. I need to know why he pulled away from our kiss like he did. It felt real, for that tiny moment in time . . . I felt a connection. I need to ask him a question.'

I'm expecting him to shout at me, stare at me a little more, but he doesn't. Instead Jez comes alive and begins shouting orders at his redundant crew and the bored experts, who have suddenly come alive.

'Go, go, go . . . Bloody hell, move it, people . . . Find out where he is. Tamzin has his contact details, so someone call his mobile. Phone his family, sister, parents, his best mate . . . Someone must know where this guy is – we need him here as soon as possible.'

I watch as the team split in all directions.

In no time it's just me and Jez in the empty foyer.

'So what's the question you need an answer to?' he asks.

I tap my nose suggesting secrecy.

'Oh really, that good, eh?' says Jez, his eyes shining with excitement. 'You best go and apologise to Jennifer – she's got the gift of the gab which has saved your bacon.'

Carmen

'Yes, Carmen speaking.'

'Carmen . . . it's Connor . . . Connor Warwick.'

My mind goes blank. My hesitation lengthens as my brain argues with itself: 'No, it can't be? Surely not Connor, but it sounds like him.' A wave of embarrassment must be flowing along the optic fibres, which I am sure he can hear.

'Carmen . . . are you still there?'

'Yes, hi, Connor, so sorry, I lost you there for a moment . . . How are you?' I feign delight and happy thoughts.

'I'm good, thanks. I was wondering how you are?'

Bloody good question, but not one I can chat about right now.

'I'm . . .OK.' I pause, fearful of saying much more in case my tears flow again. This is Connor, *the* Connor. The man I'd previously worshipped and who'd broken my heart before I met Elliot. The man who I truly thought I deserved in life, but he was too immature and self-centred back then.

'Good to hear.' There is a lengthy pause before he continues. 'Carmen, it's not your type of thing but have you been watching the new TV documentary this week, the one about dating?'

'No, but I've heard about it from the others in the boutique . . . the woman is our local florist.'

'Yep, Dana, she's lovely but, well . . . it's got me thinking, Carmen. Thinking about me and you . . . and what could have been, if I hadn't behaved so badly. I was wondering if we could meet up . . . go for a drink, a coffee perhaps . . . I just fancied a chat.'

I can't believe my ears.

I can't believe his timing.

'Well, that is pretty unexpected, Connor ... I'm currently in Paris but ...'

'How amazing! On holiday?'

'Not quite ... It's a long story, which you probably haven't got time for, but ...'

'I'm in no rush, I've got time to chat now, if you have,' he interrupts.

'OK ... I have to say you calling tonight is ridiculously spooky given the circumstances,' I say, settling down amongst the satin pillows. 'So how have you been, Connor?'

Dana

'Dana, where's Dana?' calls Jez, hurrying through the foyer, ahead of the crowd.

I sit bolt upright, having slumped into a plush chair and drifted off amongst the madness of the last ninety minutes.

'There you are! Now, get yourself together ... here he comes!'

My world is a blur as the cameras reappear, the experts follow suit and then the crowd parts and, in the aisle created, there is Brett.

Jez approaches me, offering a microphone.

'No, I'm not having a microphone for this conversation. It's private!' I snap at Jez, attempting to push aside the tiny gadget but without success as Jez pins it to my dress. 'Hi, Brett, how are you?'

His features split into a wide smile as I walk towards him, hands outstretched, and pull him into a friendly hug.

'I'm good. I didn't expect to be dragged out to the big city on a Saturday night; I was home alone.' I'm shocked by the tingle running along my spine as we make contact. He's exactly as I remembered from the other night, before his swift departure . . . I'm not about to chastise him, complain or begin moaning. I just want to ask him a simple question about that kiss.

'Brett, can we go for a walk? I need to ask what happened the other night.'

He gives a sharp nod before dropping his gaze to the polished tiles of the foyer.

I link my arm in his and we slowly walk away from the crowd of Happy Productions TV much to the annoyance of Jez and his trailing camera crew.

'I need to know why you dashed out . . . is it something I'd said or did?'

Brett smiles gently. 'It was me. I followed my instinct and kissed you but partway through I caught sight of the cameras and the shy guy in me simply came to the forefront. This whole scenario simply isn't me. I live a quiet life without drama and fuss. I forced myself to complete the online application and apply because I want to share my life with someone special. I don't ever seize the day, I don't live for the moment and to suddenly find myself kissing you in such a passionate way when we'd spent less than a couple of hours in each other's company was overwhelming. Before I knew what I was doing I was dashing down the staircase and I'd ruined my chances . . . or I thought I had.'

I listen to every word he says. In his piercing grey eyes, I see a multitude of emotions turn and shift, like the kaleido-scope making a snowflake pattern, a moment in time in which everything changes.

'I appreciate your honesty, Brett . . . it's what I needed to hear.'

'You're not annoyed by my rudeness?'

'Nope. You're as vulnerable as I am when it comes to

admitting your emotions but I think we had a great date . . .
I felt a connection, too good not be given a second chance.'

A delighted smile almost eclipses his features.

'Wow, this is not what I expected you to say, Dana. I thought
I'd really upset you, given your expression as I dashed out.'

'It just didn't make sense when I felt we'd made a connection . . . but still, what time is it?'

Brett checks his wristwatch. 'Eleven fifty.'

Dare I ask the big question?

My heart rate quickens, my pulse flutters and my palms are
clammy.

Should I seize the moment, or not? The leap-year tradition
doesn't stipulate how long a couple should know each other
beforehand. Tamzin wants to hear it. Jez would be ecstatic to
hear me pose the big question having ruined hi slive finale night,
but is this what I . . . what we want?

'Brett, one more question before we head back for a drink . . .
I feel a connection as if I've known you for a lot longer than I
actually have so I'm willing to live in the moment and ask . . .
How much do you know about elephants?'

Brett stares at me, puzzled. 'Elephants?'

I nod slowly. From the corner of my eye, I spy Tamzin and
Jez frantically gesturing at each other, yet again. The group of
experts stand open-mouthed and staring. They only had one
question in mind. I had another.

'I know that their tusks never stop growing and they spend
up to eighteen hours a day eating,' says Brett, adding quickly,
'and, female Asian elephants don't have tusks.'

My heart bursts with delight. In an instant, my kaleidoscope
has formed the best pattern ever.

'Excellent! Now can we please pick up from where we left
it the other night?'

As our faces draw closer and our lips reunite, I can hear Jez and Tamzin flapping about in the background in a desperate attempt to direct the camera crew to capture our first proper kiss, to show tomorrow night during the highlights.

'It's very late into the night but I have to ask, how do you both feel?' asks Jennifer, seated in front of us for a hastily arranged interview.

I know I've messed up Jez's finale night with my indecision and the frantic search for Brett, and the camera crew have had a nightmare trying to capture footage. But it was never supposed to be about them, was it?

'This is probably the craziest thing I've ever done, but it feels right. I have to be honest despite how it might seem to others . . . I feel like I've known Brett for a lifetime.'

Brett squeezes my hand as I speak.

'I agree. There are a million things we don't know about each other but there is a definite connection, which I've never felt before,' he says. I can hear the nervous tremor in his voice; this really isn't his thing.

'And, we're in no rush. From this point onwards we can take our time getting to know each other,' I add, glancing up to catch his eye.

'But Dana – that was one strange question you posed about elephants. Was that your plan all along?' asks Jennifer, her eyes twinkling with excitement.

'No, not at all. My aim was to complete the three dates and to be honest . . . I'm as stunned as anyone by the outcome of this evening.'

'Especially as you originally chose Connor for your final dinner date,' interrupts Jennifer with a giggle.

'Exactly. I feel bad about Connor but we both felt awkward

tonight, and, thankfully, we were honest with each other. I think his mind was elsewhere, if I'm honest.'

'Yours certainly was! But hey, Connor's misfortune is your lucky day,' swoons Jennifer, turning to Brett. 'So tell me, what are your immediate plans?'

We briefly exchange a look of surprise.

'I think we'll be making arrangements to meet up tomorrow and have a second first date in private. There are lots of things we need to discuss and I need to explain about a very special person in my life.'

Jennifer nods eagerly. Brett hasn't a clue why I asked about elephants but I sense he trusts my judgement.

'I totally agree. I fully appreciate your need to ask about elephants – it shows your devotion to others. Anyway, I'm being told that social media has gone crazy tonight as our audience try to keep abreast of the action. I think you need some privacy now to open up to your families and enjoy each other's company. Though promise you'll come back for an update in a few months?'

We both laugh and nod as Jennifer turns to address the camera.

'I'm hoping you've thoroughly enjoyed our week following Dana's journey to find love in the modern age and, fingers crossed, they'll be joining us in the near future, but for now, I'm delighted that together, they are "taking a chance on love"! Good night!'

Epilogue

Saturday 18 April 2020
at St Peter's Church

Polly

'Cody, have you got the rings?' I ask for the umpteenth time, as we gather outside the church.

'Are women always such worriers?' he says to his father, pulling two gold rings from his right suit pocket.

'Get used to it, lad,' teases Fraser, looking towards my father for confirmation, who duly nods.

'I'm just checking. Having got this far, I don't want any calamity detracting from our vows, that's all. Is it too much to ask?'

'Fraser, are you and Cody going in any time soon?' calls my mother, who, despite the peace agreement with my father, is standing a few feet away, beside Helen. It is not quite the parental pact I'd hoped for but if the two can be civil and polite for one day, my wedding day, I'll be happy. I'll take my parents truce any day over my mother's obsession with her friend Derek. Though I fear my father did more than his fair share in the negotiations to pull off today's ceasefire. I'm simply relived that Derek isn't present.

'We're all here, Pauline, so there's no rush. We might as well take our time and enjoy the sunshine,' says Fraser.

My mother's hat accentuates the tiny nod she makes, unimpressed that Fraser isn't following her orders. I know her impatience has more to do with Fraser's mother, Olive, standing close to her in silence.

Helen gives me a fleeting smile, fully understanding all sides of the situation. She's grown stronger in recent months. Her weekly counselling sessions have provided professional support for her to gain an equilibrium in her life. She's not forgiven Marc, but she no longer blames herself for his shortcomings. She hasn't found it easy coping amidst the debris of what happened but every day she's grateful for a new dawn. Had Marc been a little later arriving home that night, things would be very different. I don't take her for granted any more, Helen is Helen, and I love her as she is. Some episodes in life bring sisters closer together; sadly, it took her overdose to make us tight.

Marc stands tall at her side. Their obsessive hand-holding and constant connection has ceased – Helen now acknowledges you can't keep hold of people in that way. He's apologised profusely for his dalliance and vowed to make amends. I'm not entirely convinced, but I'm not the one he needs to reassure so I simply let him be. I'm sure time will tell.

This is exactly as I'd imagined all those weeks ago. Us two, standing in beautiful spring sunshine, with just our family in attendance to witness our vows. My mum had tried to talk me into going the whole hog, and Fraser would have happily obliged, but this is what I wanted. We three, my sister's family and my parents, and Fraser's parents and his brothers, Rory and Ross. No one else.

I know that equates to thirteen guests but nothing, not even

superstition, is going to overshadow our day. Fraser has waited
long enough to make me his wife.

The church clock strikes midday, our allotted time.

'Come here,' he whispers, pushing a stray hair back from
my forehead. 'I'll see you inside. I'll be waiting.' His lips gently
touch mine for the last time before our vows.

'See you in a while,' I whisper.

'Mum,' says Cody bashfully, then he strides off beside his
father, heading for the front pew of the church. Both my boys
look smart in their navy suits and new haircuts.

Dad and I stand, arm in arm, gleefully nodding as each
of our party dawdle past to follow the groom and best man.
Helen looks better than ever, more flesh on her bones. Marc
is more attentive, ushering Evie and Erica into the church. My
mum enters on her own, refusing to walk between her two
granddaughters, so bringing up the rear of that small group.
Fraser's parents glide past, as always pristine in their appearance, though I can't quite hold Olive's gaze; I know this isn't
what she's dreamt of for a family wedding, but she still has her
two other sons to give her the Cinderella-style extravaganza.
Rory and Ross are the last to enter – unsurprising given their
reluctance to attend – in matching attire to Fraser and Cody.

'And then there was us,' says Dad, once we're alone.

'I know, it feels strange . . . Having made all the plans in such
a short time . . . here it is.'

'You look beautiful, Polly.'

'Thank you, Dad . . . This is what I wanted.' I'd hailed simple
and elegant as my style, and Carmen had found me the perfect
dress. An understated gown in ivory, it fitted well and suited
my frame. In my hands, a tiny bouquet of lily-of-the-valley tied
with a straw binding reinforces the simplicity, thanks to Dana's
talents. Today, Fraser and I are making our vows, which is the

most important thing. Not the dress, the flowers or the people in attendance – but Fraser and I reinforcing our love for one another just like we have every day that we've chosen to be together.

Saturday 1 August 2020
at St Peter's Church

Carmen

We stand in the opening of the church doorway. The Reverend Harris waits patiently as I wrap my shaking hand around my father's offered forearm, each of us taking a deep breath and smiling at the other. This is the moment we've both been waiting a lifetime for, knowing how much it means to the other.

'Ready?' asks Reverend Harris, clutching his Bible in his large hands.

'Ready,' I say, to both men. I am determined not to cry. How can I cry on a day I've looked forward to for so long? And I don't want to ruin my make-up, which the artist spent an entire hour layering on my face for a glowing look. Though if it's a choice between perfect make-up and tears of happiness, I know which I'll prefer.

Reverend Harris takes a backwards step inside the church doors and gives the nod to the organist. Instantly, the gentle music which had previously filled the church as the guests arrived changes to a dramatic blare of 'Here Comes the Bride'. It's not my personal choice to accompany me up the aisle – I think it's too chocolate-box and twee – but, still, this is the only time in my life when it will be played for me.

I try my hardest not to look at the camera crew as I enter

the church and begin to walk up the aisle. Again, it wasn't my choice but after Connor's participation in the dating programme, it seemed only fair that Happy Productions TV should be given the opportunity to record a follow-up episode outlining his own journey towards true love. Our relationship was the unexpected outcome from their filming of *Taking a Chance on Love*, and given that Dana and Brett have delayed their wedding plans until next year, we were willing to oblige the production company's request.

As I prepare to walk the length of the rose-petal-strewn aisle, I take a deep breath and view the sea of familiar faces warmly smiling at me. It's a different mix of friends from those I'd once imagined. I didn't invite Elliot to witness the proceedings, although we have remained friends after my failed proposal. He couldn't commit and was entirely honest about that. I'm grateful that he was, though it hurt at the time. Elliot's schoolfriends, Magoo, Monty, Steve and Andrew plus their wives, have been replaced thanks to my rekindled friendship with Dana. I'm certain that the crowd didn't regard ours as a true friendship, just an association because I was Elliot's girlfriend. I haven't heard from any of them, much like Dana didn't once she and Andrew had split up.

We'd settled on a fair agreement regarding the house we'd shared – he bought my half at the market value. Which made sense given that I'd moved into Connor's home, and I could plough part of my newly gained capital into my new venture. It was a privilege to book our own wedding using all the services involved in my new business – and it reinforced my faith in their products and services. The business is just six months old and already a success story. I could burst with pride.

As I look around, my gaze meets that of an unexpected guest: Elliot's mum, Sally. Standing alone near the back of the church, she gives me a warm smile. I accept her presence as a gesture of kindness that she wishes me well.

No one is more surprised than me to think I spent eight years loving and living with Elliot only to fall back in love with Connor when he met me at the airport the day after Elliot's rejection. None of us knows what the future holds, but I never expected that one failed proposal would result in another so soon afterwards. The only difference was that Connor did the proposing and I gave an immediate answer: a resounding 'yes'.

Monday 31 August 2020
at the Royal Hospital

Dana

Brett takes my hand in his and gives it a gentle squeeze as we sit in hard-backed chairs in front of the midwife's desk. She smiled warmly on welcoming us into her room but hasn't said much whilst flipping through our notes.

My free hand is lightly draped across my stomach, stroking my bump.

I'm nervous. More nervous than I was when I was expecting Luke.

I'm nervous for me and possibly a little scared for Brett. This is his first child and, whatever the result, I want it to be right for Brett. I don't want him to feel pressure or that he can't speak up.

I've been here before. I know what it feels like to sit in a quiet room such as this and receive a result that wasn't the one I'd hoped for. I went into shock, I think. Later, I listened to Andrew's careful explanation. He had his reasons – he made his own choices based on his beliefs. Deep down, we all know what our limitations are.

I love my Luke. I wouldn't change him for the world. If the truth be told, if I was offered the chance to wave a magic wand, I probably wouldn't take away his extras – that might sound very unfair of me but my boy is definitely my boy. If Luke didn't have the extras, he wouldn't be my Luke; he'd be a James, a Thomas or even a Benjamin. But he's not, he's my Luke, a unique little boy who I'm learning to share with Brett.

Maybe one day, as time goes by, my Luke will become our Luke, shared and equally loved by two adoring parents.

Nothing would give me more pleasure – well, apart from not needing this particular test result.

But I'll accept that whatever will be will be. I'll cope.

We'll cope.

I give Brett's hand another reassuring squeeze. It's the smallest gestures which make life bearable. Like the moment Brett met Luke for the first time. He didn't treat Luke as some others do. Brett looked past his condition and greeted the little boy in front of him with big smiles, a contagious laugh and an open heart. If I hadn't connected with Brett beforehand, that would have been our moment, the moment Brett connected with Luke.

We've only been together for a matter of months but still, time doesn't define everything in life. Sometimes just one moment is all you need, for others an entire lifetime fails to deliver the experience of knowing love. For us, a basic knowledge of elephants helped to ease our path. For the past seventeen weeks, Brett's been as delighted and as nervous as I have. He's been at my side every step of the way, doing everything he can to support our little family and help me raise Luke.

Luke's thriving at the moment. I managed to discuss my concerns with the head teacher, Mrs Huggins, who was clearly embarrassed by the lack of humility from members of her staff. She immediately intervened and helped to secure an individual appointment with the speech therapist once a week. I'd like him to have more sessions but for now, he's happy and progressing. I want him to remain in mainstream school because he'll need a role in mainstream society in the future. I'll only consider a specialist school if it is right for Luke, no one else.

The midwife coughs, flicks a strand of hair behind her ear and looks up, glancing between us before speaking. She's experienced, mature – she's done this before, I'm sure.

'OK, so the result is positive.' Her sentence is rushed, a telling sign.

She falls silent and waits, continuing to glance between us as her fingers play with the edge of the paper on her desk. I can almost predict her thought patterns and the conversation which she's preparing to have with us. It can't be easy confirming news such as this.

We don't say a word. I look at Brett: he gives me a cheeky wink. His grey eyes never fail to entice and engage me.

I gently rub my thumb against my small bump as the midwife shuffles in her seat.

'Any questions?' she asks, breaking the stifling silence.

'Do you know the gender of the baby?' asks Brett.

'Yes, would you like to know?'

'Please,' says Brett, giving my hand a comforting squeeze in return. I give a tiny nod.

'You're expecting a female,' she says; her voice is deadpan. I don't like her choice of words: a female. I know she's trying to be professional, unbiased given the medical results but it sounds so unnatural.

'A girl? We're having a girl?' Brett's delighted tone fills the small office; his wide smile says it all.

The midwife's brief nod confirms Brett's joy, then she watches him as intently as I had watched Andrew years ago.

'Dana, we're having a girl!' he says, kissing my hand.

'And the results . . . ?' she whispers, tapping our file.

Brett shrugs.

I watch as her sombre expression slowly fades towards one of relief as she understands the family before her.

'And nothing – we're having a girl!'

This moment suddenly becomes a precious memory. I have never loved Brett more. I know that our pregnancy will deliver a unique human being unlike any other, whatever difficulties she and Luke may encounter, whichever direction our path in life takes us – we will be absolutely fine as a secure and happy family of four. Always taking a chance on love.

Acknowledgements

Thank you to my editor, Kate Byrne, and everyone at Headline Publishing Group for encouraging my fascination with leap years and giving me the opportunity to flex my imagination in relation to tradition and marriage proposals.

To David Headley and the crew at DHH Literary Agency – thank you for your continued support. I couldn't ask for a more experienced or dedicated team to champion my career.

Thank you to my fellow authors/friends within the Romantic Novelists' Association – you continue to support and encourage me every step of the way. I promise to repay the generosity and kindness received in recent years.

Thank you to Jo Pickering and Alan Pearse – teaching colleagues who answered my author questions regarding French and science.

Thank you to Hipparchus of Nicaea, Greek astronomer, geographer and mathematician, whose book *Peri eniausíou megéthous* ('On the Length of the Year') first determined that a year on Earth is approximately 365¼ days long (an additional 5 hours and 55 minutes longer than originally believed), resulting in an additional day every four years. Since primary school, when the principle was first explained, I've been fascinated with 29 February and how it keeps us perfectly aligned with the solar system, the equinoxes and solstices, the sunset, the sunrise and our seasons. Plus us romantics added a little bit of love for good measure! So, don't ignore 29 February – it deserves our respect!

Happy memories of Johnny Long, a family friend, who loved his newspaper cuttings, his elephants and his knotted zuzz (a handkerchief).

Loving thanks to my mum for always supporting my efforts and spreading the word about my books.

Heartfelt thanks to my husband, Leo. I appreciate your support whilst I'm AWOL in Narnia. Apologies too, as I always seem to have a thousand urgent questions when you're watching the football.

And finally, thank you to my wonderful readers. You continue to thrill me each day with your fabulous reviews and supportive emails. I'm truly humbled that you invest precious time from your busy lives to read my books. Without you guys, my characters, stories and happy-ever-afters would simply be daydreams.

P.S. Good luck to anyone proposing on 29 February – enjoy your moment, create your memories and I hope you receive a resounding 'yes!'

Taking a Chance on Love

Bonus Material

Erin Green's Favourites

Book

Pride and Prejudice by Jane Austen.

Film

Marnie – an Alfred Hitchcock film.

Food

Everything – I am a greedy gannet!

Drink

Copious cups of tea (with milk and a sweetener).

Place

Dublin, Ireland.

Season

Autumn – I love the beautiful colours.

TV programme

The Great British Bake Off, *The Great British Sewing Bee*, *Friends*, *University Challenge*, *Mastermind*, history documentaries, crime documentaries, *The Big Bang Theory*, *Tomorrow's World*, *The Krypton Factor*, *QED* and *Noel Edmonds' Multi-Coloured Swap Shop*. (I can never decide whether TV now is better than TV back then.)

Song

'Dancing Queen' by Abba or 'Town Called Malice' by The Jam. (I can never pick.)

Possession

My dog – I suspect he owns me though, not the other way around.

Item of clothing

Tartan pyjamas.

Colour

Emerald green.

Flower

Bluebells.

Perfume

J'adore by Dior.

Way to spend the day

People-watching, drinking copious amounts of tea and using my imagination.

Bird

Peacock.

Animal

Tortoise.

Word

Paraphernalia.

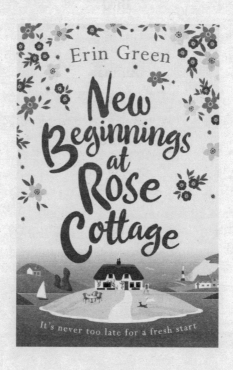